Clean romances with
fun-loving, unforgettable characters

MEG EASTON

# Also by Meg Easton

**Romancing the Spy romantic comedies**

*Spies Don't Fall for Their Asset*

*Spies Don't Fall for Their Rival (coming 2024)*

**Nestled Hollow Romances**

*Coming Home to the Top of Main Street*

*Second Chance on the Corner of Main Street*

*Christmas at the End of Main Street*

*More than Friends in the Middle of Main Street*

*Love Again at the Heart of Main Street*

*More than Enemies on the Bridge of Main Street*

**How to Not Fall romantic comedies**

*How to Not Fall for the Guy Next Door*

*How to Not Fall for the Wrong Guy*

*How to Not Fall for Your Best Friend*

*How to Not Fall for Your Ex*

**A Mountain Springs Christmas**

*The Christmas Pact*

*The Christmas Bet*

*The Christmas Clause (coming winter 2023)*

**Love Started Romances**

*It Started with a Sunset*

*It Started with a Note*

*It Started with a Glance*

**Silver Leaf Falls romance**

*Coming Home to Silver Leaf Falls*

# STOCKINGS, SNOW, AND MISTLETOE

A Christmas Romance Collection

MEG EASTON

# STOCKINGS, SNOW, AND MISTLETOE

*For my daughter, Alecia*

# Contents

# Christmas
## AT THE END OF
# Main

*A Nestled Hollow* ROMANCE

# MEG EASTON

## Chapter One

Macie sat in the middle of her bedroom floor, putting on one of her running shoes, when her black lab pushed his way right into her space. "Reese! I can't reach my shoelaces!" The dog nuzzled his face into her neck, his feet scrambling to sit on her lap. Sometimes it seemed like he didn't even realize he wasn't a puppy. Macie gave up trying to tie her shoes and rubbed her fingers behind his ears and under his collar, just as he liked.

It wasn't long, though, before his scrambling legs knocked her right over, and Lola, her cream-colored Goldendoodle, joined Reese in licking her face. "Lola! Reese! I appreciate all the love, I do. But you both want to go for a run, right?" She pushed her way back to sitting, and wove her arms through the jumble of dog legs and managed to get both hands working to tie her shoelaces. Then she led the two big dogs out of the room she rented from her sister and brother-in-law, and into the open kitchen, dining room, and family room that she shared with them.

"Good morning," Macie said to Joselyn as her sister

packed lunches for her family. Then she turned to her littlest niece, Aria, who sat in her high chair, and gave her a kiss on the cheek. Lola and Reese played their favorite game with Aria while Macie got their breakfast ready— taking turns hopping up in the air in front of Aria's high chair while Aria squealed with delight, occasionally throwing some of her food their direction in her excitement.

"So," Joselyn said, drawing out the word, "how was your date last night?"

Macie's shoulders slumped at the memory.

"Oh, that good, huh?"

Macie put Reese's and Lola's dishes on the floor, and they raced to them, scarfing down their food. "It was fine. He was fine." She paused a moment, then added, "For someone else."

Joselyn's lips lifted into a smile. "I sense a story."

"He's just really, *really* loud. And really strong. Which would've been great if I hadn't found that out because of his exuberance in playing 'Slug Bug.'" They had driven all the way to Denver to go to a concert, and with more than two hours on the road, there had been a surprising number of Volkswagen Beetles along the way.

Joselyn winced. "Besides the 'slugging,' how was the drive? Any good conversation?"

"We didn't exactly find a conversation topic that interested both of us." She grabbed an apple out of the basket and washed it in the sink. "I have no idea why in the world Sherry thought we had so much in common when she set us up. Unless she meant that I am twenty-seven and not married and he is twenty-eight and not married. Because that's the only commonality we discovered."

Macie stood at the patio doors, looking out as the predawn light just began to show the backyards that she and her siblings shared as she ate her apple. There were seven of them, and their parents had bought an entire square block of property in Nestled Hollow. Until her early teenage years, the property had been a big field they'd played in for hours each day.

Then, one by one as her siblings got married, each couple built a house for their new family on their own lot. Now her parents' house was at the top center of the square, her two older brothers' on their left and right on the corners, her twin brothers finishing off the left side, Joselyn and Marcus had the bottom center, her sister Nicole at the bottom right. All their backyards came together into one giant playground with picnic benches and fire pits and barbecues and shade trees, where all of her nieces and nephews played and they got together for family dinners every week.

Joselyn started cleaning off Aria's face with a wet cloth. "Don't worry. You'll find your Mr. Perfectly Right, I know it."

"Nope. I give up." She gestured at the one lot that remained empty— the lot that was hers that currently only held weeds and a single scraggly-looking tree that was shorter than her. "I'm just going to build a one bedroom house there, buy a spinning wheel, maybe bring home a few cats from work."

Joselyn chuckled and was joined by Marcus's booming laugh as he entered the room. Macie joined in, and Aria bounced in her seat and the dogs ran in circles around them.

"I take it last night's date didn't go well?" Marcus asked. "My brother says he's got a friend who would be perfect—"

"No," Macie said, cutting him off. "No more blind dates."

"But—"

"No." Macie's voice came out more forceful than she meant, so she searched for the right words to explain. "I'm tired of having hope. Tired of hoping that a blind date will work out. And when it does work out, I'm tired of hoping that it'll turn into something more."

"So you're just going to stop dating?" Joselyn asked.

Macie nodded. "For six months." She hadn't actually made that decision until the words were out of her mouth. "I'm just going to focus on my business, and forget trying to find a future spouse."

"You know what Dad's going to say about that," Joselyn said as she lifted Aria out of her highchair.

Of course she did. She'd heard him say often enough that her future spouse was a needle in a haystack, and that she had to be willing to search through a lot of hay to find him. She was even hearing it right now in her head, with his exact tone of voice and inflection. "But here's what I figured out last night in between 'Slug bugs.' What if my needle isn't even in the haystack I'm searching in? What if my needle is in Myanmar or Denmark or Zimbabwe or wherever, and I never go there in my lifetime? What if I keep searching through my haystack and get through every single piece of hay, only to find that there was never a needle for me? That my perfect guy just isn't out there? I think I'll just tell Dad that for six months, I'm just going to let the wind clear away some of that hay for me."

"Even if you convince him," Marcus said, "your mom won't stop finding people with 'son-in-law qualities' to line you up with."

"People in town won't stop, either," Joselyn added, Aria bouncing on her hip.

Macie's breath came out in a sigh. She knew people lined

her up with dates out of care, concern, and love, but they still felt like a force of nature that couldn't be stopped.

Lola came running up to Macie, her leash in her mouth, and seconds later, Reese joined her, also holding his leash. "Looks like it's time for me to head to work. Are you still free to chat business this afternoon?" She stretched out her calves, then bent down to attach their leashes.

Joselyn handed Aria off to Marcus. "Yep! Can you come to With a Cherry on Top at 4:30? We're usually pretty slow about that time."

"That'll work."

"Have you gotten any closer to deciding whether or not to buy your building?" Marcus asked.

The question itself made her chest tighten and her stomach churn. It was a weight on her shoulders all the time, even when she wasn't actively thinking about it. But she needed to be actively thinking about it more often. She'd been working toward opening Paws and Relax ever since she'd planned the business in her high school entrepreneur class. She knew she wanted to rescue animals from the county shelter that were desperate to be loved, and have them available for people who were desperate to love an animal but couldn't have a pet in their home.

Even after thinking about it and planning it for years, it still took a huge leap of faith to sign the lease on the building, and it renewed every six months. But the owner wanted to put the building up for sale on January first, unless she let him know first that she wanted to buy it.

And buying it was so much more than a six month commitment. If leasing the building was taking a leap of faith over a ditch, buying it was taking a leap of faith over a chasm so wide that she couldn't see the other side.

Macie put on her coat, gloves, scarf, and hat as she spoke. "Not yet. I've got four weeks from today to decide, so I'm going to try some new directions with my business, and see if I can make enough per month for it to work." It was going to be tough, and she wasn't sure she could do it. She picked up the leashes, and as the dogs pulled her to the door, she called out, "Looks like we're going then. See you all at four-thirty!"

Once outside, she said to Lola and Reese, "What do you think? Mountain trail or lake trail today?" Like usual, Lola was the first to choose the direction. Always Lola. "Mountains, then."

She started off with a slow jog, trying to get her muscles warmed up in such cold temperatures. At least it hadn't started snowing yet— snow made their morning run so much more difficult to pull off. Lola and Reese ran right alongside her as she jogged through the last few streets of homes. When she reached the area where the gradual slope of the valley turned into the steep climb of the mountainside, they turned right onto the dirt pathway.

The leaves had long since fallen and given way to the calm, crisp, clear winter air. The scene from here was different now, but every bit as beautiful. Without leaf-covered trees blocking her view, she could see the whole town from this vantage point, the sun that was just peeking over the mountain making the lake sparkle like spilled glitter.

Her home was the perfect distance from work— just over two miles. Long enough to get good exercise for her and the dogs, but short enough that she didn't show up to Paws and Relax sweaty. Even in these temperatures, there were still quite a few people using the mountain trail. Every time she would pass by someone, Lola would run forward until the leash stopped her. "What's up today, girl? You're extra excited, aren't you?" Macie hoped she'd have a busy day at the shop to help give Lola the attention she needed.

Just ahead, a man on a bike was coming from town up to the trail. As he turned from the road onto the path, heading her direction, Lola raced forward like she was shot out of a cannon, yanking the leash right out of Macie's hand. "Lola!" she yelled as the dog sprinted forward. "Come back here!"

But it was too late. Lola had run straight for the biker, causing him to swerve. As he swerved and she pivoted, her leash got caught up in his tire, and the man and his bike jerked to the side and crashed to the ground in a tangled mess of bike and man. Macie raced to his side and bent down to see if he was okay, but he was already struggling to get his leg out from under the bike. He limped to a standing position.

"Are you okay? I am so sorry!"

"I'm fine."

Except he was still not putting pressure down on his left leg. He shook it a few times, like he was trying to shake off the pain or injury. Lola just stood by both of them, looking up and panting, like she was going to get scratched behind her ears for doing a good job. The man— a good-looking, lean man who was probably around Macie's age— started brushing the dirt off his clothes. Macie reached out and brushed some of the dirt off his shoulders and back, apologizing for Lola and for not holding the leash tightly enough.

"It's okay, really." He bent down and grabbed his bike handles, pulling it upright. "I'll be just fine. If I don't hurry, though, I'll be late for work and it'll be a zoo, and then you never know what's going to turn up on your white board."

He got back on his bike, and as he pedaled, his right leg clearly doing the bulk of the work, he called over his shoulder, "Nice meeting you!"

Macie watched as the man cycled away, and felt badly that she hadn't done a single thing to help. This crash was a perfect metaphor for her relationships lately. They always crashed and burned. She turned her back on the man— and turned her metaphorical back on relationships— and faced the Goldendoodle in front of her. "Lola! We don't run ahead and cause bikers to crash!"

Lola at least had the decency to drop her head the tiniest fraction in remorse, before she stood on all fours right next to Reese, mirroring his perfect angel pose. Macie was still upset at Lola for her behavior, but then Lola looked back at her with those big brown eyes, her fur framing them in a look of innocent anticipation, and she couldn't stay mad. "Okay, we'll keep going, but you stay right here next to me. No running off."

The rest of the run went as expected. When they reached Main Street, Macie slowed to a walk to get her heart rate down, and they made their way down to the end of the street where her business, Paws and Relax, was just a small fenced-in yard away from her sister's and brother-in-law's ice cream shop.

She unlocked the door to Paws and Relax, let Lola and Reese off their leashes to play, and filled up the smaller dogs' dishes before going into the dog room. "Good morning, Piper, Cookie, and Zeus!" She let the little dogs out of their kennels and through the side door to the small yard to relieve themselves. It was one of the reasons why this building had been the perfect choice—it was the only one on all of Main Street that seemed to be made for dogs.

When they'd all done their business and came bounding back inside, she sat on the floor and let them climb all over her as she laughed and tried to pet them equally. "One day," she told them, "I'll have my own house and I will take you all home with me every single day. Hopefully I'll have a husband and kids for you to climb all over, too." Then they all raced into the main room to get their breakfast and to play with Lola and Reese, while she went into the back room to get food for the cats.

She carefully carried their dishes and opened the door to the cat paradise room. Shadow was lounging under a platform, Sam was clawing at a post, and Jinx was sitting at the highest spot on the climbing toy. They all raced to her as she sat down the food. "Come on out whenever you want," she told them as she left, leaving their door open.

After feeding the fish, the hamsters, and the geckos, she flipped the sign on the front door to *Open*, and then turned to look at her big family of animals. Just being around them was already making her less stressed. Seeing customers who couldn't have their own pets for a variety of reasons come in and hang out with these guys was the icing on top of a pretty fantastic cake. It felt good to turn her back on dating completely and to focus on her business. She didn't need to go looking for love. She had all the love she needed right here.

Chapter Two

A s soon as the discussion in the faculty lunchroom at Nestled Hollow High turned to dating, Aaron made a show of noticing the time and excusing himself. His group of friends already gave him enough grief about it— he didn't need any more.

Actually, the bell was seconds from ringing, and if it weren't for the topic change, he very well could have kept socializing and been late to class. He stopped by the copy room and picked up his stack, then hurried toward his classroom as quickly as he could while the hallways emptied. His left leg still hurt a bit, but at least he wasn't having to limp. His cell phone buzzed in his pocket, and he pulled it out and glanced at the text on his screen.

"Speak of the devils," he said to no one in particular, and slid the message open. In a group text with his friends, Matt mentioned their weekly Wednesday night get-together. Then he texted, *Can you find your own date, Aaron? Or should we find one for you?*

14

Aaron shifted the stack of papers he was holding so he could type in a return text.

*Afraid I'll win every game again if I don't have a date to distract me?*

The bell rang when he was still four classrooms away. As soon as he stepped into his room, the talking died down to complete silence, all eyes on him. Aaron eyed them. "Good afternoon." He paused for a moment, trying to see if he could tell why they were acting weird. "What's up, guys?"

"Nothing," Allen said.

"Nothing at all," Kyle added.

Morgan rolled her eyes. "You guys are so smooth. We were just speculating about why you were late, Mr. Hall. That's all. So how are you doing? How was your Monday evening?"

"You guys first," Aaron said. "I haven't seen you since class on Friday. How was everyone's weekend?" This AP History class was his favorite to teach. At just eleven students, it was by far his smallest class. The kids were all bright, and they gelled in a way that classes rarely did. It made for some interesting and enlightening discussions on history.

Several of his students told about what they'd done over the weekend or on Monday, they all riffed back and forth on each other's comments, and class settled into something more normal.

Then one of the students, Alecia, asked to use his cell phone. He nearly pulled it out of his pocket— something he'd have never done with any of his other classes, but then he realized that everyone was back to acting weird.

"You're welcome to use the classroom phone if you need to call home."

"I need *your* phone, actually." Alecia's eyes cut to her classmates.

Aaron shifted his weight to his other leg and gave them his best *I am willing to stand here for as long as it takes to get someone to raise their hand and answer* look. He had perfected this look— it was one of the reasons why he was able to get his classes to chat about history so much.

"Oh, just tell him," Morgan said.

Alecia looked at Morgan for a moment, then ducked her head and pulled a post-it note out of her binder. "We, um, made you a dating profile on the Single Professionals Match app."

She held the orange paper his direction, but he didn't reach for it. "You... What?" He couldn't quite make sense of the words. "How did you even get my—" Then the previous class with these students came to mind. Four students were gone on the Young Ambassadors field trip and he didn't want them to get too far behind, so when the last half hour of class turned to chatting, he'd let it turn into a bonding moment. "Now all the specific questions you were asking me on Friday make sense."

The kids were grinning. He couldn't ruin this for them just because he wasn't thrilled at all that they were trying to set him up too.

"You really got me to answer all the questions needed? How did you do it without a confirmation email coming to me?" He reached out and finally took the paper from Alecia.

"That was my genius idea," Cory said. "We just created a new email address for you."

"MrHallIsSingle at sentmail dot com," Kyle said.

Alecia pointed at the paper. "It's right there in your login information. The password to the email account is at the bottom."

"You might want to log in soon," Morgan said, sharing a grin with the rest of the class. "Your profile is pretty impressive. You've got quite a few interested people reaching out."

"Good-looking ones, too, Coach," Allen said.

"We've got your back," Alecia said. "We'll get you a wife by the end of the school year."

"That's our goal," Cory said.

Aaron rubbed his forehead with a thumb and two fingers, pretending like they were giving him a headache. Which was completely and totally true, but he didn't want them to know that, so he made it obvious he was faking it. He didn't mind dating. Actually, he liked dating. Casual dating. It was the marriage part he wasn't okay with. He definitely didn't need any more people trying to push him into it. "What am I going to do with you guys?"

"You could give us all A's for our troubles," Kyle said.

Like every kid in this class didn't already do everything they had to in order to earn A's.

"And bring us donuts on Thursday," Alecia said.

The last thing Aaron wanted was to be on a dating app. Their actions heaped frustration on top of frustration that seemed to come from every direction, but their hearts were in the right place. He might have to surprise them with donuts on Thursday just for being thoughtful.

Except that would probably only encourage them. He'd better not.

"Instead, how about I provide you with a feast of historical knowledge?" As he was writing *1450 to 1650: The Age of Discovery, Reconnaissance, Expansion* on the white board, the classroom on the other side of the wall erupted in cheers. "See? Even Mr. Klein's class agrees." The class gave half-hearted groans, but they dutifully pulled out their notebooks and held their pens or pencils at the ready, because if nothing else, this group of kids loved knowledge.

At the end of class, Aaron called out, "Morgan and Allen, I'll see you down at the pool in fifteen minutes for swim team practice. The rest of you, have a great Tuesday, and I'll see you in class on Thursday!"

As he stood at the door, giving each student a fist bump, hand shake, or high-five as they exited, Alecia said, "Mr. Hall, do you promise to install the app on your phone and see the people who are interested in you?"

Aaron took a deep breath. "I promise to think about it."

Alecia paused a moment, like she was deciding if that was good enough, and then nodded and left.

When the last student was gone, he walked over to his desk, stared down at the sticky note with the login information for his new email address and for Single Professionals Match. After a few moments, he opened his desk drawer, shoved the note in the back, shut the drawer, and walked out of his classroom.

By the time he left swim team practice, Aaron was mentally exhausted. Morgan and Allen had told the rest of his team— with great excitement— about setting their coach up on the dating app, and every single one of them was pressuring him to install it. He kept refocusing them on drills, and eventually on getting their form exactly right for the butterfly stroke, since that one wore them out the quickest, but they had been relentless in their coaxing.

He walked back to his classroom, put on his coat, got his bike out of his office, and wheeled it outside. He hadn't swam today, but he could still smell the chlorine on his slacks and button-down, which always happened simply by being in the same room as an indoor pool. The scent had been a near constant companion since he'd first discovered swimming at age three, and for him, was tied with nearly every emotion a human could experience. It was a scent that made him feel more himself than anything else.

Normally, he would've gone for a swim after his team left to help wash away his frustration. But today's frustrations called for something different. He had never been one to drink— not after his first and only time a decade ago. Actually, he wasn't one to put less than wholesome things into his body for any reason, with one exception. And a day like today called for exactly that kind of self-medicating exception: ice cream. His students had told him about a great shop right in Nestled Hollow, so he figured he'd stop by before heading home to Mountain Springs.

As he rode his bike through the streets of town, he tilted his face upward, letting the cold mountain scent wash over him as the wind got stronger the faster he pedaled. The wind rushing past him while biking always brought back the same sense of powerful speed that swimming brought him. That feeling of truly connecting all the senses in your body, your mind, and your muscles, with what was around you, and becoming all the more powerful because of it. It was intoxicating and exhilarating and made him feel invincible.

He slowed as he reached Main Street and turned on to the road. As he was heading to the other end of the street, a car pulled up next to him, matching his speed. He glanced over to see a student of his, Tim, and he waved.

Tim rolled down his window and said, "Hey, Mr. Hall. We've got a new hashtag trending. It's hashtag *NHH Finds a Wife For Mr Hall.* You should check it out!" Then the car pulled ahead and Tim rolled his window back up.

Aaron stopped pedaling and put his feet out as his bike stopped. Tim was one of his students, but he hadn't even had his class today. How had news spread so quickly? And how in the world was he going to stop something that had apparently taken on a life of its own?

Needing the ice cream now even more than before, he spied With a Cherry on Top a couple of buildings down. He pedaled there, parked his bike in the rack out front, and went in to the shop, the smell of sweet cream and sugary cones hitting him the second he walked in. If he was ever going to let himself have a vice, this would be it. Something about the smell of ice cream took him back to every good memory in his childhood. It didn't exactly make problems go away, but it helped.

"Do you already know what you'd like," a broad-shouldered man with a big voice said from behind the counter, "or can I interest you in a few sample spoons?"

Aaron leaned forward, but realized that angle made his ankle injury from this morning hurt, so he shifted and looked at his choices. "Let's try *Maple, Please Bring Home the Bacon.*"

The man scooped out a bite on a little plastic spoon and handed it to Aaron. He put it in his mouth, and maple exploded across his tongue, the candied bacon and walnut adding the perfect amount of crunch. "Wow. Let's do a big scoop of that."

"You don't want to try any other flavors first?"

Aaron shook his head. "I don't care about anything else at the moment. This is all I'll be able to think of until I get a scoop. No wonder so many of my students recommended this place."

As the man scooped up his ice cream, Aaron's attention wandered around the shop. A dad and his two elementary school-aged kids sat at one table, and a woman holding a baby sat across from a woman with blonde curls that fell halfway down her back. The woman was chatting using her hands, a bunch of papers spread out in front of her, a cup of ice cream next to them. He turned back as the man handed him his ice cream, which had a cherry perched on top, just like on their logo. As he was paying, his eyes went back to the woman. There was something familiar about her.

"Enjoy," the man said.

Aaron turned to leave, but the woman caught his eye again.

Then an image of her awkwardly trying to brush dirt off his coat hit him, and he smiled. They had met this morning. He walked over to her table. Just before he got there, a group of kids that all looked about ten years old, wearing matching basketball uniforms, walked in with their coach, and the woman with the baby stood up. As soon as she realized that Aaron was coming to her table, she said, "Oh, hi." Then she looked to the other woman, probably realizing that Aaron had come over because of her and said, "Do you two know each other?"

The other woman's attention had been on her papers, spoon in hand. She looked at him like she was looking at a stranger, but only for a fraction of a second, then it turned to recognition and she nearly choked on her ice cream.

"Hi," he said. "Nice seeing you again. Especially under less painful circumstances." But as he was saying it, she had stood up so quickly that her chair fell over backwards, hitting her in the shin, and she winced. So he added, "Or possibly equally painful circumstances."

"Oh hi. I, um, sorry about this morning. I'm so embarrassed. Lola isn't usually that crazy. Are you okay? Did that, the wreck, do any damage? You know, to you or your bike?"

"We're both doing great, thank you for asking."

"I'm sorry. My brain is so deep in business planning I can't even think straight. But I am very sorry about this morning. Would you like to sit?"

He was about to open his mouth to say no, but between the number of tables and chairs in the shop and the number of kids on the basketball team, they'd probably all be taken, and riding a bike while holding an ice cream cone wasn't optimal. "Sure." He slung his coat over the back of the chair and sat down, then motioned to her ice cream cup. "What flavor did you go with?"

"My standby— *Is the Doctor Pepper In*? I see you went with *Maple, Please Bring Home the Bacon*. Quality choice, there."

"Well, I'm a quality guy, so it seemed appropriate."

She cocked her head to the side and narrowed her eyes as he took a bite. "What?" he asked around a mouthful.

"Just trying to figure this out."

He looked to the left and the right, suddenly self-conscious under her gaze.

"This isn't a celebratory ice cream for you."

"Nope." He took another bite.

"And you didn't just decide that ice cream was a viable choice for dinner tonight."

"Correct again."

She crossed her arms, studying him as he bit off another bite, this one giving him brain freeze. "You're drowning your sorrows."

Aaron raised an eyebrow. "So, are you a professional Ice Cream Motivation Analyst?"

"Nah. The Professional Ice Cream Motivation Analyst Guild has exorbitant membership fees, so I decided to stay a hobbyist."

"Understandable. That's exactly the reason why I never joined the Professional Ice Cream *Eater's* Guild. So what about you? What's your ice cream reason today?"

She looked down at hers, picked up a spoonful and put it in her mouth, a look of pure enjoyment on her face. "Celebration."

He held his ice cream cone out for a cheers, and she picked up her bowl and bumped it into his cone.

"So what are you celebrating?"

She sat up straighter in her chair and said, "I'm ignoring what everyone else wants me to do, and going six full months without dating."

Aaron thrust out his hand. "Hi, my name is Aaron Hall. Nice to meet you."

The woman laughed, then reached out and shook his hand. "Macie Zimmerman. I'm guessing we might have something in common."

## Chapter Three

"So tell me," the man across from her said, as the chaos of kids on the basketball team all asked for sample spoons, "why are you choosing to go six months without dating?"

This was all still so new to her. She hadn't even thought about it much before she told Joselyn this morning, and now that she was telling this guy she just met, it felt like it was a commitment she was setting in stone. "Family is hugely important in my family. Well, it's hugely important to me, too. I would love to get married and have lots of kids, but I haven't found the right man to tie the knot with. And believe me, I've searched. Searching is exhausting mentally and emotionally, and I just need a break."

She lifted one shoulder in a shrug, and then straightened the stack of papers in front of her. "There's a time for everything, and I feel like right now, it's time to focus on seeing if I can turn my business into something more. How about you?" She studied him, trying to read his body language and reading between the lines of what little he'd said. "I'm guessing you've got some reasons for not dating too."

He turned his cone around, studying his ice cream like it held all the answers. "My reasons have to do with where dating leads, and that is always to either a break up or a marriage. And break ups get old after a while."

"And you don't see marriage in your future?"

"In *my* future? Not even a little bit."

"I'm sensing a story there, too."

He took a bite of his ice cream and chewed it slowly. "Trauma as a young adult, and a repeat as a slightly less-young adult. Not really an interesting story."

"And you're jaded. Don't forget that part."

He smiled, and his dimples were even visible through his scruff. They were cute. Actually, his brown scruff and matching short brown hair was cute, too. "You're a perceptive one, Macie Zimmerman."

"Only if you're eating ice cream. It kind of comes with the whole amateur Ice Cream Motivation Analyst gig." She ate a spoonful of hers. There was just nothing that paired better with ice cream than Dr. Pepper. First bite or the last, each one was exactly right. "So, do you have a 'no dating' pact too?"

"Before tonight I've pretty much had an 'always dating' pact, but after a day like I've had, going without sounds like an excellent idea. Why? Are you looking for an account-ability partner? Is this going to be a hard commitment to keep if you don't have someone to report in to?" He crunched into his cone.

She thought of everything not dating would entail, and suddenly she was worried it actually would be a hard commitment to keep. "I just wish I could get everyone off my back. Telling my parents definitely isn't going to be fun. Not that they're controlling or anything, but they do know I want to get married and so they're going to think I'm making a terrible choice. And then there's the matter of my siblings and everyone in town always trying to set me up. Maybe I should have Whitney write an article in the Nestled Hollow Gazette with a big headline saying *Macie Zimmerman isn't dating for six months, so for the love of her sanity, don't set her up on any blind dates.* If I could get her to put it on the front page in big text, maybe people would listen."

Aaron laughed a big hearty laugh that made Macie chuckle. "Do you think she would add my name to that headline?"

"People in town are trying to set you up, too?"

He shook his head and licked the side of his cone. "I live in Mountain Springs. But I teach at Nestled Hollow High, and my students have made it their goal to get me married off by the end of the school year. And they're a pretty relentless bunch."

"No. They didn't." Macie laughed. She knew most of the high school students at NHH, and just imagining them being matchmakers to their teacher was the funniest thing she'd heard all day. She didn't mean to keep laughing, but she couldn't help it. "And I thought things were bad with my family and all the townspeople."

Aaron laughed, too. "You know, when one of my students said that hashtag *NHH Finds a Wife For Mr Hall* was trending, I didn't think it was so funny, but it really is."

Macie laughed even harder. The ten-year-olds were all getting their ice creams one by one and filling in the tables behind her. She pointed her spoon at the man. "See, what you need is a fake relationship. Get someone who will pretend to be your girlfriend, and then the students will feel like their job is done and back off."

Aaron froze, and then a grin spread across his face. "Not only are you the best amateur Ice Cream Motivation Analyst I've ever met, but you're also a brilliant genius. That would fix everything." He met her gaze, his eyes practically sparkling. "So are you up for the job?"

"Wait," Macie said. "Me? I wasn't meaning me." She paused, blinking a few times. "You want me to be your fake girlfriend?"

"Sure! Why not? We're both in the same boat, so it's a win win. I could get my students off my back and you could get your family and everyone else in town off your back. We could go on a couple of strategic fake dates, and then in a few months we could break up. Our broken hearts would buy us at least three more months of people backing off. Then bam, you've got your six months, and I'll have made it to the end of the school year."

"Wow, I really am kind of brilliant." She paused, searching his face. "But I don't know. That's just... I don't know."

"You want to get married and I never want to, so obviously the two of us would never work out as a couple. That's what makes this so perfect. No romantic feelings will get in the way— we'll just be two teammates working together for a common goal."

The more she thought about it, the more excited she became. This could be the answer she needed that she hadn't even known she was looking for. "Do you think it would really work?"

The basketball team was all around the three other tables in the shop, all talking over one another and comparing ice cream flavors, raising the noise level and the excitement level in the room. The excitement started to bleed from them to her.

"Why not? How old are you?"

"Twenty-seven. You?"

"Twenty-nine. So pretty close. Plus we'd make an attractive couple."

Macie glanced at her sister and bit her lip. Could she keep a secret like this from her?

Aaron tipped his head Joselyn's direction. "Who is that you're worried won't believe you?"

Macie chuckled that her face had been so easy to read. "My sister Joselyn. She knows we just met today."

"She's seen us having engaging conversation. That usually precedes a date."

"True." Macie would have to keep it a secret from everyone else in her family, too. Could she do that? She was the one who obeyed the rules. She didn't lie. But the more she thought about it, the more sense it made. She could already feel the weight of the hope and disappointment that came along with dating lifting from her shoulders, and with that, she felt a smile lifting her face.

Macie pushed her ice cream off to the side, pulled the notebook from her stack of papers, opened it in front of her, and picked up her pen. "We need to figure out the details before we can enter into a contract."

"You aren't going to make me sign in blood, are you?"

"No, but we will need to head over to City Hall and have Gloria notarize it." She enjoyed the look of surprise on his face before she let him know she was kidding. But really, a part of her did want something more official than scribbles in her notepad.

"Okay, details," Aaron said. "We should probably each choose an event to show up together at that's really going to give us the biggest bang for our buck. Oh! I've got it. Can I borrow your pen?"

Macie handed it to him, and he pulled a couple of napkins out of the holder that sat on their table and wrote something on it, hiding what he was writing. Then he folded it up in a fancy way that made it look like an envelope, completely surprising her that he knew how. He slid it across the table, a look of fabricated shyness on his face.

Macie picked it up, opened the "envelope," and read what he'd written out loud. "Will you go to Winter Formal with me? Ice cream if you'd say yes." The note took her right back to her high school days and she laughed. "Winter formal, huh?"

"I'm chaperoning. If we went together, all of my students would see. We'd be dressed fancy, which will make them go crazy for it. We could dance a few dances, and in their mind, the deal would be sealed. What do you think?"

When was the last time she had dressed up fancy? It might be fun to do it again. "When is Winter Formal?"

Aaron winced. "This Saturday. Is five days enough notice to get a dress?"

"Maybe." She took her pen back, pulled out her own napkin, wrote down her answer, folded it into a different envelope shape that she'd learned back in elementary school, and handed it to him.

After opening it, he read out loud, "'That sounds *sweet*. I won't leave you out in the *cold*— we were *mint* to go together.' Aww. My students would be so proud of this exchange here. I might have to tell the story in class. Okay, why would they not eat their cones?" he asked as he gestured with both hands toward the tables behind Macie. "The cone is practically the best part!" He took a big bite of his.

Macie turned to see what Aaron was looking at. All of the basketball kids had eaten the ice cream out of their cones, and were putting them pointed side up on a tray, balancing more on top like a house of cards trying to be a castle. The noise level in the shop rose with each cone that they managed to put on top without falling.

Macie laughed at how much enjoyment the kids were getting from it, then turned and wrote *Aaron's strategic date: Winter Formal* on her paper, then tapped her pen on her lips, trying to decide what would be her best strategic date. "Really, my most strategic date would involve my family. How willing are you to go to a family thing with me? It might be the only way to convince them, since if I really had a boyfriend, I'd bring him, no questions. My family has two parties— one on Christmas Eve that goes into Christmas Day, of course, but we also have a Christmas Kickoff get-together the weekend closest to when the twelve days of Christmas starts. It's the Saturday after the Winter Formal."

"That could be fun. Sure, why not?"

"I'm the youngest of seven kids."

Aaron's eyes grew wider.

"And they'll all be there."

She paused to let that sink in.

"And they're all married."

She waited, giving him a moment.

"And they all have kids."

Really, it was comical how wide his eyes were getting. She ducked her head in apology. "Change your mind about this agreement? We haven't gone to Gloria to make it official, so it's not too late to back out."

Aaron swallowed hard and looked at his ice cream cone like it had betrayed him. Then he got up and threw it in the garbage can, then made his way back very slowly. She bit her lip, watching him, trying to guess exactly how awful that would be for him.

He sat back down, eyes on her, and said, "How many people are we talking?"

Macie looked up at the ceiling, doing the calculations in her head. "Thirty-three. Plus us."

"You've seriously got thirty-four people in your family, just with you, your parents, and siblings on down? Without counting aunts or uncles or cousins?"

She nodded. "Why? How many do you have?"

"Four, including me. Unless you count the woman my dad married, then five." His eyes shifted to the chaos that the ten-year-olds were making as two of them were now trying to see who could smash their cones into bits the fastest. "So you're saying that a get-together at your house is kind of like that."

Macie winced.

"It's worse?"

"Well, that's like what? A dozen kids? We've got nineteen. Not that nineteen is much more than twelve, though," she added, hoping that it softened it a bit.

He sat up straighter in his chair. "Do you know what? I have one class with thirty-three students. I can do this. Write it down."

"Are you sure?"

"I'm asking you to get a dress on extremely short notice. It's the least I can do."

She wrote down *Macie's strategic date: Family Christmas Kickoff party.* "We might need a couple more dates just to make sure it's believable. Should we just say that we'll keep the number even between yours and mine?"

Aaron nodded.

"Sorry to interrupt."

Macie jumped at her sister's comment. She hadn't noticed her coming.

"The night crew just got here," Joselyn said, "so we thought we'd head over to Snowdrift Springs Park and see if they need any help with decorating the city tree before the lighting. Do you want to join us?" Her eyes cut to Aaron. "You could bring your friend."

Macie's and Aaron's eyes met, and he raised an eyebrow, asking if she wanted to go. "It might make Saturday go more smoothly if we've already been somewhere together."

"True," Macie said, even though it would make the fake relationship thing go from theoretically a good plan to real life scary and committed, even though she hadn't had nearly enough time to consider all the angles enough to commit yet. She didn't take leaps like this. But, she told herself, this wasn't a leap. This was taking the safe way around in order to *avoid* leaps. She studied him for a moment, and then turned to her sister. "Emily is closing up Paws and Relax and taking care of the animals, so I'm good there, but I'll still need to stop by after to get Lola and Reese. But we'd love to."

"What's Saturday?" Joselyn asked.

This was the moment. She'd have to commit to it fully if she was going to convince Joselyn. "We," Macie said, smiling at Aaron, "have a date."

## Chapter Four

aron had been teaching at Nestled Hollow High for more than three months, but he realized that all of his time spent in Nestled Hollow had been at the high school, or, on the very rare occasion, grabbing a quick bite to eat. He'd quickly fallen in love with the students there and he had the time, so he'd volunteered for nearly every after school assignment the school offered. But all of that— every swim meet, school dance, football game, band competition, drama production, tennis match, and soccer game—had been on campus. He'd spent almost no time at all in the town itself.

Come to think of it, he hadn't spent much time at town functions in Mountain Springs either. Or in Colorado Springs before that. So the tree decorating caught him a little off guard. Apparently the lighting itself wasn't until six, and that's when everyone showed up, but there was still at least three dozen people there, helping to decorate the giant tree smack dab in the middle of the park. It stood several feet taller than all the others, and looked like it had probably been there since before Nestled Hollow was even a town.

Macie seemed excited by the event, and she was trying to get him excited, too. True, he spent most of his time with high school students and adults, but families came to NHH sporting events, so it wasn't like he wasn't used to crowds like this. Maybe it was just because as a kid, his life had revolved around swimming, school, and his sister's dance competitions. Going to town events just wasn't in his family's DNA.

"We should help them decorate," Macie said.

Several high ladders were evenly spaced around the tree, and the city had one of their cranes with the basket at the end to hold a person that was extended to the top of the tree. There were several people to each ladder, standing at different heights, and people were passing ornaments up, assembly-line style.

"I'm not sure we're supposed to," Aaron said. "Besides, it looks like they've got it under control."

She gave him a smile that clearly said she thought that was a flimsy excuse, and pulled him toward the totes of ornaments along with Joselyn, Joselyn's husband, and their baby. The people in charge must have been okay with everyone helping, because nobody stopped them. And it was actually a lot of fun— he was glad that Macie had made him participate.

The darker it got, the more families arrived. Not too many teens had been at the decorating part, but more and more of them were coming in anticipation of the lighting. At 5:45, they took down the ladders and set up a microphone and a small platform. People started finding spots in front of the tree.

"It's getting pretty cold. I think I'll go grab my bike from in front of the ice cream shop and head home."

"You can't leave," Macie said. "They haven't lit the tree yet."

He glanced up at it. "This isn't really my thing. I've seen a couple of students already, and the rumor mill will probably take it from here."

"Have you never seen a big tree lighting before?" When he shook his head, Macie said, "It's incredible. It's nothing like a tree in your living room. It took Sam three full days to get this many lights wound onto the tree. Stay. It'll change your life."

He raised an eyebrow in challenge.

"Think I'm wrong? The only way to prove it is to stay."

"Perceptive *and* persistent." He took a deep breath, looked up at the tree, and then glanced at the crowds pulling up in the parking lot or walking toward the park, all bundled up in their winter clothes. Some of them were certainly his students. And after helping to decorate the tree, he actually found himself wanting to see how it would look lit up. "Okay, I'll stay."

She led him to an area in front of the tree near the microphone, on the side that people coming from the parking lot would reach first, and they both rubbed their hands together to keep warm. Not two minutes passed, and he could already see a handful of more students. Morgan and LeeAnn headed straight for them.

Macie slipped her hand into his. He turned to her and smiled. "Nice touch." She grinned back at him.

"Hi Coach Hall! Hi, Macie!" Morgan said as the two girls from his AP class neared. He caught the moment that both girls' eyes flicked to their hands and then back up to their faces.

Aaron looked from Morgan to Macie. "You two know each other?"

"Well, duh," Morgan said. "We do live in the same town. And she gives me puppy therapy. I swear I wouldn't have made it through finals at the end of last year if it wasn't for her."

LeeAnn nodded her agreement. "And without her, I never would've been able to handle breaking up with Peter."

"Basically, if it weren't for Macie opening Paws and Relax, we'd both be blubbering piles of Morgan and LeeAnn-colored goo on the ground."

"It's true," LeeAnn said. "She, like, literally saves lives."

"Wow. A life-saver and an all-but-pro Ice Cream Motivation Analyst. You are one talented woman." How had they decided to commit to a fake relationship, and he hadn't once even thought to ask what she did for a living? That was the kind of thing a boyfriend would know. He needed a crash course in Macie Zimmerman.

"Don't forget perceptive and persistent," Macie said.

He smiled. "I'm pretty sure I couldn't forget that if I tried."

"So you two are dating?" Morgan asked. "When did this happen?"

Well," Aaron said, "we first met this morning, actually. It was a pretty explosive meeting, like a bolt came out of nowhere and knocked me right off my feet. With such a memorable meeting, I couldn't stop thinking about her all day long. One thing led to another, so we met at With a Cherry on Top—"

"Where he knocked me off my feet just as quickly—"

"And we had an amazing conversation and just really hit it off."

Macie looked up at him and smiled. "By the time we finished a *Is the Doctor Pepper In?* and a *Maple, Please Bring Home the Bacon*, we had decided that life would be perfect if we started dating."

LeeAnn put both of her hands over her heart. "Oh my goodness, that is the sweetest story I've heard in my life!"

Macie reached out and placed her fingers on his biceps. "It doesn't stop there, girls. He even asked me to Winter Formal."

Both girls squealed in delight.

Morgan glanced at the choir. "Oh! We've got to get up there quickly." She grabbed LeeAnn's wrist, and started backing toward the choir while calling out, "But we want to hear all about this in class on Thursday!"

This was working even more perfectly than he could have possibly hoped. Macie was pulling it off beautifully. As the chatting from the crowd grew, he leaned in and whispered in her ear, "You are amazing, teammate. That went beyond what I had hoped for. And pulling it off in front of those two was especially perfect."

Macie turned and put her lips right next to his ear and said, "And I'm pretty sure that you leaning in to whisper in my ear like that just set the rest of the town abuzz. Nice work, teammate."

He stole a quick glance behind them and sure enough, everyone was watching them, even Macie's sister and her family. Smiling, he turned back as Macie pressed her side into his, blocking the fist she raised from everyone's view behind them. He bumped his fist into hers as they grinned at each other. "We've got this."

A man stepped up to the microphone, and the crowd quieted. Macie leaned closer and said, "That's Mayor Stone."

"Welcome to the one hundred fifty-fourth annual lighting of the town Christmas tree! I think a lot of you remember when this beauty was a little shorter and a little easier to decorate," he said, putting his hand on one of the lower branches of the tree and looking up at its height. "She's all grown up now, so we decided she needed a few more lights than she had before. This year, it's an unprecedented thirteen thousand seven hundred lights!"

Everyone around cheered, so Aaron joined them and clapped.

"Now the Nestled Hollow High choir's here," the mayor said, "and they've got a special number for us. When they're finished, we'll flip the switch and watch magic happen!"

"I'm ready for my life to be changed," Aaron said as the choir started singing. "I hope you weren't just using hyperbole on me."

"I stand by my hyperbole. It comes with a Macie Money Back Guarantee."

As the choir sang *Do You Hear What I Hear*, Aaron found himself swaying back and forth slightly, along with the rest of the town. Like they were all Whos down in Whoville. He immediately stopped swaying.

The choir did sound pretty amazing, though. It was great to see so many of his students singing—he was used to only seeing them at school events.

They all sang louder as they neared the end. "He will bring us goodness and light." They held out the last word so long that he was so proud of the lung capacity of all of his swim team members in the group. As the conductor motioned to cut off the song and the last sounds of the word "light" faded into the mountains, the lights of the Christmas tree lit up the entire park. Aaron had to admit that it was one of the most beautiful displays of light he had ever seen.

And with a loud bang from somewhere across town, everything went dark.

Amidst the surprised murmurs and exclamations from the crowd, someone called out, "Looks like you made it a little *too* unprecedentedly awesome!"

"Well," someone else said, "we now know what our maximum awesome is. I guess we need to dial it back."

"Nonsense," the mayor said. "We've never dialed it back before, and we're not about to on my watch. Folks, it looks like we managed to flip the breaker, of sorts. I know this is a huge disappointment for everyone, and that you all had hoped to be reveling in the beauty of the tree, but don't you worry. As you can see, Sam has already taken off running to go see if he can find and fix the problem. Now help yourself to some refreshments over here, and we'll hurry to get some lamps set up so you can see what you're eating."

Joselyn neared with her husband and baby and Macie asked them, "Are you guys staying for refreshments?"

The husband—Aaron was going to have to find out his name soon—answered, "Of course! Power's out to our houses, anyway, so no sense going home. What about you two?"

Aaron looked at Macie. "I've got a twelve mile bike ride ahead of me. I think I better grab my bike and head home."

Macie shivered in the cold, probably thinking about how much colder the wind made a bike ride when the temperatures were low like this. "It's so dark! Do you want a ride home? I've got a brother with a truck. He's probably here somewhere with his family. We could put your bike in the back and I could drive you."

He smiled. "Nah. I do this kind of thing all the time, so I'm prepared. I've got a great headlight, warm clothes, and a path I could follow with my eyes closed."

"I'm going to head over with him," Macie said. "I'll grab Reese and Lola from the shop while I'm there—I'll see you all back at home."

As they walked back to the far end of Main Street where he'd left his bike outside of With a Cherry on Top, Aaron and Macie chatted about how it went and about the dance. The news that the students were going to band together to find him a wife had spread so quickly, he was interested to see how fast the rumors that he was dating Macie would spread. He could barely wait for school tomorrow to find out.

As they passed Paws and Relax, the dog that had caused his bike wreck this morning and the other big dog that Macie had with her raced to the front windows, their barking muffled behind the glass. Macie waved at them, and gave them some kind of hand signal. He remembered from what LeeAnn and Morgan had said that this was her business, so he at least knew that about her.

"Oh! Phone numbers!" Macie said as she pulled out her phone and unlocked the screen. She opened her contacts and handed him her phone.

He did the same and handed his to her. She took a picture of herself first, and then started entering in her information. Aaron thought of following suit, but the truth was, he hadn't perfected the art of taking selfies, so he just put in his name and phone number. He switched phones back and looked down at the information Macie had put in his contacts for her. The picture drew his eyes first. With all the power out in the town, she was lit only by the silver moonlight, and it made the picture look like it was in black and white. Instead of looking at the camera, she was looking off in the distance, looking for something or someone in the dark.

Then he noticed her contact information. "Macie 'My Mysterious Goddess' Zimmerman?"

She smiled and lifted one shoulder in a shrug. "In case I call or text and one of your students sees it." She glanced down at her phone. "Aaron 'Dashing Man' Hall."

Aaron burst out laughing, and Macie quickly joined him. The truth was, he'd never entered his contact information like that into a woman's phone before. But it had somehow felt right in this fake relationship of his.

"Text me the details about the dance," Macie said as Aaron grabbed his helmet off his handlebars and fastened it on his head.

"Will do." He swung a leg onto his bike and flipped on the headlight. "And I'll start preparing myself for the onslaught of your family a week from Saturday."

"Throwing yourself into the chimpanzee enclosure at the zoo might help with that."

Aaron chuckled nervously. "Good to know."

## Chapter Five

*M*acie practically skipped from task to task as she took care of the animals at Paws and Relax the next morning. Last night had been fun. This fake relationship thing was one of the better ideas she'd ever had. When Joselyn got back home, she found out that four of her siblings had been at the tree lighting, and had seen her and Aaron together. They had pulled everything off so well, apparently they all had thought she was dating someone new.

She'd been worried about whether or not she'd be able to convince her sister. But Joselyn knew that when Macie first started dating someone, before she figured out for herself what she really thought of him, she didn't like talking about it. Macie always needed to get things figured out in her own mind first. Chatting as both sisters and best friends with Joselyn, getting excited about all the little things the guy she was interested in did— that came later. The precedent she had set really worked in her favor this time, because she hadn't had a lot of practice in fooling people.

Emily, her one and only employee, didn't have any college classes today, and was more than happy for the extra hours (and the extra time with the animals) that Macie offered her by coming in today. Once all the animals were fed and petted and played with and cared for, Emily walked in. Macie filled her in on the schedule for today— a Parent, Preschooler, and a Puppy weekly event in an hour, the open Pet a Pet hour during lunch, where anyone could drop in to get a boost and a bit of relaxation, and the daily Chill After School session. Then she headed into her office, closed her door, and spread her business plans across her desk.

And then she remembered about the dance. She pulled out her phone and texted Brooke, the woman who owned Best Dressed, a shop on Main Street that sold fancy dresses. She took a deep breath, and then decided it was time to start planting more seeds about her's and Aaron's budding "relationship."

*Hi, Brooke! I started dating a man who asked me to accompany him as he chaperones Winter Formal at the high school on Saturday. I know it's short notice, but any chance you still have a dress available?*

Brooke's response came quickly.

*Yes! I have the perfect one for you. And you're in luck, because I just stepped off a plane three days earlier than I had planned. Can you come to the shop at 4?*

Macie quickly typed her response.

She pressed *send*, and then got to work on her plans.

It felt good to pour all her focus into her business. Everything went so well when she was with the animals. This— her business and the pets— was definitely all she needed in her life.

She spent the day brainstorming ways to let more people experience the joy of these animals, especially the dogs. After several hours, she had what she thought was a great list of ideas.

She had one page listing birthday party packages, where she'd team up with her sister's and brother-in-law's shop for ice cream at the end. She'd come up with different packages, along with their prices and what they offered, and she'd even come up with a list of games that would involve the dogs, a treasure hunting game to find the lost cat toys (since they were always lost within moments of finding them anyway), and time to play with and hold the animals. She had a party package where she would take the dogs to the birthday boy's or girl's house or a park, with her or Emily running the party.

She had a field trip plan for the local elementary and middle school science classes, with information about each type of animal, and what instantly became her favorite: a program where people could rent-a-pet for an hour or an afternoon or evening, so they could enjoy a pet in their own home. She hoped people would see how much they enjoyed it, and think about adopting their own rescue pet.

Each item would take a lot of time and effort to get graphic images, signage for her shop, her website updated, and advertising. She had her work cut out for her. But the dogs were good dogs who loved being around people. It made her happy thinking of how much they'd enjoy more time to play and be loved and take a nap in someone's lap.

If all these plans went well, though, she might be able to make enough each month to justify putting an offer on the building. Except that was such a huge commitment that part of her worried she'd never be able to make the choice in the amount of time she had.

Her stomach grumbled, and she lit up her phone to see the time. No wonder she was so hungry! She had worked all the way through lunch, and it was almost time to meet Brooke to look at dresses. After organizing all her new plans into a nice stack, she hurried out of her office. A half-dozen elementary school-aged kids, including one of her nephews, were playing with the dogs and cat and hamsters, and a couple of high school students were brushing Reese's fur, and one had a cat asleep in her lap.

"Everything going well?" Macie asked Emily.

"Sam went into her crazy cat ninja mode for a bit and alarmed Cookie and a couple of kids, but that only lasted about twenty seconds before she plopped down in front of Brandon here, looking to be petted. Other than that, we've been doing great!"

"Are you okay to run things until I get back? And then I'll stay until time to close things up."

"No problem. Oh, hey—I heard you were dating some-one! Why didn't you tell me last night?"

This wasn't normal dating, so it was time Macie stopped doing her normal "don't say anything until you decide how much you like him" responses. She agreed to this fake rela-tionship so that people would stop setting her up on dates or saying who she'd be perfect for, so she might as well take full advantage of the plan. She smiled big. "His name is Aaron, and he teaches history at the high school, and he's pretty amazing, actually, and that's all I'm going to say about that." Then she ducked her head, which she hoped came across like she was a little shy talking about it, instead of the truth, which was that she wasn't sure how well she pulled off the lie, and she just realized that the high school students were listening in.

Emily squealed, and out of the corner of her eye, she could see that the high school students were doing silent squealing, as if she couldn't tell that they were eavesdropping. "I've got to run. Have fun!" she called out to the room, and then raced out the door.

This would get easier, right? The more people she told, the more comfortably it would come. She just needed to think thoughts of her ideal man before talking, and pretend that she'd finally found him. She crossed over the creek that ran down the middle of Main Street at the Center Street bridge, and went into Best Dressed near the middle of the block.

A bell rang on the door when she walked in. Even with the dance just three days away, there were still a few dresses and tuxes in the shop. As she waited for someone to come up to the front, Macie wandered toward the dress side and looked at a few of them. They all had the *By the Brooke* tag on the inside of the neck with Brooke's company logo, and were all beautiful. She glanced at one of the price tags. She was a good saver, but with the uncertainty about her business, she was nervous about spending so much.

"Macie!" Brooke said as she came from somewhere in the back to the store at the front. "I swear it feels like I've been gone for a month. It's good to see you! Come on back."

"Oh, we're not looking at—" Macie motioned to the dresses in the store as Brooke grabbed her hand and led her toward the back rooms.

"No, those aren't for you. So I've only been back in town for like two seconds, but long enough to hear that you and your new man are 'so cute' together."

"It's true," Macie said. "We're a 'downright delightful' couple."

Brooke laughed. "This town really does get excited about things like this, don't we? That's why I only go on dates with people in other states."

Macie had never been in the back rooms of Best Dressed. It was easily four times the size of the front, and Brooke's two employees stood around a big design table, discussing a pattern in front of them. She was pretty sure that one of the women lived in Denver and commuted here. The other woman moved to Nestled Hollow not long ago, but Macie didn't know her. Bolts of fabric hung on the walls, and 3 sewing machines sat at big tables. It looked like there were a few offices in the back. She waved at the other two women, and they smiled back.

Brooke turned and studied Macie. "Really, though, you look happy. Are you happy?"

Macie smiled thinking about it. She was happy about how everything was working out. She channeled that in her answer. "I am. It's new and fun and I'm enjoying it."

"Good to hear. Now are you looking to keep or return?"

At first, Macie thought Brooke was talking about Aaron, and a pang of worry hit her that Brooke had seen beyond their facade. Then, probably at Macie's confused face, she reworded it. "Do you want to borrow or buy?"

"Oh! You loan dresses?"

"Not usually. Only to you, actually. You only need it for a few hours on Saturday, right? I know you're looking into possibly buying your building, and I'm guessing you'd rather not have an unexpected expense right now. Yes?"

Macie let out a huge breath. "Brooke, when I said you were a godsend, I clearly was minimizing your amazingness."

"Well, you, my fellow single businesswoman," Brooke said, holding a swatch of fabric up by her face, "are freaking adorable and I've always wanted to dress you in one of my gowns."

Macie drew back in surprise. "For real? Why?"

Brooke smiled. "And that's just one of the ways in which you're adorable."

Macie didn't have long to be confused before more questions came her way. "Do you have a color preference? Style preference?"

"Honestly, I haven't dressed up fancy or even thought about dressing up fancy for so long, I don't even know what my preferences are."

"Can I choose then? I have one I designed with you in mind."

"*Me* in mind? I don't understand."

Brooke walked to a door at the back half of the building as she talked, and Macie followed her. "With every dress I design, I have a certain person in mind. I figure that person represents a slice of the population. If I am designing with that specific person and their personality in mind, it should resonate with the slice of the world that person represents."

Macie's phone dinged, and she pulled it out as Brooke went through her racks of dresses. It was a text from Aaron.

*Hello, my mysterious goddess. The dance starts at 8:30, and they need chaperones there at 8.*

Macie smiled and typed in her response.

*Sounds great, my dashing man. I will meet you at the high school at 8:00 then.*

"Mysterious goddess, huh?" Brooke said and Macie jumped. She hadn't even noticed that Brooke had come back out of the room.

Macie blushed, and then looked back down when her phone dinged. She almost slipped it into her pocket without replying, but then Brooke said, "No—reply. Don't keep that Dashing Man waiting." So Macie opened Aaron's text, read it, and replied.

*Do you know what color your dress is yet? I just want to make sure we look incredible together.*

*I'm finding out right now.*
*P.S. We'll look incredible together even if our outfits go together about as well as eating peanuts and chewing gum.*

*True. Okay then, I'll wear bright bold stripes; you wear lumberjack plaid.*

*Deal.*

"Are you ready to see it?" Brooke asked, a zipped garment bag lying over her arm.

Macie had *thought* she was ready. But it hit her that Brooke wasn't letting Macie choose— she was giving her exactly one dress to try on. What if she hated it? She really didn't want to hurt Brooke's feelings, especially since she was so willing to help her out with such short notice. But she also didn't want a repeat of her own disastrous Winter Formal, where she wore a dress handed down through both of her sisters and had a seam in an essential place that she didn't know was one fast song away from bursting open. She put a smile on her face and said, "Yep!"

Brooke hung it on a nearby rack, then unzipped the white bag and pulled out a royal blue gown that was the most stunning thing Macie had ever laid her eyes on. The satin straps lay just off the shoulders, and fell to a V at the neck, just above exquisite beading through the bodice. The skirt was full, but not gathered as much in the front, giving it a more sleek look while still being worthy of a ball.

"Brooke," Macie breathed. "How...how did you know?" She hadn't even known herself what her perfect formal dress would look like before this moment.

A smile spread across Brooke's face as she ushered her into the room with the racks of clothes. "I told you I'm good at reading people. Now go try it on. I'll help you zip it up."

As soon as Brooke closed the door, Macie slipped off her jeans and sweater and stepped into the dress. The fabric Brooke had used on the lining made the dress feel more incredible against her skin than anything she had ever worn. She opened the door and moved her hair to one side so Brooke could zip it up.

Brooke pulled at several spots along the bodice, testing to see if it needed any adjustments, but it seemed perfect in every way already. "Come see," Brooke said, and led Macie to a full length mirror that was easily four times as wide as her mirror at home.

Macie ran her hands down the front of the dress. There was nothing about it that wasn't exactly right in every way. Dreaming up a dress this incredible wasn't even something her brain was capable of. "Brooke, I always thought you were a pretty cool person. But I had no idea that you were a mind-reading savant. A couture genius. Amazing beyond words."

"Stop it," Brooke said. "It's all you. I could design a dress out of a tarp and sew it with my eyes closed and you'd still look good in it."

Macie rolled her eyes.

"Don't let her downplay herself," Brooke's employee said. "There's a reason I'm willing to drive this far every day to come work with her. She's brilliant."

Brooke blushed and waved away the comment. "So, do you think it'll work? A lot of the girls buy their dresses here, so knowing what they bought, I think it will fit in with the others at the Winter Formal, but it won't make you look like a student."

"I know that every high school student wants to look like a princess at Winter Formal. This dress, though," Macie turned to each side, and then turned to see it from the back, "it makes me feel like a queen." She found herself standing taller and with more presence just wearing it.

Her phone's text alert started going off, text after text in quick succession. She had her phone on silent, and she only had two people on emergency bypass—Joselyn and Emily. She gathered up her skirt and raced back to the room where she'd changed, and pulled her phone out of the pocket of her jeans. The texts were from Emily.

### *Chaos Here*

The next text was a picture of the front area of Paws and Relax with kids and pets running all around, some kind of white substance scattered everywhere. Was that stuffing from one of the sitting pillows? She zoomed in. No, it was toilet paper. It had to be several rolls' worth, strung everywhere and torn to pieces.

### *Come Help?*

Macie sent a quick *On my way* text.

"Let me help unzip you," Brooke said as she stepped up behind her. "It looks like they need you quickly—I can have the dress packaged and ready for you to pick up after work."

"Thank you. For all of this."

"You just make sure you have fun Saturday. Hopefully your date will go more smoothly than that," Brooke said as she nodded at Macie's phone and winked.

## Chapter Six

*A*aron worried it might be hard to convince his class that he and Macie were dating, but he'd barely had to even tell them. By Wednesday morning, the rumors were in full swing, especially since they all seemed to know Macie. Since he didn't live in Nestled Hollow, he hadn't even thought to take the small-town everyone-knows-everyone thing into consideration. This fake relationship thing was going to be a cake walk.

As the week went on and the buzz of excitement from the students about Winter Formal grew, he found himself getting excited, too. He had already chaperoned the Homecoming and Sadie Hawkins dances, so he knew he'd enjoy himself, but he had to admit that he was more excited knowing that he was taking Macie this time. She seemed fun. And he was quite enjoying being on the same team as her in this game they were playing.

For a small moment earlier in the week, he'd contemplated calling around to some costume shops in Denver to see if they had any suits for rent that had bright bold stripes, if for no other reason than he thought Macie would get a kick out of it. But when she texted saying that her dress was blue, he changed his mind. Instead, he put on a crisp white shirt, a tie with a royal and navy blue pattern, and his favorite black dress suit.

Which just happened to have royal blue pinstripes.

Thanks to his quick thinking to get a haircut on Wednesday so it had a few days to get to that just right length, and a fresh trim of his scruff, he had to admit he looked pretty good in his formalwear.

He looked down at his watch. He'd made sure he was ready to go in the mirror of the faculty restroom, and it was now two minutes to eight, so Macie should be arriving any moment. He should get down to the gym to check in.

He had been joking around with the Polanskis, a married couple who both worked at the high school—him as a counselor and her as the Spanish teacher—who were the other chaperones for the night, when he caught movement from the corner of his eye. He turned just as Macie walked into view and he lost the ability to talk. She was all smiles as they walked toward each other and he was all—he wasn't sure. Gaping-mouthed, probably. As they met in the middle, the "you look lovely" he had planned to say never made it to his lips as he took in how amazing she looked.

No, amazing didn't begin to cover it. Words that were never part of his spoken vocabulary filled his mind. Words like *splendor* and *grace* and *brilliance*. All those words translated into a choked, "That is very much not lumberjack plaid."

Macie laughed. "And those stripes are far from bright and bold."

"I guess everyone's just going to have to deal with us

being the best-looking couple here." Aaron winked and Macie laughed, like she thought he was joking. But even if he was the least attractive person in the room, with the two of them averaged together, they'd still win. "Come here—I've got something for you."

He led her to the refreshments table next to the Polanskis, and opened the box he had sitting there. Macie's face lit up. "You even got me a corsage?"

"What kind of high school dance date would I be if I didn't?" He grinned as he slipped it on her wrist.

The lights dimmed, music started playing, and someone flipped on the hundreds and hundreds of clear Christmas lights that were placed in the fake snow that decorated the edges of the gym, wound around the archway where the photographer set up to take couples and group pictures, and hung from the refreshment tables. Another switch was flipped, and projected images of snowflakes filled the ceiling. A few at a time, students started trickling into the room.

"I haven't even thought of school dances in so long!" Macie said. "I forgot how magical dim lights, music, and cheesy decorations can make the gym."

Back when he'd chaperoned his first dance at Bunnell High in Colorado Springs, he learned pretty quickly that kids didn't go out for a smoke or try to spike the punch or sneak off to make out in a dark hallway if he interacted with them. So he and Macie went from group to group around the room, chatting with kids. They held hands the whole time, and that little detail didn't go unnoticed by the students. Macie was great with them, too. She had a way of making them feel important.

"There's a group of girls over there who came stag,"

Macie said as they walked along the outside of the dance floor. "They look like they really want to dance."

"And there's a group of boys over there who look afraid to dance. Shall we give them both a nudge?"

"Three, two, one, and break," Macie said as she released his hand and headed toward the girls. He went the other direction and met up with the boys.

He chatted with the boys, asking them easy questions until they started giving him more than one word answers. Then he asked them if they came there to dance. Every single one of them found a random object nearby suddenly very fascinating to look at.

"Come on, guys. I know you don't want to go home having not taken the chance to dance with someone. See that group of girls over there?" He turned to point out the girls. Macie already had them out on the dance floor, all of them dancing to the fast beat. She gave him an encouraging thumbs up. "They'd love to dance and are just waiting for you to ask. So go ask one of them. If you get turned down, at least you won't go home feeling bad about not trying. And who knows? You might have a great time."

A few of the boys started walking toward them, then halted when they sensed that their friends weren't all coming, and turned back around. "Shoulders back, deep breath," he said to the few stragglers. "Now go be brave."

He smiled as all seven of the boys headed toward the group of girls. As he and Macie met in the middle, all the boys were dancing in the same group as the girls. Some got into it a little more than others, who just kind of bounced in place.

"Nice work," she said.

"You too." As the fast beat came to an end, a slow song

began to play, and the now bigger group of stag students started asking each other to dance. "What do you think? Should we join them?"

She held out her hand and he took it in his, and wrapped his other arm around her waist as she wrapped hers around his shoulder and they began to move. Aaron had dated a fair amount in his life, but he didn't go dancing often. The last time he asked a date to join him as a chaperone, things had gone horribly wrong. "Now, admittedly, I haven't gone dancing with a ton of people since high school, so the pool of competition isn't huge, but you're possibly the most graceful person I've danced with."

Macie gave a little curtsey as they danced. "You aren't half bad yourself."

"You can thank my parents for that—it's not a choice that I would've initially made myself. I grew up swimming competitively, and my parents read somewhere that if your child is in a sport where a lot of precision is required, they'll do better if they also train in ballroom dance. So I joined my high school team."

"And did it help?"

Aaron shrugged a shoulder. "Probably. Hard to say."

"I joined ballroom for an entirely different reason."

Aaron's eyebrow lifted in surprise. "So your parents didn't tell you that your cell phone privileges would be revoked if you didn't join?"

Macie laughed. "Nope. They couldn't have. I didn't get my first cell phone until after graduation. I had been taking dance since I was two, though, so I figured moving from dancing solo or in a group to dancing with a partner wouldn't be too much of a stretch. Not that I was really interested in ballroom per se—but I was interested in Ezra

Knight. Based on our heights, I knew we'd get paired together, and I figured it would be the perfect way to get him to actually notice me."

"Did it work?"

She nodded. "It did. Kind of hard not to notice a person when you've got your arms around them, or are lifting them up in the air."

Aaron managed to choke on his own saliva and coughed a few times in his attempt to recover. "Yeah, you could say that." He was acutely aware of exactly how Macie's waist felt under his hand, and trying not to let it affect his ability to think. Or to swallow without choking. "But no happily ever after to the story, huh?"

Macie shook her head. "I mean, there was for a while. Then I had work after practice one day, so I got changed quickly and walked into the gym where the boys were hanging out together, long before they were expecting any of us. And Ezra Knight was leading a discussion where they were all ranking various body parts of all the girls."

"Ouch."

"Yeah, it was a bit of a crush squasher, so I only stayed on the team for a year. But I got some valuable ballroom dance practice out of the deal. I can now do a pretty mean cha cha. Or at least I could back in tenth grade."

The song ended then, and Aaron released Macie. The next song had a much faster beat. After a few seconds listening, he said, "How about the fox trot? Think we could do it to this song?"

Macie took another step back, finger tapping her lip, looking at him but studying the music, her head bopping to the beat. The more she listened, the bigger a smile spread across her face. She lifted her skirt a few times, like she was testing how much movement she would have before she finally nodded. She put her arms up in the air and moved her hips to the beat, then did a few twirls around him as he stood still. Excitement bubbled up in Aaron, and a smile spread across his face.

Then she reached her arms out straight and put both hands on one shoulder then one in the air. Aaron twirled around once, and then they both started into the footwork. Slow, slow, quick, quick. Slow, slow, quick, quick. He was definitely rusty, but it was coming back to him faster than he thought it would.

He reached out for Macie's hand and she twirled into him, and then they twirled around together. Then Macie stepped out, arms outstretched as he did, and they switched spots, circling around each other, stretching their arms out like it was a dance they'd rehearsed dozens of times. She put her hand on his neck and he put his hand on her back, and they swung around, other arm outstretched.

They moved across the floor, using the footwork he'd learned so long ago, one hand on each other's shoulder, elbows high, other hands clasped outstretched. When they reached the other side, Macie kicked her leg up as he leaned her back. They added so many flourishes to the dance as they went, matching each other so well, he wasn't sure who was leading whom anymore. They just moved to the music and to the movement of each other. They moved from side to side, touching, releasing, touching, releasing. As the song neared the end, he held her close and spun them both together, Macie's leg raised behind her. At the last note of the song, she leaned back on his arm, and he lowered her into an impressive dip and she held it, arm outstretched.

He pulled her back to standing, and they stood chest to

chest, breathing heavy, laughing breaths. Macie was practically glowing, and he suspected he was looking pretty happy himself. He wasn't sure he had ever enjoyed himself that much on a date before. "If high school ballroom had been anything like this, my parents wouldn't have had to force me to go."

"If I'd have had a partner like you, I'd have stayed on the team as a junior and senior, too. I haven't had this much fun dancing in years!"

The cheering around them finally caught Aaron's attention, and he noticed for the first time exactly how many people had cleared the dance floor, making a circle of spectators around them. He spun Macie out, and with their hands still clasped and their breathing still ragged, they lifted their arms in the air, and then took a deep bow.

The next song was another fast-paced song, and the students surrounding them looked ready to dance, so he called out, "And that was our portion of the dance-off. Now show us what you've got!" Then he led Macie to the refreshments table and grabbed them both a cup of punch.

"That was incredible," he said after taking a swallow. "*You* are incredible."

Macie gulped down her punch then said, "You were pretty incredible yourself."

Looking at Macie now, he realized he was admiring much more than the way she looked in that dress. There was something about this girl that was unlike anyone he'd ever dated—for fake or real—before. She was fun and talented and beautiful and amazing with the students and made him feel alive. And having his hand on her waist, in her hand, and dropping her into a dip was electrifying. Not to mention the way it felt to have her hand on his neck or her arm on his shoulder.

But then he reminded himself that what they both wanted out of life was at complete odds with one another. She wanted the spouse and children. He didn't. These kids all around them in this room—they were his kids. He cleared his throat and motioned at the students. "And look what we started."

Macie turned to watch as all the students were on the dance floor, dancing and cheering each other on in one united group, instead of individual couples. Even the two groups of kids who had been hanging out at the walls before were in on the action.

"You're really good with them," Macie said.

Aaron looked out at the students that he normally saw in casual clothing, sitting in his classroom or walking in the halls, or messing around at lunch. "They're good kids."

Hemi, one of the linebackers from NHH's football team, was being spun around by the quarterback. Hemi was trying to act like he was graceful when he was anything but, and the crowd was laughing and cheering.

"Whoa!" He grabbed Macie around the waist with both hands and swung her to the side just as Hemi came barreling their direction. He had barely gotten her out of the way before Hemi crashed into the refreshment table, sending the punch bowl to the ground, cookies and mints scattering every direction. Hemi tried to stand up, but he slipped on the punch and fell back down. Students raced forward to pull him up, but they each ended up slipping and joining Hemi on the floor.

"Hold up," Aaron said, his arms out. "Let's get some towels over here before we have any more casualties." Then he turned to Hemi. "Are you okay?" When the boy nodded, he said, "How about the rest of you? Are we all good?"

When he got confirmations from everyone currently down on the ground, he turned to Macie. "Well, if this wasn't a memorable date before, it definitely is now."

## Chapter Seven

It was easy to fake date Aaron. Macie found herself so naturally reaching for his hand as they had walked around the room, or running her fingers along the back of his neck as they slow danced. If his students weren't convinced before that he was dating someone, they definitely were now. It was too bad that he didn't want kids of his own, because he was fantastic with them. As they had gone around from group to group, she could tell by the way he chatted with each of them that he truly cared about them and wanted the best for them.

After the janitor mopped up the punch, the dance quickly evolved from a dance into a party. Actually, it became more of a sport than a party once someone decided that it would be fun to play hockey with the fallen cookies, and it turned into one massive game with all the students and a couple dozen cookie hockey pucks. For the first few moments, she, Aaron, and the other two chaperones tried to stop the game, but when they saw how much fun the students were having and the unifying effect it was having on them, they decided to join in.

The dance was ending in ten minutes, and although most of the students had left, Aaron had managed to arm a few kids with sweeper brooms, and they were turning cleaning up the mess into a game as well. The other chaperone couple had crashed in a couple of chairs along a wall. Aaron leaned against a wall at the end of the gym, facing the three boys who were cleaning up while simultaneously showing off to their dates. So far, their need to be impressive was working to get the gym back in order.

"I am exhausted," he said, running a hand down his face.

Macie practically fell against the wall facing Aaron, tiredness making any bit of gracefulness she had disappear. "Right there with you. How long was this dance? Like twelve hours?"

"It sure feels like it." Aaron stood up straight. "Wait. Was tonight a glimpse into what I can expect at your family party next Saturday?"

Macie laughed. "No, not at all." Then, once Aaron leaned against the wall again in relief, she added, "My parents mostly have carpet, so clean-up is a bit more hands-on," just to alarm him. And it worked. "No, I'm kidding; it won't be this crazy. Hopefully."

They both stood in silence for a moment, trying to recover enough strength to finish the last bit of clean-up, marshal the half dozen kids out to their cars, and lock the doors. For now, though, they were going to keep letting the kids work on clean-up.

Aaron grinned. "Tonight was fun."

"It was!" Macie said. "The most fun I've ever had at a high school dance, actually."

"Me, too." Aaron face suddenly wasn't looking so tired. He was studying her, his expression soft, curious, thoughtful. "It was the most fun I've had on any kind of date in a long time."

Macie wondered if this was the most fun she'd had on a date in a long time, too, but she suddenly couldn't even think of a previous date she'd been on. All she could think of was tonight's, with Aaron. How rewarding it had been to banter with him and the students, how enjoyable it had been to let spontaneity take over when the dance hadn't gone as planned, how exhilarating it had been to dance with him while being cheered on by a crowd. To feel their way so seamlessly though a dance they'd never done before, yet somehow communicated to each other what to do without using words. On the surface, she barely knew him. Yet a part of them had communicated on a level deeper than she'd been able to communicate with anyone in a very long time.

She had a list she'd made in her high school dating and relationships class of all the qualities she wanted in a future husband. As she got to know each person she dated, she put a mental checkmark next to each thing when the date exhibited that quality, or she'd mentally cross it out when they didn't. She put a check next to *Communicates with me well.*

"You're a fascinating woman, Macie." His eyes were searching her face, like he was trying to know more, to grasp clues about who she was.

Macie was just as eagerly searching his face. The more she got to know him, the more she wanted to know. She wanted to know it all. He reached out and placed his palm on her cheek, and she leaned into it, closing her eyes.

"Macie," Aaron said, and she opened her eyes as she

stepped closer, closing the remaining distance between them.

His eyes dropped to her lips for a moment, which made her notice his lips. Lips that were soft and smooth and framed by the perfect amount of scruff. She met his eyes, and leaned in, her heels making her the perfect height, just as he leaned in.

And then just as her eyes were closing, she noticed his eyes flick to something behind her, and she remembered that they weren't alone. She whipped around to see all six students who remained in the room all focused intently on the two of them, unmoving and silent, probably not wanting to break whatever spell had fallen over Macie and Aaron.

She sucked in a quick breath of air. She and Aaron had just come so close to *kissing*! What in the world had she been thinking? "Oh my goodness. I am so sorry." She turned to the left and then the right in quick succession, trying to remember what she was supposed to be doing right now.

"I'm sorry too. This wasn't part of the deal. I don't—"

"It was the formal wear," Macie said. "We can't be trusted in formal wear."

"It clouded our judgement," Aaron agreed. "That was a mistake."

Macie hurried to the wall that had the last row of chairs, and she grabbed one and folded it flat, then hung it on the rack. Aaron and the other couple joined her. *Come on, Macie!* she scolded herself. *For a second there you let hope sneak in, and that's exactly what you were stopping yourself from doing!* This relationship, out of all the relationships she'd had over the past decade, was the one she could guarantee would never work. Everything here was for show. Maybe Aaron was trying to send the last few kids off with some fodder for rumors that would seal the deal, or maybe he was just as affected by the formal wear as she was—it didn't matter. There was nothing between them, and both of them knew it.

Actually, having them both know that their relationship could go nowhere made the situation less awkward. Both of them knew that the other person wasn't going to have their feelings hurt that the kiss was stopped, because neither of them had meant for it to happen.

When they finished and Aaron walked her out to her car, Macie said, "Mistaken almost-kiss aside, I had a very enjoyable time tonight."

"I did too." Aaron smiled. "So basically, all we have to do is stay away from formal wear, and we'll have smooth sailing from here on out."

She held out a fist and he bumped it with his. A kiss would've definitely put the wrong cap on the evening. Their fist bump was a much better one, signaling what they were — teammates who had just worked together and successfully met a team goal and pulled off the next phase of their plan.

Macie slid into her seat on the fourth pew from the front of the chapel, her family taking up their customary three rows. As usual, she sat with her brother Everett, his wife Hannah, and their kids. Not only was Everett the brother nearest in age to her so they'd always been close, but he and Hannah also had four kids under the age of seven, and could use the help keeping them wrangled and somewhat reverent during the meeting. Today, Macie held two-year-old Kristine on her lap as the toddler put baby Jesus in the manger of the activity book she held and folded the blankets over him.

The pastor finished his lesson on ways to keep Christ in Christmas, and started talking about the importance of traditions—individually, as families, and as communities, and reminded everyone about the festivities going on in Nestled Hollow over the next week. As Macie listened, she noticed how contented she felt. Now that she wasn't going to worry about dating, she realized she was no longer holding one of Everett's kids in her lap, wondering and worrying about when she was going to be able to hold her own child in her lap. She just simply enjoyed being Kristine's aunt.

Her mom always said that she'd find her future spouse once she stopped stressing out about finding her future spouse, so maybe this plan was actually helping. She felt the hope creep in with that thought, and she squashed it quickly. She wasn't going to hope that this new plan was "working." That wasn't why she came up with the no dating plan. She was just going to enjoy being Macie, without having to be *Macie: the woman in search of a husband.* Just Macie. That's all she had to be.

After the closing prayer, she helped her siblings and their spouses and her parents carry, nudge, hold hands, or chase after all her nieces and nephews as they made their way with the rest of the congregation to the youth activity room for donuts, hot chocolate, and coffee. The room was a little too small for so many people, but a storm had blown in early that morning, and the first few flakes had started to fall just as she had entered the building. So the warmth and the happy chatter and the cup of hot chocolate in her hands felt right.

Several of the teenage girls had worn their Winter

Formal dress to services today, and each of them gave her smiles like they were excited to be in on her secret. She chatted with them all and asked how their night was. She tried to think of a way to say "me dating your teacher isn't a secret! Shout it from the rooftops! That part's not the secret, so tell everyone!" in a subtle way, but apparently it was too subtle, because the questions they asked were in hushed voices.

Normally, news in Nestled Hollow traveled fast. So many people had seen her and Aaron last night that she figured that everyone would be talking about it today. That didn't seem to be the case at all.

Like always happened in such a small space, the crowd moved around so much that she often found herself chatting with people who she might not have sought out on her own. Normally, that was one of the things she loved most about the months when it was too chilly to have the gathering outside.

At one point, she found herself chatting with a group of older women—Evia, Misty, and Margie. Apparently, Evia had a nephew, Misty had a grandson, and Margie had a friend with a son who were all perfect for her, and wouldn't it be simply marvelous if they set her up on a date? Maybe she could ring in the New Year with a boyfriend, because who wanted to start off the New Year being alone? As gracefully as she could, she thanked them but said she was dating someone already, and then switched to a different group when an opening came up soon after.

Unfortunately, the next group she found herself in included Bo Charleston and Don Anderson. Normally she would've been relieved, since the men usually didn't try to set her up on dates, but Don's son Paul was in town visiting.

Shortly after Don introduced Paul, he said, "Paul, this is the woman I was telling you about. Don't you think she'd be just right for your friend Jake?"

Paul seemed just as uncomfortable with setting his friend up with a stranger as she was accepting a date with a stranger. She was so glad she had an excuse that wouldn't hurt Don's feelings or make Paul look any more uncomfortable than he already was. "You're always looking out for others, Don. Thank you for thinking of me, but I've already started dating someone seriously."

"Looks like we're a little too late, son. I knew I should've called you about this sooner!"

Macie and Paul shared a smile that told her he knew exactly what she was going through. Soon after, Don and his son Paul got pulled into a different group, and her little group was joined by Chad and Shelly Brown, the couple who owned the bakery on Main Street, and Ed and Linda Keetch. Her smile grew bigger at seeing their faces. She loved chatting with fellow Main Street Business Alliance members whenever she got the chance.

But after a few minutes of small talk, Chad said, "Shelly has a little brother who is awesome. Seriously, we love the guy. He's newly single, and I think you two would be great together."

"You would be. Do you want me to set you two up?"

Macie forced a smile on her face. "I've actually started dating someone." Her phone buzzed right then, so she excused herself, made her way to a corner, and pulled it out from her bag.

It was a text from Aaron.

*HEY THERE MYSTERIOUS GODDESS. HOW'S YOUR WINTER FORMAL HANGOVER? I DON'T KNOW ABOUT YOU, BUT I'M WISHING I WOULD'VE STRETCHED BEFORE THAT DANCE.*

*LET'S JUST SAY THAT I CHOSE TO WEAR FLATS TO CHURCH TODAY. I THINK MY FEET WOULD'VE GONE ON STRIKE IF I WORE SO MUCH AS MY ONE INCH HEELED BOOTS. MAYBE OUR NEXT FAKE DATE SHOULD BE LESS PHYSICALLY TAXING.*

*SPEAKING OF WHICH...*

*I HAVE A GROUP OF FRIENDS—4 PEOPLE, ALL MARRIED. THEY'RE COOL AND ANNOYING AND CURRENTLY THINK I'M MAKING YOU UP. I SHOWED UP DATELESS TO OUR LAST WEDNESDAY GAME NIGHT, AND I DON'T PICTURE THEIR RAZZING ME WILL STOP ANYTIME SOON.*

*WILL YOU COME WITH ME ON WEDNESDAY? I'M PREPARED TO SEND MANY ANIMATED GIFS OF ADORABLE ANIMALS AND POSSIBLY TODDLERS BEGGING IF THAT WILL HELP CONVINCE YOU.*

*I HAVE A BETTER IDEA TO CONVINCE ME. THIS TOWN IS TOO FULL OF TOO MANY HELPFUL PEOPLE WHO APPARENTLY HAVE NO IDEA ABOUT THINGS THAT HAPPEN AT THE HIGH SCHOOL. BE MY DATE AT A TOWN EVENT?*

*SOLD! NAME THE PLACE AND TIME, AND I'M THERE.*

Macie thought for a few moments. The pastor had just mentioned everything going on this week, so it was all fresh on her mind. Which event would be best?

*The Main Street Business Alliance is in charge of a scavenger hunt on Tuesday. Meet me at Center and Main, 7:00. Dress warm.*

Macie smiled as she pressed send. The scavenger hunt was the perfect choice. Come Tuesday at about 7:30, and everyone here would know she had someone in her life, and that she wasn't in need of any interventions.

## Chapter Eight

aron managed to find a parking space on Main Street. Sure, he'd only been on this street half a dozen times, and never during a town event, but it still surprised him that it was still so full of people. He got out of his car, pulled on his hat and then gloves, then adjusted his scarf and his coat. Each breath was making a cloud in front of him. How did they find so many people who were willing to brave this weather?

It was easy to see where the action was—a crowd of a few dozen people were assembling in the space where Center Street crossed Main Street, on the bridge that covered the creek that ran down the middle of the road. He made his way there, and saw Macie behind some long tables, standing next to her sister, chatting and smiling and organizing some kind of papers. A big Christmas bulb-shaped container sat on the table, with a small hole in the top. Macie reached in like she was swirling its contents around.

She was just as bundled up as he was, in her long coat, scarf, hat, and gloves, with her blond hair free and straight for the first time that he'd seen. It really was too bad he couldn't date her for real, because he wanted to more than he'd wanted to date anyone in a while.

But of all the women around, she was the most off-limits of them all. He knew she wasn't looking to date casually, and that was all he had to offer. Turning this into something more real wouldn't be fair to her. They were in this fake relationship as teammates, and teammates didn't do that to each other.

Macie looked up just then and she found him in the crowd almost instantly and her face brightened into a smile. He smiled back, and then their attention turned to a woman who was standing at a microphone.

"Hello," the woman said. "My name is Tory, and on behalf of the Main Street Business Alliance, I'd like to welcome you to the twenty-seventh annual Hayride of the Santas! Those of you who've been here before probably know the drill, but for those of you here for the first time and for Sam—that's right, Sam, I saw you hop off the hay ride early last year—I'm here as your host and judge for the evening. We've got Cole here as your scribe and gift accepter, and Whitney and Eli as your documenters and additional judges.

"We've been coming to you asking for monetary donations for months, and I'm happy to report that we have enough money donated to help out a lot of kids this year who might otherwise wake up Christmas morning without any presents under their tree. You'll divide into teams of four or five people, so go ahead and get your teams together."

Aaron looked at Macie, and she motioned to him, then her, then her sister, and then pointed toward the end of the street. He turned and saw Macie's brother-in-law, the one he saw at With a Cherry on Top, walking their direction. He nodded.

"Okay, *one* of you will come up to the table here, reach inside the giant ornament, and choose *one* piece of paper. On this paper will be the age and gender of a child who you will be purchasing a gift for. It will also list any preferences, colors, sizes, or things they might be currently interested in, along with a budget. Your goal is to brainstorm with your team about what to purchase for the child and to decide which Main Street store might have what you need. You'll go to that store, pick out a gift, and take it up to the register. The store will ring it up, attach the receipt to your paper, and sign off on it.

"You'll then bring the paper with the receipt stapled to it, along with the gift, and check in with Cole. He'll verify that the present is appropriate for the age of the child and that you stayed within budget. You'll then wrap the gift *as a team*. Using only one hand each, and I expect no cheating here. Yeah, even from you, Frank. Your arm may be in a sling, but I've still seen you use those fingers on your injured arm for more things than I think your doctor ever intended."

The man who must be Frank laughed, holding up the arm in the sling, wiggling his fingers.

"Then you'll grab a new slip of paper from the ornament, and head off to find the second gift. The first team with five presents returned and wrapped wins!"

Everyone cheered. Aaron just chuckled. This town sure knew how to turn the typical sub for Santa into an event. He didn't pay attention to what kinds of city celebrations his own city did, and suddenly wondered if they were anything like this.

"Here's the kicker, though. You can't run to the next store.

We've got these two flatbed trucks filled with hay bales here." She motioned to one facing north on the road behind her and the other facing south on the road in front of her, and everyone turned to look. "You can only move from store to store on a hay ride, and May and George have been instructed that they can only move forward if everyone on board is singing a Christmas carol.

"Now I know what you're thinking. What if I'm right there at Wishstones Department Store, and I need to go next door to Toys 'n Trinkets. The buildings are practically touching! Can't I just slip next door? *No.* You can't go an inch past the edge of any store without being on a hay ride. So that means that yes, to go from Wishstones to Toys 'n Trinkets, you'll have to wait for the next hay ride to come along, sing carols while it goes down there to the end of Main, turns the corner, comes all the way along this side of Main, turns the corner again, and brings you back to almost where you started from. Sound like a blast? That's because it is! Okay, send your representatives up to get your first slips of paper, and then start brainstorming. You'll have about three minutes. When you hear the horn sound, the game is on!"

Macie waved Aaron up to the giant ornament, so he wove his way through the crowd and up to her.

"Well, hello, Dashing Man," she said as he reached his hand inside the ornament and grabbed a square paper. "You're looking mighty fine all bundled up."

"So are you, Mysterious Goddess."

She grinned at him, and then motioned to her sister and said, "You remember my sister, Joselyn, right?"

"Good to see you again," he said as he reached out and shook her hand.

"Oh, and here's Marcus," she said.

He committed Marcus's name to memory, and then shook his hand.

Marcus turned to Joselyn. "I checked with your parents, and Aria is doing great." He clapped his hands together. "Alright team, are we ready to win?"

Macie and Joselyn finished getting papers to each team, then Macie handed the ornament to Cole—the man who stood at the other table, who was apparently going to be the scribe and present-wrapping official. Then the four of them huddled around the paper that Aaron held, and he read it out loud.

"So this child is a four-year-old boy, and we're looking for a toy with a forty dollar budget. He likes dinosaurs and Legos and especially playing dinosaurs *with* Legos. His mom says he's a creative and determined kid."

"Toys 'n Trinkets," Macie, Joselyn, and Marcus all said at the same time.

"Toys 'n Trinkets it is then." The whistle blew, and Aaron pushed the paper into his pocket, slid his gloved hand into Macie's, and they raced to get on the back of the nearest truck. Aaron sat on a bale of hay, leaving room for Macie to sit next to him. She did, and leaned her head against his shoulder, snuggling into him for warmth. It felt nice having her so close. So he put his arm around her shoulders and held her tight to him so they'd both stay warm.

The twenty or so of them who seemed to be getting on the truck got on, but it didn't move. Macie seemed to be the first to realize why, and she jerked upright and sang, "Dashing through the snow..." and the truck started to creep forward.

She sang so wonderfully off key, it caught Aaron off guard. He wasn't exactly ashamed of his own voice—he'd taken a year of choir back in high school to fulfill a music requirement and had learned a few things—but he wasn't proud of his voice, either. He usually shied away from singing out of embarrassment, but off-key or not, Macie was belting it out with such unabashed gusto that he couldn't help but want to join in. "In a one horse open sleigh…"

Before long, all twenty of them were belting out the carol, and it was clear that Macie wasn't the only one who couldn't sing on key. Aaron found himself smiling as he sang. Why should people feel like they couldn't join in if they couldn't sing well? The cacophony was actually kind of nice, and in a way that didn't quite make sense, made him feel accepted.

As they neared Toys 'n Trinkets, they all perched on the side of the flatbed truck, and the moment it crossed into that store's territory, they leapt off and raced inside and to the Lego aisle.

Marcus grabbed a set of Lego Duplos. "How about these? They'll fit in our budget."

"I don't know," Macie said. "Those say they're for ages one to five, so he might grow out of them soon. We don't know how close to age five he is already. What about this kind? It says ages four to seven."

"The kid probably has chunky little hands," Marcus said, holding out his own chunky big hands as proof. "These will be easier for him to grab. Plus, if he wants to play Legos with dinosaurs, he probably wants to build something tall that a t-rex can come along and knock down. These kind are the best for knocking down."

As the two of them debated the different sets, with Joselyn throwing in her opinion, Aaron picked up a set that was labeled for ages five through twelve. It said *Island*

*Paradise*, and had blocks that made palm trees and little huts whose doors could open and close, making it perfect for the smaller dinosaurs to get inside. He would've loved that set when he was a little kid.

"He isn't looking to knock down the blocks," Aaron said, his eyes on the set. "His mom said he's creative, so he wants to build a set the dinosaurs can interact with. And he's determined, so he likely won't be discouraged by smaller blocks." He held the set out to the others. "If we get him these, he can add to the set and keep using them for as many years as he'd like."

Macie beamed at him, and looped her arm into his. Marcus took the set from Aaron, and looked at the front and then the back before giving a strong nod. "I think you're right. This is the one."

Further down the aisle, they found a bunch of plastic dinosaurs that were inexpensive, so they grabbed a variety and raced up to the front. After getting their receipt and paper signed off, they hurried outside, but the truck had just passed their building. As they waited in the cold, rubbing their gloved hands together, Macie looked into the bag. "He's going to love these."

Aaron nodded. "This is a fun way to do it."

Marcus stepped behind Joselyn and wrapped his arms around her, kissing her on her temple. As the next truck made its way ever so slowly toward them, he wondered how many of the people were genuinely here for the kids, and how many were here for the free date.

Macie shivered and scooted closer to him. "There were a couple of Christmases when we were little where our parents didn't have money for presents, but it was okay because we had each other, and that was what really mattered. But some of these kids don't have much of a home life. Can you imagine how sad it would be for them if they also didn't get any presents?"

When she said things like that, Aaron had a hard time picturing Macie as being anything other than genuine. Of course, before the very public shame of his parents' divorce had hit him, he had always thought they were genuine. Back then, he'd mistakenly thought Sabrina was, too, so now he didn't put much stock in his judgement. Aaron swallowed. "I can't imagine. That'd be awful." He squeezed Macie's hand. "Whoever this four-year-old is, he's going to love Christmas morning."

The truck finally made it to them, and the four of them hopped on, found seats on the hay, and immediately joined in singing *The Twelve Days of Christmas*. They only had to stay on for a moment before they jumped back off in the middle of Main Street, to the present wrapping station.

"Need a box?" a man asked.

"Yes!" Macie said. "I was imagining trying to wrap all these little dinosaurs with the four of us one-handed, and thought that we'd made a terrible mistake. Eli, I'd like you to meet my boyfriend, Aaron."

She had hesitated for a moment before saying the word "boyfriend," and Aaron realized that it was the first time either of them had said it.

"Nice to meet you, Aaron," the man said as he shook his hand. "Here's your box and your wrapping paper and tape— each of you can choose which hand to put behind your back, but you can't switch once you've decided."

As it turned out, having four right-handed people all choosing their right hand made things more difficult than if they'd had a couple of less-skilled left hands in the mix. A woman with wavy auburn hair was taking pictures of their struggles.

"I think it's beautiful," Macie said when they were finished.

Aaron grabbed a bow with his right hand, and held it while Macie pulled the plastic off the sticky part with her right hand, and he stuck it on top. "I'm not sure 'beautiful' is the word I'd use—"

"But it's done," Marcus said, "and that's what counts." He handed the present to Cole, and Cole checked it off the list and put it in a giant bin.

Joselyn raced to the table with the ornament and pulled out their next paper—an eight-year-old girl who was in need of pajamas, jeans, and socks—and they jumped on the next hay ride.

By the time they'd started shopping for the fifth paper they'd pulled out of the big ornament, it was clear it was down to just them and one other team to take the win. Aaron was pretty sure there wasn't an actual prize to be won, but both teams seemed very determined to win.

"I never would've guessed you were so competitive," Aaron said.

Macie shrugged. "Every year, it's my goal to win this. I've only succeeded once before, but I have a good feeling about tonight, especially with you as a teammate. You grew up swimming competitively, right?"

"I did."

"Were you any good?"

Aaron tried to hide a smile. Normally, he didn't like talking about that part of his life, but every once in a while when someone asked, the urge to tell them the truth about how good he was came on pretty strong. But the urge to know how someone felt about him when they didn't know always won out.

He shrugged. "I guess that depends on who you compared me to." That was *not* the answer he usually gave—that answer practically begged her to ask for details about who he'd be good compared to. And if he answered that, it might give her enough information to piece things together. So he shifted the focus ever so slightly. "And I love helping my team to win now. What do you say we win this?"

He could honestly say that he'd never shopped for all the ingredients for a Christmas dinner at a grocery store in two and a half minutes before, but they somehow pulled it off, got the receipt and had the cashier sign off their paper, then hauled all the groceries to the next hay ride. As they hurriedly started singing *Deck the Halls*, like they would get there more quickly if they did, Joselyn pointed out that the other team had just jumped on their hay ride on the other side of Main, and it looked like they might both reach the present wrapping station in the middle at the same time.

"This is going to be difficult to wrap," Marcus said between fa la la's. "We'll have to be fast."

Macie stood up and moved to the back of the flat bed, leaning out to look at something. Aaron got up and joined her.

She pointed back the way they'd just come. "There was a little kid in the alley between Best Dressed and the library. He was just crying. I think he's lost." She looked up and down the street, standing on her tiptoes to be able to see over the cab of the truck. "I don't see any parents nearby. We have to help him."

She moved to the edge of the truck, and Aaron grabbed the sleeve of her coat. "If we jump off, we'll be disqualified."

She met his eyes, hers pleading. "We *have* to. We're here to help kids in need—what's the point of it if we don't help a kid in need?"

He searched her eyes, trying to tell if that was what she'd really wanted, as a tear welled up in her eye. She batted it away, like it was a traitor ratting her out, and looked back toward the alley before meeting his gaze again.

"Let's go help him," he said as he wrapped his hand in hers, and they jumped off the back of the truck.

For the first time in the last decade, he trusted his own judgement when he realized that Macie might just be the most genuine person he had ever met.

## Chapter Nine

aron picked Macie up at her house, and together they made the drive to his friend's house in Mountain Springs. She studied him as they drove, and she could tell that something was different. He was quieter, and his eyebrows came together in the middle.

"Do you not want to go to this?"

"What? No. I love game night. My friends are good people."

Okay, not the answer she would've guessed, based on his face. She studied him some more. "Oh! You're nervous!"

Aaron looked confused, and then chuckled softly. "I guess maybe I am." He thought for a moment, then said, "Are you nervous to have me meet your family on Saturday?"

"Totally. I'm always nervous when dates meet my family. I worry that my family might not like them, and worried that they'll scare him off."

"My family imploded when I was nineteen, and we all pretty much scattered at that point. But even before then, we weren't much of a family. We never willingly chose to hang out with each other. But these guys, they're my family. Their opinion matters to me a lot."

"And you're worried they might not like me?"

He glanced over at her. "How could they not like you?"

She shrugged. "Beats me. I'm the youngest, so I've been told my whole life that I'm adorable."

"They're going to love you. But if anyone is a tough crowd to convince, it's these guys."

Macie tried hard to remember everyone's names when Aaron introduced them, but she only managed to retain about half. After meeting everyone, though, the guys split off into the kitchen end of the open room, and the women gathered on the couches, and Macie was quick to pick up on and memorize their names. Ciara was the brunette who looked like a model, Timini was shorter, rounder, and constantly smiling, Annah was the quiet one who kept catching her off guard with her funny remarks, and Julie was the one who was seven and a half months pregnant who everyone was gathering around.

"So, other than the fact that I can't seem to hold on to anything," Julie said, "I think we're all ready for this baby to come! Of course, if I can't figure out the holding things part, I might need to hire a nanny just to keep me from dropping her."

"Oh, that goes away right after giving birth," Macie said. "Your joints have to loosen so your hips can adjust for birth, but it loosens all your joints, including the ones in your fingers. That's also why your feet are probably not fitting into your normal size of shoe."

It had seemed like a normal thing to say, but suddenly everyone was staring at her. "What?"

"How do you know that?" Timini asked in awe.

"I have six married siblings with kids. I became an aunt at fifteen. It kind of comes with the territory."

"Will you move in with us?" Julie blurted out, and everyone laughed. "No, seriously. We've got an extra bedroom up there and I don't have a clue in the world what I'm doing."

Macie knew the woman was joking, but it still made her feel good. Accepted. She looked toward the men and met eyes with Aaron. He gave her a smile and a nod, like he was passing along his approval, too, and she smiled back.

"Wow, you two have fallen for each other *hard*, haven't you?" Ciara said.

For the smallest moment, Macie almost protested. Just because he kept proving that he was perfect over and over again didn't mean she was falling for him—she wasn't! Luckily, she caught herself quickly and kept up the show. "He is pretty fantastic."

Then it hit her—Ciara had said they had *both* fallen for each other. So they were already believing it; she and Aaron just needed to keep it up and his friends would be convinced.

Matt clapped his hands together. "Let's get this show on the road, ladies! If I have to stand next to this food much longer, I can't be held responsible for digging in early."

"Ooo, I can't wait to see what Aaron brought," Timini said.

"Aaron?" Macie asked. She knew he brought in a covered glass baking pan, but she honestly hadn't thought much about it.

"His food is divine!" Annah said. "I could hate you all and I'd still come just to eat Aaron's food."

So he could cook, too. Macie mentally checked off the *Must know how to cook* box on her *Future Husband* list. Then she chided herself for once again thinking of him that way. But how could she stop herself when he was standing there like that, holding his arm out to her with that brilliant smile and that *I care about you* face?

Instead of letting herself linger on the impossible, she focused her attention on the others. Like on the way that Ciara went up to Matt and they whispered something to each other, their noses touching, before she turned around and he wrapped his arms around her from behind and she snuggled into him.

Being here with all these happy couples was making her want, more than ever, what she didn't have. It always felt like everyone else got their happy endings. Why couldn't she?

*Stop*, she told herself. *Your perfect guy isn't even in your haystack, remember?*

After the food was cleaned up, and they all still sat around the table, Timini passed 3x5 cards out to all of them and said, "I can't wait to try this game out!"

Her husband rubbed his hands together in anticipation.

"Ian and I came up with this game last night and it's called...Oh my goodness, honey, we never came up with a name!"

Ian thought for a moment, and then blurted out "*Cloak and Dagger.*" Then, just a beat later, said, "*Duck and Cover.*

Oh wait, no. I've got it. *Sneak Attack.* Come on, honey, we have to name it *Sneak Attack.*"

"I can understand the 'sneak' part, but the other part isn't really an attack. It's a challenge."

Ian spread his arms wide. "And what's an attack if not a challenge."

Timini sighed, and Ian put his hands together in a pleading motion, which apparently worked on Timini, because she said, "Okay, this game is called *Sneak Attack.*"

Shad reached out and gave Ian a fist bump.

"You've each got three green cards. Write on the top of each 'Attack.' On these cards, write down a different challenge on each one. Something that one person could challenge any other person to do to see who wins. Like who can stand on one foot the longest, or who can make the other person crack a smile first. Something that will take about a minute or less to do. Everyone else decides who won the challenge and whoever does wins the card."

"Now on your two yellow cards," Ian said, "write 'Sneak' at the top. Write down something that the person who gets that card will have to do without anyone else knowing that they're working on fulfilling a *Sneak* card. Like a phrase they have to say, or an action they have to do. You don't want to make it too easy, like scratching your nose or something, because it's everyone else's job to guess when they're doing something that's on their card. Because if you think you've caught someone else, you can yell," he glanced at his wife, then smiled, "'Sneak Attack!' and you'll win their card, but you can only call it if you weren't the one who wrote it. Get away with it, and you win the card. The person with the most cards at the end wins."

Macie's stomach was starting to feel queasy—probably

from something she ate—but she willed herself to be okay, and started writing things on her card that she thought might be fun to do or funny to watch.

After they'd all turned in their cards and they were shuffled, Timini handed a yellow card out to each of them, and then one by one, they drew a green card and challenged someone to whatever it said. She laughed as Ian and Matt attempted to balance a pencil on their fingertip the longest while trying to blow the other's off, as Shad and Anna competed to see who could fake laugh the best, and as Julie and Timini attempted to whistle a note the longest. All while watching for opportunities to do what her yellow card said: "Tell your spouse/date 'Baby, I'm never cold, because you warm my heart.'" She had been faking this relationship for more than a week now. She could fake this line no problem.

Aaron drew a card and read it out loud. "See who can run barefoot in the snow the longest."

Everyone's eyes darted to the patio doors and the snow that covered the backyard just beyond them, worried that Aaron might challenge them to do it.

Aaron turned to Macie. "You wrote this one, didn't you?"

"Who, me?" Macie asked, trying to feign innocence.

"You did this with your siblings when you were little, didn't you?"

Macie chuckled. "Yes, and then we'd run back inside and wrap our feet in towels. How did you know it was me?"

"Because the only sane person who would do this is someone with enough siblings to talk her into it. So, Macie Zimmerman," Aaron said, slapping the card on the table between them, "I challenge you to a race barefooted through the snow."

They both took off their shoes and socks, rolled up their

pants, and then made their way onto the patio with everyone else. Aaron grabbed her hand, they grinned at each other, and then he said, "Ready, set, go!"

Luckily it had snowed a bit just before they came, so there was a layer of soft powdery snow on top. Just under the top inch or so, though, the snow was a couple of days old, and with the sun shining on it during the day, it had made it icy and a little sharp. With each step, she landed on the soft cushion, and then broke through the crust from the layer just underneath, sinking into the snow up to mid-calf. Their feet pounded step after step, all the way to the end of the yard. And as they ran, she checked off her mental list, *Will do crazy, spontaneous things with me.*

They turned and raced back, still holding hands and right before they reached the patio, Macie stopped in her tracks and dropped Aaron's hand. He didn't have time to react before his bare feet touched the snow-free patio. Apparently he had forgotten this wasn't a race to the finish line—it was a challenge to see who could stay in the snow the longest. He remembered a moment too late, though, and hurried to step back into the snow.

"You might be Poseidon in the water, bro, but you're too late in the snow," Matt said as he clapped him on the back. "She's got you."

*Poseidon in the water, huh?* There was something he wasn't telling her. She made a mental note to ask him about it the next chance she got.

"I should've known better than to challenge the only experienced person here," he said as he placed a kiss on her forehead.

"You should've," she echoed as a pain shot through her stomach. She tried her best not to wince—not in front of people she was trying to impress. She shivered as she sat down in the kitchen and reached for her towel that Dennis held out, but Aaron grabbed it first and wrapped it around her feet. "You look so cold," he said.

She couldn't have planned the setup better. Two cards were going to be hers in a matter of moments. As she reached out and put her hand on his cheek, she said, "Baby, I'm never cold, because you warm my heart."

"Sneak Attack!" several people yelled at the same time.

Macie looked up, bewildered. "How did you know?" At least Shad, Annah, and Ciara had all called her out on it. Maybe even more of them that she didn't catch.

"Sweetie," Ciara said. "Don't ever become a used car salesman. You can't pull off a fake to save your life."

She met Aaron's eyes, and they shared a smile. There was something else in his smile, though, that she couldn't quite interpret. She didn't get a chance to figure it out before everyone was ushered back to the table.

Timini passed everyone their second yellow card. Because Matt was in her field of vision, she saw that he read his card, his eyes flashed at Aaron, and then he looked at her, and then back down at his card. He laid it face down on the table and said, "We've got to go."

Ciara had been laughing at something Annah had said, and she turned to Matt and said, "We do?"

Matt stood up, his chair legs scraping across the floor. "We do." He answered Ciara, but kept his eyes on Aaron. Eyes that looked hurt and betrayed.

Aaron reached out and grabbed the card that Matt had left behind. Macie barely needed to lean in to see what the card said— it was one of the ones that she had written. *Say out loud "I lost my job today."* Macie's hand flew to her mouth as she realized what must have happened. What were the chances of her writing down something that was supposed to be difficult to pull off without being called out, and have it actually be true for someone? And then to have that person be the one who drew the card?

As Matt tucked in his chair and turned to leave, everyone at the table watching him in confusion, Aaron stood up, too, and slid the card into his pocket. He met Matt at the doorway to the entry, and the two had a whispered conversation, and at one point, Matt met Macie's eyes, and then shook his head no to Aaron. Matt said something more to Aaron, and Aaron nodded his head several times, then clapped Matt on the shoulder before he and Ciara left.

Great. The group of people that Aaron was most concerned about impressing were these people, and Macie had totally messed it up. She couldn't tell how much of her sick feeling and the cold sweat breaking out on her forehead was coming from whatever she ate and how much was coming from how awful she felt about offending Aaron's best friend. He was probably wishing he had never brought her. Maybe he'd even want to take her home right away, before she had a chance to inflict any more damage.

"Okay," Aaron said loudly as he came back to the table, taking in everyone's confused faces. "Matt wanted me to apologize that he realized he and Ciara needed to leave so quickly, and wanted me to make sure that we finish this round!"

The other three couples seemed to understand that they weren't going to get any more information about what just happened, and apparently respected Matt's wishes to act like nothing happened. Everyone else refocused on the game with renewed vigor, like they were trying to make up for what negative thing just happened, but Macie couldn't. All she wanted to do was apologize profusely for what had happened. And then crawl into bed and pull the covers over her head.

As Aaron sat back down, he leaned in close and said, "I'm so sorry that happened. Are you okay?"

*He* was apologizing to *her*? Based on her experience dating men who had a tight group of friends, that wasn't what she was expecting at all. Even though she was now sure that the nausea that was creeping over her was very much sickness, she still smiled and felt the smile all the way to her core. "I am, thank you for asking." And then she put a checkmark in her mental list next to *Shows that he puts me before his friends.*

Maybe she had been wrong all along. Maybe her perfect man really was out there.

# Chapter Ten

$\mathcal{A}$aron glanced up at the clock in his classroom to see how much time was left in class. He felt terrible that he hadn't noticed how sick that Macie had been getting last night until she was so bad that he hadn't thought she'd make it the whole way back home without him having to pull off the side of the road.

Sure he'd been distracted by Matt thinking that he had betrayed a confidence and told Macie that he'd lost his job. Macie had seemed to understand exactly what had happened and her role in it. So whenever she looked like she wasn't doing great, he thought it was because of that, and had just vowed to make the game more fun. All along, he should've been offering to take her home early instead.

He figured she'd be sleeping in to recover, so he waited to text until his second period class was watching a short documentary fifteen minutes before class got over.

*HOW ARE YOU FEELING? DON'T ANSWER IF I JUST WOKE YOU UP.*

*Ha! No, I've been up for hours, sadly. Got a shop to run, animals to feed...*

He sat up straighter.

*Please tell me you're joking. You're sick! You've got an employee—Emily, right? Can't she take over?*

*Not today. She can't come until 1:00.*

*What about family? Is there anyone who can help?*

He glanced up at the clock. 10:20 on a Thursday morning probably wasn't the easiest time of day to rustle up help, but maybe there was someone free. He thought of how sick she had looked when he got her back to her house last night, and he couldn't believe she was doing anything other than being in a soft bed under a mountain of blankets.

*Being the youngest in a big family means everyone thinking you need help and can't do things on your own. I've been fighting that for so long, I think I forgot how to ask.*

*Old habits die hard, I guess.*

*Or I don't know. Maybe I'm afraid to ask, because they might start acting like I'm helpless again.*

*And I clearly shouldn't text when I'm so sick. It makes me philosophical and vulnerable.*

*P**RETEND** I **DIDN'T** **SEND** **ANY** **OF** **THESE**.*

*R**EALLY**, I'**M** **DOING** **GREAT**. I **CAN** **MAKE** **IT** **UNTIL** E**MILY**
**GETS** **HERE** **JUST** **FINE**.*

*L**OOK**! P**UPPIES**!*

She sent a picture of three smaller dogs climbing on her as she sat next to one of her big dogs. Her face wasn't in the picture, but the fact that she was sitting on the floor and leaning against the wall wasn't a good sign.

*N**ICE** **USE** **OF** **ANIMALS**. Y**OU** **TOTALLY** **GOT** **ME** **WITH** **THAT**
**DISTRACTION**. H**ANG** **ON**, **THIS** **VIDEO** **IS** **ALMOST** **OVER**, **AND**
I'**LL** **NEED** **TO** **TALK** **TO** **MY** **STUDENTS** **BEFORE** **THEY** **LEAVE**.*

He discussed with his class some of the points the video made before the bell rang, and then excused them to go to their third period classes. As soon as the last kid was out the door, he picked up the classroom phone and dialed the front office.

"Hi, Lisa, this is Aaron. I've got a prep period right now, and I just wanted to let you know that I'm going to run an errand and won't be back until closer to the end of lunch."

She thanked him for letting her know, and then he grabbed his coat, his cell phone, and his keys, and headed out the door, locking his classroom behind him.

An impressively short fifteen minutes later, he was at the doors of Paws and Relax with a grocery bag from Elsmore Market in one hand and the blanket he always kept in his trunk for emergencies in the other. He went inside and found Macie propped up in the corner where the big fish tank met the wall, a cat asleep on her lap, her black lab laying against one leg, a small dog in her arms, and another puppy pulling her sock off. Her face didn't have any color, and she looked miserable.

"Hi," he said.

"Aaron!" She pulled the little puppy out of her hair and back into her arms. "What are you doing here?"

He crouched down next to her and leaned over the dog to put his hand on her forehead. "I have officially ditched school, and I'm here until twelve-thirty to help out."

She looked around the room, as if she was sure she'd see someone there that she'd missed. Like she didn't think he'd come if it weren't a date that was meant to convince some group of people that they were dating. "Why?"

He brushed the hair off her forehead. "Because even a fake boyfriend can be a good friend." Did he really just willingly say something that would further entrench him in the friend zone when he very much hoped for more than that? He hadn't been able to stop thinking about her ever since the dance and he was starting to wonder if maybe, possibly, there could actually be something between them. Except every time he thought there might be, he remembered that she was just playing a part. Doing what she could to convince whoever they were around that they were dating.

But just then she looked at him like she really wanted him to be something more, too.

It was probably just the sickness talking. Besides, he never wanted to get married, and she did.

"So do you think it was something you ate last night?"

She shook her head. "I wondered at first, but no. This is definitely a bug. Hopefully only a twenty-four hour one."

"What do you need help with?"

"I fed the dogs and cats already, but I haven't managed to get to the fish, hamsters, and geckos. And I've got a toddler group coming at eleven and I've really got to get stuff taken care of by then."

She started to move like she was going to get up, but he put a hand on her arm and said, "Stop. That's what I'm here for. Just tell me where everything is."

She hesitated and then nodded. "The fish food is in that door—they need two pinches. The hamsters' is in that cupboard right by their cage. Just fill their bowl to the top. And the geckos' food is next to the hamster food."

He stood up and raised the stuff in his arms. "Do you have an office or a back room where I can put this?"

"Just down the hall."

The office was the first room he found, and he set the grocery bag on her desk. The room was decently sized, but didn't have a cot hiding behind the door like he had hoped. It did have some empty floor space, though, and she did have a blanket draped over the back of her chair, so he folded the blanket he brought in half and laid it on the floor. A quick glance around and he didn't see anything he could use as a pillow for her, so he took off his coat and folded it into a somewhat pillow shape, and put it on the blanket. Then he went back into the main room.

"Let's get you up," he said as he moved the animals off her.

"But my Parent, Preschooler, and a Puppy group will be here any minute."

He scooped her into his arms and stood up. "And those parents will really appreciate if you don't pass this bug along to their toddlers. I'm going to run the group, and you're going to get rest." He carried her into her office and lay her on the makeshift bed, adjusting the coat pillow. Then he grabbed the blanket off the back of her chair and spread it over her. Without the blanket hiding it, he noticed that her coat was on the arm of the chair, and spread that out on top of her, too, because she had a bit of a fever and figured she needed the warmth.

She snuggled into the blankets, shivering at first, and then relaxing. He stood up and started pulling things out of the grocery sack. "I brought you tissues; I'll put them right next to you here. And I got pain reliever/fever reducer. Do you want one now?" Macie shook her head no, so he put the bottle next to the tissues and set a water bottle next to it.

"For when you're feeling well enough to eat, I got you some chicken noodle soup from Elsmore's deli. I'll put it in your mini fridge. Do you need—" He had turned around to ask, but saw that she'd already fallen asleep. After adjusting the blanket to cover her shoulders more fully, he pressed his lips lightly to her temple and whispered, "Feel better," then he snuck out of the room and shut the door quietly behind him.

Parents and their preschoolers started coming in the shop before he even finished feeding the animals. He didn't have a clue as to how to run a Parent, Preschooler, and a Puppy event, but the parents gave him the gist of it, and were mostly able to point out where things like balls and other dog toys were.

He made up games to play with the preschoolers and dogs as he went along, and hoped that the group had fun and didn't feel cheated that Macie wasn't there. By the time the hour was over, he was ready to collapse himself. The cats had mostly left the room after sniffing everyone out, which left him with four parents, five preschoolers, two big dogs, and three little dogs, and he decided that they were way more exhausting than even his third period Modern World History class. And that was saying something.

Once the place emptied of the kids and their parents and he got all the dog toys cleaned up, he opened the office door and peeked in. Macie was still sound asleep and looked so peaceful and less miserable than she had been that he couldn't bear to wake her up. He glanced down at his watch. There was no way he could find a sub this late, and it would only be thirty minutes before Emily came in anyway.

Then he remembered that Joselyn and Marcus worked just next door. He hurried in to With a Cherry on Top, where thankfully they were both working, and Joselyn was free enough to come man the shop.

"Thank you," Aaron said as Joselyn walked into the shop, baby Aria in her arms. "I just didn't want to wake her."

"Thanks for looking out for her," Joselyn said. "I'll make sure she gets home and in bed once Emily gets here."

Aaron gave one last glance the direction of Macie's office before he left. She had been so sick, he wondered if she'd even remember that he'd been there.

## Chapter Eleven

acie spent the day on Saturday at her parents' house, helping to prepare the food for the family Christmas Kickoff with her mom and oldest sister, Nicole, while other siblings helped out in other places. After putting the top crust on one pie, she wiped the flour off her hands and pulled out her phone for what was possibly the thousandth time, wanting to text Aaron, but holding herself back. She was dangerously close to falling for him, and if she just let herself text when she wanted to, she'd fall completely. For a guy who was only interested in being her fake boyfriend.

Falling for him would be dangerous. And dangerously easy. So instead of texting when she wanted to, she'd only texted once—on Friday, when she'd joined the land of the living again. Or at least the land of the semi-conscious. She had thanked him for coming to rescue her on Thursday, and let him know that she was feeling much better and expected a full recovery by the party that night.

So she'd kept herself from texting, yet she'd still used the tissues he'd brought, taken his medicine, eaten his soup, and snuggled up to his coat that smelled like the most wonderful combination of cinnamon and pine with hints of chlorine. And thought over and over about how thoughtful he'd been to show up when she most needed help, even when she'd told him that she'd be fine. And how it felt to have him carry her into her office. And how sweet it was that he took over her Parent, Preschooler, and a Puppy event. And how she could put a check next to *Takes care of me when I'm sick* on her list.

Come to think of it, texting probably would've been much less dangerous than thinking about him.

"Tell me about this new man in your life," her mom said as she put another filled pie on the counter in front of Macie.

*Okay, Macie,* she told herself. *Time to push the part of you that's seeing hearts for real out of the way, and pull out the part that is trying to convince everyone of the fake relationship.* The further this relationship went, the more difficult it was to switch into fake relationship mode.

"He's great, Mom," she said as she laid strips of pie crust across an apple cranberry pie. "You're going to love him."

"Well, Joselyn has had nothing but good to say about him. I'm glad you're finally bringing him to meet us."

"They haven't even been dating for two weeks yet, Mom," Nicole said as she rolled out a pie crust. "Janet, Mindy, Masen, and Chris, freeze right where you are!" Macie's attention flew to the back doors where Nicole's four kids had just burst into the house. "Get those snowy boots and coats off and hung up before you track it through Grandma's and Grandpa's house! I heard he brought you soup. I tell you, if a man brings you soup when you're sick, he's a keeper."

"Kennon, Zach, and I have the lights all finished!" her

dad called from the far side of the family room. "Can I ring the bell yet?"

"Five minutes, Dad," Joselyn said from where she and their sisters-in-law, Audra and Lia, were helping her to set the long dining tables that separated the kitchen from the family room. "Just let us finish with the tables before you add to the," she stepped over Brindley, her parents' dog, and then over Katie, her three-year-old niece who was chasing her, "crazy."

The doorbell rang just then, and everyone's heads jerked up, all knowing that the only person who was coming who wouldn't have just walked in was Aaron.

"I'll get it," Macie said, taking off her apron, brushing the flour from her hands on a towel, and heading toward the front door. Her mom did the same. She had a suspicion that her dad was on his way from the other end of the hall, too.

She opened the door, and Aaron stood on the porch, looking tall and lean and perfect and covered in snow and holding a vase of Christmas-themed flowers.

"Oh, wow. It's really coming down out there, isn't it?" Macie helped to brush the snow off his coat and scarf, and then he stomped his feet and stepped inside.

"You look beautiful," he said. "The flour on your cheek is a nice touch." He reached a hand out and brushed the flour off her face with his knuckles. "How are you feeling? You look about three hundred times better than last I saw you."

"I'm feeling all the way better. Thank you. And thank you for Thursday."

He smiled, then his eyes shifted behind her, and she turned to see that it wasn't just her parents who were crowded around the back of the entry, but at least half of her siblings and their spouses. "Aaron, I'd like you to meet my parents, Emeline and Joseph."

"Thank you for inviting me to your home," Aaron said as he handed the flowers to her mom. "It's so nice to meet you."

Her mom accepted the flowers and gave him a one-armed hug and said, "We're so pleased you could come. We've heard nothing but good things about you."

Then he shook her dad's hand, and her dad added, "Don't do anything to hurt my little girl, and you're always welcome here."

Macie held an upturned hand toward everyone else in the room, and said, "Well, I'd like to say that I'll introduce you to everyone else, but we both know this isn't even close to everyone else. Here, let me take your coat."

As they walked into the kitchen from the hall at the right, she thought about how proud of herself she was for not dwelling on how sweet it was that he brought flowers for her mom. Instead, she leaned in and whispered, "Nice touch with the flowers," and offered her fist. He bumped it with his.

When they reached the great room, her mom placed the flowers from Aaron in the middle of the dining tables, and took a step back. "There. Now everything is absolutely perfect."

"So does this mean I can ring the bell?" her dad asked.

"Yes, dear, you can ring the bell."

Her dad went on to the back patio, and rang the big bell he had attached to the patio roof, like he was calling the ranch hands in for the midday meal. He'd installed it clear back when she was a sophomore in high school and her oldest brother Oliver had just finished building his house. Twelve years later, and it still brought him just as much joy to ring it to call everyone home.

Within minutes, the patio was swarming with family, brushing the snow off their coats and hats and gloves and stomping their feet, before pouring into the house and removing winter gear. A lot of the coats and scarves made it on to the hooks, and some boots were paired and standing upright along the wall, and the rest was in one massive pile.

His dad's face was beaming as all the kids gathered around him and the Christmas tree. Like always, it was a live tree that he went into the mountains to chop down, and by the looks of it, was nearly ten feet tall. Ladders of various sizes were placed around the tree.

"Who's ready to decorate this tree?" The kids cheered loudly, then he said, "Remember, you've got to be eight to get on the taller ladders, and five to get on the shorter ones, okay? Raise your hand if you are one, two, three, or four." All the littlest kids raised their hands. "You all get something even better than a ladder. If there's ever an ornament you want to put up high, you've got me. I'll be just like a ladder on a fire truck and lift you up as high as you need. Okay, you all know what to do—let's get this tree decorated!"

"It looks like your dad loves this," Aaron said.

"He really does."

"Do you want to give me everyone's names?"

Marcus, who was standing nearby, said, "Don't do it. There's too many— they'll all just swirl into a fog. It took me months to learn all of them. I still forget some sometimes."

"He does not," Joselyn said. "Don't let him fool you. He even has their birthdays memorized."

"Well, there's a lot of competition here for favorite uncle! I have to do what I can to stay ahead of the game." He crouched down, and as four-year-old Brighton ran past to grab another ornament, he said, "Who's your favorite uncle, buddy?"

"You are!" Brighton said and gave him a high five with an impressive amount of force behind it.

"I want to hear them," Aaron said.

"Really?" Macie searched his face, to see if she could tell if he was really wanting to know, or just trying to play the part of the perfect boyfriend. How had she once thought this fake relationship was a brilliant idea? She hated never being able to tell how he really felt. "Okay, well that's my oldest brother Oliver over there on the couch next to his wife Audra. That's Larissa, Riley, Claire, Sophie, and that was Brighton. Then there's Zach with Cameron in his arms, his wife Lia is over there, and Trevor and Katie."

She looked at him to see if he was overwhelmed already, but he motioned for her to keep going. "Then my sister Nicole and her husband Noble are there, and they've got Janet, Mindy, Mason, and Chris. My brother Kennon is with his wife Rosabella there, and their sons are the ones at the tops of the ladders— Brian and Brandon. Everett is over there, and his wife Hannah is holding Madison. She's my youngest niece; she's only two months old. They've got Drew and Jason there, and Kristine is over— Kristine! No eating the dog's tail! And then you already know Joselyn and Marcus and Aria."

Aaron smiled as he watched the kids decorate the tree, and that made Macie smile. She had worried that being around such a big family might be too much for him, especially since his was small and didn't include kids. But if she had to guess, she'd say that he was enjoying himself.

Of course, he had proven himself to be a pretty good faker.

When it was time to eat dinner—their traditional prime rib, roasted Brussels sprouts, rosemary roasted baby potatoes, and a big range of salads made by each of her siblings—Aaron was gracious and kind and started conversations with everyone. He even made sure the kids weren't ignored. In fact, beyond not being ignored, he had a gift of making each of them feel important and special. Back when she was sixteen, she hadn't even known to put that on her list. She had just put an all-inclusive *Would make a good dad* on it. But this kind of thing was exactly what she had meant. She put a bunch of checkmarks next to that on her mental list.

"Who made this butternut squash and apple casserole?" Aaron asked the table in general.

"I did," her older brother Oliver answered.

"This is one of the best things I've ever tasted," Aaron said. "We need to talk after."

Oliver nodded back, and she could see in Oliver's eyes that he liked Aaron and accepted him. *Oliver.* Her brother who was the harshest judge of her boyfriends out of everyone. She tried to remember if he had ever had that look in his eyes when seeing anyone she had dated.

Maybe she didn't need a break from dating. Maybe she just needed a break from dating all the wrong people. Maybe the right guy was sitting next to her.

When the meal was finished and cleaned up, her parents gathered everyone into the family room, and they all found spots on the floor facing the fireplace.

"It's time for the annual hanging of the stockings!" her mom said, her hands clasped in front of her.

This had always been one of Macie's favorite parts of Christmas. She wondered what Aaron would think of it. Her mom pulled out the pile of stockings that were all linked together. With her own stocking in one hand, her mom handed her dad's stocking to him. They each pulled on their end, and everyone's stockings unfurled. Macie and all of her siblings' stockings were connected together between her mom's stocking and her dad's, one after another, a row of nine stockings, each linked to the next with gold rings. Each of her siblings had their spouse's stocking linked to theirs, and each of their kids was linked to the two of them, hanging down in a line before it connected with the next family's.

Each of her parents used big clamps to fix their stockings nice and sturdy to the mantle, everyone's stockings hanging between them.

"We've got three new stockings to add this year," her mom said, and pulled the stockings from the box. "We've got Cameron's, since he was born just the day after Christmas last year." She held the stocking out and everyone *Ooh*-ed an *Ahh*-ed.

Macie leaned into Aaron and whispered "My mom makes every stocking, and they're all different. You've got to see them up close."

"And then we've got Aria's," she said as she held hers up, "and of course baby Madison's."

Her parents used the golden rings to link each of the three new stockings to the bottom of each of their families, and then linked them to the next family. Then her dad took a step forward to tell the annual Christmas Link story.

"As you can see, each of you are linked to everyone else in our family up here. All those links, connecting us together, is what makes us strong. Happy. Loved. United. Every single person represented here is an important link in our family. You are important. You matter. You are loved by all the family that are surrounding you today. Nothing will ever change that. There is nothing that you can ever do that will change that fact, not even death."

Macie's mom reached out and touched the stocking with Cambry's name that was linked right below Zach's and Lia's stocking.

"We love you. You matter. Your relationships with your family matters. So when disagreements or misunderstandings or hurt feelings happen—and they will, we're all human—talk it out. Fix it. Nurture each other extra in those moments. Keeping those relationships takes work. But it's some of the most valuable work you can do. You matter. The people around you matter. Family matters. Those relationships matter. Keep working on them, and keep looking out for every chance you can get to serve each other, because that's what keeps those links strong."

Two years ago, Joselyn's stocking was just like Macie's—linked together yet hanging alone. And then last Christmas, Joselyn's had Marcus's stocking linked next to it. Now they had a stocking hanging below them.

Seeing her family's stockings all linked together always made Macie feel like she belonged and was valued. But she wanted more. She wanted her own stocking links to go down, too, just like all of her siblings' stockings did. She had wanted it for years, but never had the longing hit her as strongly as it was right now.

She snuck a glance at Aaron, and could tell by the way he was staring at the stockings and blinking faster than normal that what her dad had said had touched him too. He wrapped his arm around her shoulders.

"What do you say we work on making those links even stronger? Who's ready for their Secret Service names?"

All the kids cheered and jumped up from where they were sitting on the floor. They each came up to Macie's mom and pulled a name out of the bowl she was holding, the littler ones racing to their parents to have them read the name and tell them who they'd be doing secret acts of service for. Macie's dad brought around the bowl that had her siblings' and their spouses' names in it, and had each person pull a name out. Macie pulled one out and looked at Aaron, but his eyes were still fixed on the stockings.

## Chapter Twelve

$\mathcal{A}$aron had to admit that the tree lighting was pretty cool. You could hardly even tell that all the ornaments were clumped in clusters on the bottom half or up in lines along the edges of each ladder.

He hardly had time to admire it, though, before Macie's brother Zach leapt out of his seat and said, "Who thinks they can outlast me? I'm planning to make it around the playground."

Zach kicked off his shoes and started pulling off his socks, and Aaron's eyes grew wide. His attention flew to Macie. "When I asked if you ran outside barefoot in the snow with your siblings when you were little—"

Macie ducked into a shrug. "Yeah, I didn't quite mention that it wasn't *only* when we were little. What? It's not like we do it all the time. Just during Christmas Kickoff. So..." She looked to the left and the right. "Do you want to see if we can outlast Zach? He's tough."

Aaron laughed. One thing was for certain, life with Macie would never be boring.

Did he just imagine his life with Macie? It had been a very long time since he'd done that with anyone. He looked at her for a long moment, admiring how her curls cascaded down her shoulders, the way her smile lit up her entire face, the way she got excited about the little things. Not to mention the way she looked in that red sweater and jeans. "Sure. We survived last time, after all. And I don't have to worry about you getting too cold, because I warm your heart, baby."

"You better believe it," she said, putting her hand on his chest and sending heat zinging to it.

"I'll grab the towels," Macie's mom said as he and Macie took off their shoes and socks and rolled up their pant legs.

Aaron was surprised—most of the adults were taking their shoes off, along with all the older kids. Of course it was a family event with the Zimmermans. He should have guessed. They all raced out to the covered patio, braced for the cold, and came to an abrupt halt. Snow covered everything so deeply, it was difficult to make out what any of the bumps were.

"When did it snow this much?" one of Macie's sisters-in-law asked.

"Look at how much it's still coming down, too," Nicole said. "The forecast said it would only be a couple of inches!"

Macie gazed across the lawn, a look of wonder and disbelief on her face. "This has to be up above our knees."

"Well," Zach said, "I guess we'll be swimming to the playground then." He dove off the patio into the snow, like he was diving into water to swim laps.

"Zach!" his wife yelled. "You're going to be frozen down to your bones!"

"Especially if I can't figure out how to swim any faster

than this," he said as he made motions that mimicked freestyle, but didn't make him move forward at all.

They all made their way back into the house, including Zach, whose wife made him brush all the snow off him before entering. Macie's oldest brother pulled his phone out of his pocket and furrowed his brow at the screen. Then another brother pulled his out. Aaron had felt a ding from his about the same time, so he pulled his out, too.

*ALERT: HEAVY SNOWFALL AND AVALANCHE WARNING IN THE CLEAR CREEK AREA; I-70 IS CLOSED FROM MOUNTAIN SPRINGS TO COPPER MOUNTAIN.*

"Oh. I guess I need to...Oh."

All around, everyone pulled out their phones and showed it to the people nearest them. Aaron just kept staring at his, trying to make his head work through the implications, then he hurried into their living room and looked out the front window at his car. It was covered so deeply in snow that he could barely tell what color it was anymore. And with the roads closed, he wasn't going to be going home. "I guess I should probably go before I can no longer find my car and see if I can get a room at the hotel."

"Nonsense, son," Joseph said. "We've got a guest room right here you can use. Even if we got your car unburied, you wouldn't make it two feet until they plow these roads."

"Of course we'll put you up here," Emeline added. "I'll go get the bed made up."

As they walked back toward the family room and kitchen, one of the older kids said, "With this much snow, Grandma, I don't think we'll be able to make it home either. It's probably deeper than Brighton! If we go home, we'll lose him in the snow and he'll be gone forever. I think we're all snowed in, and our only option is to have a giant sleepover like we do on Christmas Eve."

"The boy has a point," Macie's dad said.

Before Aaron knew it, it was no longer just him sleeping at Macie's parents. It was everyone. All thirty-five of them, all sleeping at the same house.

"You know the rules," Emeline called out. "Mine and Grandpa's bedroom is off limits, and so is the guest room. Anywhere else is free game."

"But not the bathtub," Larissa said, giving Brian a pointed look.

"Oh, don't worry, I learned my lesson last year when I had to get up and leave every time someone had to go to the bathroom in the middle of the night."

As Aaron and Macie helped all the kids get their beds set up in all corners of the house, Aaron thought about all he'd witnessed this crazy, unexpected night. He'd never known a family like this in his life. His parents had always said that family was important, and they supported his swimming and Aliza's dancing every step of the way, right up until the end. But they never cared about each other the way that this family did. Strangely, during Joseph's talk about the family and the links that connect them, it made him miss Aliza. His parents, even. He called them every six months or so, and visited occasionally, but usually out of a sense of obligation. Missing them was new.

Some of his friends were closer with their families than he was with his, but none of them had families that were anywhere close to this either. He didn't even hear people talk about families like this. It had to be a show. A front that

Macie's parents were putting on, just like the front his parents put on. Like his ex-fiancée had.

But even so, as he and Macie worked side-by-side, he couldn't deny the attraction he felt toward her. She was one of the few people he had ever met who looked just as beautiful when she was working through the flu as she was in a ball gown. And as much as he wanted to reach a hand out and run his fingertips along her cheek and neck, it was more than just her looks. He was drawn to her because of everything she did. Because of everything she was.

When they finished with the beds, and a group of nieces and nephews started climbing on Macie to have her read them a story, he excused himself to go get his own bed set up, since he'd stopped Macie's mom from doing it.

As he worked, he realized how much his heart was getting tied up in this. Just like it did back with Sabrina when he was twenty. And if he ever needed a reminder of how painfully that turned out, all he had to do was Google his own name. He couldn't invest his heart in something again that could turn out to be just a front. And there was no way a family like this wasn't.

He walked out of the guest room and paused. Macie's parents were right across the hall, standing in the doorway of their darkened room—the one place they thought they had to themselves, their back to him and oblivious of his presence.

"Every time I think I can't love you more," Emeline said, "I look at this family we created together and the way you love them, and my heart just bursts."

"Forty-one years," Joseph said. "Forty-one years, and my heart still leaps every time I see you. Life has been heaven on earth with you in it, my dear Emeline."

Aaron stepped back into the guest room, stunned at what he just witnessed. They weren't putting on a show for their kids or for anyone else. They were completely alone, and that was how they spoke to each other when they thought no one was looking.

It was all true then?

Everything he witnessed in this family tonight. It was real? Genuine? The last time he truly believed that love like that was possible, he was just a kid.

Now he understood what Macie wanted. He finally grasped why she was searching so hard to find the perfect spouse. She wanted this—a marriage like her parents had. And he finally learned why. This was what he wanted too. Deep down inside, it was what he had always wanted; he had just never known it before now.

When he got back to the family room, Macie and a couple of her siblings were tucking the last few kids into bed. She looked up at him and smiled, then stepped over the sleeping bodies and made her way toward him as her siblings went to other rooms, probably to check on other kids.

As she neared, he whispered "You're even graceful when you're stepping over sleeping kids."

"You haven't seen me trying to do the same thing after being woken in the middle of the night to ward off monsters when a kid needs to go to the bathroom."

"True." The moonlight bounced off the snow, making outside unusually bright for eleven p.m. The moonlight spilled through the kitchen window and lit up the side of Macie's face. This entire night, something inside him had been building and building—a connection to the heart of Macie that pulled him to her. He reached out and put a hand on her cheek, needing to feel its silkiness against his skin, and she responded by putting her hand on his chest. He closed his eyes as the electricity from his whole body rushed to meet her hand.

Snow fell cold and beautiful just outside the window, but Macie stepped close enough that he could feel her warm breath against his neck. It wasn't just him who felt the connection, then. It was as if the two of them were forces being drawn together by something unconcerned about whatever protests they had. And maybe nothing else beyond showing Macie how much he cared about her did matter. He moved his hands to her waist, and she brought her second hand up next to the first on his chest. Her eyes shifted to his lips, and suddenly her lips were all that he could focus on as the snow fell all around them.

Macie leaned into him, a hand slipping up to the back of his neck, her fingers in his hair, and he brought his lips to hers. Her lips were soft and moving on his carefully, testing to see if this was okay. He responded, his kisses being just as careful and questioning. After a few moments, her second hand flew to the back of his neck, and she pulled him in closer. He pulled her in tight and kissed her with an urgency that matched hers, pouring everything into it that he had felt not only in the past few hours, but since the day he'd met her.

Macie broke contact first and whispered, "Wow."

Aaron tried to steady his ragged breathing enough to whisper back. But before he did, he heard, "Smoochie smoochie! *Mwah, mwah, mwah*." And then more kissing sounds followed by a whole lot of giggling.

"Trevor! And Janet, Mindy, and Sophie! You all are supposed to be sleeping!"

"But we're not," Janet said, "and we caught the whole show."

"I'm not asleep either," three-year-old Katie said.

Aaron felt heat rushing to the back of his neck, and Macie's blush was visible in the moonlight. She motioned to them and then the general vicinity of his room and then somewhere else, like she wasn't quite sure where to direct her focus, then said, "We better, um—"

"Yeah, we should," Aaron agreed, and they both went off to their own separate parts of the house.

## Chapter Thirteen

Macie was in her office, studying spreadsheets and brainstorming, when the bell at the front door chimed. Reese and Lola, who had been lying at her feet, jumped up and ran to the main room. School wasn't out yet, and she didn't have any events planned, which meant it was a walk-in customer. Those were some of her favorites! Sometimes she got tourists, or just stressed out adults who needed a mid-workday boost. Since she'd been spending more on advertising, it was happening more and more frequently.

She walked out to the main room and saw her dad crouched down next to her dogs, trying to give them both equal attention, when both wanted his undivided attention.

"Dad!" she said as she hurried forward and gave him a hug. "This is a nice surprise. What are you doing around here in the middle of the day?"

"I just needed to stop by home and change clothes before heading to a business meeting in Denver. I thought I'd drop in and see how my favorite youngest daughter was doing."

They sat down in two of the chairs along the wall. "I'm doing great, Daddy."

"That Aaron sure seems like a nice boy."

"He really is," Macie said, thinking back to the Christmas Kickoff party, their kiss in the kitchen, and the family breakfast the next morning before he headed back home.

"You make sure he knows he's welcome anytime, okay?"

"I'm pretty sure he got that message by the sendoff you and Mom gave him yesterday morning."

He reached out and gave her hand a squeeze. "Alright, alright. I'll stop trying to nudge the relationship and just let it play out on its own. Now tell me, how's the decision on whether or not to buy this building coming along?"

Macie took a big breath, and then let it out in a fast huff. "I don't know, Dad. As I've been pushing to grow the business more, the numbers have actually been coming in where I was hoping they would. Not that one month's worth of data is enough to base a decision off of. There are just so many variables."

"So the numbers are coming in good, but..." he prodded.

"But getting sick really scared me. If Aaron hadn't stopped in to help, I don't know what I would've done. I was trying to convince myself that I could just push through it and everything would work out, but Dad, I was really sick. Too sick to have done what he did, no matter how hard I tried or wanted it.

"I know I was only sick for a couple of days. But the truth is, if I'm ever out of commission, even for a little while, this business is, too. It relies too heavily on me being one hundred percent." It was a fear that she hadn't actually voiced before, and now that she said it, she felt it even more strongly.

"Can you get another employee? Then you'd have enough overlap that if any one of you was sick or hurt or what have you, there would always be someone to cover for you."

Macie shook her head. "I can't and still have the numbers be where they'd need to be to buy the building."

"Is there more growth potential? If so, maybe you could move forward knowing that things would work out."

"I don't know. That's impossible to tell without more market research and testing. And those things take time."

"Would you like me to take a look at your books with you, maybe see if there's something you're missing?"

"That's okay, Dad. You've got a meeting you need to get to. I'll get this figured out."

"I know you will. You're a bright, determined girl who knows how to use that business degree you've got. Just know that the offer stands anytime you want it." He rubbed Lola's head and ran his fingers back and forth behind Reese's ears, just like they liked it, then pet the two dogs and one cat that had sidled up to him, then left.

Macie headed back to her office to work her way through another scenario. The more she thought and planned and figured things out, the more things popped into her head that she would need to account for. And the more she got worried about committing to something so big.

Eventually Emily came in to work, and things got much busier out front. Still she worked through plan after plan. But all the playing and laughing going on in the other room was distracting, and she found herself spending more and more time glancing over at the coat Aaron had left cradling her head when he'd lain her down on the makeshift bed he'd made for her on the floor last Thursday. She'd taken the coat home with her, and had meant to bring it to the Christmas party to return it to him, but she'd forgotten. She still wasn't ready to analyze her forgetfulness to see if it had been strictly on accident, or if a part of her wanted to keep it a little while longer just to feel him near. Or to give her an excuse to go see him.

Whatever the reason behind it was, she did have the coat, and she did need to return it to him. She glanced up at the clock. School was out, but he'd probably still be there. She put on her own coat, grabbed her purse, and slung his coat over her arm.

The front office let her know that he had swim team practice today that was probably just about over, so she headed toward the end of the school with the gyms and the indoor pool. When she went through the doors, his entire team was out of the water, pressing their towels against their suits and hair as they listened to him give details about when their next practice and meet was. A chlorinated humidity hung in the air, so she immediately set his coat on a bench, removed hers, and laid it on top of his. Aaron dismissed them all to the locker rooms.

Macie figured that he would probably turn around and walk her direction, but he didn't. He pulled his shirt off, tossed it on the benches along the sides, and dove into the pool. She didn't mean to just stand there, watching him when he didn't even know she was there. But his strokes as he glided through the water were just so... beautiful.

He swam freestyle, one arm at a time coming up out of the water, then sinking back in with such powerful force and perfect rhythm, his head turning to take a breath every fourth stroke. His legs kicked so strong and lean and every line and angle of every movement was breathtaking. Each turn at the ends of the pool was flawless, not a wasted motion, not a muscle out of line. Watching him was mesmerizing, and gave her the strangest sense of déjà vu. Then he switched to swimming the butterfly stroke, his arms coming out of the water at the same time, those powerful legs kicking together.

The third time his arms came out of the water, she gasped.

This wasn't the first time she'd seen him swim. It had been a long time since she had, but she immediately knew it was true. The more she watched him swim, the more details came back to her. The pool. The crowds. The suit, the swim cap, the diving blocks, the judges, all on her family's TV. She had been what? A senior in high school? No, not quite. It was the summer Olympics, right between her junior and senior years. And he had been the golden child of the USA Olympic Swim Team, swimming in several individual and team events.

How had she not recognized the name? Probably because it was just normal enough to not stand out. There was something people used to chant. She racked her brain trying to remember.

"Aaron Hall," she whispered the chant. "Take gold in all."

Something happened, though. The details just hadn't been in her head enough. Like she hadn't seen it happen herself; she'd only heard about it, so it didn't stick.

He swam up to the end of the pool nearest Macie, touching the side of the pool with both hands at the same time. Then he stood and brushed the hair out of his face.

The moment he noticed her standing there, his face broke into a smile. He must've been able to read the expression on her face, though, because the smile fell right along with his shoulders. She could tell that he suspected she knew.

Yet still, he put on a smile and acted like nothing happened. "You're a nice surprise. What brings you to the chlorine-scented, humidity-filled part of town?"

"Aaron, you are an Olympian! A gold medal-winning Olympian!"

He didn't respond—he just glanced at the lane beside him, like he was wishing he'd kept on swimming.

"Aaron, why would you not mention that? Why would you not tattoo it on your arm or print it on all your t-shirts?"

He took a long breath, then put his hands on the side of the pool and pushed himself out. He walked toward her, the pool water running down his chest, arms, and legs, accentuating muscles that she had only felt a hint of when she'd put her hand on his chest. Then he turned, grabbed a towel from the rack, and pulled it down his face, then dried off his neck. "Because I don't have the best of memories associated with the Olympics."

Macie's brows crinkled and her head cocked to the side as she tried to remember what had happened. He blew out a breath. "Okay. I'll tell you the story—I'd rather you didn't find it out by Googling it. Give me ten minutes to shower and change."

She sat down on a bench to wait, and had to repeatedly stop her fingers from inching toward her cell phone, where the internet was waiting, ready to give her answers. But no —she respected Aaron and could wait to hear them from him.

As long as he hurried.

Her cell phone was so close, though. *No, Macie,* she told herself. *You can wait.*

When he came back into the pool room, he was dressed in slacks and a button down shirt. She grabbed the coats and he led her out of the pool, through the gyms, and into the atrium, an octagonal room with tall windows on six sides. They sat on one of the couches that she'd curled up on to study plenty of times back in high school.

"Okay," Aaron said, "tell me what you already know."

"I know that you were young. Now that I'm doing the math, nineteen." He nodded, so she continued. "And you were supposed to swim in a lot of different races."

"Five."

"And you were a gold hopeful in several of them."

"Three."

"And you won gold in some..."

"Two gold, one bronze."

"But then something happened, and you didn't compete in your last event. I can't remember what."

"My parents happened. I didn't know it, but apparently they'd been having disagreements for years over the money all the coaching and traveling to national meets cost, versus the endorsement deals I'd eventually get by being an Olympian, over which one of them was doing it so they could have a trophy family and the bragging rights that came with it, and which one was doing it with my best inter-ests in mind and just wanted to set me up for a successful future. And since their private marriage had 'ended' years ago, which one of them was flaunting extramarital affairs in the other's face the most."

"Oh, Aaron."

"My parent's public marriage had been pretty close to

perfect, even from my point of view. I got my first endorsement offer between races, and it blew the lid off an argument that had been brewing between my parents for years. They had hid every fight they'd ever had from me and my sister Aliza and the rest of the world. That final explosion, though, happened right in front of me. And Aliza. And everyone else in the press room. Moments before my final race."

He was quiet for a few moments, his fingers flipping the zipper pull from her coat that was lying on his leg back and forth, back and forth.

"I was at the Olympics, I'd had three medals hung around my neck, and had received my first endorsement offer. I was nineteen and at the highest of highs. But at that moment I watched my family implode, and every truth I'd ever known about them was shattered. It...It was a long way to fall."

"I am so sorry, Aaron." Macie didn't know how to even comfort someone who had gone through something like that. She wrapped her arms around his shoulders and squeezed him in a tight hug.

He lifted one shoulder in a shrug. "It's not pleasant to talk about or relive, but it was a long time ago."

"How did you manage to get past that?"

He laughed a humorless laugh. "Well, I started by walking out of the Olympics right then and vowing never to return. Then I decided to move on to drinking. That seemed like the customary response to a problem of that magnitude. So I went to a bar in the Olympic Village with some teammates and had my first drink. Got drunk, even. Then I went back to my room and puked and was absolutely miserable." He laughed for real this time. "I had spent my life fueling my body with the healthiest of foods that would make me capable of being an elite athlete, and drinking felt like dumping poison on what I'd worked so hard for. So the night of my first drink was also the night of my last drink."

He shrugged. "So drinking was out. When I got back home, I decided the best course of action would be to get engaged, so I got right on that."

"Wait, what? Were you seriously engaged?"

Aaron nodded.

"Well that's a...less conventional way of dealing with grief. I guess it's true when they say that everyone deals with it differently."

"You could say that." Aaron's eyes looked up, thoughtful. "I think I was looking for a way to prove that my parents' marriage was just a terrible, horrible fluke. That marriage wasn't really like that. That real love was possible. That a marriage like I had *thought* my parents had was possible."

"And?"

"Well, finding candidates wasn't really a problem. It's not hard to get dates when you have a couple of gold medals tucked away in a drawer." He looked down where his hand rested on the seat not far from hers. "It sounds like that kind of situation would be ideal. A real ego booster. But in reality, it just means that you have no idea who likes you for who you are, and who likes you for what you just did and the notoriety it brings. Especially because the press felt the need to get involved in all of it. I actually had enjoyed the press back when they were covering my swimming times and my meets. I liked them less when all they could focus on was my parents' divorce and who I dated.

"But then I met Sabrina. She seemed perfect, and I was convinced that she actually liked me for me. I proposed, she said yes, and we started planning a wedding. We were both twenty."

Somehow in the middle of getting to know Aaron better and him meeting her family and that kiss in the kitchen, she'd managed to forget that he was against the one thing that mattered to her the most. "I'm guessing she didn't restore your faith in marriage." What was she thinking, falling for someone like Aaron, when she'd known he never wanted to get married?

Aaron shook his head. "I found out four months into our engagement that she hadn't broken up with her previous boyfriend. They were still very much together."

"No."

"Yep. So drinking had been a failed way to cope, which I hear is pretty true for everyone. And jumping into an engagement was also a failed coping mechanism. After floundering for a bit, I realized that I had three loves: leading, swimming, and kids. So I came up with the brilliant plan of becoming a teacher, so I could teach teens how to be stellar people and to set goals and to work hard to achieve them and to treat others with respect. It hasn't failed me yet."

She put a hand on his shoulder. "Those kids are lucky to have you."

He squeezed her hand that was on his shoulder and met her eyes. "Thank you for showing me Saturday night that families can be different from the one I've experienced. It restored some of my faith in humanity."

She gave him a smile filled with so many conflicting emotions, not the least of which was the dichotomy between the zing that his hand on hers sent through her body and the fact that he'd said her family had restored his faith in *humanity*, not his faith in families. Or in marriage.

He sat up straight and shifted so he was facing her. "Now, if I haven't scared you off too badly with that story, I was planning to stop by your house tonight to ask a favor."

Macie raised an eyebrow.

"I have a class of overachievers—my AP History class. It's a smaller class of just eleven kids. They're involved in everything—taking every Advanced Placement and Honors and Concurrent Enrollment class offered. They are in every extracurricular, after school offering imaginable—several clubs each, with most of them in club leadership, sports, National Honor Society, volunteering for charity work and other service opportunities, and some of them even manage to squeeze in after school jobs. Anyway, the end of the semester is this Friday, the last day before Christmas break, and as you can imagine, these kids are out of their mind stressed with end of semester projects and making sure they maintain their four point oh GPAs."

"Several of my students have mentioned how much dog therapy has helped them." He grinned in a way that told Macie that this was his puppy dog pleading face. "Do you think you could bring yours to my class with these kids tomorrow during fourth period?"

Macie smiled. She didn't know how to help with the betrayal he felt from his parents and his ex-fiancee, but this she could do.

## Chapter Fourteen

When Macie texted to say that she was almost at the school, Aaron tossed the remains of his lunch in the faculty room garbage can and hurried outside to meet her in the parking lot. It hadn't snowed for a couple of days, so even though the snow was deep on the lawn and in big mounds at the ends of the parking lot, the parking lot and sidewalks were cleared and dry.

"Good afternoon, my mysterious goddess," he said as he opened her door for her.

"Why thank you, my dashing man." She stepped out of the car and placed a hand on his cheek. It was only for a moment, and such a small gesture, but it still sent warmth coursing through him right in the middle of the Colorado cold.

He lifted out the carrier with the three smaller dogs, and grabbed the cat one with his other hand, while Macie led the two bigger dogs on leashes inside the school.

She glanced over at him. "How do you feel about going to my work Christmas party this Friday?"

"Work party? Like with just you and Emily?"

Macie laughed. "No, actually, it's with all of the Main Street Business Alliance members. Dates aren't required, but I thought it might be fun."

"I would love to." They paused outside the windows of front office, and Lisa looked up, saw that Macie was with him, and gave him a thumbs up.

The hallways were filled with students chatting with friends at the end of lunch, and as they walked, they were met with a chorus of *Awww*'s and "Look! Puppies!" People swarmed to them, asking if they could pet the dogs.

"I am so sorry," Aaron said. "I didn't even consider this."

"No problem. I don't think it would be possible for Reese and Lola to get too much attention. The littler dogs and Sam, though—"

Aaron looked at the animals in the carriers. The dogs were yipping and jumping and were definitely getting a little overly excited, and Sam was scratching away at the floor of the carrier. "Make way, coming through," he called out in his *Listen to the teacher* voice. And they did. They still lined the halls and bent down to wave at the dogs as they passed, but they left the middle open, so Aaron led Macie up the stairs and to his classroom like they were in a parade.

Once they were in his room and he'd set the carrier down, he stepped up close to Macie. Close enough to kiss her, actually. But instead he breathed, "Thanks for coming."

She smiled nervously and then glanced at the door. "Should we be doing this with an audience?"

Lola nosed her way right in between the two of them, forcing the space between them to be wide enough to fit a large Goldendoodle. Aaron chuckled. "It seems Lola has an opinion about that too. And she's probably right." He picked up the dog carrier and took it back in to his office. He didn't want to let them out until the students entered the room and he could close the door.

Macie crouched down to take the leash off Reese's collar, so Aaron crouched down and did the same with Lola. "So," she said as she laid the leash on the table that held his little classroom Christmas tree, "how are you?"

"Good. The end of the term is Friday, so I've been preparing the students for their tests tomorrow and grading their end of semester projects."

Macie nodded and leaned in to take a closer look at the Christmas tree.

"How about you?" he asked. "How are things going with your business?"

"Good. It's been picking up."

How had things become so awkward between them? It was like the magic of Saturday night had worn off. He had felt so certain about where he stood with her when they had kissed, but he'd second guessed it a million times since then. He'd replayed their conversation from that night in his head dozens of times, and had realized that she hadn't said that she felt the same way about him that he did about her. Actually, he wasn't even sure he'd told her how he felt. So maybe the kiss was all just part of trying to convince her family.

He'd already had enough people in his life who had been fake about their relationships. Why had he thought that doing it on purpose was a good idea? He took a stride closer to her. "Listen—"

"Mr. H!" Cory said as he strolled into the room. "I heard you have a surprise for us!"

Morgan squealed and raced past Cory. "It's true!"

The other students filed in close behind Cory and

Morgan, dropping their backpacks and binders at their desks, and then gathering around Reese and Lola. Aaron leaned against his desk right next to where Macie leaned against it, close enough that their arms were touching.

"Reese and Lola are in heaven with all this attention," Macie said.

"And look at the smiles on the students' faces." He watched Macie watching the students, and thought she looked like she was in heaven, too. She had really opened the perfect business for her.

The bell rang, and the students dutifully stopped petting the dogs and sat in their seats. It made him chuckle, but he should've seen it coming. So he went up in front of the class, and explained about how class today was going to be hanging out with the dogs.

"I don't understand," Alecia said. "There isn't going to be a lesson?"

"Nope."

"But the end of the semester is three days away," Kyle said. "Shouldn't we be studying?"

Aaron blew out a breath. The easy-going, fun class he'd had just a couple of weeks ago had grown into a ball of stress. "I purposely scheduled the next test for your class well after the break so you'd have one less thing to study for and worry about. Today, this is for you."

Morgan raised her hand. "But—"

Aaron cut her off. "Alright, listen up class; I've got an assignment for you." They all sat up a little straighter. "I need everyone to come up to the board and grab a marker." Once they all stood at the board, a whiteboard marker poised and ready, he said, "I want you to think about what you've got going on today. Okay, now think about yesterday.

And now Wednesday, Thursday, and Friday. Keeping those days in mind, on a scale of one to ten, I want you to write down how stressed out you feel."

He watched as nine of eleven students wrote the number ten on the board. Some big, some small, some with a big circle or square around it, and a couple underlined. Allen was the only one who wrote a nine, and Bethany wrote 837.

He walked up to the board and studied the numbers, then turned to the students. "Stress can be good. It can propel you to action. But stress at this high of numbers is not only unhealthy, it's unhelpful. Your assignment over the next..." he glanced at the clock, "hour and thirteen minutes is to work to get that number cut in half. I'll have you report back in at the end of class. Now get to work!"

Macie went with him to his back office, and got Zeus, Piper, Cookie, and Sam out of their carriers and released them into the room. Then Macie pulled a couple of small balls out of her bag and tossed them to a couple of students. Piper lay on the floor as Morgan and LeeAnn petted her. Macie crouched down next to them and said, "I brought some Christmas ribbon. Do you guys want to fancy her up?" The two girls' faces lit up, and she passed them a little container.

When she came back to lean against the desk with Aaron, she said, "If things keep picking up, I might be able to rescue another dog from the shelter to add to the Paws and Relax family." Her face had been so excited when she was telling him, but then the smile fell a bit. "If I decide to buy the building. If I don't, I'll have to find homes for most of these dogs."

"You'll be able to buy it," he said. "I believe in you one

hundred percent. Before you know it, you'll have that new shelter dog."

As his kids played with the dogs, he swore he could see the stress fleeing from them. He twined his hand in Macie's and brought it to his lips and kissed her knuckles. "Thank you for doing this. It really means a lot to me."

"It's a great idea—I'm glad you thought of it. I think I might add it to what we do at Paws and Relax. There might be other teachers who have students in just as much need. And look at how much the dogs are loving it! And look how adorable Piper is looking with those bows."

A few students were tossing a ball to Lola and Zeus, and Cookie was sitting right on Kyle's shoulder, looking like she was wondering if she might want to climb right on top of his head.

"We should talk about that kiss."

"It was a great kiss," Macie said. "I give it a solid ten out of ten."

Aaron laughed. "You know that wasn't what I meant." He searched her face, trying to see if he could find any answers to his unasked questions. All kinds of emotions flitted across her face, but he couldn't figure them out. He needed words. "For you, was it just something to help convince your family?"

*Oof!* He exhaled as one of the balls hit him in the stomach.

"Sorry, Mr. H!" Cory called out. "My bad!"

He picked up the ball and threw it back to Cory, and then his eyes went back to Macie's. She searched his face, too, and then whispered, "No."

His face split into a grin. "So it meant something more?"

"I've got it!" Bethany called out, and from the corner of

his eye, Aaron saw her race across the floor on her hands and knees toward a ball, before he heard a *thud*.

He jerked forward right as Bethany yelped and backed away from a desk, her hands flying to her nose. It started bleeding almost immediately. Aaron grabbed five or six tissues from the box and rushed to her. "Kyle, get on the classroom phone and let the front office know that I'm bringing Bethany down and that she's going to need the nurse."

He made eye contact with Macie and she said, "You go. I've got this."

Once he got Bethany in with the nurse, he called the phone numbers on record for her parents to explain what happened and to see if they could pick up their daughter. They were both in meetings, but he eventually got her older brother who had just come home from college for Christmas. Aaron stood in the door opening and asked the nurse, "What do you think?"

"Could be broken," she said. "She'll want to see a doctor."

Bethany sobbed.

"Your brother is on his way, and he's going to get you to the doctor and take good care of you."

Bethany nodded, then, muffled through the wad of gauze covering her nose, said, "Mr. Hall, I'm feeling like my stress is even higher than eight-thirty-seven right now. Does that mean I'm going to fail this assignment and get a horrible grade in your class?"

He chuckled and shook his head. "You're not going to fail it. I'll tell you what. I'll give you extra credit for being a trooper."

"Thank you," she croaked out, looking like her injury

might be worth it if it meant extra credit. He wasn't sure why extra credit mattered so much to someone who already had a 99.4% in his class, but it looked like it did.

As he was trying to make it back to his class before the bell rang, his phone vibrated, so he pulled it out of his pocket and saw a text from Matt.

*Can you come over the second you get off work?*

He quickly typed in a response.

*Is everything okay?*

*Just come.*

There was so much Aaron wanted to talk to Macie about. So much time he wanted to spend with her. So much more he wanted to find out. And he really *really* wanted to kiss her again.

He was hoping to get a chance to do at least some of that after all his students left. But when he got to the classroom, there was barely enough time to put the room back in order. Before they left, he had the students erase their old stress rating and replace it with the post hang-out-with-puppies-during-class score, which he was happy to see were all sixes and lower, with the exception of Bethany's 837 that was still on the board.

Distracted by what could be going on with Matt, he helped Macie get the dogs and cat back to her car, she gave him a quick kiss on the cheek, and he said, "I'm sorry I have to run. I'll call you after I leave Matt's."

And now thoughts of Macie and worry about Matt fought for dominance in his mind. He pulled up to the front of Matt's house, the yard filled with Christmas lights and decorations with the lights still on, even though it was mid-afternoon.

He knocked on Matt's door, and heard a shouted, "Come in," so he did. The place was feeling strangely empty. Like some of the furniture was missing, or maybe the things on the walls, but he couldn't quite put his finger on what. It just felt as though the essence of the home was gone. Matt was splayed on the couch, looking unshowered and bedraggled.

"Matt, buddy, what's going on?"

Matt sat up and leaned forward with his elbows on his knees. Aaron sat in the chair across from him and waited.

"Ciara and I are separated. She just left with all her stuff right before I texted you."

Of all the things that had run through his mind of what could be wrong, this didn't even make the list at all. Matt and Ciara were the perfect couple. They were rock solid. "How did this happen? I thought you two were happy together. You always seemed...happy."

"We were! But then I lost my job."

"She left you because you lost your job?"

Matt shook his head. "She wasn't upset about that. Well, she *was* upset that I didn't tell her before our game night last week."

"You didn't tell her? Matt!"

"I know, I know. But I knew she'd ask why I got fired, and I didn't want to tell her."

Dread filled Aaron's stomach like a lead weight. "Matt, why did you get fired?"

He ran his hands over his face, and then ran them through his hair, making it stand up in all directions. "I was caught in a compromising situation in the break room with a co-worker. Subordinate, actually—I'm her boss. *Was* her boss."

Aaron fell back in his chair. All he could manage to say was one word. "Why?"

"I don't even know! Because I'm the biggest idiot on the planet? It's never happened before...It was just that once...And we didn't actually..."

"Matt! Regardless of how far you got before you were caught, you cheated on your wife!"

"I know," Matt said, and dropped his head into his hands. "What do I do?"

Aaron took a few slow breaths. "I want to be a good friend and give you good advice. I do. But I'm going to need a few minutes to process this before I can." He stood up, let himself out of the house, and started walking around the block.

# Chapter Fifteen

In preparation to eventually start Paws and Relax, Macie had worked at a pet groomer's in college so she'd learn everything she needed to know. She had mostly used the skill to groom her own dogs, but now that she opened it to the public and had started advertising, business was coming in quickly. If this kept up, she might even be able to get a second employee.

As she trimmed the fur of a poodle named Pebbles, she looked around the back room. If she had a second employee, she could probably turn this part into a place to board animals when people went on vacation, just like she'd envisioned when she'd first leased the building.

And if she opened up boarding, along with everything else she was doing, it'd likely bring in more than enough to justify buying the building.

But all that was just dreaming. There was no way to tell if any of those things would be profitable over the long term, so they couldn't be relied on when making her decision. She just needed more facts! More assurances that things would work out. More certainty that buying the building was the right choice. Because if she couldn't be certain, she couldn't tell her landlord that she wanted to put in an offer.

She glanced at her phone, like she had every couple of minutes for the past three hours. Logically, she knew that Aaron could be at Matt's for a while. All night, even. But that didn't stop her heart from a little too often hoping she'd get a call from him. Every couple of minutes, apparently. He had started a conversation in his classroom that she desperately wanted to finish. It seemed like maybe he had felt the same way that she did, but she wasn't sure. She wanted to know for sure.

After Pebbles' owner, a war veteran named Jim, stopped by to pick her up, Macie got a phone call. It wasn't Aaron, but it was Joselyn, and that was just what she needed right now.

"Hey, sis! Are you still at work?"

"Yes, why—do you want to go do something?"

Joselyn laughed. "Yes, actually. I am just leaving the shop right now and was hoping to get the last little bit of Christmas shopping done. It sounds like you would love to go with me."

"I very much would. I'm grabbing my stuff right now."

"That's good, because I'm already at your door."

Macie poked her head out of her office, and saw Joselyn as she reached the front door, baby Aria in her arms. She waved, then hung up the phone and put on her coat. She let Emily know that she was going to be gone for a couple of hours, and if she wasn't back by closing time, Emily should just close up, and she'd be by shortly after to get Reese and Lola.

A light snow was falling as they walked. Just enough to

add a little magic to Main Street, the Christmas lights above shining in the darkness. They took Aria to go touch the poinsettia garlands wrapped around all the hand rails on the pedestrian bridges, to see the giant wreath on the clock tower, and watched the creek as the lights from above danced in the water that was starting to form ice crystals where the snow met the slow-moving water. Eventually, they even made it to Wishstones and started shopping.

"Okay, tell me what's up," Joselyn said as they paused next to the boxes of wrapping paper. "You've checked your phone dozens of times since we've been out."

She had? And here she thought she had been doing a good job of distracting herself. "I was just hoping for a call from Aaron."

"Here," Joselyn said, putting Aria in her arms. "You need something to keep your hands busy, and I need to find the perfect paper. You'll hear it when he calls."

Macie made faces at her little niece and was rewarded with some big smiles and a few laughs.

"You really like him, don't you?"

Macie sighed. "I really do. I'm just unsure about how much he likes me."

"Are you kidding? It's obvious how in love with you he is!"

Not really. It was painfully un-obvious.

Joselyn stopped searching through the rolls of wrapping paper and narrowed her eyes, scrutinizing Macie's face. "Why are you so unsure? Did he say or do something? Because from what I saw on Saturday, you two were both looking pretty smitten."

Macie reached down into Joselyn's bag, grabbed out a toy, and handed it to Aria. She looked at Aria for a moment as the baby squealed in delight and then started shaking the toy, and then she took a deep breath and looked at her sister. The two of them used to argue a lot back when they were in middle school, but by the time Macie was a sophomore in high school and Joselyn was a senior, they had become best friends. She was used to telling Joselyn everything. And right now she needed to be real with her sister and to get some help figuring things out way more than she needed to have her believe that she and Aaron were dating.

"I'm unsure because…" She hadn't realized how difficult it would be to tell her sister that she had been lying to her. But if it was so hard, why had it not been so hard to pull off faking the relationship in front of her? Macie wondered if that possibly meant that she hadn't been faking. Maybe she had liked him since that first day. "Okay, remember that day when we first met and were eating ice cream together in your shop?"

Her sister nodded, her hands still frozen on the rolls of wrapping paper.

"I was complaining about dating and said I wanted to take a break for six months. He said he didn't want to ever get married, but his students were set on finding him a wife by the end of the school year. So we decided to fake date each other so that everyone would back off."

"You've been faking?!"

"Shhh!" Macie said. "I don't exactly want it to be public knowledge!"

In a much quieter voice, Joselyn added, "And you didn't tell me?"

"I am so sorry. It was just somehow easier to pull off if I was acting the same way around everyone. I'm not exactly proficient in lying or faking things, so if only the two of us knew, then it was us teaming up together to do something. And he is really great to team up with."

"But then you actually fell for him."

"Pretty fully. I haven't felt this way since..." Macie racked her brain, trying to figure out when, "probably Jack."

Joselyn smiled, remembering. "Wow. When was that? The summer after your senior year? I remember, he was the guy you thought you'd ride off into the sunset with. This is huge."

"Well, huge for me. I have no idea where he stands. But that kiss Saturday night felt pretty real."

"From what Janet, Sophie, Trevor, and Mindy said, it was pretty smoochie smoochie."

Macie blushed, still embarrassed that her nieces and nephew had witnessed it. "And then earlier today, he started to ask me about it, and it seemed that maybe he had felt something too, but then his students needed him and then his friend needed him, and I just don't know." She adjusted the way Aria was sitting on her hip and pulled out her phone, just to make sure she hadn't missed the ring tone or the buzz.

Joselyn pulled out two different wrapping paper rolls, and held them next to each other, her head cocking to the side. "Well, from where I stood, things looked pretty authentic on his part. Do you think you want to continue dating him—for real?" Joselyn must've decided on the paper, because she moved down the aisle to bows.

"I don't know. I like him a lot. For so many reasons. But I've found myself hoping again, and that's a dangerous thing. It's like my heart has PTSD when it comes to hope. It knows that when it starts to hope, it has to prepare for being shattered."

"Unless this is the one time that it doesn't get shattered. Maybe this will be what restores your heart's faith in hope." She picked up a box of bows, and then looked toward the front of the store. "We really should've grabbed a cart if we want to get any shopping done."

They headed to the front of the store, then Macie buckled Aria into the seat in the cart and handed back the toy she had tossed onto the ground. "I think shattering is the more likely outcome. Plus, I think God's been giving me signs all along that we shouldn't be together."

Joselyn crossed her arms and raised an eyebrow in only the way an older sister could.

"No, really. Every time we've been together, something bad has happened. That first day, we went to the tree lighting, remember? And for the first time in probably all of Nestled Hollow history, the tree lighting caused a power outage for the entire city."

"That's because it was the first time in Nestled Hollow history that we had that many lights on the tree."

"At Winter Formal, we got the kids dancing, and one danced into the refreshment table, and punch and cookies went everywhere. At the hayride, that little kid got separated from his mom, so I got us disqualified." She tried to think through the order of the dates they'd gone on. "And then at his friend's house, not only did we have to leave early because I was getting so sick, but I totally and completely offended and embarrassed his friend. At the family Christmas party, we all got snowed in."

"Which ended up working in your favor, if you remember. Plus, the kids had a blast with the bonus sleepover."

"Today," she plowed ahead, sure that if she presented enough evidence, Joselyn would understand, "I took the dogs to his AP History class, and one of the girls got a broken nose. A broken nose, from playing with my dogs! What are the chances of that even happening?"

Joselyn still had her arms crossed and they still hadn't moved from the front of the store. Macie grabbed hold of the handle to the shopping cart and steered it back toward the toy section of the store, so Joselyn followed. "Oh! And let's not forget the first moment we met—it was because Lola ran ahead and her leash caused him to crash his bike. We met because he *crashed*."

"Maybe that was God intervening, because neither of you would've given each other a chance if he hadn't."

Macie just shook her head. "There have just been too many evidences that it's a bad idea. I mean seriously, Joselyn, even the idea was bad, because when I went to Best Dressed, I wasn't even with Aaron. I was simply getting a dress for when I would be with him, and chaos erupted at Paws and Relax just during those few minutes I was gone."

Joselyn reached out and stopped the cart, stopping Macie. "Have you actually *asked* God? Or are you just making assumptions?"

Macie sighed. "I haven't. But the fact remains that my goal is to get married. His goal is to not get married. So none of this matters anyway. My brain should've known all along not to let hope in, because there's really no hope to be had when it comes to things working out between us. Subconsciously, my brain hasn't been doing its job of protecting my heart from harm. I need to start doing it consciously."

Joselyn shook her head like she saw that Macie was just going down a path she'd seen her go down before. But this one really was different. "Just...Before you decide to do that, wait for his call. Ask him your questions, and see what he has to say, okay? Just wait for that?"

Macie hesitated, so Joselyn said, "Your 'boyfriend' and you have been fake dating, and you *didn't tell me.* I think the least you could do to make up for that is to promise me you'll wait until he calls to decide anything."

Macie nodded. She could do that. "Okay, I will."

Except Aaron didn't call at all that night.

Or at all on Wednesday or Thursday.

By the time Friday morning rolled around and her texts were still going unanswered, she wasn't even sure they were going to be going to the Main Street Business Alliance Christmas party together.

## Chapter Sixteen

$\mathcal{A}$aron knew he should've called Macie or responded to her texts. But Matt's news had hit him hard, and he'd barely managed to stay focused enough to make it through the last few days of school. If he'd been dating any girl other than Macie, he'd have already texted, letting them know that he was out—that he couldn't date right now.

But this was Macie.

So Friday during lunch, when he only had one class period left before the semester was over and school let out for two weeks for the Christmas break, he finally felt strong enough to reply. Before today, he'd planned to let her know that he couldn't make it to her work Christmas party, but now that the day was here, he decided that maybe he could handle it. Plus, he just really wanted to see her. He typed out a text and pressed send.

*I apologize for not calling. It's been a rough few days. Are we still on for tonight?*

The text showed as being read, but it was still a few agonizing minutes before the bubble showing that she was replying appeared.

I'M SORRY ABOUT YOUR LAST FEW DAYS! IF YOU NEED TO SKIP TONIGHT, THAT'S OKAY. LIKE I SAID, DATES AREN'T REQUIRED, AND I DON'T MIND GOING ALONE.

I WANT TO GO. WHAT TIME AND WHERE SHOULD I MEET YOU?

8:00, AT THE LIBRARY ON MAIN STREET. GO AROUND TO THE BACK, AND YOU'LL SEE DOORS THAT LEAD TO THE BASEMENT.

He knew he should've offered to pick her up so that they could arrive together, but he just didn't have it in him.

Aaron arrived at the doors to the basement of the library just a few minutes after eight, took a deep breath, and went inside. Macie's face lit up when she saw him, but then fell pretty soon after. This was a party. He really needed to figure out how to smile while he was here. He worked on it while she made her way to him.

"How are you doing?"

"I've been better. Matt told me that he cheated on Ciara, so of course Ciara moved out a couple of days ago."

Macie gasped. "Oh no. But they seemed so happy!"

He didn't know why he brought it up. He didn't want to talk about it—he mostly just wanted her to understand why he wasn't feeling the Christmas spirit. He shifted his gaze to the Christmas tree and a refreshments table instead of at Macie. She picked up that he didn't want to talk about it pretty quickly.

"Come," she said. "You need punch." She led him to the table, seeming a little unsure of herself, but covering it decently well. As she was ladling the punch into a cup, she said, "I know you don't want alcohol to harm this beautiful body of yours so I'd reassure you by letting you know this punch doesn't contain any, but it probably does have a near lethal amount of sugar, so there's that."

She smiled so big when she was handing it to him that he couldn't help but smile while he took it, his hand lingering on the cup, brushing up against hers longer than necessary.

"I think I could use the sugar today."

Macie led him around the room, introducing him to everyone. In his current state, it made him seriously question whether he should've come.

The woman with auburn hair who had been taking pictures at Hayride of the Santas stood in front of an area where chairs were set up, wearing a shirt that said, *I'm dreaming of a white (and black and read) Christmas*, and had a picture of a rolled up newspaper under a Christmas tree. She called out, "Everyone come on over—it's time for our first game!"

Macie leaned in and whispered, "Are you sure you want to stay?"

He nodded, grabbed her hand, and headed to the chairs. He had needed something to get his mind off Matt, and maybe this would do it.

"For this first game, everyone's going to need a partner, so if you didn't bring someone, find someone to be yours."

Macie looked at him and batted her eyes. Bad mood or not, she still managed to get a laugh out of him. "Will you do me the honor of being my partner in this game?"

"That would make me as happy as a kid who just found out he made the 'nice' list."

Aaron's eyes went back to the front, where the woman said, "This game is called 'TV Art Show Host,' and you guys are the artist hosting! The always incredible Eli, here, is going to help me demonstrate."

A man came up and joined her, and by the way they looked at each other, they were obviously dating. Or married. He glanced down at their ring fingers. Ahh. Engaged.

"Okay, the taller person goes in the front— that's you, honey— and the shorter behind." They scooted closer to a giant notebook of paper, the kind teachers sometimes used, that was propped up on an easel. "The taller person is the voice, and the shorter person is the arms, and cannot talk. The taller person puts their hands behind their backs, and the shorter person puts their arms under the arms of the person in front and sticks them out like this." Eli was facing the audience, but the woman's arms were the only arms they saw, and she waved at the crowd, making it look like Eli was the one waving.

"When it's your partnership's turn up here, I'll show the shorter person a paper that says what scene they are going to draw, and what things need to be in it. Since they're shorter, they aren't going to be able to see what they're drawing. While they're drawing, the taller person has to narrate what's happening, as if they are the host of a show that is teaching the audience how to draw this scene. And since the taller person can't see what's on the paper, they're just going to have to figure it out as they go. Now who wants to be first?"

Everyone looked around at each other, like they weren't sure if they wanted to start out a game they'd never played before, including Macie and Aaron.

"Okay then, I nominate..." The woman looked around the crowd. "Macie!"

"Thanks, Whitney," Macie said, then looked at Aaron. "What do you say, teammate? We've partnered up on everything else pretty well."

"True. Let's win this. Is this a game where there are winners?"

"Even if it isn't, let's win it anyway."

They went to the front of the crowd, and Eli adjusted the giant notepad so that everyone could see it. Aaron put his hands behind his back, and Macie slid her arms between his arms and his sides, and the touch sent heat rushing to his chest. Whitney showed Macie a paper, and he felt Macie lean back just enough to read it, then she closed the gap between them.

"Welcome," Aaron said, turning to face the group, "to today's episode of Draw a Christmas Scene. I am your host and resident artist..." He tried to quickly think of a couples name for him and Macie while she spread her arms out like he was about to introduce something awesome. "Aaracie." Okay, that one was awful. Maybe he should've thought about this first. He turned his back most of the way toward the group, so that he was facing the big sheet of paper.

"I'd like to tell you what scene we're drawing today, but I thought it might be more fun to keep it a surprise. Oh, and we're drawing. For those of you following along at home, we are starting by drawing two horizontal lines right in the middle of the paper. And then some vertical lines— one on the left side and one, um, kind of in the center? Never mind. Scribble that one out. We don't make mistakes here; we make happy little scribbles, like a garland on a Christmas tree. Doesn't that just add to the festiveness?"

After spending a full four days away from Macie, away from her family, and in the middle of the mess made by someone he trusted more than anyone in the world, he'd been ready to walk away. But seeing her here today brought everything back.

"Next, kind viewers and budding artists, we draw a box underneath the horizontal lines. Oh, and then inside the box, but also kind of outside the box, we are drawing... Actually, I'm not going to tell you just yet, I'm going to let you have a moment to see if you can guess. If you're doing this at home, just make things that kind of look like rectangles, but with the short sides curved, and just throw a bunch in there at all different angles. Now draw a jagged line above, kind of like the teeth of a shark. Oh! And that, my friends, is how you draw logs and a fire in a...I'm pretty sure that's a fireplace."

And feeling her pressed up against his back like this made him want to turn around and hold her tight and never let go. He wanted to lean into her, to have that cheek she had laying on his back to be laying on his chest. He wanted to kiss the top of her head.

"Okay, now above the fireplace, I want you to draw a big circle. That's right, don't worry if where you started the circle doesn't match up with where you ended. It's those kinds of details that really give this artwork personality. Now inside the circle, in the... bottom half, it looks like, draw a circle that's less than half the size of the bigger one. Then above it, draw two more smaller circles. Now see how great that looks, having a giant face above your fireplace, giving you the *Wow* look?"

Everything to do with Macie right now confused him. Things were no longer clean and clear in his mind—it was all one muddled mess. He couldn't figure out if he desperately wanted to be with her, or if he desperately wanted to run away. All he knew was he loved being with her. And that being with her was scaring him senseless. And the one person he would usually go to when he needed to talk things through, Matt, was the very last person he could go to.

"Wait a moment, we're adding more eyes to the face. And more eyes." He could feel Macie laughing into his back. "Lots more eyes. Yep, a *Wow* face with lots of eyes. That's the secret to drawing a wreath hanging above your fireplace!"

He knew what Macie wanted. All along he'd known what he wanted. But then getting to know Macie and being around her family had made him question that. It made him want what he hadn't wanted since he'd first separated from Sabrina. It made him want a wife who would be with him through thick and thin, facing all of life side by side. It made him feel like he might have been wrong about marriage all these years.

"But don't stop yet, young artists," he said, "because we have a few more details to add. Yes, right in the middle of your canvas, we want to add a squirrely line. Remember what I said about that adding festiveness? Oh, wait. We don't want to stop at the squirrely line; we want to curve it around and I think we maybe wanted to keep going until we get sort of in the vicinity of the beginning of the line. Because then when we're done, we'll have... a lump of coal, maybe? Those things are flammable, so don't keep your lumps of coal this close to the fire in your own homes, young artists."

Seeing what happened with Matt's and Ciara's marriage made him realize he hadn't been wrong, though. He should've known better than to turn his back against guards he'd had in place for a reason. Guards he'd had for years. They were there to protect him, and he had let himself tear them down. He could already feel the pain that was causing, and knew from experience how much more it had the possibility to inflict.

"Keep going with those and pretty soon, you'll have three very lovely...stockings! Yes, three lovely stockings hanging on, or floating above—your choice—your mantle. He turned to face the group and said, "And now we've reached the end of our episode. I do hope you'll join us next time when we discover how to draw a new and very unique Christmas scene. Until then," he could no longer remember the couple name he'd used for them, so he paused, trying to figure something out, "this is Macron, signing out."

Macie spread her arms wide and he took a bow. The group roared with laughter and cheered. Macie came out from behind him and they grasped hands and did a second bow. She grinned at him, and he grinned right back and wished that partnering with Macie—in every random way they had over the past few weeks—didn't always come so naturally. Because having so much fun with her just muddied the waters even more than they already were. Why couldn't she just be awful? That would make this so much easier.

## Chapter Seventeen

After three and a half days of not hearing from Aaron and her heart aching to connect with him, she was happy that he had texted that they were still on for the Main Street Business Alliance party. She was also more than a little wary. She had been hoping that he liked her more than just as a fake date, but three and a half days of no texting was a pretty big sign that he probably didn't.

Of course, she figured that those days of no contact could very well have been because of what was going on with his friend Matt, but thinking along those lines was the same as holding out hope. And she was working to keep herself far from hope.

Still, though, she had hoped for some kind of answers. But all night long, she had been getting the opposite of answers. When Aaron had first arrived, he'd seemed like he didn't want to be there at all. He was gracious enough as she was introducing him to everyone, but his usual spark was gone. Was that spark something he normally had, even when he wasn't around her, and other things had taken it away? Or was that a spark that was a special reserved-for-her spark, and whatever connection they'd had was now gone?

She didn't know him outside of having close contact with him, so she had no idea what his usual was. All she knew was that, her own fears and doubts aside, she missed the old Aaron.

And then, during the Art Show Host game, he had returned. He was back, *and* she had gotten to snuggle up to him. The smells of cinnamon and pine and chlorine and something else that was so uniquely and so perfectly Aaron that had clung to his coat was right next to her, and she had basked in it. Having him near her was so much better than having his coat. And he'd been fun and they'd worked together so well, just like they always had, and she'd felt connected to him again. She'd even put a second check mark next to *Will do crazy, spontaneous things with me.*

But after they sat back down, that disappeared. A few more pairs went up to do the Art Show Host game, and they'd all laughed pretty heartily, but his spark was gone again. Confused and frustrated by the mixed signals of apathy and fun and disappointment and irritability that was coming off him in constantly changing but buffeting waves, she got up and went to the refreshment table. Maybe some liquid sugar would help. Actually, what she really needed was water. Cool, clean water. And a walk in the brisk outdoor air. She tried to think of something in her car that she could say she forgot and had to run outside to get. Maybe the cold air would help her think.

Before she came up with something, though, Aaron was at her side. She had so many questions for him, and suddenly couldn't think of a single one. But then he stood there, spark-less and unreadable, and she knew exactly what she needed to ask. "Do you like me?"

So many conflicting emotions played on his face so quickly that she couldn't tell which one was strongest. After a moment, he carefully said, "Yes."

"Fake-like me or real-like me?"

"Real." Again with the careful, one word answers.

One word answers she *didn't* want to hear. What she wanted to hear him say was that he didn't actually like her—it was all a show, just like they had planned. Because if that was the case, then she could easily abandon all hope in this relationship, because that's what she'd been after all along. An escape from hoping something would work out.

But he just gave her a yes. Knowing that, was this relationship one she could move forward with? She didn't know if it was even possible. There were too many obstacles standing in their way. Not the least of which was the fact that he looked like he was pretty unhappy about liking her. Almost like he was mad about it.

He opened his mouth like maybe he wanted to ask a question. The same one she had asked him, possibly? But then he closed it, grabbed a cup of punch, and kept his eyes on it.

Macie said, "Your words are telling me one thing, but your actions—"

At the same time Aaron said, "I don't know if I can—"

But just as both of them stopped talking to let the other talk, Brooke stepped up to the refreshment table. "Hello, you two! How are you...Oh."

Just then, the whole group started making their way over. Macie was not about to advertise the troubles she and Aaron were having to all of her peers, and she didn't want to put

Aaron on the spot when he was struggling enough just talking to her about what was bothering him. So she pasted on a smile, even though it felt forced and not actually resembling a smile. "Is the game finished?" She slid her hand into Aaron's as a wordless plea for help, because she knew she wasn't pulling this off well on her own at all.

In a swift movement, he pulled his hand out of hers. "I'm sorry. If you'll all excuse me, I need to leave. Right now."

He hurried to the chairs at the side of the room where all the coats were stacked and pulled his out of the pile.

"Oh," Cole said. "We're sad to see you leave early. It's been fun having you."

It took a moment before Macie recovered from the shock of Aaron's sudden reaction. Then she rushed to the chairs and pulled out her own coat, and ran after Aaron as he opened the door and went out into the cold night.

"Aaron!" she called out.

He stopped in his tracks and then turned to face her. "I'm sorry. I really am."

"What just happened in there?"

Aaron ran his hands over his face. "I wasn't lying when I said I liked you. More than like, actually. And I really thought that maybe we could make it work, but then I realized that the chances of it actually working were pretty minuscule." He took a few deep breaths before continuing. "Seeing my parents broadcast a fake a relationship to the world when in reality it was decayed, and then going through it again with Sabrina took me somewhere more agonizing than I had known existed. And then the thing happened with Matt. I had forgotten how painful it is." He swallowed. "He reminded me why I never wanted to get married."

Macie tried to figure out how she should respond to that, but words didn't come. She just stood there, mouth slightly open, but silent.

"And then seeing you in there, pretending everything between us was fine when it very clearly wasn't—it was just too much. I couldn't."

"I wasn't trying to—"

He stepped closer, putting up a hand. "No, I know. But I can't—" He paused, searching her face. "I just...I'm sorry. I can't." Then he turned and walked away.

## Chapter Eighteen

The saying "misery loves company" must be true, because there wasn't another good explanation of why Aaron ended up on Matt's doorstep at eleven A.M. on Saturday with a pizza in one hand and chicken wings in the other.

"She's just so perfect," Matt said. "How could I have forgotten for a second how perfect she was? Do you think there's ever going to be another woman as perfect as Ciara? I'll tell you right now there's not."

"Just like there's never going to be another woman I get along with as well as Macie."

"You two were pretty fun together. You pair up well."

"We really did. I've never had that before. In all the girls I've dated, and you know that's been a lot—"

"By-product of never getting serious."

"—none of them has been a *teammate* before. Someone who felt like a partner, who stood side-by-side with me in whatever we happened to be facing."

"That's valuable stuff, man."

"It really is."

"And we threw it all away."

"Because we're stupid."

A knock sounded at the door, and Matt called out, "Whatever you're selling, we're not interested!"

There was another knock, more persistent this time. Aaron would've gotten up to get it, but he'd been half sitting, half laying in this same uncomfortable position for a while, and it'd take more effort than he could muster to move. A moment later, the door opened, and Ian & Timini, Dennis & Julie, and Shad & Annah all walked in.

"Ew," Timini said. "How long has this pizza been sitting here?"

Matt glanced up at the clock on the wall. "Like six hours. What are you guys doing?"

"Getting you lowlifes off the couch," Shad said as he opened the curtains. Aaron and Matt both shielded their eyes from the brightness of the setting sun.

Ian kicked the bottom of Aaron's shoe, making his leg move from where it had been resting for way too long. "I expect Matt to wallow. No offense, Matt."

Matt raised a hand. "None taken."

"But not you, Aaron. This isn't like you at all."

He shrugged. It really wasn't like him. "Well, I've never thrown away a chance at a real relationship with someone like Macie before, so it seemed appropriate."

"Up," Julie said, offering her hand to help pull him up. "We all know you don't go Christmas shopping until school gets out for the break, so we're going to take you."

Dennis held a hand out to Matt. "Because we know if we don't, none of us will be getting presents from you turkeys."

It actually felt good to get out around people in the one department store in Mountain Springs. And to move his legs again, see bright lights, and talk to people who weren't as miserable as he and Matt were.

All though it felt *good*, it still didn't feel *right*. Macie had redefined what "right" was for him, without him even realizing that it happened. He was twenty when his engagement to Sabrina had ended. Here he was, a full nine years later, and he was pretty sure that he was worse at dealing with a breakup now. Should he be missing Macie this much? He had only known her for a few weeks, after all. But the impact she'd left on him was so much greater.

He'd only brought her to his city once. Yet everything here reminded him of her. A dress on display in the center aisle was almost the same color of blue as the one Macie had worn at Winter Formal, when they'd danced like they'd been dancing together their whole lives. In a Lego display, he saw the same set they'd gotten the little boy during Hayride of the Santas. The shoe section reminded him of running barefoot in Dennis and Julie's backyard. Some Christmas stockings hanging on a printed cardboard cutout reminded him of the picture they'd drawn at her work party. And of the stockings hanging on her parents' mantle.

Maybe he would never get over her.

"So, I was talking with Ciara," Annah said, and Matt straightened like he was on full alert. "She said she might be open to going to marriage counseling with you."

"What?" He grabbed Annah's shoulders. "She really said that?"

Annah smiled. "I'm sure it will take some heavy-duty repentance on your part."

"And major, major groveling," Ian added.

"And never ever ever even *thinking* about another woman again," Timini said.

"You hurt her a lot," Annah said. "And that's not going to be an easy or quick thing to get over. But deep down, she still loves you. And before all this happened, you two had something special."

"Do everything you can to make things right," Ian said. "Keep doing them until you can convince yourself and her that there's no chance it'll happen again, and you never know. You might get a second chance."

Matt practically floated down the aisle, but Aaron stayed at the back of the group, lagging behind everyone else. Julie slowed to Aaron's speed and bumped her shoulder into his. "You're being awfully quiet."

"I'm just surprised, I guess. Why would Ciara even think of taking him back?"

She shrugged. "Sometimes things aren't as broken and unfixable as they can appear to be."

*P*aws and Relax still needed Macie. The animals still needed Macie. Emily still needed Macie. So she went to work on Saturday like she always did. She gave all the shoppers chances to relax and recover and prepare for their second trip into the fray. She gave little kids who were stir-crazy from being strapped into shopping carts too long a chance to run and play with pets. And she gave people who were saddened by the holidays a chance to brighten their day.

And then she took Reese and Lola home, walked straight to her room, and shut the door behind her.

She wasn't sure how much later—a couple of hours, maybe?—Marcus knocked on her door. "We're about to watch a movie. Come join us."

She didn't respond.

"It'll do you good." He paused. "Come on, Macie. Emily said you shut yourself in your office at work whenever you could, too."

Macie grabbed a blanket out of her closet, walked out of

her room, put her coat, gloves, scarf, hat, and boots on, and then walked out the back door. She walked out to where the snow was nice and deep and untouched, spread the blanket out right on top of the snow, and then flopped down on it, the snow beneath her forming to her body, feeling as close to lying on a cloud that she could imagine.

There. She was out of her room.

Her breaths made little cloud puffs in front of her face as she stared up at the stars, Christmas music wafting across the backyards of her family. It was probably coming from Everett's house. She heard songs a little further away, coming from Christmas carolers at one of her neighbors'.

A few minutes later, light spilled onto the snow from the back door. She closed her eyes, hoping it wasn't Marcus or Joselyn coming out to talk. A moment later, though, Reese leapt onto the blanket with her, wearing his booties so his paws wouldn't get too cold in the snow. She sat up to say thank you, but she only saw the back door close.

Reese seemed to know exactly what she needed—someone to just be next to her as she grieved, and to have zero expectations. He stretched his body out next to hers, and she petted the fur at his neck.

"I really liked him, Reese." She took a few slow breaths. "And because I know you won't tell anyone, I'll confide in you that I think maybe I even loved him. Okay, I know I loved him, and I loved him a lot. I think I started falling in love on that very first day, but I wasn't willing to admit it, because it wasn't part of the plan.

"And now he's gone."

Reese whined, and Macie wrapped her arms around his neck and hugged him tight.

"He was just unlike anyone I've ever dated. I mean, it's

not like I've never dated anyone where we connected in the way we have fun before. Or connected in the way we work in a partnership. Or connected in the way we treat kids. It's just I've never experienced all of that with the same person before. Plus, you saw us, Reese. Standing next to each other, we just look like we belong together, don't you think?"

Reese barked and then licked her neck. Macie chuckled and rubbed behind his ears.

"Remember how I said that I wasn't going to hope? Zero hope for six months. I said that, right? Well, I guess I opened the door just a teeny crack, and when I wasn't looking, hope snuck its way in. And I'm talking a *lot* of it. I didn't even realize how much had gotten in until Aaron broke things off yesterday."

She turned her face toward the stars again, and listened as the Christmas carolers started a new song, to the east of where they were before.

"What do I do, Reese? What do you do when you you've been searching for your needle in a haystack ever since high school, so for nine years, and then right when you give up, you feel one in your hand, and you think it might be your actual needle? And before you've even had enough of a chance to bask in the sunlight that's glinting off the needle, it disappears, *poof!* right out of your hand." Reese whimpered and nuzzled in a little closer.

She looked off to the side, twisting to see the empty lot that was hers, covered in a blanket of untouched snow.

"What do you say, Reese? Me and you can build a house there. We'll find you a wife— an adorable, stalwart lab who will stand by your side, and the two of you can have a houseful of puppies. We'll find a great husband for Lola, too, and they can have a bunch of puppies, and all your puppies can romp and wrestle and play together like they're cousins. And then every time I'm sad that I don't have my own spouse and houseful of kids, you can just come lay next to me and listen to me and whine at all the right places, because you're super good at that."

Reese rolled onto his stomach and put a paw on her shoulder, and just looked at her like he understood. Then he leaned his head forward and licked her cheek, wiping off a tear that had slipped out, making her laugh. "Okay, you know you just left my cheek more wet than it was, right? You're a good boy, Reese. Thanks for always being by my side."

# Chapter Twenty

*A*aron finished his Christmas shopping during the day of Christmas Eve. Alone. That had never bothered him before—he enjoyed doing things in groups, but he had always been perfectly fine doing pretty much anything solo. But today somehow felt like a window into his future. A future where his friends were with their spouses, off to visit family, and he was alone.

Braving the traffic and the crowds of last-minute shoppers, he had headed to the closest mall on the outskirts of Denver. He had just bought the last gift on his list when he felt his phone buzzing. He pulled it out of his pocket and looked at his screen. It was his sister Aliza.

He frowned at the screen. He, his sister, his mom, and his dad always did a group video call on Christmas day. That way, they all didn't have to make multiple calls to get in their obligatory chat with everyone, and if there was a lag in the conversation, there were four people to fill it instead of just two. His sister didn't just call out of the blue like this. He hoped that everything was okay.

"Hello?"

"Hey, big brother."

"Hi, Aliza. Is everything okay?"

"Can't a girl call her big brother on Christmas Eve even if nothing is wrong?"

"She can call anytime. It's just a little unprecedented."

"Well, you know me—I like being unpredictable. How deep is the snow in icicle-land?"

"A few inches above my knees. How hot's the oven in Phoenix?"

"A little chilly, actually. Sixty-eight. Although if you were here, I bet you'd be wearing shorts, even though it looks like it might rain."

Aaron laughed. "Probably."

"Okay, enough with the idle chit-chat. I called for a real reason, and I wanted to tell you before the family video chat."

Aaron paused a moment, then realized he was stopping right in the middle of the hallway of the mall and kept walking. "I'm listening."

"A while ago, I met a guy. His name is Frederick, and he's pretty great, actually. We've been dating for most of this year, and Saturday night he proposed to me right below the lanterns at Lights of the World."

"You're...*engaged*?" Aaron spotted a chair five feet away and practically fell into it.

"Can you believe it? One of the offspring of Ken and Sheri Hall somehow survived their parents' fiasco of a divorce and is going to get married."

"An impressive feat indeed. I'd like to offer my congratulations. You sound really happy."

"I am. Thank you."

"Aren't you worried that—what?" Aaron's attention flew to the man standing in front of him with his hands on his hips, wearing an elf suit.

"You're in my seat," the angry elf said.

Aaron looked around and noticed for the first time that he'd fallen into a seat in Santa's court, where kids were lined up to sit on Santa's lap, surrounded by giant-sized candy canes and lollipops and gumdrops. And the seat he was sitting in looked more like a throne than the mall benches nearby.

"Oh, sorry. Here you go. Merry Christmas."

He grabbed his bags and started walking again.

"Aaron? What's going on?"

"Nothing. Except I think an elf just put my name on the naughty list. Okay, so you're engaged. Don't you worry that things might turn out like they did for Mom and Dad?"

"Or like they did for you and Sabrina?"

"I like that you don't tiptoe around subjects that might be sensitive."

"You know me, bro. I call it like I see it. Besides, it's been nine years. I figured you were over it by now."

"I am. It's just that all that kind of stuff resurfaced lately, so it feels fresh."

"Uh oh. Do you want to talk about it?"

"This call is about you, not me." He pushed open the outside doors and headed into the parking lot.

"Okay, you asked if I worry that my marriage will turn out like Mom's and Dad's, and the answer is no. It's a worry I've had pretty much constantly in the past, though. I'm a drop-dead gorgeous dancer with an MBA—this wasn't the first time I've been proposed to. A couple of them were really great guys, too. Ones who would've made pretty fantastic husbands. But this is the first time where I felt like not only was he a great guy, but a great guy for me specifically. And it was the first time where I felt like I had gotten past the way I got screwed up as a teenager going through Mom's and Dad's divorce."

"So there's a way to get past that then?" He pushed the button on his key fob to pop his trunk and then put his bags inside.

"There is. It kind of surprised me, too. I mean, there's not a magic way or anything. A lot of it just happened over time. It probably has for you, too, and you just haven't realized it. I just got to a point where I realized that I am not Mom and Dad. Frederick is not Mom and Dad. They faced some challenges, sure. But they made a choice to put other things before each other, and I've chosen not to. I'm marrying someone who is just as dedicated as I am to putting each other first. When we're faced with challenges, we aren't going to make the same mistake."

Aaron opened his car door and got inside. "And he's a good guy?"

"One of the best I've ever known. This woman who's on your mind—"

"I never said there was a woman."

"Well, maybe not with your actual words, but it's coming across loud and clear. Is she a good person?"

He put the key in the ignition, but didn't turn it. "The very best there is."

"A decade ago, Mom and Dad caused us a lot of pain, and I think we've both been carrying it around with us. It's kind of scary to lay down a load that's become a part of who we are. But Aaron?"

"Yeah?"

"It also feels pretty great. People aren't meant to be alone. It took me a long time to realize that applies to me, too."

Aaron had always figured it didn't apply to him, either. And before Macie, he was perfectly fine with being alone. She had opened a door in him that hadn't ever been opened before, and now he wasn't sure if he'd ever be fine being alone again. Could he lay down that pain he'd been carrying with him? It really had become a big part of who he was. Did he dare lay it down and walk away from it? Could he have enough faith and trust in himself and in Macie to believe that they could make it work?

"Thank you, Aliza. Out of all the people who could've helped me figure things out, I would've never guessed the best advice would come from family."

"Remember when you were going through your big breakup and we used to talk all the time?"

"Yeah."

"We should do that again. If I've learned anything in the past few weeks, it's that family matters. I would love to have a more than twice-a-year brother."

*Family mattered.* It's something he had just begun to learn, too. "I would like that too." He thought about what Macie's dad had said when they put up the stockings at their Christmas Kickoff party. *Your relationships with your family matters.* He'd told them the importance of talking things out and fixing things and nurturing each other. That relation-ships take work, but it was the most valuable work he could do. That it was important to keep those links strong. Aaron now knew that it was important with his own family, and it was important with the woman he wanted to become family.

He turned the key in the ignition and let the phone call switch over to the car. "Thank you, Aliza. I'm really glad you called. Now if you'll excuse me, I've got to go—I've got to get in touch with someone. I might call you before the family video chat tomorrow."

Aliza paused, and then said, "Before?" with a little too much excitement and question behind the word.

"Maybe. I guess it all depends on how good I am at apologizing and making up for being a complete jerk to someone who didn't deserve it, and in convincing her of how much I love her."

"Then I'll definitely be rooting for before."

*M*acie walked into her room, carrying bags filled with all the papers from her office. She pulled her phone out of her pocket when it buzzed, looked at the text, and groaned before tossing all the bags on her bed.

"Not a happy text?" Joselyn asked from the doorway.

"It's Max Cohen. He said that he's not trying to rush me, but he'd like to start preparing everything for the building to go up for sale on January first if I'm not going to put in an offer, so the sooner I let him know the direction I'm going, the better. He's hoping for a quick sale."

"And have you decided what you're going to do?"

"I just don't see how I can possibly put in an offer. But if I tell him no, what do I do with the animals when the building sells? I've looked, and haven't found a location to move the business to. Do I just close up shop and have the animals I rescued from the shelter go back there?" The whole thing made her stomach churn just thinking about it.

She opened the flap of the bag containing the binders

with all her financial information. One more look at the information, and she was going to have to decide. It was Christmas Eve, which meant she only had one week left, and nothing that happened with the business was going to change drastically during that time to warrant putting the decision off any longer.

Joselyn walked into the room and sat on her bed. "So tell me what you're thinking. And stop giving me that look, because it's been years since I have pulled the older sister card and told you what to do."

"True."

"And not only am I family, but I'm also your *best friend*. And best friends and family talk this kind of stuff out with each other."

Macie sat down cross-legged on the bed facing Joselyn and opened the binder. "Okay. Here's what my monthly income looked like from each of the different programs I run before I started making changes, and here's the one from after."

Joselyn took both of them in her hands, looking back and forth between the two. "Wow. This is pretty incredible."

Macie nodded. "Part of me is actually kind of grateful that Max gave me a deadline like that, because it pushed me to try some things that I had been a little wary of trying. If I would have known they'd work out so well, I would've tried them a while ago. I just wish the deadline didn't also come with me losing my business."

"You're not going to lose your business."

"I don't see how I can keep it. I have no guarantee that these numbers will stay the same month after month. And I have no idea if something will happen with me or the business that I haven't predicted."

Joselyn set the papers aside. "I know you're a good saver. How are your bank accounts looking?"

"For my business account, I have about six months of expenses saved up."

"That's fantastic, Macie. How about your personal accounts?"

Macie handed her the spreadsheet with her personal finance information, and Joselyn's eyes grew big. "Whoa! You've managed to save up that much money? Macie, you could practically pay for two-thirds of the entire building cost with this!"

Panic coursed through Macie at the thought of there not being a big chunk of money sitting in her account, ready for any emergency that came along. She wiped her sweaty palms on her pants, and tried to slow her breathing.

"Relax, Macie. I'm not suggesting you should dump it all into your building. I'm just saying that if something happened, you'd have options. This opens so many possibilities."

Macie shook her head. "It's not enough of a safety net. It won't cover everything. There's no guarantees that if I buy the building that bad things won't happen." She looked down at the papers. Papers that she'd been studying for the past three weeks. There were just so many unknowns that she couldn't prepare for. And the unknowns that she did know to prepare for, like what would happen if she got sick or injured or any of a million things that could stop her from being able to work for more than a day or two, were all things she hadn't made a great plan for yet.

"I think you're letting fear of unclear outcomes stop you from some pretty great things. In both your business and your relationship with Aaron."

Macie's head jerked up. "With Aaron?"

"Oh, come on. Don't tell me you don't see the parallels between where you're at with your business and where you're at with Aaron."

In truth, she hadn't. So she just looked at her sister, blinking.

"Macie, you have planned and prepared for this business since you were in high school, getting every single duck exactly in a row. And you have planned and prepared to find the person you're meant to be with for the rest of your life since high school, getting every single duck there in a row too. And you have put time and energy and your whole heart into both of them. But when it comes down to making a really big commitment with either of them, you back away."

"I didn't back away—Aaron did!"

"And have you gone after him? Have you let him know how you feel, and that you think the relationship is worth fighting for? And what about before the break-up? That day when we were out Christmas shopping and you confessed that the two of you had been fake dating, you were backing away plenty. Were you backing away before then, too?"

Macie opened her mouth to respond, but nothing came out, so she closed it again. After a few moments, she looked down and said, "He said he doesn't want to get married. To anyone, ever."

"I know he did. Do you know if he still feels that way? Because the man I saw at the Christmas Kickoff party wore the face of someone who'd had a change of heart." Joselyn got up from the bed and walked to Macie's desk. "Where's your *Future Husband* list?"

"Middle drawer, right on top."

Joselyn brought the sheet of pale blue card stock filled

with Macie's handwriting as a seventeen-year-old, written nearly a decade ago, and put it on the bed between them as she sat back down. The edges of the paper were a little bent and more rounded than they once were, after years of pulling the paper out and looking and re-reading it, making mental checkmarks with each guy she dated.

"Which of these attributes does Aaron fill?"

Macie went down the list, making a little checkmark with her finger with each item. Communicates with me well, is fun to be around, encourages me and supports me in my choices, takes care of me when I'm sick, will do crazy spontaneous things with me, knows how to cook, shows that he puts me before his friends, would make a good dad, is kind to others.

"So basically all of them."

"My business looks good on paper too," Macie said, "but that doesn't tell the whole story. There have been times over the past few weeks where I've thought Aaron and I communicated super well, and on a level deeper than I've connected with anyone in a really long time. Maybe ever. But then he ran into something that affected our relationship, and he didn't come to me with it. And since he didn't, we couldn't tackle it together and come up with a solution. He just let himself fall down a dark hole, and only came to me once he was resigned to living in that dark hole. How could we have a good partnership like that? I had thought he was a great communicator before this. See? There are just no guarantees. With Aaron or my business."

Joselyn reached out and held Macie's hands in hers. "You've planned and prepared well, Macie. You've built yourself an impressive safety net. There aren't guarantees that things will work out the way you planned. You know this better than most people do. When you make a huge big commitment and things go a different direction than you thought they would, you adjust, just like you've been doing all along without there being a big commitment."

Macie looked at the papers spread before her that, in black and white, showed the qualities of her business, and in blue and pencil lead, the qualities of Aaron, and whispered, "But I'm afraid." Her voice came out squeaky and small. She was afraid of making huge commitments to both of them, and risking something going wrong. She was afraid of losing her business since so much of her heart was wrapped up in it. But most of all, she was afraid of losing Aaron, after having so much of her heart wrapped up in him.

"Do you know what the opposite of fear is?"

Macie looked up and met her sister's eyes, her head shaking a fraction.

"It's faith. Faith and fear can't co-exist, so if you choose one, the other disappears. I *know* it takes a big leap! It did for me, too. But you aren't going to get the truly great rewards if you choose fear over faith."

"Do you really think I can take a leap of faith that big?"

"As your best friend, as a fellow businesswoman, and most importantly, as your sister, yes. I know you better than anyone, Macie. And without a doubt, *yes*."

## Chapter Twenty-Two

*A*aron knocked softly on the door and waited, shifting the big box that sat in his arms. A few moments later, Macie's mom carefully opened the door, a wide smile spread across her face, and whispered, "Hi, Aaron. Come in."

"Hello, Emeline. It's so good to see you again. Does anyone know?"

She shook her head. "Still just me and Joseph."

Aaron set the box down on the ground, took off his gloves and put them in his pockets, then handed his coat, scarf, and hat to Macie's mom.

"Macie is about to make an announcement," she said, still in whispered tones, "so I need to get back in there. But first," she led him to a small table under the big family picture that hung on the entry wall opposite the front door, "here it is." She handed Aaron a fancy box about the size of a shirt box, then reached out and placed her hand on Aaron's arm. She looked up at Aaron with a look of silent but complete approval on her face.

Aaron nodded down at the box in his hands and mouthed *Thank you for this*. Then Emeline turned and hurried around the corner into the family room that sat on the other side of the wall.

Muffled sounds and occasional laughter came from the other room. Aaron took a deep breath and crept near the opening so he could hear what was happening.

"Okay, enough with the balled-up wrapping paper war," Joseph said. "I believe Macie has an announcement she'd like to make."

"Grandpa!" one of Macie's older nephews said. "You can't throw one more after you called a cease-fire!"

"Oops. I better throw two more, then."

Judging by everyone's laughter and shouts, Macie must've intercepted the second one and tossed it right back at her dad. Then, except for the sounds the littlest kids were making and an occasional dog bark, everyone quieted down.

"Yesterday," Macie said, "Joselyn went all 'big sister' on me— but don't worry, not 'bossy big sister'—"

"Because she knows she'd have to fight me for that title," Nicole said, to lots of laughs.

"And she helped me to realize that I have been holding back in a couple areas of my life, and that I was shying away from making long-term commitments because of some pretty deep-seated fears. She also told me that faith wipes out fear. Apparently there were a lot of things I was unknowingly doing, and I can't say I really wanted to believe that she was right about it."

"*Oof.*"

Based on the sounds and Marcus's burst of belly laughter, Aaron guessed that Joselyn had thrown a ball of wrapping paper at Macie.

He chuckled, knowing that by the sounds of things, Macie threw it right back.

When the noise died back down, Macie said, "So I did some pretty hefty soul-searching all day yesterday. And then last night when we were doing the live nativity and Riley, you were wearing your angel wings and halo and Janet, you were dressed as Mary and had just found out that you were going to have baby Jesus, the angel said to Mary, 'Be not afraid.' And then Janet, you got this look of blissful contentment on your face, and I knew that's what I wanted. I wanted to not be afraid, and to be willing to take two huge leaps of faith, even if it was over chasms so wide that I couldn't see the other side. Because with you guys cheering me on, how could I fail?"

Aaron could barely breathe as he waited to hear the rest of her announcement. A small scuffing sounded behind him, a shifting of position, and his attention went to the box still sitting near the door, wrapped in colorful Christmas paper.

"So last night, after everyone was all tucked into their sleeping bags all through the house, visions of sugarplums dancing in your heads, I took the first of two leaps. I logged on to Mom's and Dad's computer and signed the papers to buy Paws and Relax's building, and sent them off."

Cheers erupted from the room, and Aaron's heart swelled. Macie had done it. He knew how tough the decision had been for her to make, and he was so proud of her. It was obvious how much she cared about her business, and how much it meant to the people of Nestled Hollow, and he was thrilled she'd be able to keep it. He set the fancy box back on the table, and went over and picked up the box by the door.

The box was big enough to be rather awkward to carry, especially with its shifting weight. He turned the corner to the family room to see thirty-four people, all dressed in Christmas-colored pajamas and hugging and congratulating Macie, and all eyes flew to him.

"Aaron!" Macie said, a look of surprise on her face. But it looked like a happy surprise, which was much more than he expected after the way he had treated her. He breathed out relief. He had suspected that her second leap of faith involved him, but he wasn't sure if that leap was going to be away from him or toward him.

But either way, he was proud of her for making a tough decision, and he wanted to let her know that, and to show that he believed in her, even if it was coming a bit late. And then he'd need to convince her of how much he wanted that second leap of faith to be toward a future with him.

He didn't even have to say a word, and everyone found seats on the couches, chairs, and floor, leaving an open pathway between him and Macie. She stood in front of the crowd, wearing red, white, and green striped leggings, and a nightshirt with a Christmas tree printed on the front. In his jeans and button-down shirt, he suddenly felt very wrongly dressed for the occasion.

"I heard your announcement," he said, the smile spreading across his face. "I knew you could do it. I brought you something to show how much I believe in you." He lifted the box a bit, and walked right up next to her.

Her eyes searched his face, and then she glanced at the box. Her face was full of questions, and he wanted to answer them, but first, he really wanted her to open the box.

Her older brother Oliver got off his chair and moved it near Macie, so Aaron set the box down on top of it. But still, Macie's eyes wouldn't leave his.

"Open it already!" one of the kids called out.

Aaron wanted to give him a high five for saying what he was thinking, but he didn't want to take his eyes off Macie.

She lifted the tag on the top of the box and read out loud, "To my Mysterious Goddess, from your Dashing Man who believes in you one hundred percent." She gave him a smile before lifting the lid off the top and then she gasped.

"Oh my goodness, you got me a dog!" She pulled the dog out of the box to the sounds of *Aww*'s and "he's so cute" from everyone in the room, and the dog immediately gave a happy bark. His coat was a milk-chocolate brown, and the reindeer antlers Aaron had put on the puppy right before coming in the house were still in place. The dog was still young enough that he had the chunky toddler-like features, and his feet scrambled to find her as she pulled him to her, hugging him to her chest. He gave a second yip and licked her neck.

"From the shelter?" she asked.

"Of course," he said, and she looked at the dog like she loved him even more.

The dog was trying to climb her or get into a different position or just burn some energy after waiting so patiently, and she was struggling to keep hold of him and still be able to look at Aaron. He seemed to find a position he liked, though, and settled into her arms. "That was a huge risk, Aaron Hall! You knew I could only get a new dog if I bought my building. How did you know I would put in an offer?"

"You're an amazing woman, Macie. It's not hard to believe in you." She gave him a look that took his breath away, and made him think that maybe he had a chance. He was suddenly very aware of how many people were in the room, and he cleared his throat. "He's just little now, but they said he'd likely be a medium-sized dog, and I figured that since you had big ones and smaller ones—"

"He's perfect. As perfect as could be. Does he have a name?" She rubbed a thumb behind his ears, and the dog leaned his head back, mouth open in obvious enjoyment.

Aaron reached out and petted the dog's head. "Nope. They found him wandering alone without a collar."

Macie looked the dog in the eyes, studying him. "A Christmas puppy—with antlers!—from my Dashing Man. Hmm. I think I'll name him Dasher."

As Macie looked at the puppy, her face bright and happy, Aaron knew, once again and with absolute certainty that what he wanted most in the world was to be able to wake up every morning for the rest of his life next to her. To face whatever challenges life threw at them, and to do it side-by-side with Macie, meeting those challenges together. "That's not actually the only thing I came here for."

"Oh?" Macie looked at him, her lips parted, an eyebrow raised. She set Dasher on the ground, and a few of her nieces and nephews gathered around him and petted him.

Aaron turned toward the door opening, but Macie's mom was already out of her seat and motioned that she would get the box. A moment later, she came back into the room and handed it to him.

The box shook slightly in his hands. For as sure and confident and at peace he'd felt this morning, he had hoped that he'd be able to pull this off with a little more fearless-ness. After having such a monumental change in heart and his entire way of thinking—something that only Macie could've affected in him—he was suddenly very worried that she didn't feel the same way.

And there were so many people in the room watching. It was a lot of people to make himself so vulnerable in front of. But it also felt exactly right to have them here.

Their relationship had begun under the guise of dating, and he'd be forever grateful for their pact, because he'd have never gotten to know and love her without it. He'd realized that from the beginning, the parts of themselves that they'd been sharing and the ways in which they'd been connecting with each other had been anything but fake. As he'd been drowning in his sorrows and looking back at the last several weeks with her, he knew he'd been connecting to the truest, most genuine, sincere, authentic person he'd ever met.

The thoughts calmed his nerves, the box stopped shaking, and his tight throat relaxed.

"Macie," he said, and all the chattering in the room hushed. "I met you at a time when I was most determined not to fall in love. I thought I was just getting out of the deal a teammate with a common goal—I didn't know I was partnering up with the one person in all the world with the power to shatter the stone around my heart. That day in the ice cream shop, I thought you were the most beautiful woman I had ever seen. Since then, I've found out that the beauty you have in here," he reached out and touched three fingers just above her heart, "far outshines it. You've introduced me to a kind of love that I didn't know existed, and I want to show you that same kind of love back. I want to be your teammate in life, Macie. Your partner in everything."

He took the lid off the top of the box and set it aside, revealing the stocking Macie's mom had made with his name on it, with two links already attached to it—one that he hoped Macie would want to link with hers, and one to link him to her family.

He got down on one knee to the collective sound of gasps from everyone in the room. "Macie Zimmerman, will you marry me?"

## Chapter Twenty-Three

Macie looked down at the stocking in the box, with her mom's signature beading and stitching, and with Aaron's name on it. Every year when her parents put up the linked stockings, she had imagined how it would look to have one up there with her future spouse's name on it. Seeing that stocking with Aaron's name on it felt exactly and completely *right*.

"You...You want to get married?"

Aaron chuckled. "I hadn't seen this coming, either. But apparently all along it wasn't that I didn't want to get married—it was that I didn't want to get married to anyone who wasn't you."

She realized that she could deny it all she wanted, but Aaron was exactly what she'd imagined every day since the seventeen-year-old her had first made her *Future Husband* list. He had been her needle in the haystack all along, and deep down, she had known it even during the times when she'd allowed fear to try to convince her that she'd just been holding another piece of hay.

"So," he said, his voice coming out more unsure, "what do you say?"

"Oh, Aaron, yes! Yes! Of course the answer is yes." She pulled him to his feet, wrapped her arms around his neck, and said, "Yes, I want to be your teammate in life, your partner in everything, your wife. I want to be the person you turn to, the shoulder you cry on, the one you laugh the hardest with, and the one you dream the biggest dreams with. You and me, hand in hand, facing everything life has in store for us, together."

Aaron set the box aside and wrapped his arms around her waist, holding her close. Their noses touched, and he said, "I've seen the way we are as partners, and I'm pretty sure there isn't anything we can't conquer."

She grinned and he grinned, and then she kissed that grin. His kiss back wasn't hesitant like the last time they'd kissed. It was soft and wonderful and full of confidence. Their lips moved together in perfect unison, like a dance that they'd practiced the steps to. She pulled him in closer. And then she realized that she was being kissed by her *fiancé*, and her kiss turned into a smile once again.

"Too much smoochie-smoochie!" her four-year-old nephew Brighton said. "Everyone quick—cover your eyes!"

Macie burst out in laughter and Aaron's cheeks reddened.

"Oops," he said.

Macie just turned to face her family, then grabbed Aaron's hand and lifted it high, and then they both bowed, just like they'd done at the Winter Formal. She smiled at him to cheers and clapping. One room, and it was filled with all the people she loved more than anyone in the entire world. After not seeing Aaron's face for several days, and fearing that she'd never see it regularly again, seeing him smile back at her brought her even more joy than she'd ever imagined she'd feel in this moment. "I love you, Aaron Hall. With my whole heart, with my whole soul, with my whole *everything.*"

"And I love you, Macie Zimmerman. About a hundred times more strongly than I thought was even possible."

They stood there side by side, looking in each other's eyes, as happy chatter filled the room.

Macie's dad stood up and shook Aaron's hand, and said, "Welcome to the family, son. You're in our hearts for good now." Then he turned to the group and clapped his hands together. "I think there are two things that need to happen before we move on to the gingerbread house competition. Now I know you are just freshly engaged and don't even have a wedding date yet, but do either of you have any objections to linking Aaron's stocking right now?"

Macie saw the look on Aaron's face and thought that maybe, just maybe, having his stocking linked to everyone else's was just as important to him as it was to her. Her dad must've noticed, too, because he said, "I'll take that as not having any objections. What about the rest of you? Any objections?"

Marcus raised his hand. "I object to having more competition for Favorite Uncle."

Macie's dad laughed, and said, "I'll also take that as not having any objections. Emeline?" He held out his hand, and Macie's mom stood and put her hand in his. Then they turned and linked Aaron's stocking to Macie's, and then to the rest of the family. Her parents both turned back to face all of them, and Macie's dad said, "More than anything else, family matters. And we would like to officially welcome you to ours."

Aaron reached out like he was going to shake their hands and give them a heartfelt thank you; but instead, her parents enfolded him in a hug. And then Macie's brother Zach slammed into their group hug, wrapping his arms around them all. "Welcome to the family, bro."

"Stop hugging," six-year-old Sophie demanded, one hand on her hip and the other holding out a present. "Grandpa, you said there were two things that needed to happen, and hugging wasn't one of them. *This* was."

Macie accepted the present, and saw that the tag said it was to Aaron, and the *from* line was blank. When they'd opened presents earlier, she hadn't even noticed that there was one still unopened. Who had gotten a present for Aaron? She hadn't even guessed he would be there. But her mom motioned for her to give it to Aaron, so she did.

Aaron took off the wrapping paper, took the lid off the box, and started laughing. He pulled out a pair of Christmas pajamas. "I knew I was underdressed." He turned to her mom. "Thanks for having my back."

"Now hurry and change," Macie's brother Everett said. "I'm going for the 'tallest gingerbread house' award, and I need some better competition than these fumble-fingered troglodytes."

"I had fun today. Your family is very accepting." Aaron rubbed his hands down his pajama pants, and then tapped his fingers on his knee.

"It's because they all have the Christmas spirit. Just wait until Valentine's Day—that's when the claws come out."

Aaron looked at her in alarm.

"Kidding! They love you." She watched as he jiggled the mouse connected to her laptop. They escaped the festivities not long after lunch and headed back to her place to wait for the video chat with his parents. "Why are you so nervous?"

"I'm pretty sure you've gathered that my family is not like yours."

"And you've never 'brought home' a girl before?"

"Not since Sabrina. And that was nine years ago." He looked up for a moment. "Looking back, that meeting didn't actually go very well. It's not too late to back out. Do you want to back out? I can tell Aliza to just let them know that I couldn't make it."

Macie put her hand on Aaron's leg. "Family is important. Whether it's big or small, functional or not so much, accepting or exclusive, they're important." She grabbed his hand with hers. "Side by side, together, we've got this."

Aaron looked at Macie, his gaze intent and searching and welcoming. He leaned forward and gave her a kiss. His lips had barely touched hers when the incoming call alert sounded. Aaron took a deep breath, then said, "We've got this," and clicked to answer the video chat.

"Aaron! So good to see you. Merry Christmas!" His mom leaned closer to the camera, squinting. "Are those Christmas pajamas you're wearing?"

"Hi, Mom. Merry Christmas to you too."

"Seriously, son, it must be like two in the afternoon where you are. Why on earth would you still be in pajamas? Remember when you used to dress nice for our calls?"

"Mother, you're wearing a swim suit."

"That's because I'm vacationing in Cabo San Lucas. Check out these white sand beaches." She turned her tablet around, giving them a view of the landscape.

"It looks beautiful there. And warm."

"Oh it is. And I am here with a very good-looking and— Oh, it's your father." Aaron's dad's picture showed up on the screen. "Hello, Ken."

"Hello, Sheri." Aaron's dad's voice had been just as cold in his greeting to his mom as she had been in his. "Aaron! How you doing, son? Wait, are those...Are those *Christmas pajamas* you're wearing?"

"Hi, everyone! Sorry I'm late," Aaron's sister Aliza said as her face popped up on the screen, and Aaron's grip on Macie's hand loosened just a bit.

"It's okay, honey," his mom said. "We already talked to you recently."

"Did I miss anything?"

"Just your brother showing up in pajamas," his dad said, and Macie quietly chuckled, just out of view of his family. Her laughing nearly made Aaron laugh out loud, so she put her hand over her mouth.

"So, no *announcements* or anything have been made yet?" Aliza asked.

"You already told us your announcement, honey."

"But it sounds like Aaron hasn't told you his."

Both of his parents looked into their cameras, their faces full of questions and impatience, while Aliza leaned back in her chair, arms folded, a smile spread across her face. Aaron looked at Macie and said, "Are you ready?" She nodded, and he turned the laptop so that the camera captured both of them in the frame. "Mom, Dad, Aliza, I'd like you to meet Macie Zimmerman. She's an amazing woman who, as of about five hours ago, is now my fiancée.”

“Congratulations, son,” his dad said. “Congratulations to both of you.”

Aaron's mom's hand flew over her mouth. “You're getting married? Ken, our son is getting married!” She shouted loudly enough that everyone on the beach probably heard, “My son is getting married! And so is my daughter!” She held the tablet out toward all her fellow beach goers so they could see the evidence, but none of them seemed the least bit interested. She turned the tablet back to herself. “Oh my goodness, neither of my kids are going to die old and alone. Oh, I'm so happy!”

“Thanks, Mom,” both Aaron and Aliza said at the same time.

“Oh, come on you two. You know you were both giving me plenty to worry about.”

“Truthfully,” his dad said, “I'm thrilled for both of you. I hope you're as happy as me and Felina are.”

“And as happy as me and Carlos are,” his mom quickly cut in, aiming the tablet toward a muscular, shirtless man in the lounge chair beside her.

Aaron looked at Macie, his face all love and smiles, and said, “I think we've got the happiness thing down.”

## Epilogue

*W*ith a blanket in his arms and Macie by his side holding two bowls of ice cream, Aaron made his way from the back door of Joselyn's house out across the grass, Reese, Lola, and Dasher joining them.

"It's still so muddy—I'm sinking!"

"Here, take this," Aaron said, holding out the blanket.

With both bowls of ice cream in her hands, Macie grabbed the blanket between her elbows, and then Aaron scooped her up into his arms, the blanket and bowls of ice cream now resting on top of her.

"Mmm," Macie said. "The last time you did this, it felt like an angel lifted me out of the land of the nearly dead and carried me to the land of salvation. It feels every bit as amazing even when I'm on top of the world."

He made a mental note to hold her in his arms like this every chance he got. As he picked his way across the back-yards that all came together in one, Macie snuggled in close enough that he could smell the scent of her shampoo—milk and honey from heaven—and he kissed her on top of her head.

Reese stayed right by their side, while Lola ran ahead to the picnic table she must've sensed they were headed to, and Dasher ran circles around them, yipping his excitement about being able to run around in grass that was turning green again.

When they reached the picnic table, he joined her and wrapped the blanket around both of their backs as they sat on the table, their feet on the bench. She passed him his *Maple, Please Bring Home the Bacon*, and picked up her *Is the Doctor Pepper In?*, and they each took a bite as the tractor rolled into place on the very last empty Zimmerman family lot, and started digging the hole for their future house.

"And the first scoop of dirt is out!" Macie said, and held up her cup of ice cream.

Aaron bumped his bowl into hers, and thought about their very first meeting over these same flavors. He had been so clueless back then about how much the trajectory of his life was about to change. What if he hadn't decided that the events of that day had called for ice cream, and he missed out on knowing how rich life could become?

"It's freezing out here!" Macie said as she scooted even closer. "Whose crazy idea was it to celebrate this moment with ice cream anyway?"

Aaron laughed. "I believe that one was your crazy idea. It's one of the reasons why I love you."

"Right back atcha. I hear that marriages full of mutually crazy ideas make for the best ones." Macie grinned and then leaned in for a kiss.

Aaron pressed his lips against hers, their cold noses

touching, the simple kiss sending a wave of warmth to his chest. Then, still less than an inch apart, he said, "We're going to have a house soon."

She smiled into his lips and said, "And we're going to be married soon," before kissing him again.

They both turned to watch as the tractor dug another scoop of dirt out of what would eventually be their basement. After going over so many plans, the weather had finally cooperated enough to start. Aaron took a bite of his ice cream. The past three months had been more blissful than he thought life could possibly be. With as against marriage as he had been for so many years, he surprised himself by not having a single moment where he wondered if he had made the right choice or not. He just knew, without a doubt, that marrying Macie and starting a family with her was what was going to make him the happiest he could possibly be.

Feeling Macie's intense scrutiny on him, he turned to face her again. "Uh oh. You've got your amateur Ice Cream Motivation Analyst face on."

Macie tapped her spoon against her lips. "I better analyze you then. Let's see. With that look, you must be...trying to decide what the chances are of you being able to finish your *Maple, Please Bring Home the Bacon* before Dasher jumps up here and eats it for you."

Aaron laughed as the puppy finally managed to jump onto the bench, bouncing and yipping. He pulled his bowl in closer to him. "That wasn't what I was thinking. Strike one for the amateur analyst."

She nodded. "Okay, you were thinking that I look really great in this sweater you gave me for my birthday."

"While I have thought that *many* times today, it is not what I was thinking just now. Strike two. It's a good thing you didn't join the Ice Cream Motivation Analyst Guild. I don't think they'd be thrilled with your record right now." He took another bite of his ice cream.

"No, I'm going to get this. Just give me a minute." She studied his face, her own face so intensely serious that he had a hard time not either flinching or chuckling under the weight of it. "I've got it! You're thinking about how many children we should have."

His eyebrows shot up in surprise. "Impressive. The Guild is reviewing your application as we speak. They'll waive the application fee if you can also figure out how many I was thinking."

"Four."

She hadn't even paused to think about it first—her response was immediate. He actually hadn't come up with a number himself yet. "Why four?"

"Because that's how many it takes for a swim medley relay."

Aaron laughed so loud, he was positive that all her siblings heard it inside each of their houses. "Kids, you don't have a choice. You—you're the firstborn, so you must perfect backstroke, you've got breast stroke, butterfly for you, and I know you're the baby, but you need to bring some serious speed with your freestyle."

Macie grinned and took a bite of her ice cream.

"Unless, of course, you want a setup like this eventually." He motioned around to all of her siblings' houses. "Then we'll need seven kids."

"I don't know. I already promised Reese that he could have a houseful of puppies. And I sideways promised that

Lola could too. I'm not sure how many we can fit in this house."

"Hmm. We're going to need more room." Aaron set his ice cream aside and stood up, letting his side of the blanket fall to the top of the picnic table. "I'll go tell him to dig a bigger hole."

Macie laughed and pulled him back down. "However many kids we end up having, I'm sure we'll find a way to fit."

He wrapped the blanket around them more tightly and pulled Macie in close. "As enjoyable as it is to be your fiancé, Macie Zimmerman, I am very ready to be your husband."

"Waiting stinks," Macie said. "It's like we're at the starting line to a wonderful life together, and we're just standing there. Waiting. It's right there, so close we can see it, and no one is *ever* going to sound the 'Go' horn."

"I would suggest that we elope, but I don't want to miss out on seeing what the Zimmerman family is like when you add aunts, uncles, cousins, and grandparents, from both sides, to the mix." Truthfully, he couldn't even imagine how big that group would be.

"And if all those students of yours who were so determined to find you a wife by the end of the school year didn't get to come to the celebration, I think they might just plan a secret one for us, and then find some sneaky way to get us there."

Just picturing what they'd do made him chuckle. They were good kids. A little presumptive, but good. "So I guess we wait."

"Which comes with the added bonus of giving the contractor enough time to finish our house. Because otherwise, we'd be sleeping out here under the stars and cooking all our meals over that fire pit."

"As long as I get to be there with you, I wouldn't complain a bit."

"Who cares what temperature it is?" Macie said. "Baby, I'm never cold—"

Aaron laughed and finished the sentence, "— because you warm my heart."

Macie sighed and leaned her head on his shoulder, looking out at the tractor as it continued to dig the hole that, as they watched over the next few months, would slowly become their together home. "You know, I've imagined this moment so many times over the past...fifteen years, I guess—since I was thirteen and watched this same moment happen for my oldest brother and his fiancée. And in all my imagining, never did my brain come up with something this wonderful." She turned her face toward his. "You, Aaron Hall, are even more incredible than my very impressive imagination."

Then she turned toward him, put her hands on his cheeks, and pressed her lips against his. Lips that were soft, confident, and sure. He moved his hand up her back to rest at the nape of her neck, his fingers in her hair, and returned her kiss, his own lips filled with hope, possibilities, and excitement for their future together.

### Author's Note:

I hope you enjoyed *Christmas at the End of Main Street*!

Are you in the mood for more Nestled Hollow? There are five more books!

But keep reading, because coming up next is A *Kiss at Christmas*, from my Royal Palms Resort series. I hope you love it!

Happy reading!

—Meg

# A Kiss at Christmas

## the Royal Palm Resort

# MEG EASTON

# Chapter One

## KELLI

*K*elli Ellis drove her car into Building C's parking lot and saw over the piles of freshly plowed snow that her favorite spot was available.

"Yes!" she shouted to her empty car, "I got here first!" She immediately looked around, sure that Parker Brockbank from Trade Shows was already in the lot, ready to steal it from her. But there wasn't anyone else.

Then, just as she was almost to it, Parker drove in from the opening at the other end of the lot and pulled into her parking spot. The spot that so perfectly had the boughs of a big Ponderosa Pine sticking straight out above it, completely shading the entire parking space in the summer and keeping the snow off her car in the winter.

She shook a fist at Parker's car, pretty sure he was chuckling at having snuck in and grabbed the space when she was so close. Then she went to her second choice spot—C15, which wasn't anything special at all. She looked up just in time to see Parker as he strode down the sidewalk toward the building, looking infuriatingly perfect in his slacks, overcoat, and perfectly imperfect hair.

After grabbing her bag and exiting the car, she checked, and yep—she was evenly spaced between the lines and exactly straight. Unlike Parker's car, which was a good six inches closer to the line at the front than it was at the back.

She had woken up still in a sour mood from the bomb her dad had dropped on her when he and his new wife had stopped by her house last night. But she was determined not to let that, or Parker stealing her spot, ruin her day. She had put on her favorite pair of heels, a pink blousy top, a navy skirt, and the necklace that never failed to get her compliments.

She pushed away the negative thoughts, purposely put a spring in her step, and reminded herself how much she loved her job as she used her keycard to open the front door of the ZentCube offices. After taking the stairs to the second floor, which housed the entire marketing department, she sat at her desk and pretended she had been the first in the office.

It wasn't easy to arrive first—or the second—at the office, but it was worth it. Her constant goal was to be the perfect employee, so getting in early was important. It was when she came up with her best ideas. And when she made the effort to get them, she didn't have to rely on something coming to mind on the fly during marketing meetings—she had ideas, plans, and proposals waiting in the wings.

She smiled at the adorable little Christmas tree on her desk, straightened her papers and pens, made sure her keyboard was perfectly straight, and then got to work.

At eight-forty, when the first of her coworkers stepped

foot on the second floor, she was putting the finishing touches on her ideas for their new advertising campaign. Five minutes later, she went into the break room and grabbed a cup of coffee. She had just taken the first step out of the break room when she heard Parker's boss say to him, "Two o'clock on Wednesday works for Adrian, and I'm guessing it will for the others. Will you get the conference room scheduled?"

Kelli ducked behind a cubicle and pulled out her phone. After opening her email app, she quickly typed an email to Greg, asking if she could schedule the conference room for two on Wednesday, then sent the email before Parker and his boss even finished talking. She chuckled all the way back to her desk, already imagining the look on Parker's face when he realized it was payback for stealing her parking space.

Valeria, her best friend and normally on-time coworker, didn't arrive until ten after nine. She blew into their team's quadrant like a snowstorm, ushering in a rush of air and a flurry of excitement with her.

"Good morning, Sunshine," Kelli said. "You're rather happy today."

Valeria collapsed into her chair at the desk kitty-corner from Kelli's with a sigh. "It was a really good morning. I thought I was going to be here early, but then Rhett—"

Kelli slapped her hands over her ears. "La la la! What's the rule about being late?" She took her hands off her ears when it was clear Valeria wasn't going to finish her sentence.

Her friend let out a huff of air. "That I can't tell you why if it involves something Rhett and I did until we've been married for at least six months. Preferably twelve." She grabbed the poofy fluff ball that they usually tossed back and forth when they were brainstorming and threw it at Kelli. "I'll tell you what the real solution is, though—Oh. You didn't have so great of a morning, did you?"

"Parker Brockbank in Trade Shows stole my spot, so that wasn't great." Kelli threw the poof ball back and turned to her computer. "But I came up with some great ad copy for the Business Success magazine campaign." Her boss, Liz, was sure to be impressed. Kelli didn't need promotions, the corner office, or a fancy title. What she did need was for her boss, Liz, to be impressed. To see her as a valuable member of the team.

An email notification popped up on her screen and she quickly clicked on it when she saw it was a response from Greg, and she grinned. "I heard that Parker wanted the conference room tomorrow at two, so I emailed Greg right then and it looks like I got it. He even said, 'You emailed just in time, too. Someone requested it less than a minute after you did.'"

Valeria laughed and gave her a high five. "That's my girl." But she'd been studying Kelli the whole time she'd been talking. "Okay, today's good. It was last night, then, that was bad."

"How do you always know?"

Valeria smiled and threw the poof back to her. "If I say what your tell is, then you'll stop doing it. Now, about last night. Spill."

"My dad came over."

"Oh, good. I know you've been feeling like you haven't seen him enough lately." Then Valeria's face dropped. "Oh. He brought the evil stepmother with him."

"JoAnn isn't evil. She's just..." Kelli wanted to end the

sentence with, "a thief who stole my dad," but she was trying to be an adult about this. "She just wants to work on blending the newly combined family."

"A family that she doesn't want you to be a part of."

Kelli nodded but didn't let herself think of it fully. She wasn't about to let the door open on that much pain—no one needed to know how much it hurt her. Not even Valeria.

"What happened?"

"Well, my dad texted to ask if he could bring me over a couple of éclairs from Petrocelli's. I should've known right then and there that he was buttering me up. He didn't tell me that he was bringing JoAnn with him—that was a surprise I got to enjoy when I opened the door, threw my arms around my dad's neck, and saw her standing there.

"So they come in, sit down in my living room, and my dad awkwardly hands me the pastry box. Then he and JoAnn look at each other, and I can see that my dad is nervous, but JoAnn gives him an encouraging smile. So he starts talking about how this is the first Christmas they are celebrating since getting married and about how difficult it is to bring two separate families into one and all that. So they decided that for Christmas, it might be best to do that in isolation and get away to have some bonding time."

"So..." Valeria said, "he wants you to go hang out with him and JoAnn and your three new stepsisters over Christmas at some secluded cabin in the mountains? Like with no escape?"

"Honest to goodness, that's right where my mind went, too. And I was wondering if I could get along with three teenagers who want nothing to do with me and want every second of my dad's attention. But no. Instead of a cabin in the mountains, it's a beach resort in Cabo San Lucas. And when he said they needed to bring two separate families together for bonding, they meant my dad and JoAnn's daughters."

"They didn't invite you?" Valeria's voice was every bit as incredulous as she needed it to be. It was one of the reasons why she made the best friend ever.

"Nope. My dad tried to sell it by saying how awesome it would be for me to celebrate Christmas with him early and to have some one-on-one time. And how much more special it would be to spend all day with him on the twenty-first instead of the entire week of Christmas because the twenty-first happens first. And how great it will be for me to be free to do whatever I want over Christmas break instead of being tied down by family things."

"Please tell me you told him what you really think of that."

"What was I supposed to do, Val? Tell him to cancel the trip?"

"Or tell him to invite you. And to remember that you are every bit as much a part of the family as JoAnn's daughters are."

Kelli shook her head. "It was just me and my dad against the world since I was in eighth grade. I got to hang out with my dad more than most people do. JoAnn's girls are in junior high and high school. They've been without a dad for a few years, and they're desperate for time with mine. Maybe I should just give him up. I mean, I'm twenty-six years old. I shouldn't need to see my daddy all the time anymore."

She didn't even consider mentioning to Val how it had felt like she'd lost the only family she had when her dad got remarried, but she could tell by the look on Valeria's face that she knew it without Kelli saying.

"I know!" Valeria said. "Come spend Christmas with me and Rhett. Spend the week, even. We can pretend we're twelve and having a sleepover."

"In your teeny apartment."

"You can sleep on the couch. Or we'll put an air mattress in that space between the tree and the kitchen."

"Most people call that space a 'hallway.'"

"It'll be cozy."

"Valeria. I appreciate the offer. You know I do. But this is your first Christmas as a newly married couple. I don't want to ruin that for you."

"It'll be fun!"

"Remember how I said I didn't want to hear about your morning with Rhett?"

"Yeah...On second thought, you really don't want to be around us at Christmas."

At the sound of someone loudly clearing their throat, Kelli and Valeria spun in their chairs to see Liz.

"Sorry to interrupt your sleepover plans, but Kelli, do you have the mock-ups for the print ads?"

Of course, Liz had to stop by when she was socializing instead of during any of the time she had been working diligently already today. She turned back to her desk and grabbed the folder that had been leaning against her binders, revealing an upside-down white paper cup that had a picture of a spider drawn on it with the words *Don't lift until you're ready to squash it!*

Kelli screamed and shoved herself away from her desk, her chair rolling backward until it hit something, and then she jumped out of her chair to get more space between the cup and her. "I've been sitting next to that thing for more than two hours?!"

Her heart raced, her breaths were ragged, and it was likely that everyone on the second floor had heard her scream, but right now, she didn't care. All she cared about was that a spider had been crawling around who knew how much of her desk before someone trapped it with that cup, and it had been probably pacing with those spindly legs around that little circle of space on her desk the whole time she'd been working.

And now, all she could think about was how that little stealthy, moving, vial of poison with its shiny or hairy—either was gross—abdomen and its eight beady eyes were right there in that cup, just waiting for its chance to escape and come after her. "Someone kill it!" Her hand was on her chest like she could manually stop her heart from beating so fast and hard.

"Don't worry," Valeria said, "I've got you." She grabbed a notepad and held it level with Kelli's desk right at the edge, then slid the cup onto the notepad. Then she flipped it over and, in a move that made Kelli's heart shudder, Valeria lifted the notepad off and looked inside the cup. She put the hand holding the notepad on her hip and tipped the cup toward Kelli. "There's nothing in it."

Kelli's first thought was that it had escaped and could possibly be on her, but in a flash, she knew there had never been a spider. This was a prank. She looked over the top of her cubicle to the crowd of people that had gathered to see what her scream was about, and she saw Parker Brockbank giving a sly smile big enough to bring out that adorable dimple in his right cheek, a mischievous gleam in his eye. But, at least he had the decency to look contrite before ducking away.

"If you're ever having a sluggish morning where coffee

isn't doing the trick," Kelli said to all the coworkers gathered around her cubicle, "and you need a good old-fashioned scream to get the heart pumping, you know where to find me."

They all chuckled as they headed back to their desks, and then Kelli turned to Liz. "I am so sorry. I might have a slight fear of spiders. Um, here are the mock-ups. Let me know what changes you'd like or if you want to meet to discuss." She tried to make her voice sound extra professional to combat the dose of unprofessionalism she had just shown.

"Thank you. I will."

She thought she caught a slight smile on Liz's face as she was walking away. Great. That's all she wanted—to be the office entertainment.

After pushing her chair back to the vicinity of her desk, she took a moment to shoot a glare in the direction of Parker Brockbank's desk, even though she couldn't see it from hers. Then she sat down and faced her computer, re-straightening everything. "Can you take your lunch hour at one tomorrow and join me for a project?"

"Of course!" Valeria said. "What do you have in mind?"

Kelli started typing an email message. "I'm letting Greg know that I need the conference room at one instead of two, so whoever wanted it at two can have it."

"And what are we doing in there at one?"

"We are spending the hour blowing up balloons and filling the conference room as full of them as we can. Unless..." She turned in her chair to face Valeria. "Do you think Parker has a phobia? Like, of snakes? Maybe we can fill it with plastic snakes instead."

"Whatever it is, I'm in."

That's what she loved about Valeria. She gave her support, even when it meant helping with a prank, and she had fun with every bit of it.

But Kelli wasn't doing this for fun—she was doing it to get even.

# Chapter Two

PARKER

*P*arker had been running behind all day. His days usually consisted of talking to person after person—on his team, in his department, in other parts of the company, and on phone calls outside of the company. So the only time he could get any good planning and research in was if he came in at seven, before everyone else got in.

But this morning before he left for work, his buddy Josh, who was the marketing director at a business training company, had called. He said that they were looking for a brand marketing manager, and they wanted him. Parker hadn't even been looking for another job—especially after Stephanie had pulled the rug out from under him and made him second guess how capable he was at making valuable contributions.

Brand marketing manager had been a job he'd had his eyes on since he'd graduated college, though. The offer had hit him like a snowstorm blowing in. ZentCube was a great company to work for, and he'd be crazy to leave. But the current brand marketing manager at ZentCube would be crazy to leave, too, so the same job here wasn't likely to open anytime soon.

Maybe now was a good time for multiple fresh starts.

As soon as he'd hung up the phone, all Parker had been able to do was think about the job while wandering around his apartment in a possibilities-fueled daze that had been both exciting and exhausting. He had pulled into work more than an hour later than he liked and of course, Kelli Ellis from Digital and Print Marketing had already taken his parking spot.

He smiled thinking about yesterday, though. Who would've thought that a simple paper cup and a Sharpie could've caused such a reaction? Enough of a reaction that he'd felt a little bad about it for a moment.

He knew their pranks were a bit childish, but they'd become almost a tradition at work. They added so much life to the day—like a shot of espresso. They were a bright spot, especially when he'd been going through hard things.

As he was preparing the final mockups for their trade show displays for his two o'clock meeting in the conference room, he thought of Kelli again. When Greg had responded saying that he'd just missed being able to reserve the confer- ence room because someone had requested it a minute earlier, he knew that someone was Kelli. She had been the only other person in the office that early.

And then it suddenly became available moments after she had discovered the spider cup. She was up to something, and he got more and more wary as two o'clock neared. He finished packing up his stuff and headed into the conference room five minutes before he was supposed to meet his boss, the product manager, and a couple of people on his team.

Everything was fine, though. His meeting went great, and

they finalized decisions on which mockup to use and what last-minute changes needed to be made. He left the room feeling energized and ready to get started on the changes. He had been second-guessing the direction he'd gone with this coming year's event display and worried that it was the wrong choice entirely, but after that brainstorming session, he knew it was going to be the best they'd ever had.

He was practically whistling his way back to his desk alongside his coworkers, and then he stopped dead in his tracks when his desk came into view. Darren and Hannah stopped too, and then they burst into laughter. They were the first to race forward and check it out. Parker stayed back a bit, unsure if he wanted to see it closer. Then, curiosity got the better of him, and he walked up to it.

His entire cubicle was covered in cat pictures. No—on closer inspection, he saw it was just one cat; the pictures were just taken at all different angles. There were poster-sized cat pictures on the walls of his cubicle, one-inch high pictures completely covering all four sides of the outside frame of his monitor, a framed picture of the cat on his desk, and an *Ode to My Cat* poem on the wall.

On one wall, the one most open to everyone's view, of course, there was a full-length picture of Parker that was a good two feet tall, cut out, with a speech bubble that said, "I love you, Princess Olive." And of course, there was a speech bubble on a picture of the cat that said, "And I am willing to share my space with you, Parker. Most of the time." The cat was wearing a Santa hat.

There were even pictures of the cat—Olive, apparently— covering every inch of his desk, underneath all his papers and office supplies. And little tiny pictures of Olive on the C, the A, and the T letters on his keyboard. In one corner sat a stuffed cat whose back legs were seated but whose front legs were standing tall, looking regal and judgmental, with a Christmas wreath around its neck like a necklace.

He couldn't help it—he burst out laughing. This was good. And so not what he had expected. He turned to Darren. "Did you tell Kelli that I have a cat allergy?"

"It may have come up in conversation."

He shook his head and then pulled his phone out of his pocket when it started buzzing. Seeing it was his mom, he said, "You'll have to excuse me," to Darren and Hannah and then answered it as they both walked back to their cubicles.

"Hi, Mom."

"Hi, Sweetie. Is this a bad time? I hate bothering you at work—"

"It's totally fine, Mom. If it was a problem, I wouldn't have answered. You know you can call anytime."

"You're a good son, you know? Okay, so today is the last day that your dad and I can cancel our cruise reservations without penalty and—"

"Don't cancel, Mom. This is your thirtieth anniversary. You guys deserve to go live it up to celebrate."

"I know. It's just that it's over Christmas."

"You love having your anniversary on Christmas Eve, and you should get to go on your anniversary trip during your anniversary."

Truthfully, Parker was going to miss them. Christmas Eve at home always consisted of celebrating his parents' anniversary with a feast, followed by making gingerbread dream homes, then bundling up and going caroling as a family. It was going to feel wrong to not do that.

Until this year, Christmas was one holiday that he looked forward to as an adult every bit as much as he had when he was a kid. But ever since Stephanie broke off their engagement, he'd lost all desire to celebrate Christmas at all. The magic it held was just gone. Still, though, he was going to miss it this year. But it wasn't like he was going to have his parents skip the trip they had been planning practically his whole life.

"I don't know if it's right to leave."

Parker twirled his pen, which now had a little eraser pushed on the top—like they used in elementary school—in the shape of a cat. Of course, it did. "Ethan is fine to spend Christmas with the Garlands at their cabin?"

Parker's boss Adam walked over to his desk, some of the sketches from their meeting in his hand. Parker held up a finger, motioning for him to wait a moment.

"He's thrilled about it. It's on a lake, so he'll be in heaven the whole time and we'll be lucky if he even stops to think about us once."

"Then it's right for you two to go."

"It's *you* I'm worried about, honey."

"If your fourteen-year-old son is fine with it, I think it's safe to assume that your twenty-seven-year-old son is okay with it, too."

"I never would've planned it if I hadn't truly believed you'd be spending Christmas honeymooning it up on your own cruise."

He tried not to feel the stab of pain at her mention of how different his life should be right now. "I really will be fine if you go. I will find a way to celebrate Christmas on my own."

It was a lie—he hadn't planned on celebrating at all. But he didn't lie to his mom, and the guilt hit him instantly. He vowed to listen to a Christmas song, or get a foot-and-a-half tall Christmas tree like Kelli had on her desk and put it up in his apartment. Some little thing that could be considered "celebrating Christmas" so it wasn't a lie.

"You will?"

"I will."

"Okay, then, we'll keep our trip. But if you change your mind, even last minute, you let me know and we'll cancel and take the penalty."

"I will. But don't worry—I'm not going to change my mind."

"I love you, son."

"I love you, too, Mom."

Parker hung up the phone and turned to Adam, motioning at the papers in his hand. "More thoughts?"

"Oh, yeah." Adam looked down at the papers for a moment, like he'd forgotten he was holding them. "I was thinking about this section here, where it says, 'higher,' the display should physically go higher." Then he turned his attention from the papers back to Parker. "You don't have anywhere to go for Christmas?"

Parker shook his head. "Not really, but who knows? I might spend the holiday with friends." Not a lie, because he didn't say he was—just that he *might*. If all his friends weren't either married or going home to their parents for Christmas, or both, which he was pretty sure they all were. "How much higher are you thinking? Subtle, or aim-for-the-ceiling?"

Adam dropped the hand holding the plans to his side. "Come to my house for Christmas. Erin and the kids would love it. You can have a Christmas Eve feast with us, and watch Luke and Holly be Mary and Joseph, with Holly holding her baby doll, and a bunch of their stuffed animals playing the part of the stable animals. It'll be unpredictable in the way only a two-year-old and a four-year-old can make it.

"We've got a guest room. We'll open presents on Christmas morning, you can see how great it is to experience the magic of Christmas through the eyes of little kids, and we'll eat warm cinnamon rolls for breakfast. It'll be great. What do you say?"

It would be great. It was exactly what Parker wanted. His breakup with Stephanie had been difficult all along but especially right now, since they were supposed to get married the week of Christmas. The last thing he needed was to hang out with a guy who had everything Parker wanted, at a time when he was acutely aware of how much he didn't have it. Especially when it was just a pity ask. His boss didn't really want him there.

"I'll think about it and let you know. Show me what you were thinking about that display."

Adam studied him for a moment, and by the look on the guy's face, he knew Parker's promise to think about it was just a way to stall him until he told him no. He lifted the papers he had been holding so they both could see and discuss them.

Parker just needed to accept that the magic of Christmas was just a childhood thing that he should've grown out of. The magic was gone, along with any need to celebrate this year. He was fine spending it alone.

# Chapter Three

KELLI

As soon as Kelli heard voices mid-conversation as the conference room door opened, she grabbed her tape dispenser and the few random cat pictures that they hadn't yet found a place for, and she and Valeria ducked into the break room before Parker and his team rounded the corner. They peeked through the one window that had a perfect view of Parker's desk and waited.

"I think you should start dating again," Valeria whispered.

"What?" The randomness of the comment caught her off guard.

"You know, get back on the horse again. They say the longer you wait, the more you'll fear getting bucked off again."

"It's not the right time."

"It's been a year since you and James broke up. It's time."

She was very sure it wasn't time. One of the hardest things about the break-up had been with James's family. She had fit in with them, and could even see where her place was in his family. Breaking up with James meant breaking up with his family. And now that her own little family of two—she and her dad—were doing their own kind of breaking apart, she couldn't expose herself to that possibility again with someone else.

It wasn't until months after she and James had stopped dating that she realized she'd fallen for him because she'd wanted a family so badly, and his was so great. She didn't trust herself to date anyone right now for fear that she'd make the same mistake again.

Especially because, right now, she desperately wanted a family. For the first time, she hated that ZentCube gave them nearly two weeks off for Christmas and New Year's. It was a long time to be alone and feel like she didn't belong anywhere. This year, she was dreading the break.

Yeah. It was definitely not the time to start dating. It would surely be a mistake.

"Shh! They're coming!"

She held her breath as Parker came into view and wished more than anything that from this angle they could see his face and not just his backside. Parker froze when he saw their handiwork, and Darren and Hannah raced forward to look at it closer.

Parker's dress shirt was fitted enough that she could see his back muscles perfectly, so Kelli watched them closely, along with his arms and hands. But not so that she could admire them—she'd stopped herself from doing that long ago. And then stopped herself again every day, just like she stopped herself now. No, this time she watched so she could interpret his reaction.

The muscles in his shoulders twitched and his arms were

rigid. She chuckled. He looked properly annoyed. Score one for team Kelli and Valeria.

Then Parker *laughed*. A big, hearty laugh. That was unexpected. And, surprisingly, it made her feel like she'd won this particular battle in their "Let's see who can annoy the other person more" war. Interesting.

He walked forward to check out their display of cat affection, which was pretty great if she did say so herself. She knew he was seconds from turning around to see if he could see the person who had done it—like he'd guess it would be anyone other than Kelli—so she said, "We better get out of here."

Instead of walking out the door on their usual side, they took the door on the opposite side of the break room and walked the long way around, so Parker wouldn't see them. She chuckled the whole way.

They had almost made it back to their desks when her phone buzzed with a notification. She looked at the screen, eyebrows scrunched together, while she tried to make sense of what she was seeing.

"What is it?"

Kelli held the phone so Valeria could read it.

"Carla Cook... Isn't she the assistant to one of the bigwigs?"

Kelli nodded and opened the text with a shaking finger and read the message out loud. "'Hello, Kelli. Merit Casselman and Graham McNeil would like to meet with you today at three-thirty in Building HQ, on the third floor. Please let me know if you'll be able to make this meeting time.' Why do the CEO and the CTO want to meet with me?" She glanced back in the direction of Parker's desk. "Do you think I'm in trouble for the cat prank?"

"How would they even know about that? Besides, it's not exactly something you'd get called on the carpet for."

But Kelli's stomach had already fallen, her ears were on fire, and she was feeling very lightheaded. "I don't know. It's got to be something." Her mind raced, trying to figure out what she could be in trouble for. Wouldn't they just have her boss talk to her if she wasn't doing something right? Or maybe even someone from Human Resources? Why in the world would the two co-founders of the company need to see her?

She looked at Valeria. "Did you get a message?"

Just as they reached their desks, Valeria picked up the phone that she'd left behind. "Nope. No emails or texts at all. Maybe it's for something good."

"You don't get called to the third floor of headquarters for something good."

Valeria glanced at her watch. "Well, you've got twenty-two minutes until you need to be there. What can we work on that will take your mind off of it for a few minutes?"

"Nothing." Kelli shook her head. "I think maybe I should just head over there now."

Getting there early had been a mistake. A winter snowstorm was just rolling in, and big, fat snowflakes were covering her coat and hood by the time she'd walked three buildings over to headquarters.

She stomped her feet in the lobby, shook the snow off her coat, and then took the elevator to the third floor. She had seen Merit Casselman quite a few times over the two-and-a-half years that she'd worked at ZentCube, and had met Graham several times, too, but she had never been to the third floor before.

The receptionist on the third floor led her to Carla, who directed her to a seat outside of Merit's office, facing a Christmas tree she couldn't even focus on, to wait for him to finish the meeting he was in. The walk hadn't helped to calm her racing heart. The cold air hadn't cleared the lightheadedness. Forcing herself to do calm breathing as she sat and waited didn't stop her leg from bouncing.

And nothing stopped her from feeling like she was sitting outside the principal's office, about to find out exactly how much trouble she was in.

Finally, at three-thirty-two, the door opened, and Kelli stood. The two head honchos were shaking someone's hand and talking in happy voices to him, but Kelli's brain was so full of worries that she hadn't thought to notice if the guy was wearing a ZentCube employee badge or not. As the man was walking away, Graham turned to Kelli. "Welcome, Miss Ellis. Please, come in."

She shook both of their hands and then swallowed as she walked into the office. Instead of sitting down across the very large desk from them, as she had imagined, Merit motioned to a seating area in the other half of the office, where two chairs and a couch were arranged around a coffee table.

Not knowing which seat to take, she sat in the closest one —a padded armchair—and wiped her hands on her slacks, straightening them while also making her hands less clammy.

Graham sat down in the other armchair and Merit sat in the middle of the couch, his arms spread wide on the back of the couch, looking about a million times more comfortable than she felt. Of course, he wasn't the one being called in to talk to the big boss.

"Every year," Graham said, "we take about a dozen employees on a Christmas retreat. Have you ever heard anyone talk about it?"

Kelli shook her head. Should she have? Or was it something she wasn't supposed to hear about?

"Every year it's a little different, but we always go to our managers and ask if they know of anyone on their teams who doesn't have a place to go for Christmas. Then we take a look, narrow down the list as needed, and form a group."

They wouldn't be smiling so much and chatting about fancy retreats if she was in a lot of trouble, right? So maybe they wanted her to do something? Like, make some kind of marketing materials for the retreat? It was weird they were coming to her directly instead of going to her boss or the marketing director, but she could do that. Or should she already have been doing that and she somehow missed the message that she was supposed to?

"We've gone several different places in the past," Merit added. "But during the summer, Graham sent me to The Royal Palms resort in Myrtle Beach, South Carolina, and it was amazing."

Graham chuckled. "And he's not just saying that because he met the love of his life, Elise, while he was there."

Merit grinned, and Kelli saw a hint of a blush. This was all great, but she still didn't understand why she was here, in Merit's office. She wanted to run her sweaty palms across her slacks again, but she was trying to be professional, but it left her not having a clue what to do with her hands. So she just set them beside her legs on the seat.

"I've been there, too," Graham said, "and I think it's a

perfect place for our retreat. We want to take a group there this Christmas, especially, because Elise is over all the Christmas events. And since Merit and I do this thing together, I think I might be on my own if I took us somewhere other than where Elise is."

The two of them were smiling like kids at Christmas, but Kelli still didn't get why she was even in on this conversation.

"So," she asked, "are you wanting me to do some kind of pamphlets for it, or come up with some images to—"

Merit laughed and interrupted. "No, we want you to come!"

"You... What?" She looked at both of them, trying to make sense of the words. "I don't understand. You want me to work at the retreat?"

Graham chuckled, shaking his head. "The first year we did this, ZentCube was probably one-tenth the size it is now and we were all in the same building. We found out that a few people had nowhere to go for Christmas, so we decided to do something about it. We know it can be hard around the holidays to not be with family, and we know how much fun it can be to spend it with a group of people that you may or may not know.

"And this year, we'd like you to join us. *As a guest*. And don't worry—we pay for everything. Will you come?"

She gasped as their words finally sank in, a lightness filling her chest and making it seem like she was floating right out of her chair. Were they really inviting her to go on vacation? And giving her a place to go for Christmas so she wouldn't be alone? "For real?"

"For real," Merit said.

Kelli's heart practically burst out of her chest with so much happiness and gratitude that it made her jump out of her chair and hug Graham, and then go around the little table and hug Merit. "Yes! Yes, I want to go!"

She was going to have a place to go for Christmas. It was all she could do to not let happy tears spill down her cheeks right in front of the company's founders. When they led her out of the room to pick up a packet of information from Carla, she hugged it tight to her chest. She kept hugging it tight as she put on her coat and speed-walked back to her building, not even caring that she was getting covered in snow.

She wasn't going to be alone. She was going to belong somewhere.

# Chapter Four

PARKER

*P*arker worked on putting in the last of the design element's changes so he could get them finalized and sent to the trade show exhibit company they used before the end of the day, running his mouse over the cat-themed mouse pad his desk now had.

Darren's chair creaked as it turned around behind Parker, just before he heard his teammate and friend say, "So, I see you haven't taken the cats down yet."

"Well, you know me. I *love* cats." Kelli—and probably Valeria, he was guessing—had put a lot of effort into this. It would be a shame to waste such hard work. A prank as good as this one deserved to stick around for a few days. He tweaked the dimensions on the plans a bit until they looked perfect.

"I don't think it's the cat that you're so fond of."

"Ha ha," Parker said without even turning around.

"I think you're fond of the girl who put it up."

"Kelli?"

"Obviously."

Parker shook his head. "We just like to annoy each other. Like you're doing with me right now."

He clicked save on the plans and then sent a message to his boss. *All done. Take a look?*

Darren didn't respond, but he also didn't hear his coworker's chair turn back to his desk, so Parker turned around in his chair to face him.

"I'm just saying that deep down, I think you want to ask her on a date."

"Darren, I *just* got out of a serious relationship."

The guy shook his head. "Nope. That was over two months ago. It's time."

"Who says that two months is the standard amount of time to get over an engagement and move on?"

"Dude. There's no standard. It's different for every person and for every relationship. I'm telling you that for you, with that breakup, it's time." Darren stood up and walked over to Parker's desk, leaning against the framework of his cubicle.

Parker turned back around in his chair to face his computer screen. "And I think you don't have any idea what you're talking about."

"We all know why you do the initial spiel at trade shows. I mean, you've got that face that's all symmetrical and that deep voice. People like listening to people with pretty faces. Now tell me why they have me talk to the ones who are interested in learning more."

"Because even when people tell you they're not interested, you won't stop bugging them about it?"

Parker barely caught sight of the stuffed cat as it flew toward him, and barely turned in time to catch it.

"No, pretty boy. It's because I'm good at reading people." He caught the cat that Parker threw at him and then pointed at him with it. "And I'm telling you that you're ready to date again, whether you think you are or not. Ask her out already."

"We already went out."

The look on Darren's face was comical. A mix of shock and surprise and disbelief. Apparently, he wasn't good at reading everything.

Darren grabbed his chair and pulled it across the aisle and sat down facing Parker. "When? Why did you not tell me about this?"

"Relax, Darren. It was like two-and-a-half years ago. Right after I first started working here."

"What happened? How did it go?"

Parker let out a breath of a laugh, shaking his head. So much of that date had been awkward. "Not well. My aunt Aftyn bumped into us at the restaurant and asked, 'Aww! Is this the girl you were telling me all about? I'm so happy to see you together. No, wait. The girl you told me about had brown hair... Why aren't you dating her anymore?'"

"You're making that up."

"I swear to you I'm not. And then as I'm paying for dinner, my card gets declined. If that wasn't embarrassing enough, the next one gets declined, too—apparently, there was some fraudulent activity on my account and they were 'protecting me'—and I didn't have enough cash to cover the meal.

"So she paid. Luckily I had bought the movie tickets online in advance. Although it probably would've been better if I hadn't, because she got sick from something at dinner, and I couldn't even take her home because my mind had still been back on why my cards had been declined, so I locked my keys in the car."

Darren shook his head.

"Let's just say it was a bad enough first date to convince us both it wasn't meant to be and guarantee we'd never have a second date. And then I started dating Stephanie and we got engaged and she went on to almost get engaged to James."

"Shut up. So, wait. Is that why you two started pranking each other? Because you had an awkwardly embarrassing first date, which made working on the same floor with each other awkward, so that was a way to turn the focus off the date and onto something else?"

Huh. He'd never really thought of it that way before. Maybe Darren could read people better than he'd given him credit for.

"You can't tell me that you'd let a little thing like an awkward first date *two-and-a-half years ago* stop you from asking someone out who you very clearly have chemistry with."

Parker shook his head. "It's not just because of a bad date. I'd never be good enough for someone like her."

Darren's head jerked back in surprise. "Are you being real right now?"

Parker didn't even bother answering. If Darren knew everything that was on the list Stephanie had given him when she broke off their engagement that detailed all the ways in which Parker was deficient, he wouldn't be questioning it at all.

"You used to own every room you walked into, Parker. You used to have the confidence to ask any woman out. What did Stephanie do to you?"

Parker was spared having to answer when his computer chimed its email alert. He turned to it and opened the email.

"I really think you should talk about this," Darren said.

Like that was going to happen. Parker stood up and grabbed his coat from the hook on his cubicle. "Maybe some other time, buddy. It looks like I have a meeting at HQ right now."

"At HQ? Why do you have a meeting at headquarters?"

"You got me," Parker called out as he headed toward the elevators. "Whatever it is, wish me luck!"

It was nearly five, and it was already getting dark outside. All of the streetlights were on in the parking lots of the buildings as he walked toward headquarters, the falling snow lit up in the rays of light below each one. He stepped into the building at the top of ZentCube's campus, stomped off his shoes, shook his coat, and brushed the snowflakes out of his hair before heading to the elevator.

When he reached the third floor, the receptionist took him to Merit Casselman's assistant, Carla. She thanked him for coming, then led him to Merit's office and poked her head in the door. "Parker Brockbank is here. He's your last appointment of the day." Then she opened the door the rest of the way, motioned for him to go inside, then left and shut the door behind her.

The office was nice. Good furniture, not overly decorated. He had met both Merit and Graham several times. He'd even chatted with Graham for quite a while at last year's Christmas party. They had both been sitting on the armrests of a chair and a couch, chatting, but stood when he walked in.

"Parker," Graham said as he shook his hand, "thanks for coming to meet with us. Have a seat."

Parker shook Merit's hand, too, and then sat down in the one seat that neither of them had been leaning against when he walked in. The two of them sat, too.

"It's been a long day," Merit said, "and we know you probably want to get home, so we won't beat around the bush. We've heard you don't have anywhere to go for Christmas."

*Ouch.* Not only was it a reminder of the broken engagement, but also that he wasn't going to have any family around.

"And we want to change that."

Parker raised an eyebrow.

Graham looked at Merit, laughing. "Well, that definitely couldn't be called 'beating around the bush,' that's for sure." Then he turned to Parker. "You'll have to forgive us. You're our twelfth and last meeting of the day, and I think we peaked in our delivery of this message somewhere around the third or fourth person."

"Maybe you should've made a slideshow," Merit said.

"A slideshow! I can't believe I didn't think of that! Ah, well. It's too late now, so we'll just spell it out. Every year, we have a Christmas celebration with a group of employees who don't have family around to celebrate with."

"And this year," Merit said, "we are doing it at a resort on the coast in South Carolina. A week-long, all expenses paid. Twelve employees—"

"Assuming you tell us yes," Graham cut in.

"—plus me and Graham for most of it. We'd love to have you join us."

The shock made Parker lean back in his chair. "Wow. That's incredible. Really."

"Is that a yes?" Graham asked.

A week-long vacation at a beach resort with a dozen coworkers, or home alone in his apartment with a foot or two of snow. The two didn't compare at all. If he stayed here, he'd be surrounded by people who wanted to celebrate Christmas, when he just wanted to skip it this year. If he was on a beach where there was no snow, it wouldn't even feel like Christmas.

And if all the people going didn't have anyone to spend Christmas with, either, they likely were just as opposed to celebrating as he was. It sounded like a perfect way to get away from it all and pretend like the holiday wasn't even happening.

But how could he say yes to ZentCube paying to fly him across the country to a resort on the beach when he had a job offer on the table that he hadn't decided about yet? It was a really good position with good pay. How could he accept this trip, and then quit the company right after? The guilt was already creeping in.

Sure, he could decide to stay at ZentCube, but there was no guarantee of that. Saying yes would be a jerk move. He wasn't a jerk, so obviously he couldn't accept.

"I'm sorry. I can't."

Both Merit's and Graham's faces fell.

"You really can't?" Graham asked. "Why?"

Maybe he was a jerk after all—the guy looked crushed. He tried to grasp a reason that wouldn't be lying but would explain why he couldn't go, but everything he came up with sounded flimsy. An excuse that would only add insult to their offer. Like he was going to turn his nose up at their big plans because he needed to water his houseplants or something.

He ran his hands over his face. There was nothing he could say that wasn't going to offend, so he might as well tell the entire truth. Then he could at least live with himself.

"I got a job offer at another company."

"Oh," Merit said.

"Not that I was looking! A buddy of mine just contacted me and said his company wants me as their Brand Manager."

Merit's eyes were still on him. "And you told them yes?"

Parker shook his head. "I haven't decided yet—they just asked yesterday. I have to let him know by the first of the year."

The room was silent for several long, excruciating moments while the two leaders of ZentCube pondered and looked at each other, giving nothing away in their expressions. Did he just commit career suicide with this company? Maybe he'd be walking out of this office with termination papers in hand.

Then Graham leaned forward, his forearms resting on his knees, hands clasped in front of him. "Come with us over Christmas."

Parker's eyebrows shot up. But still, he shook his head. "I can't. Because then if I decided to take the other job—well, I wouldn't be okay with the kind of person that would make me."

"Think of it this way," Merit said. "Did you play any sports in high school?"

Parker nodded. "Baseball."

"Any colleges try to recruit you?"

"Two."

"The recruiters—did they wine and dine you to convince you to go to their school?"

Parker smiled at the memory. It had felt pretty cool as a kid who had so little of life figured out. "They did."

Merit leaned forward, nearly matching Graham's pose. "Then pretend this is the same thing. We're trying to recruit you to stay on here. If, after the retreat's over, you decide to leave, then no hard feelings. We'll rest easy knowing we tried our best, and you'll know you made the decision that's best for your career path. Deal?"

Being able to spend the week of Christmas away from Christmas. Not only did that sound more heavenly than his younger self ever would've guessed, but it might also put him in a better mind frame to make the decision. And if Merit and Graham both knew where he stood going into the trip, he wouldn't have to feel guilty about it.

He looked at both men for a long moment. Then he said, "Okay, I'm in."

Merit and Graham both grinned big, shook his hand, and gave him slaps on the back before sending him out to Carla to pick up a packet with the trip details.

As he walked back out into the snow, he released the burden of Christmas that he hadn't realized had been so heavy until he experienced how light he felt without it. The thought of skipping Christmas brought a big smile to his face. This was going to be perfect.

# Chapter Five

## KELLI

Kelli pushed her rolling suitcase as the line for airport security inched forward, and then opened Valeria's text that had just popped up on her phone.

VALERIA: Do you promise to have so much fun without me?

Kelli smiled and typed back *Pinkie promise.*

VALERIA: And find someone to date?

She pushed her suitcase around the switchback in the fabric barrier and then typed her response.

KELLI: Val, I'm going to a company Christmas retreat, not a singles cruise.

VALERIA: Kels. These are all people who have no one to spend Christmas with, so they are likely all SINGLE. Cozy up to one of them. It'll be good for you.

She was scrolling through the facial expressions emojis to find one that perfectly encapsulated what she thought of Valeria's comment and glanced up to see how close to the front of the line she was getting. Only about eight more people in front of her. Then she noticed who had just gone through airport security. She abandoned her emoji search and instead typed a message.

> KELLI: You are never going to believe who just went through airport security!

> VALERIA: Who?

> KELLI: Parker Brockbank from Trade Shows! What do you think he's doing here?

She pulled her ID out of the pocket of her shoulder bag and opened her phone to the boarding pass. A notification at the top of the screen popped up with Valeria's response.

> VALERIA: Well, if I had to guess, I'd say he's looking to get on a plane.

> KELLI: Ha ha.

> VALERIA: He's probably going home for Christmas.

> Oh, hey, Christina Jensen in SEO is flying home today, too. If you see her, tell her I said hi.

Of course. Parker was probably flying home for Christmas. This was the first day they were off work for the holidays, so it made total sense.

Kelli handed her ID to the TSA agent and then put her

phone on the scanner to have it read her boarding pass. The agent let her through, and she entered the screening line across from the line Parker was in. He had just removed his laptop and placed everything on the conveyor belt. He was so wrapped up in what he was doing that he hadn't even noticed her. So she just watched him as she waited.

Because really, he was a very attractive guy. She rarely let herself admire him because then her stomach would get all fluttery and then she'd have to remind herself how awkward their first date was years ago and how obviously unsuited they were for each other, and that was usually all she needed to stop.

On the rare occasion that didn't work, she'd remind herself about the time a month or two later when she had first started dating James, and she had ducked out of work in the middle of the day to have a super sweet phone call with him in the print and copy room.

They had been talking for much longer than Kelli had guessed they would, and Parker had come into the room not long before they hung up. When she turned around, Parker chided her for taking personal calls on company time.

Only a few weeks after that, she went into the break room to grab a soda to hopefully help her wake up from a late-afternoon slump, and she caught him making out with his girlfriend before she was even his fiancée. Remembering what a hypocrite he was helped, too.

She was just putting her stuff onto the moving belt when Parker went through the scanner. When he stepped through, the security officer stopped him, but she wasn't close enough to hear what he said and had to turn her focus to getting her own things through security. She wasn't stopped at all, and couldn't help but give him a smirk as he was being patted down and having his fingers tested for bomb residue while she strolled to her bags and grabbed her things.

"Have a great Christmas!" she called out to him as she pulled her rolling bag behind her, grinning all the way to her gate.

She had barely found a seat, hooked her shoulder bag on her suitcase, and pulled out her phone when she saw Parker walking down the wide aisle. She quickly typed a text to Valeria.

KELLI: Sleigh bells! I think he's coming to my gate!

He can't be going on this retreat, too.

There's no way he doesn't have somewhere to go for Christmas.

No way.

Oh, no. He's sitting down. Please tell me he has family in South Carolina.

We just happen to be going to the same state. That's all.

VALERIA: No way there's that big of a coincidence. He's going to the retreat.

Kelli! DATE HIM!

Oh my goodness, that's perfect.

Kelli rolled her eyes.

> KELLI: We tried that once before, remember? It was a disaster. Most awkward date ever.

> VALERIA: Just because you accidentally wore two different boots on the date doesn't mean you can't try again.

Kelli cringed at the memory. When she had put on two different boots, she had planned to see which one looked better. But then Parker texted, saying that he was lost and thought he got the address wrong, and she'd forgotten that she hadn't swapped into the winning pair before he got there. As people kept staring at her the whole date, she assumed it was because her outfit was pretty incredible. Because minus the boot issue, it was.

> KELLI: You forgot about me knocking his soda into his lap at the movie theater during that jump scare.

> Or that I had to leave the movie early because I got food poisoning from dinner.

> Or that our waiter just happened to be someone I had dated and made comments about it the entire meal.

> Those kinds of things don't exactly lend themselves to second dates.

> VALERIA: Yep. Any relationship between the two of you is doomed before it even starts.

> No use even trying.

> KELLI: Stop it. They're boarding us now, so sorry—no more time for sarcasm. Talk to you tonight!

Kelli pushed the phone into its pocket on her bag and then wheeled her suitcase over to where everyone was lining up. Once she got on the plane, she put her suitcase in the overhead bin and her bag under the seat in front of her. The seat on her plane ticket was the middle one, which was fine by her. That meant double the people to talk to during take-off, the part that made her the most nervous.

Plus, the middle seat was close enough to the window that she could see out without having to ask two people to move if she needed to go to the restroom mid-flight.

She looked up just in time to see Parker sit down in the aisle seat of the row right in front of her. What she'd told Valeria was true—this was a bad time for her to get into a relationship. But still, a part of her heart had hoped for a little bit of Christmas romance in her life, even though she knew the pain it would bring.

Except not with Parker.

That obviously wouldn't work. That one date they'd gone on two-and-a-half years ago had been only a couple of months after she started working at ZentCube, and it had made work so awkward. She had constantly been reminded of the experience and embarrassed all over again. It was not something she was looking to repeat anytime soon.

Even if he did look mighty fine in his jeans and t-shirt—something she never saw him in at the office. Nope. She was completely ignoring him and not even noticing how good he looked at all.

Instead, she chatted with the nice young man to her left

who was flying home for Christmas and was very excited about it, and the mom on her right who was flying with her kids to visit their grandparents. The woman was nervous because she hadn't seen her ex-in-laws in over three years and they always made her so uncomfortable. But she'd gotten a call last minute saying that her ex-father-in-law was sick and probably didn't have long to live, so they booked flights just the night before and couldn't even sit together.

The woman's story was fascinating, so before Kelli knew it, the plane was at cruising altitude and she had barely even noticed anything else during takeoff. Both of her seatmates seemed to be done talking, so she pulled out her headphones, plugged them into her phone, and started listening to an audiobook.

Through the teeny space between the seats, she had the perfect view of Parker. So she just enjoyed the curve of the muscles on his arm and the perfect amount of scruff along that strong jawline.

He leaned forward to get his water bottle out of his bag, and she got to see his back muscles in action through his t-shirt. He flipped open the spout of the water bottle, and because of the change in pressure on the plane, a big burst of water shot through the straw and up in the air in a perfect arc, right in her direction.

She didn't have time to do anything—not that she could've done anything, since she was trapped in the middle seat and wearing a seatbelt—before the water landed right on her lap.

She let out a yelp of surprise, along with the handful of other people who witnessed it, as the cool liquid soaked through her pants.

Parker immediately turned around, an embarrassed,

apologetic look on his face, before he noticed that it was her that his water had landed on. Then she swore his expression turned to one that said this was payback for her spilling his drink in his lap on their date so long ago.

He did press the button to call a flight attendant, though, and the nice lady got her plenty of paper towels to soak it up. But her efforts didn't exactly leave her jeans dry. *Please let them dry before we land*, she silently prayed. She could only imagine how embarrassing it would be to walk through the airport once they landed looking like she'd had an accident on the plane. Especially with Parker there to see it.

She didn't know the eleven others who were going on this same retreat (and she refused to believe that Parker was one of them), but she suspected she would know them well by the end of the week. She didn't want wet pants to be their first impression of her.

Once the excitement of the surprise fountain and the soaked lap died down, the cabin lights dimmed, and everyone with window seats around her started closing the shades. Between the lowered lights and the hum of the airplane, drowsiness hit her pretty strongly.

Her dad had come over to "spend Christmas" with her last night before they both left on their separate trips, and she couldn't bear to cut the evening short to pack when she got to see him so infrequently lately. Plus, she kind of wanted to remind him that she was his daughter and they had a bond. She had to do all she could to make sure she wasn't forgotten.

So he left late, and she stayed up even later packing. Then she had to wake up super early to get ready for the day, finish packing, drive to airport parking—which had been a bear of a drive with all the holiday traffic—take the shuttle to the airport, go through security, and still make it to her flight without being rushed. And she was feeling the lack of sleep now.

The audiobook could wait. She wrapped her headphone cord nice and neat, slipped it into its pocket in her bag, slid her phone in alongside it, then pulled out her neck pillow and drifted off to sleep.

# Chapter Six

## PARKER

*P*arker pulled his ear buds from his ears. He'd been watching a movie on the screen attached to the seat in front of him when the five-year-old seated next to him whom he'd been chatting with at the beginning of the flight started crying.

"Hey, buddy. Do you need help with anything?"

The kid shook his head, but he still kept crying. Not a loud cry—just an upset one.

"Are you hungry? I still have my cookies from when they brought us snacks."

Still, the boy just shook his head. Parker glanced at the teenage girl sitting by the window, and she just shrugged, like *Don't look at me—I don't know what to do.* He heard the flight attendant right behind him talking to someone. Maybe he could get her help afterward.

"Do you need something to drink? Or do you need to go to the bathroom?"

The boy shook his head. "I just want my mom."

The flight attendant tapped Parker on the shoulder, so he

turned his attention to her. "Excuse me, sir. But do you mind switching seats with the boy's mother?"

"Oh, not at all. Of course." He hurried to pack his headphones, water bottle, and cookies into his shoulder bag, said goodbye to the kid, and then stood up to see where she wanted him to move to. The flight attendant was motioning to the aisle seat in the row directly behind him.

"Thank you so much," the boy's mom said before slipping into Parker's seat.

Parker nodded and then stared at the seat the woman had vacated. It was the one right next to Kelli. Maybe he should've asked where he'd be moving to before agreeing. At least Kelli was asleep—maybe they could avoid any awkward chatting. Especially if that chatting was going to end up being about his water landing in her lap. He sat down next to her and put his ear buds back in his ears.

He started the same movie again, hoping to pick up where he left off, but he was having trouble keeping his mind on it when he was so close to Kelli. Ever since he had caught the tail end of her phone conversation with James in the copy and print room years ago, he had forced himself to only think of her as a coworker. Even though James, from what he saw at a couple of company parties, wasn't nearly good enough for her.

And then he had started dating Stephanie. But now they were both single, and he was noticing her again in a way he hadn't allowed himself to for so long.

He didn't know why he was allowing himself to think about her now. As Stephanie had not-so-nicely pointed out, he had enough flaws of his own to prove that he wasn't good enough for Kelli, either. Besides—he had thought he and his ex were happy and hadn't seen their breakup coming. He didn't trust himself to know when things were going wrong anymore.

He turned the volume on the movie up even more and made himself concentrate on it.

Which worked pretty well for a good thirty minutes. Then Kelli turned slightly in her sleep, and she leaned to rest her head on his chest and shoulder. The scent of her freshly-washed hair was right there.

He should wake her up.

Except she looked so peaceful and so relaxed. Maybe she needed the sleep. Maybe he could just nudge her enough to stay in her seat without waking her up. He slowly moved his shoulder, nudging her toward the middle of her seat. It took a minute, but he got her there. He carefully started pulling himself back, testing to make sure that she wasn't going to fall over when he wasn't holding her up.

Eventually, he got to where his shoulder wasn't touching her anymore, and he started breathing again as he moved back to his normal position in his seat.

But within five minutes she shifted again, her head finding his shoulder. She had the neck pillow, so that wasn't what had pulled her toward him. Maybe she just needed to lean on something.

Once, back when he was in college, he was on a bus headed home for Christmas, and he fell asleep. He'd woken to find that he'd been leaning against the shoulder of a woman who was the age of his grandma. He'd been embarrassed, sure, but also really grateful. It had been the best sleep he had gotten in a while. Sometimes you're really tired and you need the kindness of the person sitting next to you to be a support. He could do that for Kelli. He just needed to turn the volume of the movie up louder to keep his thoughts off her.

When the captain's voice came over the intercom asking everyone to prepare the cabin for landing, Kelli jerked awake with a scream. Still looking like she was in the fog of sleep, she realized that she'd been leaning against someone's shoulder and seemed embarrassed and unwilling to make eye contact. She wiped the edge of her mouth with her knuckles, which must have told her that she had been drooling because her eyes flew to his shoulder. Then she did make eye contact with him and jerked to more alertness.

"Parker! What are you doing here? Was I sleeping on you?" She reached out and wiped at the small wet spot she had left on his shirt, and then whacked at it with the back of her hand. "Why did you let me sleep on you?"

He couldn't help the smile. "Hey, don't blame me. I was just sitting here, minding my own business. You're the one who invaded my space. I tried to push you back."

Her cheeks were flushed, and against her blonde hair, which was straight and down—something he rarely saw when she was at work—it was beautiful.

"Well, maybe you should've tried harder."

"I should've. Your snoring was making it difficult for me to hear my movie."

Her eyes narrowed at him. "I did not snore." Then she turned to the guy on the other side of her. "Did I snore?"

He looked every bit as amused as Parker was, but shook his head no.

She faced forward in her seat, hands folded in her lap, a vindicated smile on her face, but he could see beneath the smile a residual embarrassment at having slept against his shoulder. Maybe he should've woken her up. Except if he had, she still would've realized that she'd fallen asleep on his shoulder and still would've been embarrassed—she just would've gotten an hour less sleep out of the deal.

The plane landed and taxied to the gate. When it was their turn to deplane, he stood up in the aisle and took a step back, motioning for Kelli to go first. An olive branch. She must've been feeling some embarrassment still, because she stood up, slung her bag over her shoulder, and then jerked her suitcase out of the overhead bin and started power walking up the aisle.

"Hey," the guy who had been sitting at the window said. Then he turned to Parker. "What's her name?"

"Kelli."

"Hey, Kelli! That's my bag!"

Kelli froze, her back to them, then she turned around, cheeks flushed even more, and walked back to their row as Parker pulled out the bag he was fairly certain was hers and set it on the floor in front of her. She strode with purpose out of the plane, head held high, shoulders back. Parker smiled at her the whole way.

They were heading in the same direction, so even though Kelli had gotten the head start, she eventually must've brushed off the embarrassment, because she stopped moving like she was trying to win a speed-walking competition and started walking at a normal pace. He thought it was safer to be near her then, and before he knew it, they were walking side-by-side. He told himself he was drawn to her simply because she was the only person he knew in the state. It was just human nature.

"So," she eventually said, partially glancing in his direction but not enough for their eyes to meet, "is this a layover for you, or is this your final destination?"

"Final destination."

She gave a tight nod. "Do you have family in South Carolina?"

The tone of her voice was hopeful, but he had no problem dashing that hope. "Nope. I'm here for the Zent-Cube retreat." It wasn't hard to guess that she was, too.

She turned her head away from him, but he didn't miss the grimace on her face before she did.

As they were riding down the escalators leading to baggage claim, she grabbed his arm with her free hand and said, "Look! They sent drivers to get us!" As soon as she realized she was holding onto his arm, though, she let go.

All Parker could think about was the way it felt to have Kelli's hand on his arm, and how empty it felt to have it disappear so quickly. But he did look in the direction she had pointed to see two drivers in black suits with black driving caps, and they were both holding signs that said ZentCube on them.

After getting their luggage, it became obvious who the twelve of them going on the retreat were as they all gathered around the two drivers. Parker recognized several people from company functions, and one from working on a project with some people in building B—he was pretty sure the guy's name was Davis—but didn't know anyone else well enough to know their names. The twelve of them split up, six to a car, which ended up being a limo. The kind with two bench seats that faced each other.

As they made the drive from the airport to the resort, Kelli kept looking from window to window, trying to take in all the sights. He didn't think he was the only one in the car who probably would've missed them if Kelli hadn't been so enthusiastic about seeing everything.

He liked it when people appreciated all the amazing things surrounding them. He always had. How had he forgotten that so fully when he'd been making wedding plans with a woman who was impressed by nothing? How had he lost that part of himself while they'd been dating and engaged? It was a good thing that Stephanie had called it off.

*Huh.* That was a new thought. He had been crushed when his ex had ended things, and he hadn't quite gotten over feeling bad about that. His realization that it was a good thing felt like a piece of his shattered heart was just put back in place.

But that didn't mean he should be thinking of Kelli. She deserved someone better than him. She deserved someone whose list of faults wasn't a mile long.

Kelli turned around and knocked on the window between them and the driver. It slid down. "Yes?"

"Um, that sign said that the check-in for the Royal Palm Resort was right back there."

The woman driving said, "That's not where you're checking in."

Suddenly everyone in the car was more on alert, watching exactly where they were going, all with confused faces. Their driver made a left turn, then drove past the main buildings for the hotel, past cottages, and turned right onto a road that ran slightly uphill but alongside the ocean to where several mansions stood tall and proud, and pulled to a stop at one.

"We're staying in a mansion?" Kelli exclaimed.

Their driver got out and opened their door, and Parker and the others all climbed out. "You can head inside," she said. "I'll get your luggage taken care of."

The other limo had pulled up right behind them, and

the twelve of them stared up at the mansion in awe as they made their way to the front door. When Graham and Merit first told Parker about the retreat, this wasn't exactly what he had pictured.

Graham opened the front door right as they reached it and said, "Welcome! Come on, come inside—we're excited to get this week started!"

Parker stepped into a tall foyer of a mansion that opened in one direction to a living room and the other to a twisting staircase leading to a second floor, with a towering Christmas tree nestled in the curve of the staircase, all of which looked like a Christmas explosion had gone off. This place was even more decorated for the season than his Grandma Ines's house always was.

It appeared that escaping all of Christmas was going to be more difficult than he had planned.

# Chapter Seven

## KELLI

When Graham welcomed Kelli and the others into the mansion, he immediately led them to a gigantic room that had a family room on one side, a dining room on the other, and a kitchen in the middle, and Kelli was in love. The dining table seated sixteen people. Sixteen! A lunch buffet was set up along one side of the room, which was good because Kelli was starving.

Once they had their plates filled with a variety of cute little sandwiches and different kinds of salads, they all sat down at the big table. With Graham, Merit, and a woman who didn't come in with them but was looking at Merit like she was in love, they nearly filled the entire table.

For a while, they just chatted while they ate, and it felt like heaven, being surrounded by so many happy people. Parker was sitting straight across from her, and he looked like he was enjoying it, too. Then, as they got close to finishing, Graham stood up, and everyone stopped talking.

"Welcome, everyone. We're thrilled you joined us this Christmas."

Someone in a Royal Palms Resort uniform appeared from some side room and started clearing away everyone's plates while he spoke.

"I understand how it feels to not have anywhere to go for Christmas. I spent two years living away from family, and the holidays were especially rough. I know how it can make you long for all the traditions of home. Or how it can make you not want nothing to do with Christmas at all. I completely understand that some of you are going to want to gravitate toward activities at the resort that don't have to do with Christmas, and you plan to skip anything we do here that's Christmassy, too."

From the corner of her eye, she saw Parker exhale in relief like he was so glad that Graham understood. Did he not like Christmas?

Merit stood up. "Our goal," he said as he motioned between him and Graham, "is to make sure that you don't."

Kelli didn't want to be obvious by turning to look at Parker so she couldn't see his response to Merit's declaration, but she chuckled inside knowing that he probably wasn't thrilled about it.

"Okay, *make sure you don't* is kind of harsh. We're going to *encourage* you to participate. Because we know that when we get to the end of this week, you're going to be happier and more refreshed if you do."

"Now hop up," Graham said. "We have explaining to do, and explaining is always better with a slideshow!"

Everyone looked at each other, seeming just as wary of the slideshow as she was. Especially because this was supposed to be a break from work. But they still stood, of course, looking around to see where they should go.

"Don't look so afraid," Merit said. "Graham's presentations aren't boring."

Joy, a quiet, sweet, and adorable woman who had ridden in the same limo as Kelli, walked up to Kelli and said, "I don't know a soul here. Do you?"

"Just Parker." She motioned at him as they walked toward the couches on the family room side of the room.

"He is one good-looking guy."

"Yeah," she sighed. "If only he wasn't Parker."

"Oh. He's bad news, then?"

She shook her head. "Only for me."

The couches were a giant half-circle facing a fireplace with a huge TV above it. An undecorated Christmas tree stood next to the fireplace, looking regal and ready to be loved. Kelli sat on the couch with everybody else and, once again, realized she had sat with Parker in her line of sight.

"Welcome to the ZentCube Christmas Celebration!" Graham said, the first slide of his slideshow appearing on the screen. It was of each of their faces—pulled from their employee ID badges—on tiny bodies, looking like bobble-heads dancing. The sound of a crowd cheering played with it, and everyone laughed, including Kelli. She knew the cheering wasn't real, but still, it made it feel more festive and exciting.

"Now, we have a little contest to get you all in the Christmas spirit. There are two parts to this—individual activities and group activities." Graham switched to a new slide, and a little bobble-headed Merit danced onto the top of the screen, with a list of activities below him. "Now, during your time here, you can do any of these activities, and each one will earn you one point. All you have to do is send a picture of you doing the activity to Merit and me."

Two phone numbers came up on the screen, and Graham paused while they all pulled out their phones and entered them in. Kelli couldn't believe that Merit and Graham were giving them their personal cell phone numbers. She was putting the CEO's and the CTO's phone numbers into her phone!

"Feel free to take a picture of this slide if you'd like, but just know that all of these activities, along with where to go to do them, are posted on that wall over there. Now, Merit is going to talk about the group activities."

Graham changed the slide as Merit stood, and this time, all twelve of their bobble-heads danced their way to the top of the screen, to the sounds of people shouting things like "Yay! My favorite!" and "I can't wait!" along with a lot of clapping.

"I would like to introduce you all to Elise Stevens." Merit motioned to the woman who had been sitting next to him, with a look of utter adoration on his face. Like she was his world, and everything shone brighter with her in it. And Elise looked back at Merit like she had discovered the secret to happiness when she had met him.

The woman was probably a couple of years younger than Kelli, yet she had already found a love like that. Someday, Kelli was going to find a man who would look at her that way when he introduced her to people. And she was going to look at him the same way Elise was looking at Merit.

"Elise is the activities director for the Royal Palm Resort, and the reason why this resort is so popular at Christmastime."

Elise blushed, which made Kelli smile. And then, for some stupid-crazy reason, Kelli found her eyes darting to Parker. She had to remind herself that she was in no position to date right now. And especially not if that date was Parker. The two of them had already tested those waters, so they already knew they'd sink. She didn't want to date *anyone* in her building again, actually. It made for too much awkwardness.

"Be down here for breakfast every morning at nine," Merit continued. "For those of you counting, yes, that's seven Denver time. Don't worry—we'll make the meal worth your while. And that's when Elise will talk about the itinerary for the day, including the group activities. You'll want to join in on them because they'll be worth two points each. Graham, want to tell them what their points will buy?"

Graham stood again, a grin spread across his face. "Do you remember that work satisfaction survey that went out to random employees via email a week or so ago? Yeah, that only went out to the twelve of you. And the question we were most looking for your answers to was the one that read, 'What kind of non-monetary reward would most motivate you?'

"So we took your answers and came up with a prize package. We're hoping there's at least one thing on this list that will make each of you want to earn as many points as possible so that you can win it."

Graham changed to a new slide, and a little game show host walked onto the screen, motioning big with her arms at one of three wrapped presents. "The first prize we are offering is," he dragged out the word, then the present burst open, "three bonus vacation days, to be used whenever you'd like over the next year."

There were lots of "Ooh!"s and "Wow!"s from the group, but that prize didn't really interest Kelli. She glanced at

Parker and saw that he didn't seem particularly interested, either.

"And the next prize is..." The game show host moved and then motioned big at the second of the three prizes on the screen. It burst open and Graham said, "A free catered lunch for everyone on your team, delivered once a week every week for a full year!"

Kelli's eyes went wide. She instantly wanted this prize, and she wanted it badly. She imagined how much everyone on her team would enjoy it. How much all their faces would light up each week when it came. How valuable it would make her to the team, and how much she would enjoy being the one who won it for them. How much of a great bonding thing it would be for everyone on her team. With that kind of experience every week, her team would be unstoppable.

She could feel Parker's eyes on her, so she glanced over at him and saw a look of curious interest—but only until she looked. He quickly dropped the expression and turned his attention to the TV again.

"And for the last prize." The little character Vanna White-ed the last gift, and it burst open. "The best parking spot at your building for a full year! We polled a bunch of people at each building to find out which was the most coveted spot." Then he read the list of buildings and the parking spot they were giving away at each one. "And for building C—so marketing, sales, and accounting—spot C-seven."

Kelli gasped and her eyes immediately found Parker's, and they stared at each other. Kelli hadn't looked at him when Graham mentioned the second prize, but based on the expression on his face right now, even if he hadn't been interested in the lunch, he was definitely interested in the parking space.

The competition was on, and Kelli intended to win it.

"It looks like we've got you interested," Merit said, chuckling. "You'll see that right next to the list of individual activities on that wall, there's a bar chart with each of your names, and we'll update it with the number of points you currently have as soon as you report them. And just to the right of that, we'll have the daily group activity posted."

"And this won't stop on Christmas Day," Graham added. "We aren't a fan of the let-down you feel when all celebration stops the moment Christmas is over. We'll be celebrating up until the morning of the twenty-eighth, which is when the retreat ends.

"At that point, you are welcome to fly back home or you can stay here until New Year's Day. We won't be doing the retreat for the extra days, so you'll be on your own for most things, but we'll still have the mansion. So you can keep your room and take advantage of all The Royal Palm has to offer. Just let us know in the next few days which day you'd like to fly home."

Kelli's eyebrows rose. She hadn't expected at all that they might offer more days. Her dad was going to be returning from his trip on the 29th, and she kind of wanted to be home when he arrived.

Merit nodded. "I'll be here until New Year's Day, but Graham is going to head home on Monday for a family Christmas party. He'll be back in time for our Christmas Eve celebrations, and when he comes back, he'll have his wife, Tessa, and his little baby, Hope, with him."

"Who just happens to be the cutest baby in the universe!" Graham added, which made Kelli smile.

Graham switched to a new slide, one with Santa sneaking into a room. "We are doing Secret Santas, too, and Merit's assistant, Carla, randomly chose a name for each of you. When you get to your room, you'll find an envelope on your nightstand with the name of the person you'll be a Secret Santa for. Throughout your time here, try to get to know that person, and then get a small gift for them to open on Christmas morning."

"Your luggage is already in your rooms," Merit said, "which are on the two floors above us, and your room assignments are posted on the same wall over there with the points. The theater and the exercise room are downstairs. But before we let you go up and get settled, we have our first group activity!"

Elise, the woman Merit had introduced as the resort's activities director, stood for the first time. "We have a tree that needs decorating, but there are no decorations because you all are going to be the ones to make them."

All twelve of them looked at each other as if any of them understood what the plan was.

"We've got some supplies set up on the table back there," Elise said.

Kelli turned to look—someone had apparently come in while they were watching the presentation and set everything up. She hadn't even heard it happening.

Elise shook a box. "And I've got a bunch of different themes right here. Everyone partner up. Each partnership needs to come grab a theme, then make at least four ornaments with that theme."

Without letting her brain have a second to think about it or to give her eyes permission, Kelli's attention flew to Parker. Apparently, he'd done the same, because they were suddenly looking at each other. It would've been awkward to just turn away, so she raised an eyebrow in a silent question, asking if he wanted to be her partner for the activity. Parker only hesitated a second before a strange look crossed his face and he turned to the woman next to him—someone Kelli hadn't met yet—and asked her to be his partner.

Stupid eyes, thinking they could go and do the asking on their own. Her brain knew not to ask Parker—she didn't know why her eyes couldn't get the message. She exhaled, and then she stood up as everyone else did and looked around the group.

A man stepped over to her and said, "Hi. I'm Davis. Would you like to be my partner for this?"

He was cute. Nothing like Parker, of course, but he had a kind face and welcoming eyes, and looked like he might be in his late twenties, so that was perfect. His dark hair was the right amount of tussled, too. And he looked a little bit nervous to ask, which was pretty adorable. Not that she was looking to date anyone, but she wasn't against a little harmless flirting. Especially with someone who worked in a different building.

"I'm Kelli, and I would love to."

They grabbed their theme from the box Elise held—a paper that read *Santa's Workshop*—and headed over to the tables to get to work.

As they were looking at what kinds of supplies they had to work with and started brainstorming what they could make, Kelli's eyes couldn't help but find Parker again. He and the woman he teamed up with seemed to be having fun. They were picking up craft supplies and talking and laughing. She told herself that it was a good thing. Parker and his fiancée had called things off just a couple of months ago, so he probably really needed a chance to chat with a woman in a low-pressure situation.

Kelli wasn't jealous.

She wasn't wishing it was her with Parker instead of this other woman.

Nope. She was perfectly happy doing this activity with Davis. Her mind wasn't on Parker at all. Not one bit.

# Chapter Eight

PARKER

By the look on Kelli's face, she'd known that Parker understood that she wanted to be partners. And she knew that he'd pretended not to notice and instead turned to the person next to him. But he also knew that she hadn't meant to look his direction—she had just turned to him because they were the only ones from their building who were there, so he was likely the only person she knew. It was human nature. It wasn't because she wanted to be his partner.

Besides, she seemed super interested in all the Christmas activities, and he wasn't. At all. So he didn't want the simple human nature of seeking out the familiar being the thing that stopped her from enjoying the festivities.

Kelli had chatted with so many people since they had gathered together in a group at baggage claim that he figured she could easily partner with one of them. But couldn't it have been anyone other than Davis who asked her? Parker often worked with product development in Building B, since they needed to show off the latest in trade shows. He didn't work with Davis directly and didn't know him well, but he had been in the building enough to know that he was a pretty decent guy. He wasn't sure why that bothered him. He should be happy for Kelli.

Besides, he was kind of enjoying turning a bunch of random craft stuff into "Christmas on the Range" ornaments with Addison. She was funny, and they came up with some pretty brilliant ideas. And since it wasn't something he did as a tradition with his own family, it didn't make him feel sad about not being around them.

But he kept finding his eyes going to Kelli and Davis every time they laughed or every time they were working on something intricate and both were leaned in close together.

Which was ridiculous, especially since he wasn't in a position to date anyone—most of all Kelli. And if he had no interest in dating Kelli, he had no business caring how close she and Davis were right now. Or that he just brushed a lock of hair over her shoulder for her so it wouldn't get in the glue she was using.

"So, which of the three prizes do you most want to win?"

Addison's question had caught him off guard enough that he told himself that he needed to focus more on what he was doing instead of on what Kelli was doing. "Oh, um, parking spot, hands down."

"Really? The parking space?" Addison scrunched up her nose in confusion.

"It's a great parking spot."

"Is it hard to get a good one at your building?"

"Not really. I usually get there at seven, so I mostly have my pick. Except for that one—it always gets taken first."

"But your second place choice can't be more than five steps further from the door at seven."

The second place choice was closer to the door. That wasn't what it was about. And suddenly he wondered what it was actually about. How much did he love the space because of the space, and how much did he love it because of the competition to get it between him and Kelli?

He didn't know why, but simply the thought of it made him suddenly need to compete for that parking space while they were here. Maybe if he just stayed away from the things his own family normally did at Christmastime, it wouldn't be so hard.

"How about you?"

"Time off," Addison said. "I love traveling to new places, and an extra three days would make that even better."

"What have been your favorite places to travel to?"

Addison started telling him, and he tried hard to listen, but he kept noticing how organized Kelli was with the craft supplies she was working with. There were twelve people around the table working, and it looked like an explosion of scissors, glues, paints, brushes, and all the craft supplies they'd been given to make the ornaments with.

Except for right in front of him and right in front of Kelli. Everything was lined up so neatly and orderly that she could find anything she needed quickly.

"How about you? Do you have any favorite places you've traveled?"

Okay, he had to be more serious about not letting his eyes or his mind wander to the other side of the table. So he talked with Addison as they finished making their four ornaments.

When Elise called time, Parker and Addison looked at their ornaments. He admired the horse they'd made out of brown felt that stood next to a cactus that was decorated like a Christmas tree, and the cowboy hat with mistletoe on the brim. He was pretty proud of what they had created once he'd quit looking in Kelli's direction. Elise had them all gather up their ornaments and bring them to the tree, and then Graham said, "Let the Christmas tree decorating begin!"

Addison hung two of them, and Parker searched for the perfect spot for their other two, as all twelve of them were gathered around the same tree, trying to find places for theirs.

Before he knew it, he was reaching to put one of his up high while someone was reaching in front of him to place one, and he looked down to see that Kelli was pressed against him, their faces less than a foot apart. There was so much jostling around the tree that someone knocked into Kelli, and he had barely placed his ornament in time to put his arm on her shoulders to keep her from falling.

Her eyes held his for a small moment as they stood inches apart, sharing the same air, electricity seeming to crackle between them, before she cleared her throat and said, "Thank you," and then looked away. He quickly turned away from her gaze, too, and his eyes landed on her ornament.

"Wow, Kelli." He leaned in closer to it. There were little elves with wooden marble faces and felt bodies, wearing tall pointed hats with a mini pompom on top. They were both kneeling on the floor, wrapping gifts. Differently colored wrapping paper covered the floor, and she had even taken curling ribbon, cut in half so it was thinner, and made little tiny bows out of it. The amount of detail in such a small space was mind-blowing. "This is incredible. So intricate. I'm impressed."

He looked back at her to see that she was beaming at the compliment. She should be.

Once all the ornaments were placed and they had all stepped back, Graham turned the tree lights on and led them all in the *ooh*ing and *aah*ing. It did look decent. Nothing like home, though, which caused a wave of melancholy to wash over him. But then he glanced at Kelli and saw the joy on her face as she stared at the tree in wonder. It made him look back at it again. For not being like the one at home, it was a good tree.

Graham clapped his hands together. "Okay, you've got two hours to head to your room and get settled. Your packing list asked you to bring the most formal outfit you had. When you come back, be wearing that, because we're headed to the Tinsel and Tidings Christmas feast and ball!"

Parker headed to his room, which was so much more impressive than his room in his apartment. His suitcases were waiting for him, just like Merit said they'd be, so he started unpacking them and hanging up his clothes. Then he saw the envelope on his nightstand and remembered about the Secret Santa. He set down the shirt he'd been about to hang up and walked over to it. He opened the envelope, looked at the name printed inside, and smiled.

*Kelli Ellis*

Once he got all of the items put in a closet, drawer, or in the bathroom, he still had about an hour and fifty minutes before they had to be dressed and downstairs.

He looked around the giant room and exhaled. Getting ready would only take about thirty minutes. Being in this room just made him realize even more strongly how alone he was, and he couldn't spend the extra hour and twenty minutes here or he was going to go crazy.

He headed down to the second floor, but there wasn't a soul in the family room or kitchen, so he headed to the basement to check it out. The exercise room had several machines and a good number of free weights. He'd have to take advantage of them while he was here.

The theater was impressive, too. It seated twenty-one people in three rows, all in reclining chairs. And in between the theater and exercise room were several table games. He walked over to the ping pong table, grabbed a paddle and ball, and started bouncing it on the paddle over and over.

Down here was just as depressing as his room. Maybe he just needed to leave the mansion and explore a bit. He set the paddle and the ball down and had taken one step toward the door when Kelli walked into the room. "Oh, hi. You're not spending the extra time resting from travel, huh?"

Kelli laughed. How had he not noticed how amazing of a laugh she had before now? "I got my rest from travel on the plane, remember?"

He chuckled and smiled again at the memory of her being so close as she lay her head on his shoulder. "You up for a game?"

"We *could*," Kelli said. "Or we could get a jump start on everyone else and do something that will earn us some points."

Parker looked at the pool table. The game sounded like a lot more fun—he really wasn't in the mood to do anything else that was Christmassy after making the tree decorations. "What do you have in mind?" He wanted to know exactly what they'd be doing before he would be willing to commit.

Kelli pulled out her phone, probably to see the picture she had taken during the presentation. "Oh! One of them is to walk along the beach and write a Christmas message or draw a Christmas scene with a stick in the sand. That would be fun, and I have been dying to check out the beach."

A walk on the beach wasn't Christmassy, and he didn't have to draw a picture if he didn't want to. He could do that.

Less than five minutes later, they were both walking along the beach. It had only been a short pathway from the mansion, and the weather was nice. Easily over fifty degrees and sunshiny, so it felt warm enough without wearing jackets.

The beach was nearly empty, which surprised him. Sure, it was too cold to play in the sand and water, but it was still beautiful out. Kelli had changed into flip-flops, and she took them off and ran along the sand at the edge of the water, scrambling out of the way whenever a wave came in, and squealing when it washed over her feet because she didn't make it far enough onto the beach in time.

He smiled as he watched her.

"Take off your shoes! It's not that cold. Still tons warmer than anywhere in Colorado right now."

That was true. Why not? Anything to take his mind off Christmas. He left his shoes and socks on a bench and went out to the water's edge. The sand was soft beneath his feet and felt great. He hadn't been to a beach in far too long.

Before he knew it, he wasn't only dodging the waves

coming in—he was also dodging Kelli's kicks of water she was sending in his direction. He sent plenty back in her direction. And as she said, it wasn't too cold, especially since he had already acclimated to the Colorado winter.

At least, it wasn't too cold until he didn't dodge Kelli's splash of water. He gasped as the cold water soaked his pants. "Is this to get even for my water bottle on the plane? Because that wasn't my fault."

"And it wasn't my fault that you didn't move fast enough to get out of the way of that last one." There was a teasing glint in her eyes and a grin on her face as she sent another splash of water his way that he *did* move away from fast enough, and then she took off running to get away from any retaliation.

So, of course, he ran after her. He would run after her as long as it took to catch her.

"Whoa," he said out loud as he slowed to a walk. Where had that thought come from? He was not chasing Kelli. He wasn't trying to date her. He wasn't looking for a relationship at all. He hadn't guessed that coming out here, seeing her running free and happy along the beach would be a bad idea. A dangerous idea.

The walk got his mind off Christmas and how he thought he'd be spending it. Now he just needed something to take his mind off Kelli.

Kelli had stopped running, too, but she had stopped because she had found a few sticks that had washed ashore. He could've left right then and gone back to the mansion. But just because he was having a crisis of motivation didn't mean he was just going to leave her out there alone.

Plus, he wanted points for this activity, too. He couldn't let her get ahead already.

That was all. He was here for the points.

Kelli drew a gigantic, very fancy "Merry Christmas" in the sand. Parker wasn't going to draw anything Christmas-related, but then a memory of one of his favorite Christmases came to mind. His brother Ethan had somehow talked their parents into letting them sleep in sleeping bags in front of the tree so they could see Santa when he came to bring them presents, so he decided to draw that.

When he was finishing up, Kelli came over to look at it. "Wow. You're quite the artist."

"Isn't everyone who is drawn to marketing as a career?"

She shrugged. "To some degree, I guess. Not often this much. Is this you and your brother?"

Parker nodded as he finished drawing the scene in the sand. "We had fun. It was when Ethan was three and I was fifteen. I'd stopped believing in Santa before he was even born, but having a little brother who was that much younger than me let me relive the magic of Christmas all over again. I mean, you should've seen the excitement on Ethan's face when we woke up and saw that Santa had come while we were asleep."

When he finally looked up at Kelli, she had a curious expression on her face. The afternoon sun was right behind her, making her look like an angel as she gazed at his scene, and it made him wish all over again that he was good enough for her. "It sounds like you love Christmas."

He set down the stick and brushed off his hands, then stood up, brushing sand from his knees. "Usually. I've always wondered which had made me like Christmas more—my parents' love of the holiday, or getting a second chance at experiencing the magic of Christmas through a brother who was so much younger than me." He hoped that one day soon he'd be able to experience that all over again with his own kid. "But this year's different. I'm not a fan of Christmas this year, and I would happily skip it all."

"Is your family not around this year?"

He shook his head. "My parents went on a cruise to celebrate their thirtieth anniversary. They didn't think they'd be leaving me alone because I was supposed to be on a cruise myself right now."

He didn't know why he'd felt the need to get that off his chest. Maybe he just needed someone to know. Maybe he needed Kelli, specifically, to know. He knew the second that she had figured it all out because her hands flew to her mouth and she gasped. "Oh my gosh, it was supposed to be a honeymoon cruise, wasn't it?"

He nodded.

"I am so sorry."

He shrugged. "It was for the best. I hadn't believed it was at the time and didn't think I ever would, but now I get it that it was."

They both looked down at the pictures they had carved in the sand, but he wasn't sure either of them was actually seeing their drawings.

"I know what you mean."

Parker's eyes flew to Kelli, hoping she would say more.

"James and I broke up too, you know. He was the one to break it off, and it had crushed me. I didn't think I would ever feel like it was a good thing. But it's been a year, and I realized months ago that I had been in love with his family, not him. It was a big, beautiful family with so many different personalities, and I felt like I fit right in with them. Like they were my family.

"It wasn't until several months later that I finally understood that my relationship with James hadn't exactly been stellar. I had been letting the love I felt for his family color everything, so I hadn't even noticed that things weren't okay between us."

He knew exactly how it felt to not notice. He shook his head and chuckled. "Well, then, it looks like we both have our exes to thank for figuring things out for us."

She laughed, too. "I'll be sure to send him a thank you card." She looked at the things they had drawn in the sand. "Want to take pictures?"

Parker used Kelli's phone to take a picture of her standing just above her Christmas greeting, in a mid-air leap, arms thrown into the sky. Then he stood next to his, doing his best impression of the animated character in Graham's slide show that announced the prizes, and Kelli took a picture with his phone.

He was happy with the scene he had created. Even if it did make him miss Christmas at home.

As they headed back along the beach toward the mansion and the shoes they had both left behind, they texted their pictures to Graham and Merit as proof that they had completed the challenge.

"I can't believe we are texting the owners of ZentCube like they're our BFFs. I never thought I'd be doing this."

Parker looked over at Kelli as they walked along a beach, fifteen hundred miles from home, with the sun low in the sky, casting her in golden light. "I never thought I would, either."

# Chapter Nine

KELLI

Kelli loved dressing fancy. She had packed three elegant dresses when she saw it on the packing list, but she knew the one she was going to go for all along. It was the perfect shade of Christmas red, it was shimmery, and she always felt on fire when she wore it. Like she could do anything. She paired it with some equally fabulous red shoes.

Then she pulled her curled hair up in a loose bun that was speedy to do but looked all fancy, which made the dangly silver earrings she wore stand out even more.

Valeria texted to ask how things were going, so she texted back a picture of her in her dress, taken in the full-length mirror in the room.

VALERIA: Wow! You are going to knock the socks off all the guys there!

I mean MY socks just jumped off my feet.

Kelli smiled and texted the emoji with a girl dancing in a

red dress. And then added lasers to it before sending it, laughing to herself.

> VALERIA: I see you chose the red dress. Does that mean you met an interesting, single guy?

Parker came to mind first, which shouldn't have surprised her, since she'd just spent an hour on the beach with him. But she reminded herself that a relationship with *anyone* wasn't a good idea right now, and a casual one with Parker would only make working on the same floor with him even more awkward than it had been after the last time they had dated. *Davis. Think only of Davis.*

> KELLI: I did, actually!

> His name is Davis, and he works in Development.

And, because she knew Valeria would ask for details, she added a text that said, *AND HE HAS NICE EYES.*

Valeria responded with the surprised emoji. Then the gasping emoji. Then the heart-eyes emoji.

> VALERIA: Wow. This is huge. Dipping a toe in the dating pool after so long. I'm so proud.

> Okay, I'll stop distracting you. You just go get your flirt on, girl!

> But don't you dare forget to text me the details later.

> KELLI: I won't.

She slipped her phone into her handbag, took one last look in the mirror, and then headed out her door. She was sure she wasn't heading down late at all, but as she walked down the curved staircase, she saw all six of the men already standing in the lobby, waiting. And she didn't miss their appreciative expressions. It was a little confirmation that she hit the mark with her outfit.

Her eyes were on Davis as she walked down the stairs. He looked nice dressed up so fancy. His suit was well fitted, his hair looked good, and those kind eyes were like an accessory that made the outfit.

But as much as she tried to keep her eyes only on Davis, they went to Parker anyway, and she forgot how to breathe. His dark suit looked on him like suits had been designed for the express purpose of making Parker Brockbank irresistible. It was a deep, warm gray that brought out colors in his eyes that she hadn't seen before. Those eyes looked captivating. Intoxicating. Like they were reaching out to capture her.

His hair, which had looked beautifully windblown on the beach, now looked tame enough to be respectable, while still having a hint of wildness. His scruff was trimmed short and neat and she wanted to run her hands along that strong jawline of his. If Davis was a ten out of ten, Parker was an easy nine hundred and fifty-seven.

She was in so much trouble. She needed blinders tonight, like the kind they put on horses. Then she could just keep her eyes on Davis and not see Parker at all. Davis was attractive. He seemed like a good guy, and from what she knew of Graham and Merit, they wouldn't have invited him if he wasn't.

*Davis*, she told herself. Then, a little more firmly, she repeated *Davis. Keep your eyes on Davis.*

When she reached the bottom of the stairs, she stood on the side of Davis opposite Parker. Elise had talked with them earlier about this dinner and dance, and how she and her team had worked hard to make it a night that the people at the resort would enjoy. They all knew to head over to the ballroom, so as soon as the last person came down the stairs, the twelve of them went outside to find four golf carts in a row, waiting for them.

She and Davis weren't dating, though, and she didn't want him to get the impression that this was a date. Joy was walking next to her, so she linked arms with her new friend and they chatted as they walked to one of the carts, and both sat in the back seat. Another guy, Thomas, who she had seen Joy flirting with earlier, came and sat in the front seat next to the driver. Perfect.

Kelli hadn't seen much of the resort yet, but it was magical at night. Golden Christmas lights had been strung all over the grounds, across buildings, wound up palm trees, and lighting the pathways. This place was heaven.

And she was so grateful for the golf carts. It wouldn't have been a bad walk in regular shoes, but in four-inch heels when you wanted to dance the night away, not so much.

Their line of golf carts pulled up to a building, and before she knew it, Davis was at her side, offering her a hand out of the cart. She gave him a nod of thanks, took his hand, and stepped out of the cart. She didn't keep hold of his hand, though. She might be willing to dip a toe in the dating pool, but that was about it.

The ballroom was massive and had round tables in a half circle around the outside of the room. In one corner, three of the tallest Christmas trees she had ever seen were next to each other, each decorated with a different color scheme.

One in silvers and blues, one in reds and greens, and one in golds. Garlands ran all along the room, all of which were decorated, and each table's centerpiece was practically a work of art.

When she imagined tonight as she was getting ready, she had been thinking about who she wanted to sit by and how she could maneuver things so that she wouldn't be near Parker. She knew that getting close to him was dangerous, and she had felt herself slipping when they'd been on the beach. Especially when he had been looking at the scene he had drawn in the sand that showed him with his little brother. But now? With him in that suit? Now would be particularly dangerous to be around him.

Figuring out how to get everyone to sit where she had imagined had been futile, though, because the hostess directed them to two tables, and each one had their name at a specific place. She found hers and sat down, and Davis sat to her right. And then, a moment later, Parker sat at her left.

It was fine.

She could pretend she had blinders.

Blinders, and amazing food. They hadn't been seated for long before the waiter brought in cinnamon-spiced sweet potato soup with maple croutons, which not only was an explosion of tasty goodness in her mouth but made her whole body rejoice at whatever was in it. She chatted with everyone at the table, and if she ever caught her mind wandering to Parker, she just took another bite.

And then the waiter brought in the main course—roasted pork loin with herb stuffing; Italian roasted cremini mushrooms, cauliflower, and tomatoes; and the softest, fluffiest rosemary dinner rolls that Kelli had ever tasted. The entire meal was so full of flavor and texture that she couldn't have asked for a better distraction. She cut each item into the perfect bite-sized pieces.

She speared a grape tomato and cut it in half, then attempted to spear one of the mushrooms to do the same. But somehow the fork slipped and, in a move she couldn't duplicate if she was paid to, she managed to send it airborne instead, and it landed with a plop in Parker's water goblet.

Several people at the table saw and let out an audible gasp and then restrained chuckles. The people who hadn't seen, Davis included, turned to see what had caused everyone's reaction.

Parker just lifted his glass and considered it. "I've had restaurants put lemons, limes, oranges, cucumbers, and even strawberries in my water before. This is the first time I've had a mushroom." And then he took a drink.

With as hot as her face and ears felt, she knew her cheeks were as red as her dress.

"I didn't get a mushroom in mine," Davis said, clearly not understanding what had just happened.

"I bet if you asked Kelli nicely, she could help you out with that."

Kelli closed her eyes, trying to make the embarrassment go away. She did everything right and planned precisely so that embarrassing things didn't happen. Yet they always seemed to happen around Parker no matter how hard she tried.

She speared a perfectly-cut piece of the stuffed pork and made herself focus on the bite by trying to pick out what spices were used. Was that cardamom? And maybe Juniper? She would keep trying to figure it out for as long as it took for her face to get back to a normal temperature.

When the waiter removed their dinner plates, she

exhaled in relief because maybe she could get to the dancing and away from Parker. But then the waiter set dessert in front of each of them—a plate of vanilla bean clafoutis with raspberries and nectarines. It tasted amazing, but she only had three bites before she declared herself full and set down her fork.

A man's voice came over the sound system, and Kelli's attention turned to the man at the microphone who introduced himself as Christian, the dance instructor at the resort.

"We have a little custom here for the Tinsel and Tidings Ball. We like to start the first dance with our guests who have come in this week for dance lessons. They'll be showcasing the Viennese Waltz, and once they're done, we'd like to welcome you all to join us on the floor for an evening of dancing!"

As they watched the guests waltz, Davis leaned in her direction and said in a quiet voice, "Pretty impressive for only a week of dance lessons, don't you think?"

Kelli nodded. She had taken years of dance lessons, but never any ballroom. She could hold her own at a dance, but she always wished she knew how to ballroom dance.

The moment the song was over, Davis turned toward her, palm held upright, and said, "Would you like to dance?" like it was a race and he had to rush out of the gate.

"I would love to." She took his hand, stood, and let him lead her to the dance floor. She didn't even turn enough to glimpse Parker's face. She was staying so strong she should get an award. Plus, Davis hadn't witnessed all the embarrassing things she'd done—not just tonight but on this whole trip—so it felt nice to head to the dance floor with him.

As they danced, it was clear that Davis was getting his flirt on, too. It made her feel pretty. They weren't doing the Viennese Waltz, exactly, but dancing with Davis was easy. Nice.

More and more couples came onto the dance floor, and as they turned and moved around the floor, she saw some she recognized. Joy and Thomas were dancing, and it made Kelli smile. The two looked adorable together, and she hoped they might decide to start dating before the trip was over. They saw Merit and Elise, too, and Kelli once again felt that pang of longing for a relationship like theirs. They just looked so happy and radiant.

And then she saw Parker dancing with Addison, and she didn't care if she was supposed to let Davis lead—she turned them so that she wouldn't be seeing him. She didn't know why it was bothering her. It shouldn't. She and Parker knew they wouldn't work out. And even if she was wrong and things had changed over the past two-and-a-half years—which was a possibility—she knew *she* wouldn't work out with anyone right now. She was too vulnerable and needed to be cautious.

So she put on her blinders and focused on Davis, and he rewarded her with a big smile. They danced together for the next dance, too, and it was also nice. Then they headed back toward their table to grab some water.

As they neared, her eyes found Parker, like her attention was magnetically pulled toward him whether she liked it or not. He was chatting and laughing with a few people. A couple people were standing just outside the circle they made, looking at Parker's group like they wanted to join in but were shy or unsure. Parker spotted them, and so subtly shifted in a way that opened his circle. He said something to one of them, and just like that, the two others were in their group, chatting and laughing, too.

Why did he have to go and do sweet things like that? Couldn't he just shout at someone for stepping on his foot, punch someone in the gut, or bump into someone, knocking them down, and not apologize so she could get over him already?

Getting drinks of water put them right next to Parker's group and they quickly found themselves pulled into the group, and laughing and chatting themselves.

As they talked, she felt Davis's fingers brush up against hers. A question, a nudge, asking if he could hold her hand. She had imagined this being a night of fun, dancing with a lot of different people. Doing a little flirting, but nothing serious. Davis silently asking to hold her hand felt an awful lot like he was trying to claim her for the night. She liked dancing with him, but she didn't want that. So she just brought her hands together in front. A subtle move, but one that should get the point across to Davis.

A new song started, but she wasn't quite ready to leave the conversation yet, so she didn't so much as glance in the direction of the dance floor. Parker asked her, specifically, to say what her favorite cheese was when everyone was saying theirs, and right after she answered, Davis wrapped his arm around her back, placed his hand on her shoulder, and leaned in to whisper, "Did I mention how great you smell?"

And then he left his hand there. He had done it like he was pulling her close to tell her something, but it was as blatant as a guy stretching at a movie theater before draping his arm on a girl's shoulder. She didn't want to embarrass the guy by pushing his hand off her shoulder. He was a nice guy and was probably only doing it because he was feeling threatened by Parker. Who wouldn't? Parker looked like a movie star tonight.

So she waited a moment, then leaned forward to look at Joy's bracelet and shook his hand off her shoulder at the same time.

Except instead of taking the hint and dropping his arm to his side, he dropped it to her waist. She took in a slow, deep breath. If Davis was a jerk, there were several things she could do to make sure he got the message. But he wasn't, and she didn't want him to think that she wasn't interested in him at all or that she was mad at him. She simply didn't want someone to claim her as their date tonight.

As everyone in the circle chatted, she ran through options in her head of what could send the message but hadn't come up with any good ones when her eyes fell on Parker. He was studying her, reading the situation. He met her eyes, and it felt like a question. Like he was looking for confirmation that he was reading the situation correctly. She could've given him a slight nod but hadn't, yet somehow he still saw it in her eyes.

As soon as Joy finished what she was saying, Parker stepped into the circle toward Kelli. He held out a hand. "Would you like to dance?"

She smiled and put her hand in his. "I would."

She was sure that Davis got the message as she and Parker walked onto the dance floor, and she was so grateful.

The song ended seconds after they got to a spot on the dance floor, which was great because then she knew she'd get at least a full song with Parker. He kept one of her hands in his and placed his other hand in the middle of her back. Interesting. He didn't go for the waist. Not that she would have any problem with his hand on her waist, but between that and the amount of space between them, it felt like he was silently showing that he respected her.

She put her hand on his shoulder, resting her arm on his, which made her take in Parker in his suit with touch in addition to sight, and the extra sense nearly overwhelmed her.

"You are impressively graceful," Kelli said.

"I was going to say the same about you, but I was also going to add that you are extraordinarily beautiful."

"Wow. A good dancer and a good complimenter. Your mom must be so proud."

"She is. But to be fair, if Graham and Merit had us make macaroni art and I texted her a picture of it, she would be proud of me for that, too."

Kelli smiled. "She sounds like a great person."

"She really is."

Dancing with Davis had felt nice. Dancing with Parker felt amazing. Maybe it wouldn't be so bad to have someone claim her as their date tonight.

Wow, did that thought feel dangerous. It would definitely be bad to fall for him because she would still see him daily when this was over.

As the song was nearing the end, Parker pulled her closer and said in a voice that couldn't have been heard by anyone but her, "I got the impression that you don't want to be tied to one person tonight, right?"

She tried to nod, but now that she had Parker's arm around her, she wasn't so sure. She was currently having trouble simply remembering to breathe. He must've seen past that, though, because he said, "If you'd like to make sure that message gets across fully, Roman from QA is a good guy, and with as often as his eyes have gone to you, I'm sure he'd love to dance. If you'd like, I can lead us over there so it'd be natural for you to walk in his direction after the dance."

"Thanks," she managed to breathe as she marveled at this man.

She might have still been marveling at him when he thanked her for the dance and walked away just as they neared Roman from QA. Parker looked back at her once, but she hadn't been able to see his expression long enough to interpret it before Roman walked over and asked her to dance.

# Chapter Ten

PARKER

*P*arker woke up and dressed for an early morning run along the beach. When he opened his door, he saw the outside of it had been decorated with a paper Christmas tree and decorations made out of pipe cleaners and other items left over from their craft day. For the first second, he thought maybe it was something Merit and Graham had done for everyone, but the moment he saw the sash draped on the tree that read *#1 Christmas Fan Behind this Door*, with a cat drawn curled up beneath the tree, he instantly knew it was Kelli's doing.

He stood in front of the door just smiling at it for several minutes. Then he shook his head and glanced down the hallway in the direction of Kelli's room, feeling drawn toward her at the same time he wished he had never seen Stephanie's list. Before dating his ex, he'd had all the confidence he needed, but he hadn't gotten his groove back since they had broken up. Maybe because he feared that everything on her list about him was actually true.

He had to remind himself that he was supposed to stop

thinking about Kelli and headed outside. The sun hadn't risen yet, so it was still fairly dark. Even so, it was warmer than it was in Denver at midday this time of year. It was more humid here than he ever guessed it would be in December, though, and that took a bit of getting used to.

After his run, he showered and even made it down to breakfast a few minutes early.

Once he found out that they didn't need to meet for the group activity until three—serving a Christmas dinner to the homeless—he went for a walk along the boardwalk and explored the town a bit. Not that it helped to get his mind off Kelli, especially since he needed to buy a Secret Santa gift for her. Having his arm around her while they had danced last night had felt so perfectly, exactly right, that he had been afraid to dance with her a second time. It had been hard enough walking away after the first song.

He got back just a few minutes before three, afraid that if he came back any earlier, he might run into her, and he was having a hard enough time staying away. He knew he wasn't good enough for her and that he wasn't ready for another relationship.

While he waited in the family room for everyone to show up, he walked to where the points were posted. Everyone had at least four points since everyone made the ornaments and went to the dinner and dance. He had gotten his fifth point on the beach with Kelli, but several people had more than five, including Kelli, who was up to eight.

How had she gotten so many so quickly? If he didn't step it up, he was going to have to say goodbye to his parking spot for a full year.

A driver knocked on the mansion's front door not long after everyone gathered in the family room, saying he was ready to take them to the soup kitchen. They all headed outside and got in the twelve-passenger van. There were a couple of empty seats, so apparently not all of them were set on winning the prize. He purposely didn't sit next to Kelli, hoping that the distance would help his heart recover.

But once the ten of them were inside the building and got their instructions on how to help prepare the meal they would be serving to people who were homeless or otherwise struggling, he realized he wasn't going to be able to stay as far away from her as he needed. They were both put on turkey-slicing duty, working side-by-side, and he knew he couldn't bring up the dance without his feelings about the night showing as plain as day on his features, so he instead chose a safer subject.

"I see you're up to eight points now."

She smiled as she cut the meat. "And I see you're not. I think that's proof that parking spot C-seven really is mine. You might even say that it always has been."

They'd asked them to cut one-fourth inch thick slices of meat, and she cut so carefully that he thought they probably could've come along with a ruler and measured all of her slices and they'd each be exactly one-fourth an inch thick, all the way from one side to the other.

"Someone's counting their chickens. There's still a lot of week left." He didn't know why he was goading her to get more points. He really wanted that spot, but there were a lot of things on that list that he didn't want to do. And from what he'd seen at work and the fact that she was there by seven every day, he knew that she was someone who could set a goal and achieve it. He was going to have to step it up.

"Don't you worry about me. There are a lot of things on that list and a lot of hours in the day."

He moved a group of slices to the platter and turned on the electric knife again. "What did you do to earn points today?"

Her face lit up as she talked about answering letters that kids wrote to Santa, helping as an elf at the shopping center by taking pictures of kids on Santa's lap, and then wrapping gifts at a Toys for Tots charity.

Before they were finished, one of the volunteers in charge came over and asked them to move to the serving line to help the people who had just started coming in while she finished up the turkey. Because they weren't assigned which items to serve, he purposely chose a spot where there would be someone between him and Kelli.

But as he put a scoop of mashed potatoes on everyone's plates, he still found himself looking further down the line at where Kelli was placing a roll on each person's plate. She was smiling and chatting with each person. She wasn't acting like they were any less than her just because they had found themselves homeless at Christmas. The look on her face was that of zero judgment and genuine care.

He wondered if it was authentic, or if she was just very good at putting on a front. From the way everyone's faces were bright and smiley as she talked with them, they thought it was plenty genuine.

But Stephanie was pretty good at projecting the image she wanted people to see and then complaining about them afterward, and he suddenly needed to know if Kelli was the same.

After they had finished serving everyone, spent time socializing with all the people who had come to eat, and packed up the extra food in boxes for their guests to take with them, the lead organizer started assigning each of them clean-up duties. Parker took a subtle step toward Kelli, knowing that as the woman in charge reached them, she would be more likely to pair them up on a task. And she did. They both were assigned to wash the big pans.

The day had been long and exhausting—mentally and physically. Knowing that people tended to show their true colors a bit more when they were worn out, he was curious to see Kelli's. As the sinks were filling with water, she leaned against them, looking so tired. Perfect. So he asked what she thought of the people she had met. They were mostly gone, and they were far enough in the back that any that remained wouldn't be able to hear her.

Answering seemed to give her more energy. "They had so many incredible stories! Did you talk with the guy in the gray coat? He was the one wearing a beanie and mismatched boots."

"I did."

She started putting some dishes in the soapy water and washed them as she talked. "He had so many tough things happen in his life. Enough to make most people go off and be a hermit somewhere. But he was so happy and so funny. Did you see how many people he made laugh? Oh, and there was this woman who had three kids, but she'd lost custody of all of them. It was so heartbreaking to hear how sad she was around the holidays. I wanted to just wrap my arms around her and hug her for days."

As they talked, he rinsed each item as she finished, then put it in the rack, then dried and put it away while she told story after story. He was surprised that she had talked to so many people in the time they had.

Okay, all that seemed authentic. She had even talked about trying to set up rotating help from ZentCube employees at their local homeless shelter once they got back, and he had no doubt she would. But maybe that was just her thing—something that spoke to her heart.

So he searched for a different subject. Everyone had complaints about their boss, even if the boss was a great one, so he started asking about Liz. If Kelli had complaints, she didn't voice them, no matter how many opportunities he gave her.

On the ride back to the resort, he started a conversation with all ten of them in the van about things that annoyed them. Kelli did join in with her own list of annoying things, but she mentioned things like taking out her contacts at night and putting on glasses, and that the curvature of the lenses always made her question whether she was on the bottom step or still had one to go. Or thinking she had plugged in her phone to charge, then realizing that the cord wasn't pushed in all the way. Annoyances about *things*, never about *people*.

He still wasn't convinced, so he decided to check on one of the many things that really annoyed Stephanie. When they pulled to a stop light, he saw a man wearing a navy sweater and jeans walking down the street next to a woman. He hadn't known it until the end of their relationship, and had probably annoyed her countless times over the nearly two years they had dated, but Stephanie thought it was wrong and was personally offended by anyone who wore any shade of a blue shirt with blue jeans.

"See that guy?"

Kelli nodded.

"What do you think of his outfit?"

"I think he feels good in it. Look at how confident his walk is."

"But what do you think of the color of his sweater?"

She gave him an amused smile that said she knew what it was he was *really* asking. "I think that color would look great on you. Why? Did you buy one like it while you were out shopping today?"

He chuckled inside. She very much didn't understand why he was asking. He pushed further. "What do you think about it paired with jeans, though?"

He got that same amused smile from her, and she motioned at his pants. "You look mighty fine in jeans, Parker. How about the hair? I can compliment the hair, too, if you'd like."

This time, he laughed out loud. But he pushed, making sure he was specific this time. "But if you're talking style, the color of the sweater is fine when worn with jeans?"

She gave him a look that told him she was confused as to why that could possibly be something he was wondering. "I think people should wear whatever they like, especially if it makes them feel great. If whatever you're wearing makes you feel as confident as that guy looks, what you're wearing is going to look good to everyone. That's all anyone needs to worry about."

He leaned back in his seat and smiled. He might be sitting next to the least judgmental woman he'd ever known, and she'd been right under his nose for two-and-a-half years.

# Chapter Eleven

KELLI

Kelli wasn't the only one crowding around the points board in the family room before heading to the activities building to make gingerbread houses. A few people were trailing and probably had no plans to catch up. She had hoped that she was enough in the lead to skip gingerbread house making, but she was sitting at eleven points and so was Parker. And a couple of people were only one point behind them, so she couldn't risk it.

Especially because it was a two-point activity, and especially because she really, *really* wanted to win that weekly lunch for her team. And close behind that was her desire to not let Parker have her parking space for a full year.

Addison must've noticed her looking at Parker's points, because she glanced around to make sure he wasn't in the room and then said, "You work with him, right?"

Kelli shrugged. "Not really. We're in the same department but on very different teams. So I see him daily, but all along we've been rivals more than anything else." She felt like they still were, but they were also something that they weren't before, and she wasn't quite sure what exactly that was. But she found herself wanting to figure it out.

"Do you know if he's seeing someone? Or hoping to? Because he said he was single, but I'm having the hardest time getting him to pay any attention to me."

Kelli opened her mouth but had no idea what to say. Luckily, she was spared trying to come up with a reason because Addison said, "Shh. Never mind—he's coming in."

A text on her phone buzzed, so she stepped away from the points chart and to an area where she was alone and pulled out her phone. It was from Valeria.

> VALERIA: Hey, girl! How's the vacation? Full of the magic of Christmas?

> KELLI: You know it.

> VALERIA: Does that magic include a certain single man?

Her cheeks blushed just thinking about Parker before she realized that Valeria had probably been asking about Davis. She had danced with him twice more at the Tinsel and Tidings Ball, but with Parker's very timely help, Davis had seemed to understand that she didn't want anything resembling serious or exclusive, and he had backed off and just danced with her for fun. Davis really was a good guy, and at another point in her life, she would've gladly dated him and probably would have been happy. Davis was a light in the darkness.

But Parker harnessed the power of the sun, and her mind couldn't seem to do anything other than crave its brightness and warmth whenever she wasn't focused enough on what she was doing to keep her mind from wandering.

She hesitated a moment, staring at Valeria's text, before typing in, *Yes, but not the single guy you're thinking of.*

The text showed as *read* for a slight pause before she got Valeria's response.

> VALERIA: PARKER?!

> It's Parker, isn't it?

> Oh my. After all this time, it's Parker, isn't it?

> My girl has a thing for Parker Brockbank in Trade Shows!!!!

Kelli held her phone closer, glancing around to make sure no one was near enough to see.

> KELLI: Shh! I don't even know. He's just...

> And I'm...

> I know he just sees me as the awkward girl. But he's pretty great.

> And now I don't know what to do.

> My current plan is to run far away.

She glanced up and saw that Parker was no longer studying the chart, and he looked like he might be doing his own running away.

> KELLI: Gotta go.

"Parker," she called out, and he turned toward her. She took a few quick steps to reach him. "Where are you going?"

He glanced back at the points chart and then made a face. "I'm just not feeling like making gingerbread houses."

"I appreciate you being the gentleman and letting me win the parking space, but I would rather win it fair and square."

"I still plan to win it."

She shook her head. "You're practically gift wrapping it and putting it under the tree with my name on it if you walk out on this one."

She didn't want to go herself. And she would be fine—grateful, even—for less competition. But she wanted to win, and against her better judgment, she wanted him there, too. So she had no problem taunting her biggest rival.

He took a longing gaze at his escape route before meeting her eyes. "Okay, but only if you promise that when I win, you'll wrap it and put it under the Christmas tree with my name on it."

"Deal," she said, thrusting out her hand. He shook it, and they joined the group heading to the activities center. Why was she doing this? She could've let him leave and stayed away herself.

But there were still the two others who were only one point behind her and Parker, and they'd pull ahead if they both didn't go.

They gathered in the activities building—eleven of them from ZentCube and fifteen or so from other parts of the resort—and a woman in her early twenties stood in front of them. "Hi, y'all! My name is HallieMae, and I've got a great activity for you today. Now as you can see, there are tables all around the room. Each spot at the tables has the same supplies—frosting and candies and a base to build your creations on. Y'all have a stack of gingerbread rectangles in front of you, and we do have some more right there in the middle of the tables in case you need them.

"At the end, we'll have a few judges we've grabbed from among our more elderly full-time residents, and we'll give awards to the tallest, the most creative, and the most beautiful. But the catch is, you only have one hour. Now go find a spot! We've got them on both sides of the table."

Kelli found a spot first and was looking at what she had to work with, organizing and straightening everything. When someone took the spot across from her, she looked up and was surprised to see Parker. Especially since there were still other open spots available.

He had seen her embarrassingly less than perfect so many times. And not just on the plane or at the dinner or doing a million little things at the mansion, but over *years*. In fact, anytime she did something embarrassing, it seemed to be when he was around to witness it. It was baffling that he sought her out.

Especially since there was a spot conspicuously open next to Addison.

Not that Kelli was complaining.

But as much as she felt herself being pulled toward Parker, a warning voice kept nagging at her, reminding her that things might not work out. She didn't have the best track record with guys, and she knew she was feeling more vulnerable than usual right now and needed to be cautious.

"Ready?" HallieMae called out. "Go!"

She smiled at seeing Parker straighten and organize all of his supplies before he got started, too.

But then she turned her focus to her gingerbread house. She had gotten the idea last year to do a standard house with a pointed roof, then have a slightly smaller house stacked on top of it, the front and back each with a triangle cut-out so it could sit nicely on it, then a third house on top that was slightly smaller than the second. Then she wanted to decorate it whimsically and fun. But an hour wasn't much time, so she'd have to work quickly.

Every once in a while, she'd glance over at Parker's creation, which looked like a cute beach cottage, and those art skills of his were definitely at work. He was working just as focused and furiously as she was.

She glanced up when his phone buzzed on the table and saw a picture of an adorable woman, with the name showing as "Mom." With as little time as they had, she figured he would ignore it and call her back later, but he didn't. He picked it up and answered as he was walking toward the other end of the big open space to chat.

Watching him compromised the time she had to work, but she couldn't help glancing up every few seconds and trying to guess how well he and his mom got along. Every time she looked, he was laughing and smiling. It might have possibly made her heart melt into a giant puddle of goo. She knew several people who had perfectly wonderful moms, and they got annoyed when she called. They didn't have a clue how lucky they were to even have a mom!

She knew she could never seriously date a guy who didn't respect his mom. He got bonus points if his mom was amazing and wonderful, and if there was a possibility that she could one day be her mother-in-law. And when that day came, she wasn't going to call her by her name—she was going to call whoever it was "Mom."

*Kelli!* She practically shouted to herself so she'd stop. Thinking those kinds of things, while she was watching this beautiful man she shouldn't date, seeing him smile as he put everything on hold to talk to his mom, was as good as walking right into the danger zone and completely ignoring the flashing warning lights.

So she turned all of her focus back to her gingerbread house, and before long, Parker finished his call and came back and did the same thing.

Once she got the structure all in place, she started with the decorating. For the bottom house, she decided to use the pastel-colored circular flat wafer candies as the shingles. It was her dad's favorite way to decorate the roof, so she did it to bring a little bit of him here. She put the frosting on as glue and then started placing the wafers.

As she placed the first row of shingles, her annual discussion with her dad about whether the colors should be random or done in a pattern came to mind. She let her dad win this one and placed them randomly.

With each one she placed, though, the sadness at not doing this with him started to creep in. Making gingerbread houses wasn't something she had ever done with her mom—it was something her dad had started their first Christmas without her. He said they needed to come up with some new traditions that were just for the two of them since that was their family now.

That first Christmas had been hard, and Kelli hadn't dealt with everything very well. But she and her dad creating something unique and very much them had made her feel like maybe the two of them could take on the world, as long as they had each other. She missed him.

Before she knew it, a tear was running down her cheek. She brushed it away and kept working. It felt wrong to be doing this without him. This was their thing. She and her dad together. Doing this alone wasn't right.

Not sharing all of their Christmas traditions together wasn't right.

Not spending Christmas with him wasn't right.

More tears fell. One even splashed down onto the table next to her gingerbread house.

Her dad taking off with his new family and not inviting her wasn't the same as her mom leaving. She could still text her dad, after all. But somehow that familiar grief of being left behind by a parent, of not being good enough to keep them around, settled on her and made her feel like she was going to crumble in on herself.

Her breathing quickened and hitched and she tried to keep it under control and quiet so it wasn't obvious to anyone else. Before long, she could no longer see the gingerbread house through the tears, so she hurried away in the direction of a hallway where she guessed the restrooms might be.

It had been the wrong choice. She tried the knobs on all three doors, but there weren't restrooms there—just locked storage areas. She turned to run out of the building itself if she had to and ran right into Parker's chest.

"Hey, are you okay?" He put his hands on her shoulders and pushed her back just enough to see her face. A face she very much didn't want him to see because it was tear-stained and mascara-stained and probably all red and blotchy and she knew she wasn't a pretty crier. That was why she never did it in public. But she was a mess and couldn't exactly stop the tears.

He only glanced at her face long enough to see she was upset, though, before he wrapped his strong arms around her and held her tight. She felt like she was completely falling apart, but he held her, keeping all the pieces together as she sobbed. As she grieved over the mom she lost half a lifetime ago and the dad she had been losing slowly over the past year, and then very quickly over the past week. She grieved for the scared little girl she was, the girl who couldn't seem to be perfect enough to keep either of them.

Parker didn't talk; he just held her as she silently cried, soaking the shoulder of his shirt. She felt the losses so strongly and so deeply, yet as she wept in Parker's arms, she felt more safe and protected than she'd felt in her life.

Finally, the tears ran out, and she was still in one piece. She let go of her fierce hold on him, and he loosened his arms enough that she could've stepped out of his embrace if she wanted to, but close enough that they were still there if she needed them. She wiped at the tears on her face, horrified that he was seeing how awful she must look right now.

Then she let out a breath of a laugh. "I am so sorry for doing this to your shirt." She wiped at the massive wet spot on his shirt. A wet spot that also held a good amount of mascara.

"The shirt's fine." He glanced in the direction of the main room. "There's an exit only about eight feet past the end of this hall. What do you say we get out of here?"

She nodded and wiped at the remnants of tears on her face while he went back into the main room and grabbed their jackets, then came back and held hers as she slipped her arms into the sleeves. Then she stayed tight to his side as he put an arm around her and led them outside and away from people she might see at work.

"Who do you normally spend Christmas with?" His question was soft and concerned and felt like a warm blanket on a cold day.

"My dad. He's spending this Christmas with his new wife and kids."

Parker led her through the dark and onto the lighted path that she knew would take them around the gardens and up the road to the mansion. "And I'm guessing that you normally make gingerbread houses together?"

She nodded.

"It's a tradition in my family, too. It's hard not being with them."

She looked up at him, so grateful that he understood and that he was leading her away from the crowd.

"Is your dad a Hallmark Christmas movie fan?"

She shook her head.

"Good. It's not a tradition in my family either. Watching a movie and drinking peppermint hot chocolate are both on the list—how about we head back and have a marathon? Then we won't need the two points from the group activity."

She smiled—something she wouldn't have guessed she'd feel like doing at all tonight. "Deal. But only if I get to pick the movie."

# Chapter Twelve

PARKER

*P*arker woke up to the most beautiful weather he had ever experienced over the holidays before. As much as he was dreading everything that was also a Christmas tradition for his own family, there were parts of celebrating the season that he was actually enjoying. He hadn't seen that coming.

And today, an excitement ran through everything. It was Christmas Eve, all twelve ZentCube employees were helping out at the Christmas village that ran through a huge portion of the resort grounds, and Graham was returning with his wife, Tessa, and baby Hope. The Christmas Eve dinner was tonight, and Kelli was back to smiling again.

He had been curious last night and had wanted to hear more about her family situation, but he wasn't about to ask and have her go through more grief. But as they were making hot chocolate, she told about how it had just been her and her dad growing up, and that he recently got remarried and didn't want her to spend Christmas with his new family.

And if that wasn't bad enough, she didn't have a mom. He had assumed that her mom had passed away, but then Kelli told him that she'd left them when Kelli was thirteen. When he asked, she'd said she got a birthday card from her for the first three years, but she hadn't seen her after that day, and she hadn't heard from her in ten years.

He thought back to how awkward he was at thirteen, and couldn't even imagine having one of his parents leave at that age. It had to have been devastating to her.

It made him grateful all over again that he had been lucky enough to have two parents who were both great people and who loved each other and loved him and Ethan. They had even been willing to cancel an anniversary trip that they'd been planning for decades just so he wouldn't be alone at Christmas. And knowing them, if he hadn't been invited on this trip, they might've canceled even after he told them not to.

Last night, he'd been careful to pay attention and follow Kelli's lead. As much as he would've loved to just hold her all evening, protecting her from harm, he hadn't known what she'd needed. She'd been vulnerable, and it would've felt like a violation if he just stepped in and assumed that he knew how she needed to grieve.

And, based on the movie she picked, a lighthearted, funny Christmas romance was her coping mechanism of choice. He had sat in the recliner next to her in the theater room, and they'd laughed hard and often. That laugh that he loved. That smile that he loved. That teasing back-and-forth banter that he loved.

As he had been sitting there with her, feelings he hadn't fully understood or even known he had burst to the surface. And now that they were fully noticeable, he realized that those feelings weren't new. He had been falling for her since the beginning when he first started working at ZentCube.

He'd been falling through their awkward date, through the awkwardness of working together in the weeks afterward, and through all their office pranks over the years.

He'd thought he'd pretty successfully suppressed all feelings he had for Kelli during the two years he'd been dating Stephanie, but now he wondered if, deep down, during all that time, he'd been subconsciously filing all his feelings for her in a storage box in his heart that he hadn't even known he had.

And by coming here, he had opened that box, letting his feelings for her burst free, filling him with a happiness he hadn't felt in a long time, and allowing him to fall for her completely.

Before long, they were joined in the theater room by Merit and Elise, and eventually by a handful of other ZentCube employees. With all the laughing, it felt like a party. He didn't know if Kelli was amazing at bouncing back after hard things, or if she was just excellent at putting on a happy face over inner turmoil. Whichever it was, she was a lot stronger than he had given her credit for.

The Christmas village that Elise and her team had set up was amazing. A big North Pole archway led into the village, and a train ran around the outside of the grassy area, enclosing the village within. A pathway led through a sugarplum forest, another led through Bethlehem to see a living nativity, and another led through Santa's workshop, complete with Santa and his elves at the end. There were tables with crafts, booths with food, and kids and parents everywhere.

Each of the ZentCube employees was helping with a

different part of the village, and he and Kelli were, sadly, not assigned to the same place. Parker was helping get kids onto the train, letting it run around the track, then helping one group of kids unload and the next ones get on board. But from where he worked, he could see Kelli at a table, helping kids make headbands they could wear that had reindeer antlers wrapped with little blinking lights.

Just as he was getting a new group of kids onto the train, Merit, Graham, and Tessa—whom he had first met at a ZentCube Christmas party—came into the village. Graham was holding his wife's hand and cradling their baby with the other arm, looking blissfully happy.

As soon as Parker got the train started, he turned to them and said hello, shaking hands.

"Parker," Graham said, "I'd like you to meet my daughter, Hope."

"Wow," Parker said, leaning in closer to the perfect child in Graham's arms. "She is beautiful."

"Would you like to hold her?"

His eyes flew to Graham's, then Tessa's. They both looked like they were saying yes, so he looked around, hoping to find somewhere to wash his hands—he'd been around a lot of kids today—but he didn't spot anything. Tessa opened her bag and pulled out a wipe. He quickly cleaned his hands, and then carefully cradled the baby as Graham transferred her into his arms.

The baby was sleeping, so her eyes were closed and her face was perfect and peaceful and so beautiful. Silky soft brown hair curled on top of her head, and as he cradled her in his arms, she snuggled into him. Holding her was like holding a bit of heaven.

He knew that most guys his age or younger didn't spend

their time dreaming of starting a family, but Parker had been dreaming about it for a while. He couldn't wait until it was his own child he was holding. When he'd been engaged to Stephanie, he thought he'd get that chance before long. When she had broken it off, losing not just her, but the family he'd thought they'd one day have, had been hard.

But she had revealed a part of herself during the breakup that he hadn't seen before. Or that he hadn't wanted to see. He was grateful that she'd broken it off because he never would have. And now, holding this baby, it hit him all over again what a mistake marrying her would've been.

He smiled at the baby. He still hoped for this one day. There was something about holding the beautiful bundle that made him feel like any worries or troubles he had just washed away. He felt as peaceful as she looked, and he could've stood there holding her for hours. He shifted his arms a bit so he could pass her back, but when Merit stopped the train as the kids came back around and started loading and unloading the next group, he took the opportunity to hold her longer.

"You two must be in heaven every second of the day," he said, looking up at Graham and Tessa.

"We are," Graham said.

Then Graham's eyes shifted from him and baby Hope to his left, so he turned to see what had pulled Graham's attention. Kelli was watching him with a curious expression on her face. She smiled when their eyes met, and he held her gaze for a moment—long enough that he was sure that Graham would ask about the two of them, but he didn't. The man just looked down, like he was trying to hide a smile.

When Graham raised his head again, he looked to the sky. "Beautiful weather, isn't it?"

Parker nodded, keeping his eyes on the baby.

"A cold front is supposed to blow in later tonight, though, and there's a chance of snow if you can believe it. So we might get a white Christmas even on the beach."

This time Parker did look up. That was too bad; he had been hoping that Christmas would be very unlike the snow he was used to having at Christmastime.

When the train full of kids came around the second time, he figured he really should get back to work. He reluctantly passed the baby back to Graham, and the proud parents went to show off their baby to the rest of the Zent-Cube employees. He figured Merit would go with them, but he stayed and helped get the next group of kids onto the train.

Once the train pulled away, Merit nodded over at Kelli, who was now fawning over the baby herself. "How are things going with you two?"

Parker flinched in surprise at the question. He hadn't realized that Merit had witnessed his silent exchange with Kelli, too. "Um, fine?"

Merit looked back at Parker. "You like her then?"

"So much more than I should."

Merit shook his head, chuckling. "Graham really does have a gift."

"What do you mean?"

"He can..." Merit looked up like he was trying to find a way to explain. "It's like he can see connections between people, even if they've never met each other. It's helpful when you're negotiating contracts with other companies, and ZentCube wouldn't be where it's at without him. But he has an uncanny ability to tell when two people have happily-ever-after potential."

Parker just stared at Merit, not fully taking in what he was trying to say.

Merit glanced toward another part of the village, smiling, and Parker suddenly wondered if that was where Elise was currently. "Graham needed to send me on vacation—long story—and he chose here because of Elise. I hadn't even met her yet, and he knew."

"That's actually pretty sweet. And helpful."

He chuckled. "Yeah. Even if it feels anything but when he makes you take a break from the company. But he didn't only do it for me. Even if you don't see all of it, he knows the people in our company pretty well, and he keeps a list of people he'd like to bring on this trip. Then he just hopes they're free over Christmas. Some of them get recommended by their managers, and some he specifically asks the managers to check on."

"He uses the Christmas trip to set people up on dates?"

"Nah. He doesn't like to meddle like that. He's always confident enough in the connection he sees that he figures all he needs to do is get the two people in a place where they can interact and magic will happen."

"And does it?"

"A lot of times, yes. It's his goal that whoever comes to this won't be alone the next Christmas. They rarely are."

Parker stared off at the ocean, blown away. "He's got that good of a track record?"

Merit nodded.

"I'm not sure why he brought *me* here, then—I'm too flawed. And I just got out of a serious relationship at the beginning of October. I'm not exactly the kind of person you can set up with someone and expect a successful happily ever after."

"Graham has had both you and Kelli on his list since last Christmas."

Parker drew back in surprise. "But he met Stephanie at the Christmas party last year. Did he not know I was engaged?"

"He knew."

Parker's eyes flew to Merit.

"You brought her to the summer social, too." Merit studied Parker's expression, which he guessed was showing something close to bewilderment. "He talked to both of you enough to know that the connection between you and her wasn't right, and he was hoping you'd figure it out before this trip." Merit studied him cautiously before carefully adding, "Because he also saw a connection that was right between you and Kelli."

Parker's mouth went dry. He tried to swallow. "I think he's wrong about me. I've got too many issues to ever be good enough for her."

The train came back around again, and Parker stopped it. He and Merit got the group of kids off and a new group on, and then started the new group around the village.

"What makes you think you're out of her league?"

He let out a huff of a humorless laugh. "My ex-fiancée spelled it out for me."

"How?"

Parker hadn't told anyone the specifics. Not Darren, not Adam, not any of his other friends, not even his parents. He had no idea why he felt compelled to tell Merit. Maybe he just needed it off his shoulders for a bit.

"She said she was just going to walk away, but she cared about me, so she gave me a list of all the ways I didn't measure up. Apparently, she'd been adding to the list from the start and, without telling me, had given me a date to overcome those flaws. The day she ended it was that date.

"I guess she should've added 'Not self-aware' to the list, because not only had I not guessed that she had a list, but I hadn't figured out what was on it, and I definitely hadn't been working on fixing them."

"Ouch," Merit said, wincing. "That's harsh. What kinds of things were on it?"

It still hurt to think about it, and he was embarrassed by every single item on it. "Some little things, like the way I pronounced some words, that I didn't have the content of the notifications on my phone hidden, that I didn't use an umbrella in the rain, that I danced in the car, some of the clothes I wore, stuff like that. And then some bigger things, like getting too focused on projects and not putting her as my number one priority."

The list was long. Some of the things he stopped doing immediately. For others, he didn't understand what he'd been doing wrong, so he'd had no idea how to fix them. Those had been the most maddening ones. The ones that brought him down the most. The ones that he didn't even let himself think about, because they stabbed him in the heart too painfully if he did.

And out of all the people he could've listed his flaws to, he couldn't believe he just told the CEO of the company he worked at.

Merit shook his head. "It sounds like a list only someone who didn't have that connection would make. I wouldn't put too much stock in it."

Merit was assuming too much. He hadn't seen the list. He hadn't seen the look on Steph's face when she'd given it to him. He hadn't heard them in her voice.

Parker had.

"Let me ask you this, then," Merit said, studying him. "Is Kelli very similar to your ex?"

Parker looked over to where Kelli held Hope, who must've woken up because Kelli was making faces at her. He watched her smiling and laughing for several long moments. Kelli was every bit as bright, happy, and nonjudgmental when she was entertaining a baby as she was talking to a stranger, a coworker, or a homeless woman.

He shook his head. She very much wasn't.

Did Graham think that Kelli would be able to look past all of Parker's faults and shortcomings and see the man who had fallen for her so completely? Maybe. He wasn't sure that Graham was correct, but he very much hoped that he was.

# Chapter Thirteen

KELLI

Kelli had imagined that the Christmas Eve dinner in the mansion would be idyllic. The sixteen of them would all eat amazing food and talk and laugh and even if you were on the outside looking in and couldn't hear what was being said, you could tell that it was a happy group, enjoying each other's company.

In a lot of ways it was. The food was fantastic and there was lots of talking and laughing. There were also hilarious stories of Christmases gone wrong, a few spontaneous bursts into song with everyone joining in, a dish of roasted butternut squash spilled, Davis and Addison looking at each other like maybe there were some sparks between the two of them, some impressions of actors in Christmas movies saying iconic lines, a couple of people who had a bit too much to drink and became quite entertaining themselves, and some sharing of favorite Christmas traditions. It felt more than idyllic; it felt like a family.

The best part, though, was sitting next to Parker through the whole thing. He was funny and sweet, and for as long as she had been working on the same floor as him, nothing at all like she had assumed. And he kept looking over at her in a way that made her heart somehow melt and do flips at the same time.

Then, Tessa told a story about how she grew up in a rural area and their family was super poor, but they decided that a neighboring family needed gifts for Christmas worse than they did. As they were sneaking across the fields to deliver them, they ran into the family they were headed toward, who just happened to be sneaking through the fields at the exact same time to give everything they had for Christmas to her family.

While Tessa told the story, Parker had his hand resting at the side of his chair and Kelli's was resting at the side of her chair. And all she could think of was how much she wanted to touch his hand. To reach out and close that distance, make that connection.

But it was scary. No, it was terrifying. What if she wasn't ready for this? What if it was a big mistake that she would regret once they got back to real life and saw each other at work five days a week?

What if he didn't want that connection? What if she reached out but was denied, and then she just ended up feeling stupid and had to find a way to avoid him for the rest of the trip?

She was feeling pulled to him so strongly, though, that she had to try. With a hand that managed to only be a little shaky, she reached across the six inches of space separating the two of them and ironically, just like in the story Tessa was telling, he was reaching across the space between them as well.

Their pinkies touched first, just brushing up against each

other so softly that she held her hand there, just taking in the gentle, sweet feel of his skin barely touching hers. Then, in a burst of bravery, she linked her pinky with his.

It was such a simple thing, and it was such a small part of her that was touching him, but it was so much more than a casual or accidental brush. Their pinky fingers were entwined, *choosing* to hold onto each other.

He had caught her from falling. He had danced with her. He had held her in his arms as she cried, keeping her in one piece. Yet somehow this felt more intimate. More daring. More like a line had been crossed. A choice had been made. A choice to be reckless and brave and vulnerable and fearless.

When Tessa finished her story, Parker turned to look at her, his expression so deep and layered that she could've stared into his eyes for days trying to figure out all of it. But before she got enough of a chance, Graham clapped his hands and said, "Alright, everyone head into the family room —we're playing Christmas Charades!"

Parker and Kelli were placed on different teams, so they sat on opposite sides of the room. But she found his eyes wandering to her just as often as hers went to him. Now, though, the night felt charged, and she wondered if she was ever going to feel tired enough to head to bed. Most people seemed to feel that way, even after all the laughing from the bad acting and the hilarious guesses, so all sixteen of them played game after game, until people finally started to break away, and one by one, go to bed.

Merit walked to the windows and looked out. "I guess when we brought sixteen adults and a baby from a place as snowy as Colorado, we couldn't help but bring some snow with us."

"It's snowing?" Kelli jumped up and ran to the window, pressing her hands against the window at the sides of her face so she could see past the light in the room. "It's snowing! Is it even supposed to snow here?"

"It can sometimes," Parker said as he stepped up to her side and looked out. "Just not very often. I checked before we came."

"We should go out in it. You all brought coats, right?"

The handful of people who were still in the room looked at her with confused faces.

"You want to go out in the storm?" Graham asked.

She looked around at everyone. "Don't you all go outside whenever it storms?"

"Not if I can help it," Elise said.

Roman shook his head. "Me neither."

"But storms are so exciting." It was baffling to her that none of them raced outside whenever it rained or snowed so they could experience it in person instead of just from behind a window.

"I'll go with you."

Parker's words were as attractive as the smile on his face. She gave him a big, grateful smile back. Then she hurried up to her room to put on her coat, boots, gloves, hat, and scarf before he had a chance to change his mind. When she came back down to the main floor, he was already waiting by the door, all bundled up, and they headed outside.

The air was cold, and with each breath in, it felt like the cold was zinging into her body. In Colorado, it always seemed to warm up when it snowed. Like the clouds were a blanket in the sky, holding in all the warmth. But the wind had blown hard to bring in this storm, and it had blown all that warmth they'd felt earlier in the day to someone else.

"Do you think we just got too acclimated to the warmth since we got here, and that's why the cold is such a shock?"

"Maybe," Parker said as he looked out across the ocean. "It definitely feels colder."

Kelli held her hand out to catch a snowflake as they neared the bottom of the road that their mansion was on. "Or maybe it's just because this snow is wetter."

"Are you cold? Because we can head back."

"I'm fine. Unless you're cold?"

He smiled at her in a way that made her warm down to her toes. She would be just fine out here as long as she was with Parker. "I'm fine, too. But we could just watch the storm from the balcony at the mansion. That way we'd be close if things get too cold."

"No, because look!" Kelli pointed to the main resort area as it came into view. "Look at all the Christmas lights! Oh, it's so beautiful. We *have* to go see them in the snow."

The Christmas village was completely lit up in colorful lights, and so were all the buildings and pathways, even more than they had been when they'd gone to the dance. Every building and the trees and pathways around it were lit up in a different color, so one building was all purple, one was all green, one was blue, one was red, and one was white. An archway of lights went down the main pathway, each arch a different color, making a rainbow. It was the most incredible display of lights she had ever seen.

And with the snow falling, all the lights seemed to twinkle, like a magic spell had been cast over the whole resort. "I am so sad for everyone who stayed back in the mansion."

Parker looked at her, smiling, and she thought it was possibly the most amazing smile she had ever seen. She snuggled in close to him as they walked down the first pathway of lights, and he wrapped an arm around her, keeping her warm and protected. She hadn't even thought about snuggling into him before she did it—it had just seemed so natural. Maybe all her fears had just been stupid excuses to not be brave.

It wasn't like she had the best track record when it came to dating, though. She usually just went with what made her heart happy and kept logic out of it. She was trying to use logic this time around, and logic told her that she shouldn't be dating someone who could make things awkward at work.

It told her that she shouldn't be dating *anyone* right now. She knew that a man with a great family was her kryptonite, and with things being so unsettled with her dad, she knew her heart was extra unprotected. She needed to keep it far from danger, not snuggle up to danger.

So she ran. A bunch of pathways converged in one big open crossroads, with lights twisting up the five street lamps surrounding the area. She just needed to put a teeny bit of space between them, and she hoped Parker saw it as her running to the magical spot instead of running from him. She put her arms straight out and turned around in a slow circle, her face turned up at the sky, soaking in the beauty of the meandering snow falling softly on her, the lights casting a warm glow on everything.

She stopped turning and looked at Parker, who was looking at her with the same expression that she'd just had as she'd marveled at the lights and snow. It made her want to go to him. To snuggle into him. Maybe she didn't need to run from danger. Maybe all she needed was to know what her weaknesses were, to be cautious when it came to them, and to be brave when it came to everything else.

Because this man smiling at her from a dozen feet away was so very perfect.

A loud crack sounded off in the distance. The lights all over the resort shut off at once, plunging everywhere into darkness, and Kelli screamed. She hadn't even noticed there was a new moon until she didn't have even its light. And with the clouds from the snowstorm covering the sky, even the light from the stars was hidden. The silence was everywhere.

She wasn't afraid of the dark.

But this wasn't the dark. This was the absence of everything, including sounds. It made her feel as though there wasn't anything around her. Like everything had fallen away, leaving her drifting and alone with nothing to hold on to, nothing to ground her. "Parker?" she called out, her heart racing as she shuffled forward, hands out, desperate to grasp hold of anything. She wished she had brought her cell phone so she would have her own source of light.

"I'm here. I'm coming."

Hearing his voice helped her to slow her panicked breathing. She hoped that her heart would take the hint and calm down, too, but it didn't.

Parker must've pushed a button to light up his watch because she could suddenly see a faint light heading toward her. The light was enough to give her something to fix her eyes on, making it feel like she wasn't alone in a void. She stopped moving her arms in front of her, frantic to find something to grasp, and just kept her eyes on the light as it bobbed its way toward her.

And then Parker was there and she grabbed hold of him tight, pulling herself into that strong chest of his, and a peace washed over her. He wrapped his arms around her, rubbing the middle of her back in calming strokes. She felt safe in his arms, and this time, both her breathing and her heart started to calm.

"It's unnerving. I know. But I'm sure they'll have backup generators going soon. There will be enough light to find our way back before long."

She nodded and laid her head on his chest as the snow fell all around them in the complete darkness, wishing she could hear the comforting sound of his heart through his coat. But she could hear his breathing, and that was enough. She was so grateful that he was so quick to help, so good at comforting her, and so sweet and thoughtful. He was a source of light all on his own.

For so long, she hadn't let herself notice all of the good things about him. At first, it had been out of fear that things would be even more awkward at work than they'd been after their first disastrous date. Then it had been because they had both started dating other people. They'd both been single for a while now, but she'd still held back out of fear that her heart couldn't handle being open to the risks again.

He moved one of his arms that had been on her back to her side and said, "Will you tap my watch?"

She reached a gloved finger up and gave his watch a tap, lighting up the screen and illuminating his beautiful face as a smile spread across his lips.

"Merry Christmas, Kelli Ellis."

"It's after midnight?" He nodded, and she smiled so big that she felt it breathe excitement into her whole body. "Merry Christmas, Parker Brockbank."

She had gotten to know and admire him here so much more deeply than she ever had at work. She had seen the goodness in him. As he held her in the darkness, the two of them seeming to be the only things that existed, she realized that when they got back to the office, things *couldn't* be the same. They had already both been changed too much to ever go back to the way they were.

So maybe there wasn't harm in moving forward. She knew her heart needed protecting, but Parker had shown that he was pretty good at protecting her when she was most vulnerable—maybe she could trust him with her heart, too.

A hum sounded in the distance, followed closely by the buzz of the streetlights above. Only every third light turned on, and only at a fraction of its usual brightness, but it was enough to show that things other than the two of them existed. Enough to show the faint outline of Parker's face.

And enough to show a sparkle of light in his eyes as he looked at her. At her back, his arms shifted as he pulled one glove off. Then he brought his bare hand to her face, wiping a few melted snowflakes from her forehead and temple with his fingertips. His hands were so warm and soft and gentle, and as his fingers got to her cheeks, she leaned into them, soaking in his touch.

Then she took off one of her gloves and reached her warm hand up to his face. She brushed her palm against his neck, her thumb resting just in front of his ear, her fingertips finding their way under his hat and into his hair.

Linking pinkies with him at dinner had felt bold and risky. As her eyes went back and forth between his eyes and the faint outline of his lips in the darkness, the thought of kissing him felt so far beyond bold and risky that she was afraid she would back out.

Except it also felt so right.

And from the way he was looking at her, she could tell that it felt right to him, too.

So she rose on her toes slightly and pulled him toward her with both the hand on his neck and the hand clutching onto the coat at his chest. He responded by wrapping his warm hand around the back of her neck and pulling her closer at the waist.

She pressed her lips against his, soft and careful. As they kissed, their cold noses brushed each other's cheeks, but their lips warmed quickly. He let out a whisper of a groan, and she melted into him, loving that their kiss was having as strong of an effect on him as it was on her.

Everything in the world seemed to fade around them, but instead of it being terrifying like when the power had first gone out, this time it made her feel like she had everything she needed right there in her little bubble.

He deepened the kiss, and she knew she was a goner. She was handing him her entire heart, and he was putting his strong hands around it, keeping it safe.

# Chapter Fourteen

PARKER

*P*arker woke to the sound of Graham and Merit strolling down the hallways, singing a very loud and very off-key rendition of *We Wish You a Merry Christmas* as they knocked on everyone's doors. Parker rolled over to look at the alarm clock on his bedside table, but apparently, the power was still out. He picked up his phone—which he'd plugged in, but was now down to ten percent power—and saw that it was barely seven a.m. Five a.m. Denver time.

He pushed his phone into the pocket of his pajamas because his parents hadn't known when they'd be on shore and available to call, and he didn't want to miss it. Then he took a look outside. It was still dark and everything was wet and very cold-looking, but it was beautiful. And not exactly the white Christmas Graham had been rooting for.

He headed downstairs with every other bleary-eyed ZentCube employee, most of whom had blankets wrapped around their shoulders and shuffled more than walked. He was used to waking up at five-thirty Denver time, so this wasn't too far out of the ordinary, but he also never went to bed as late as he had last night if he had work the next day.

They all gathered in the family room around the tree. As soon as he saw Kelli and the way her face lit up as soon as she saw him, he decided that any amount of sleep deprivation was just fine with him if it involved being able to see her.

The sun hadn't risen yet, but Graham and Merit had placed dozens of candles around the room. He couldn't take his eyes off Kelli, marveling at how beautiful she looked in the golden glow of the candles. He wished he could place kisses on those beautiful lips, on her temples, and all along that beautiful jawline.

Instead, as he stepped up to her, he reached for her hand, brought it to his lips, and brushed kisses across her knuckles. She closed her eyes and sighed. Maybe believing in the "magic of Christmas" wasn't something just for childhood.

"Sit down, sit down," Graham said. "Everyone find a seat."

Parker sat down next to Kelli on one of the couches and listened as Merit told a story about his childhood Christmases. They had been super poor, and any presents they got were inexpensive. So his mom had started a tradition of going around and having everyone say what they were grateful for before opening anything. By the time they had all finished, they felt like they already had everything they could want. So the presents were just icing on the cake and they were always happier with Christmas than any of their friends—even the ones who got everything they had wished for.

As they went around the circle, each person saying what

they were grateful for, he thought about how much he had been dreading this Christmas, and how it had turned out so much better than he could've ever hoped. He had a lot to be grateful for.

Including last night. He'd wanted to kiss Kelli for quite a while, but he had wanted that moment to be perfect for her. He never would've chosen their first kiss to be in the freezing cold, their coats and shoes getting soaked, with the power out, scaring her. But even with all that, it had ended up being perfect after all. There may not have been electricity at the resort, but he had felt electricity coursing through him plenty.

The kiss had blown his mind. Never had a kiss felt like that before. As they had stood there in their winter gear and he held her close, everything fell away, all his worries and cares, and all that was left was a beautiful woman who was more amazing than he'd ever known, who seemed to want to be with him as much as he wanted to be with her.

His imagined perfect evening with her also would've included an unseasonably warm night, a clear sky full of stars, and Christmas lights surrounding them. But they had found a bench and sat down in the near darkness and enjoyed a peaceful silence that could only come from a power outage and falling snow, her head against his shoulder and his arm around hers. They had talked for hours on that bench, and he couldn't think of anything more perfect. And he couldn't imagine himself falling more fully for anyone.

But now that it was morning, fears started settling in. He wanted things to work out between him and Kelli more than he'd ever wanted it with anyone else. And things were going so well between the two of them. But he had thought that things were going well between him and Stephanie, too, so he didn't trust that he could tell when things were going well or not.

As it came time to open Secret Santa presents, Merit and Elise sat next to the tree and started handing them out, one at a time. After a handful of people opened their presents and then found out who their Secret Santa was, more often than not it was from someone each person had clearly shown signs of liking throughout their trip.

When Thomas stopped grinning enough that he could talk after opening a Chia Pet that was a sculpture of Bob Ross and finding out it was from Joy, he said, "I'm having a hard time believing that the names we drew for Secret Santas were random."

"No, at one point they were," Graham said, "I swear. Carla gave me the random list. And then I shifted things around just a bit when I thought it might be more...beneficial for someone to try to get to know someone else a little better." The man just grinned unapologetically for switching around names.

Parker wondered if his Secret Santa had been selected by Graham, or if it had been random. He had gotten Kelli's name, and with what Merit had told him at the Christmas Village, he assumed it wasn't random. He wasn't all the way sure, though, until Elise handed him a package and the wrapping paper on it was of cats, all wearing Santa hats. He laughed out loud and looked at Kelli as soon as he saw it.

He carefully took off the paper and opened the box. A shirt was folded in an exact rectangle, with a handwritten paper on top that was so perfectly written it could've been a font. He read it out loud. "I'll tell you right now that you will look great in this. Paired with jeans that you also look great in. And your hair looks pretty fantastic, too." And, of course, the shirt was blue.

Kelli hadn't known the significance behind the shirt, which made it mean even more to him. He smiled at her, and said, "Thank you," and she grinned back until Elise handed her a gift. Then she looked at it with curiosity, and he was suddenly nervous.

But he loved the sound of her laugh when she saw the wrapping paper. He'd been so excited when he found the paper at a gift shop on the Boardwalk. It was silver and gold and sparkly, so it kind of fit the Christmas theme, but it was probably meant to wrap a New Year's gift because it was covered in glasses of champagne. They weren't water goblets, exactly, but he'd gotten a Sharpie and personally drawn a mushroom at the bottom of every glass.

She unwrapped the gift and lifted the lid on the box. He watched her face closely as she picked up the paper where he had written, "For next time, when we continue our new Christmas tradition." Then, still holding the paper in one hand, she lifted the "Hallmark movie-watching blanket" out of the box and hugged it to her chest.

He had sat at the desk in his room for a long time, pen hovering over the paper, trying to figure out what he wanted to write, and then being nervous about writing something so bold and presumptive. Eventually, he just did it and hoped for the best. By the heart-stopping way she was looking at him now, he'd made the right choice.

Not long after the last present was opened, he felt the buzz of a text and pulled out his phone, expecting it to be from his parents or his brother, but it was from his friend, Josh.

JOSH: Hey, buddy! Merry Christmas!

I was just thinking of you, and wondering if you're leaning one way or another on that job offer. I would love to start working with you again.

No pressure. You have until New Year's to decide, of course. I'm just curious.

Parker excused himself and headed away from the group in the family room and found a seat in the living room at the front of the mansion, trying to figure out how to respond to the text. He hadn't spent much time even thinking about it while they'd been on this trip. Before he left, he had been seriously considering taking the job. Josh was a good friend, and it would be great to work with him again. And it was a great offer.

Although he hadn't put a ton of thought into it, he knew himself well enough to know that his loyalties lay with Zent-Cube. And whenever the job offer did happen to cross his mind while he'd been at The Royal Palm, all he could think of was Kelli. He had spent two years and seven months working on the same floor as her as co-workers and occasional pranksters. How great would it be to see her daily as they dated?

He took a moment to imagine it, his smile growing bigger the longer he pictured it.

But what if he messed things up? What if he hadn't been ready to start dating again like Darren thought he was? What would happen when she discovered all the negative things about him that Stephanie had discovered?

By that same token, how awful would it be to see her daily if things didn't work out between them? Sure, they had known each other for quite a while, but their relationship was new. There were so many ways he could screw it up, and it didn't matter how awkward their first date was and the months working together following it—that would be nothing compared to how awful it would be to see her daily if they broke up.

He knew her now. He loved her now. He wasn't the same person who had shown up at the airport last Saturday morning. Even the thought of their relationship not working out felt like a stab in his chest. He wasn't sure he could fully comprehend how painful it would be to see her daily if they broke up.

Maybe getting this other job offer right now, where he not only got to spend the equivalent of a month and a half dating Kelli during a single week, but he got space to decide if the job change was right, was some divine timing. He took a deep breath and then responded to the text.

> PARKER: There are a lot of things keeping me at ZentCube.

> A lot of people, too. One in particular.

> I'm not ready to say no to your company's offer yet, though. I just need to see how a few things here work out first.

> JOSH: Ahh. I understand. No worries. You've got time to figure it out.

> And remember that I'm happy to answer any questions, anytime.

> Or do anything else I can to sway you to join our team, especially since you have so many things swaying you in ZentCube's direction.

PARKER: Thanks, Josh.

Parker put his phone back in his pocket and hoped—even made a Christmas wish—that he would be able to turn down Josh's job offer. Because nothing would make him happier than spending every day at ZentCube with Kelli.

# Chapter Fifteen

## KELLI

Kelli admired the impossibly soft blanket that Parker had given her as she took it up to her room, folded it neatly, placed it at the bottom of her bed, and put his note on the nightstand. She was still on a high from their kiss last night and from their conversation on the bench. It had felt like a magical place where the two of them were the only people in the world, and they had all the time they wanted to just talk about everything.

The more she learned about Parker and the more time she spent with him, the more in love she fell.

Around the Christmas tree, she had caught him looking at her several times, and the look on his face was so sweet that it had made her heart do little leaps of joy. It was still doing little leaps of joy.

Someone yelled, "The power's back on!" and even though she could hear the hum of electricity, she still ran to the light switch in her room and turned it on just to check.

Yes! It really was. Her phone was still plugged in and sitting on her nightstand from last night. It had died before the power went out, but she hadn't made it upstairs to plug it in before they'd gone outside to enjoy the storm. She had hoped that the power would come on during the night and she'd wake up with a charged phone, but of course, it hadn't.

She sat on the bed, trying not to bounce in anticipation as she waited for it to charge enough to power back on. It took *forever*. After a minute or two, she checked to make sure that the cord was plugged in tight to her phone. It was. And then another minute or two later, she checked behind the nightstand to see if it was plugged tightly into the wall. It was.

Finally, the screen lit up as it booted back to life. There were probably going to be about a million messages from her dad, telling her Merry Christmas, asking her how things were going, and wondering why she wasn't responding to his texts. She couldn't wait to tell him all about the retreat and all about Parker.

But when the lock screen finally appeared, she only found one text—a video from her dad. He was in his suite in whatever Cabo San Lucas hotel he was staying in, an explosion of wrapping paper all around him.

"Hi, Sweetheart! Merry Christmas! I hope you've been having a blast on your trip. Sorry, I don't have time to chat—JoAnn and the girls have our day packed so full—but I'll call in a day or two. In the meantime, you keep living it up in Myrtle Beach and soaking in that sun. Talk soon. I love you."

He didn't have time to chat for even a couple of minutes. She didn't respond to the text. She took a slow, deep breath then placed her phone back on her nightstand and walked out of her room.

As she was walking past Parker's room on her way back

downstairs, he called out through his partially open door, "Hey, Kelli, wait!"

She paused, and he was at his door in a flash. "I'm video chatting with my family, and they want to meet you. What do you say?"

She should say no. Family was her weakness, and she knew it. But she was so curious about his, and she wanted to learn everything there was to know about him. Family was a big part of who a person was; how was she supposed to get to know him without getting to know his family? She should meet them.

*No, you shouldn't*, a voice said. But she reminded the voice that everything was okay, as long as she recognized her weakness and was cautious about it.

Besides, she was falling hard for Parker, and she really wanted to. And all she had gotten from her dad was a seventeen-second video text, so she felt a little cheated and was very much craving a family chat.

She smiled, said yes, and went into his room to where a laptop was open on his desk, showing three faces smiling at her. Parker offered her the desk chair and dragged over an armchair for him to sit next to her.

"Kelli, I would like you to meet my mom, Jessica, my dad, Bennett, and my brother, Ethan. Everyone, this is Kelli Ellis."

His mom had the same dark eyes and hair, only with grays throughout that looked elegant on her. And she had crow's feet at the sides of her eyes like she was a woman used to smiling. Kelli liked her instantly. His dad had lighter brown hair, but the same strong jawline and strong shoulders as Parker's. And his little brother was adorable. Like he was just as used to getting into good-natured mischief as he was to helping old ladies carry their groceries.

"Oh my goodness," his mom said. "Parker told us you were beautiful, but that was an understatement."

Kelli knew she was blushing. So much heat rose to her cheeks that they must be bright red.

His dad nodded. "He also tells us that you are smart, creative, talented, and dedicated, and that ZentCube wouldn't be as successful as it is if it weren't for you and your marketing skills."

She looked over at Parker and saw that he was blushing, too, and looking down to hide it. It was so cute.

They started by asking questions about her, but they all seemed to enjoy chatting, so she started asking them questions about them and about Parker. Then they were all just chatting about random things—their three different trips, how Ethan was liking school, what his parents did for a living, favorite Christmas traditions—all five of them.

She had thought she would be in his room for five minutes or less, but before she first even thought about what time it must be, a good half an hour had already passed.

As they said their goodbyes, Kelli realized she was falling in love with the whole family, and as she was getting ready for their carriage ride later that evening, she felt like she was floating.

By the time they walked out front to meet their carriages, she had to remind herself to pull her heart back and give some space between it and Parker's family. Without even realizing she had done it, she had fallen in love with James because of his family, and she didn't want to do the same thing ever again. And she knew that right now she was especially vulnerable since she was feeling particularly lacking in the family department.

Four beautiful horse-drawn carriages were waiting

outside, majestic horses at the front of each, standing tall and occasionally pawing a hoof on the wet road or making a snorting sound. There were spots for four people per carriage, so Parker and Kelli sat in the back seat in one carriage and Joy and Thomas sat in the seat facing them.

"They have blankets for us, too," Kelli exclaimed, pulling theirs up to her shoulders and snuggling up to Parker. He put an arm around her shoulders, so she reached up and adjusted the blanket so it would go over her shoulder enough to cover his arm. It wasn't as cold as last night, but it wasn't the warm weather they'd had the first few days, either.

As the carriages pulled away and started heading down the road, Joy said, "I can't believe they are awarding points to us for this. I don't know about you guys, but I didn't need to be bribed."

Parker chuckled. Kelli was sitting close enough to him that she could feel his laugh rumble in his chest. "Even the people who have no chance of winning are here, so I think you might be on to something."

"Who do you think's going to win?" Joy asked.

"Me," both Kelli and Parker said at the same time. They all laughed, and so did she, but it wasn't a joke—she was still determined to win.

Thomas tapped a finger to his bottom lip. "So you're saying I should either kick it in high gear or just accept the fact that I'm not going to win."

Kelli liked Joy and Thomas. And by how close they were sitting, they liked each other, too. Maybe she and Parker could go on double dates with them once they were back in Denver.

Her stomach fluttered at the thought of her and Parker

dating when they got back. Everything here felt like a magical dream—one that would disappear and be forgotten once they left. But it wasn't. She was going to be able to see Parker every day at work. After their hours of chatting on the bench in the snow last night, she knew that was what they both wanted.

But what if she wasn't as ready to head into another relationship as she had thought she'd been last night? Her fluttery stomach turned into a quivering one.

Then Parker pulled her in a little closer as they went over a little bump when the carriage turned off The Royal Palm's property and onto the streets of Myrtle Beach. She just fit so well next to him. And he was so kind and chivalrous. Any time she saw him, her entire body felt like it was filled with twinkle lights and Christmas magic. Maybe she was ready after all.

As they drove through the streets of Myrtle Beach, looking at all the Christmas lights stretched across the main streets and decorating the buildings, Kelli laid her head against Parker's shoulder. He had unzipped his coat, so apparently he was plenty warm with just the blanket. She put her hand right over his heart, feeling the strong, steady rhythm of his heartbeat.

He kissed her forehead, and when she looked up at him and smiled, he said, "Stay until New Year's Day with me."

She sat up straight so she could get a better look at him. "You've decided to stay?"

He reached out a hand and brushed a lock of hair off her cheek, then ran his fingers down her cheek, across her jaw, and stopped at her chin, using one finger to trace her lips. His touch sent electricity zinging through her and made her long to have his lips on hers again.

"If I could stay here with you forever, I would."

She was so hopelessly gone at his words. She just stared into those dark eyes with the honey color nearest his pupils and forgot how to speak. How to think. How to do anything but fall into their depths.

He cupped his fingers under her chin and leaned forward to brush his lips against hers and then smiled, showing a dimple that she loved so much. With his lips only an inch from hers—close enough that she could feel each beautiful breath—he whispered, "Is that a yes?"

She laughed, realizing that she hadn't managed to get an answer out. "Yes, Parker. I would love to stay here with you until the very moment they kick us out."

She felt a buzz in her coat pocket and jumped before she remembered that she had brought her phone along just in case her dad got a chance to call or text. She pulled it out and looked at the screen, surprised that it was someone other than him.

It was a text from James's sister Catherine, the sister that she had gotten closest to while she had dated James. The text simply said, *I MISS SEEING YOU AT FAMILY THINGS*.

She tried to push down the memories of good times with Catherine and James's family that the text brought back, and shoved the emotions right along with them. She'd try to respond later, but she couldn't now. She pushed the phone back into her pocket.

Parker looked at her, concern all over his face. "Are you okay?"

What was she doing? She had let herself bond with James's family, so she knew first-hand how painful it was to get close to a boyfriend's family, knowing that if you ever broke up with the boyfriend, you could never see his family again.

She was trying to not let herself fall for Parker so quickly and so fully and so completely. But it was *Parker*. And the man was just way too easy to fall for. She still had no idea how she had worked on the same floor as him for two-and-a-half years without falling blindly, madly, fully in love with him.

"I'm great," she said and flashed him a big smile.

# Chapter Sixteen

PARKER

arker woke up happy before his brain was even awake enough to remember why he was so happy. The carriage ride last night had been so amazing, and he'd spent the whole time memorizing how it had felt to have Kelli in his arms. To have her head on his shoulder, her breath on his neck.

He picked up his phone to text her good morning and hoped a little that maybe there would be a text from her. Instead, his screen was filled with social media notifications. He just stared at them, confused, not understanding why so many random comments were showing up on his screen. He tapped on one of them.

And then he wished he hadn't. They were all comments on a post that his ex-fiancée had made. He scrolled up to Stephanie's post, dreading reading it, but feeling like he needed to know what was going on.

*Hey, everyone! You all know that my wedding with Parker Brockbank was supposed to be last week. I've had*

*QUITE A FEW PEOPLE CHECK IN TO ASK ABOUT IT, SO I THOUGHT I'D GIVE AN UPDATE. MOST OF YOU KNOW THAT PARKER AND I CALLED OFF OUR WEDDING A FEW MONTHS AGO. I KNOW. BUT DON'T GO CLICKING ON THAT SAD EMOJI, BECAUSE THERE'S NO REASON TO FEEL BAD FOR ME. I'D LIKE TO ANNOUNCE THAT I'VE MET THE MOST WONDERFUL MAN ON THE PLANET. HIS NAME IS ROGER, AND I FEEL SO BLESSED TO BE ADORED BY HIM. SOME-TIMES WE HAVE TO GO THROUGH THE PAIN OF A CATASTROPHIC HURRICANE TO GET TO THE SUNSHINE AND BLUE SKIES AND TRUE LOVE ON THE OTHER SIDE.*

The picture she posted with it was of her and Roger on vacation together, and it looked like they were on one of the islands his honeymoon cruise with her was supposed to stop at. And now she was there with her "true love," and feeling blessed that she was no longer with Parker, her "catastrophic hurricane."

And of course, she had tagged him in her post. That way he was sure to also see all the comments from her friends—people he used to call friends, too—about how she shouldn't feel bad because Parker wasn't good enough for her, and how glad they were that she had found someone better.

He un-tagged himself from the post and closed out of the app, his teeth grinding and all the muscles in his body tensing. Instead of heading straight to the shower as he'd planned, he got dressed in his gym clothes and shoes and took off for a run along the beach. He needed to do something constructive with his racing heartbeat so he didn't do something stupid instead.

But running gave him too much time to think and question if he ever was or ever could be relationship material. Stephanie certainly didn't think so. Dozens of people commenting on Stephanie's post didn't seem to think he was, either. And they were mostly people he had known. People who hadn't given him any kind of indication that they thought he wasn't worthy of Stephanie.

What made him think he could start a new relationship and be successful? Especially with someone as incredible as Kelli?

Even after showering, he still couldn't shake the weight he'd been carrying since reading Stephanie's post. Running usually helped, but since it hadn't, he didn't know what else to try. So even though he didn't feel like it, he met up with everyone else in the family room to go make snowmen out of sand. It didn't sound possible, but maybe it had a chance of distracting him.

When he walked into the family room, though, his eyes immediately found Kelli, and her face lit up again just from seeing him. He couldn't let Stephanie bring him down. Not when a relationship with Kelli was on the line. *Kelli is different*, he told himself. *You are different.*

Since the storm passed, the weather climbed back into the sixties, and with the sun shining, the beach felt amazing. As it turned out, it wasn't impossible to distract himself when Kelli was around, and it also wasn't impossible to make a snowman out of sand. It just involved creative stacking and packing of wet sand, the same way making a castle did. They were just making a "castle" that was taller than he'd ever made, so it took some extra good packing, which they'd found out the hard way. Joy and Thomas were working with them, and for the most part, they were having fun.

But something seemed off with Kelli, and his mind never drifted far from that fact. She wasn't smiling as easily as normal, and when he asked her if she was okay, she responded with "I'm fine." He was pretty sure that meant she was anything but fine. Maybe she had been coming up with her own list of things about him that annoyed her. Every time he worried about her even for a second, the weight of Stephanie's post settled on him again.

They needed some wetter sand, so when Kelli grabbed a bucket and said she'd get some, he grabbed a bucket and said he would, too. Once they were away from everyone else, he said, "It seems like something is bothering you. Do you want to talk about it?"

She glanced toward everyone who was busy working in groups of four to make their snowmen, as if she was making sure they couldn't hear, then let out a huge breath. "I logged in to work, just to check the numbers from my campaign that was running over Christmas. Now don't give me any grief about being a workaholic, because you put in as many hours at the office as I do, and I haven't logged in the whole time we've been here."

She shook her head, looking down at the bucket she was shoveling sand into. "I don't even know what made me log in this morning. I've been enjoying the trip and hadn't even thought about work most days. I guess I was just feeling worried or unsettled or something, and I kind of just wanted that boost you get from seeing a job you worked hard on doing well, you know?"

He nodded. He knew exactly what she meant—it was one of the reasons why he was a workaholic, too.

She glanced up, looking even more worried that someone might hear, her cheeks flushing. Then she whispered, "It's going terribly, Parker. So, so, so bad. I made a huge mistake and wasted a big chunk of our marketing budget. Liz probably doesn't even know about it yet, but when she finds out, she's going to fire me."

"She's not going to fire you."

"She is! I took a big risk, thinking it was going to go well and knock everyone's socks off, and it tanked. And then after she fires me, Graham and Merit are going to find out and they're going to wish they never brought me on this trip."

"Kelli." He held onto her hand and pulled her to standing. "She's not going to fire you. Taking risks is a good thing, especially with your record. Taking risks is also what gives the biggest return on investment. Liz doesn't expect every risk to pay off." Even as he said the words, he hoped that she would be willing to keep taking risks—like taking a risk on him, specifically.

"I've been trying to be the perfect, model employee because I really like working at ZentCube, and that mistake showed that I'm the exact opposite of a perfect, model employee. I'm not even sure if winning a weekly lunch for my team for a year is going to make up for a mistake that huge."

The skin just under her eyes was turning pink, and he could tell by her erratic breathing that she was on the verge of tears but didn't want to cry with everyone around. He wrapped his arms around her, enveloping her in a hug.

"Kelli, Liz has been your boss for how long now?"

"Two years and nine months."

"Which has been plenty of time for her to witness your marketing skills. Besides, didn't she have to sign off on the ad? She's not going to fire you over bad numbers on one campaign when she's seen everything you can do."

"Do you really think so?"

"I'm positive. Everything is going to be just fine."

She breathed out a huge breath and then looked up at the sky, probably trying to convince her tears to go away. After a moment, she looked back at him and smiled before she gave him a quick peck on the lips. "I don't know if it's going to be fine or not, but thank you, Parker."

He kissed her forehead and then crouched down with her to finish filling the buckets. He knew this had been a difficult thing for her to share, and he liked that she was willing to share it with him.

But at the same time, it also felt like a test. Like maybe she shared with him to see how he would react to finding out she wasn't perfect, and he wasn't sure if he passed. Whether or not she was perfect had nothing at all to do with how much he loved her. He wasn't sure he got that across at all. Or if he had comforted her in the way he should have. His mind had been so much on his own issues that he was no longer sure.

# Chapter Seventeen

KELLI

Kelli went to bed feeling like she had a lump of coal in the pit of her stomach, and she woke up feeling exactly the same. She kept checking her email on her phone, expecting one to come in from Liz at any moment that told her that she'd really messed up and that they needed to talk about her future at ZentCube as soon as she was back in town.

And to top that off, their group activity had been to bake cookies during the afternoon, and then go Christmas caroling down the halls of the main Royal Palm Resort guest quarters, singing and delivering cookies to anyone who opened their door to listen to them sing.

All of that would've been fine, except that she had tripped on a rug and fell into Parker, spilling her plate of cookies on the floor.

Then, she sang the wrong verse of a song, and when she tried to correct it, the words of both songs mixed and came out completely wrong and very inappropriately, much to the delight of most of the ZentCube employees around her and the older gentleman they were singing to, and to the horror of the man's wife.

And if that wasn't enough, things only got worse when she and Parker went on an actual date to The Green Olive, the fancy restaurant at the resort. She had left for the restroom when they had first arrived, just after the nice man, Declan, had shown them to their seats.

While she was walking back, she stepped wrong on her heel, twisting her ankle. It hurt pretty badly, but she wasn't about to let Parker know of one more thing she messed up on. A table with four women about her age had front-row tickets to her missed step, so she just smiled at them, and then walked the rest of the way to her table, pretending her ankle was fine.

Within moments of sitting down, their waiter brought a cocktail drink to Parker and said, "This is from the ladies at that table right over there."

Parker turned to look at the women who had just witnessed her twisted ankle and were now looking some-what embarrassed that they just sent a drink to a man who was on a date. Well, at least three of them were. The fourth made her hand into a phone and mouthed, "Call me."

And then, the cherry on top of the cake was actually a stuffed cherry tomato they'd gotten as an appetizer. She laughed at one of Parker's jokes at the worst time, causing her to choke on the tomato just as she had put it in her mouth. And choked badly enough that Parker had to do the actual Heimlich maneuver just so she could breathe.

She had never had so many embarrassing, less-than-perfect moments with one person before. Especially not within a time frame of less than three hours.

No, she had once before. But the last time that many

things had gone wrong on a single date, Parker hadn't asked her out again for two-and-a-half years.

When it came time to leave, she realized that although her ankle wasn't badly damaged and would probably be fine in a day or two, it still hurt too badly to walk back to the mansion in four-inch heels. So she had to tell Parker about it after all. He was so sweet about it—he asked the host if he could arrange to have a golf cart drive them back to the mansion, and he even picked her up and carried her to the golf cart and set her down ever-so-gently on it like she was a princess and he was her prince.

But still, she had worried all the way back to the mansion that he must've been thinking that he should've never asked her on the date.

They got back just in time to take a slow breath and grab some ice for her ankle before they met with everyone else at nine p.m. in the family room. "Welcome to our final gathering for this retreat!" Graham said.

They all cheered, and Kelli looked around at the group, feeling a sentimental longing for the group even though they were still together. After spending so many hours a day together for so many days in a row, they were feeling like family, and she was sad to see it come to an end.

"Please correct me if I'm wrong, and I do mean please correct me, because if I am, then your plane tickets are wrong. Most of us are leaving tomorrow on the ten a.m. flight back to Denver. The people who took us up on our offer to stay until New Year's Day are Parker, Kelli, Addison, Davis, and Merit. And I think we all need to cheer for that last one because he's such a workaholic; you wouldn't believe what I had to do to bribe him to come on vacation here during the summer."

Everyone laughed and cheered, then Graham said, "Actually, Elise, stand up. This is who we really should be cheering for, or we probably wouldn't have seen Merit here for more than two or three days. She's in charge of the New Year's Eve celebration here, and since she's here, Merit's here."

Elise stood up as they all clapped and whooped, her cheeks blushing, but then she looked at Merit and Merit looked at Elise and Kelli sighed. The looks they gave each other were just so sweet and so like the looks she had been getting from Parker. At least they were before her disastrous last couple of days. She chanced a glance at Parker, and he responded by entwining his fingers in hers and giving her hand a little squeeze, which warmed her heart.

And also surprised her a bit. She figured he would be trying to back away by now. She hadn't been good enough for her mom to stay, for her dad to want her in his new family, and probably to keep her job at ZentCube. And she hadn't been good enough for a brand new relationship to take hold. Maybe Parker was backing away, and the hand squeeze was just his way of letting her down very gently. That would be a very Parker thing to do.

Davis and Addison seemed happy to be having their own little love story going on, though. After the awkwardness at the dance, things had gone back to being easy between Davis and Kelli. And since he hadn't spent the night claiming Kelli, he had danced with Addison quite a bit. Who knew the two of them would've hit it off so well? She was glad they were staying.

She was a little nervous about staying herself.

"We've taken down the point sheets, but I'll say that we've got several people who are very close on points,"

Graham said, "and we're excited to announce the winners. Meet down here tomorrow at seven-thirty—I know it's early, but we're hoping that you've acclimated to South Carolina time a bit—and we'll announce the winner and have a final goodbye. We'll also have some breakfast items that you can just grab and take with you before you hop on the shuttles to go to the airport."

Merit stood up next to Graham. "Okay, we are done for the night, so feel free to go get some beauty sleep, go out on the town, earn more points, enjoy the game room and theater downstairs, stay up all night, whatever you most want to do. And thank you for spending your Christmas with us. We hope it was as great for you as it was for us."

Kelli jumped to her feet along with everyone else and clapped for Graham and Merit. Then she walked up to them and thanked them personally. They had put so much into planning this for just the twelve of them, and her heart was practically overflowing with gratitude.

Then Parker came up to her and said, "So, how do you want to spend—"

But her phone was buzzing, so she pulled it out of her pocket, looked at the screen, and squealed. "It's my dad! Sorry—I've got to—" He just smiled at her and nodded, and she answered as she raced up to her room.

"Daddy!"

"It's so good to hear your voice, Candy Cane."

"You, too, Dad." It had been too long since she'd last talked with him, especially since it seemed like she'd been vacationing for weeks—or months—already. But she pushed her emotions down and said brightly, "How has your trip been?"

"Not the same without you. I've missed all of our traditions!"

"I've missed them, too," she said, only partially able to keep the emotion from her voice. She brushed a knuckle just below her eye to keep a tear from spilling over. "And I've missed you."

"I've missed you, too. Once we both get back, we need to spend a good amount of time together."

She held the speaking part of the phone away from her mouth as she let out a relieved breath that came out choked with emotion.

"I know that integrating with this new family has taken a lot of my time lately, but I'm anxious to get things going smoothly there so that I can work on integrating you in with them."

He had pushed her away, but he had a plan for bringing her back in. She was going to get her dad back, and eventually JoAnn and her new stepsisters, too. She wanted to reach through the phone and give him a giant hug.

They were only able to talk for about five minutes before he had to go, but it was a really good five minutes that left her floating on a cloud of happiness. She couldn't wait to tell Parker.

# Chapter Eighteen

PARKER

Parker didn't know how long Kelli would be talking to her dad, so he decided to use the time to go to his room and look up things he could do with Kelli during their bonus four days at the resort. The resort had a lot to offer during the winter even when it wasn't over Christmas and New Year's, and they hadn't even begun to check them all out yet. The town of Myrtle Beach had even more things to do, and he couldn't wait for the two of them to do it all.

He barely had time to look, though, before Kelli came into his room, alive with happiness. Her dad hadn't seen her at all over Christmas, and all he could spare her was a five-minute phone call?

"I just had the best phone call with my dad."

"Oh yeah?" He met her partway into his room and wrapped his arms around her waist, then kissed her on her temple. "Tell me about it."

He didn't keep his arms around her, though, because she seemed too full of energy and excitement to stand still. So he sat on his bed as she moved about the room, telling him the story.

"So when my dad first said that they were going away for Christmas, and it was just going to be JoAnn and his new daughters and not me, I felt like I was being pushed away. No—more like left behind. Tossed aside. But I just told myself that it was temporary. It was only coming from JoAnn, not from my dad. Just like how she'd asked her three daughters to be her bridesmaids at the wedding, but didn't ask me. But then my dad asked me to be his best man, so everything was fine in the end."

She seemed so happy and full of life as she was telling him, but he felt stabs of pain in his gut on her behalf. It was all awful, and he was even more impressed that she was as open and happy as she was when she had every right to be closed off and cynical.

"But apparently, I *had* been worried that my dad just didn't want me anymore and would be just as happy if I wasn't around even more than I thought I'd been. Because during our phone call, which was so perfect and amazing, he told me that he missed me that he missed spending Christmas with me, and that he hoped that he'd get integrated with JoAnn's family soon so that he could start integrating me into the family. So it *is* just temporary, and not only am I going to get my dad back, but I'll also be getting a bigger family out of the deal!

"I had no idea how much I believed that would never happen until he told me it would, and it's like a giant weight has been lifted off me and now I'm flying."

He loved seeing Kelli this happy. Part of him wanted to spin her around in a circle and celebrate with her. But another part of him—a bigger part—was worried that she was just being set up for a fall from a very dangerous, very scary height. That her dad wasn't going to follow through with all that he promised, and she would be back to having a very part-time dad in her life.

And with as excited as she was getting, that fall was going to be crushing and he worried what it would do to her. He just wanted to wrap his arms around her and protect her from such a devastating fall, and to be a soft place to land when she did.

"Kelli," he said, trying to figure out how to tiptoe his way in, "are you sure you want to get so excited yet? I mean, maybe it's better to wait until you see it happening."

She cocked her head to the side and grabbed hold of her elbows with her hands. "You don't think he's telling the truth?"

"No, it's not that. It's just…I don't know. It sounds like JoAnn has a lot of sway over him."

"She does. My dad never would've shut me out of Christmas if it wasn't for her. But I think all of that is because they just got married, and she's trying to look out for her girls. They all still live at home, you know. As my dad said, she just needs time to feel secure in their relationship."

He let out a deep breath and looked out the window before meeting her gaze again. "Maybe just be careful with hoping that things are going to go back to the way they were with you and your dad before he met JoAnn."

"Well, of course, they won't all be the same. He has more people than just me in his life now. But that also doesn't mean things are going to keep going the way they were this Christmas."

"You never know. I mean he did it once." He closed his eyes for a moment, knowing he shouldn't have said that. But he could feel the heat rising in him that her dad had treated her the way that he had, and he really didn't want him to have the chance to do it again. "I just don't want to see you get hurt."

"Parker." She was blinking rapidly now. "I don't know why you aren't being happy about this with me. Everything is going to work out just fine! My dad always has my back. He'll look out for me."

"Except he *didn't* look out for you. Even if this was all JoAnn's choice, your dad didn't say no. He chose a wife and daughters who had only been his family for less than a year, and ignored the daughter he's had for twenty-six years."

Parker wanted to throttle the guy. It was awful that he would make Kelli feel the way that she had, especially when there was so much he could've done so that she wouldn't have had to go through all that. It was so frustrating that he hadn't. While they'd been on the retreat, he'd seen just how badly she'd been hurt by what her dad did, and he wished he could protect her from every bit of pain.

"You don't even know him."

"I just don't get why you are giving him another chance. What he did was..." *Unforgivable* was how he wanted to end the sentence. But he was her dad, so instead, he just shook his head, looked down at the carpet, and said, "Terrible."

Kelli was quiet long enough that he looked up. She was standing next to his desk, one hand on her hip, and she was looking at him with her eyes narrowed. It was a look he'd never seen on her before.

Finally, she said, "So you think I should just cut him out of my life. The only family I've had for thirteen years. The link to the possibility of becoming more of a family with my new stepmom and my new stepsisters."

"Kelli, I—"

"You don't cut someone out of your life just because they made a mistake." Her voice gave him chills down his back, and he suddenly knew she wasn't talking about her dad anymore.

As soon as he thought about it from her point of view, he realized how what he said could've been taken so wrong. Especially if she was imagining herself as the one making a mistake. But he would never do that to her.

"No, Kelli, I didn't mean it like that. It's just that he's your dad, so family should come first for him." He was scrambling, trying to come up with a way to explain it to her after he had probably done irreparable damage.

His phone, still sitting on the desk where he'd left it, lit up with a message, and both of their eyes were automatically drawn to it. But then Kelli's eyebrows drew together, a confused and hurt look on her face. She stared at it until the screen went dark again, then she looked at him. "You have a job offer?"

*Oh, no.* He got to the desk in three strides and picked up his phone. The message was from Josh, and although the lock screen didn't show the full message, it showed enough.

JOSH: I get that this job is your backup plan if things go south at ZentCube (I'm guessing this is about a girl?), but I still plan to work hard to entice you to accept...

He stared at it, and of all the thoughts that could've gone through his head first, Stephanie's list made it to the front. One of the items that annoyed her was that he let his notifications show on his lock screen. Maybe he should've taken that particular critique more seriously.

"I wasn't looking for a job. Josh and I worked together before ZentCube and we became friends. So when his company was looking for a brand manager, he recommended me."

"And you decided that you'd like to stay at ZentCube, but you didn't tell Josh's company no. You're holding on to the job offer, because you're afraid that things won't work out between us, and you don't want to work at the same place as me if they don't."

It sounded so much harsher when she said it, but she'd spelled it out exactly. He couldn't think of a single thing to say that wouldn't make things worse. He pled with his eyes that she would understand that it wasn't as bad as it sounded —he had just been scared. Scared that he wasn't good enough, and scared that he wouldn't be able to tell when he wasn't, so he wouldn't be able to fix things in time.

"You've got a backup plan so that if I make a mistake, you can easily cut me out of your life."

Her words hit him like a blast, nearly knocking him backward. "That's not it." He reached his hand out halfway to her, but she didn't close the distance with hers. Her hand didn't so much as twitch, so he dropped his arm.

"You are so wrong about my dad. He's a good guy, but you've decided he isn't without even meeting him first."

He ran his hands over his face. There were times when he was able to dismiss Stephanie's whole list as just something created out of her special brand of rudeness. But other times—most of the time—he felt like she'd been spot-on. He could picture her in the room right now, standing with a hand on her hip, an eyebrow cocked, telling him all the ways in which he'd messed up during this one single conversation.

"Parker," Kelli said, her voice softer now. She stepped right up to him and this time she was the one who reached out her hand. He reached forward, almost mechanically, like his mind hadn't decided what to do yet but his body responded anyway, and he let Kelli hold his hand. "I really like you. A lot. A crazy amount. If the two of us are going to work out, you need to trust me more. Be on my side."

He sucked in a deep breath, closing his eyes. The first thing on Stephanie's list was that he hadn't put her as his number one priority. Kelli saying that he hadn't been on her side felt like the same thing. It felt like evidence that Stephanie had been right about him all along. He wasn't anywhere near good enough for Kelli.

Even though he didn't want to see what his words were going to do to Kelli, he made himself open his eyes and look at her. "I don't think the two of us are going to work out."

She looked at him for a long moment, sadness seeming to fill every inch of her.

"You should take the job," she whispered. Then she dropped his hand and walked out of his room.

Parker spent what was left of the evening in his room, feeling awful about how completely he'd messed things up and replaying all the monumentally stupid things he'd said to Kelli about her dad and the job offer. He had just been awful to her. The look on her face when he'd said that they weren't going to work out was burned into his memory, and it kept playing on repeat. *He* was the one who had caused that expression of devastating grief. Even as much as he loved her, he did that to her.

But he was in the main rooms by seven a.m. the next morning. He was hoping that she would be down a little before the closing ceremony started so he could begin to apologize for being such a jerk. And maybe explain why he had said that he didn't think they would work out. And maybe tell her how wrong it had felt to end things.

Thomas was the only one in the kitchen area that early, so he tried to focus on chatting with him enough to somewhat carry on a conversation when his mind was so far away from it.

A few more people trickled in, most of them going through the items that had been set out to eat for breakfast during the closing ceremony, in the car on the way to the airport, or on the airplane. Still, Kelli didn't come down. She was usually so early to everything. Especially to something like this, where they were going to say goodbyes and announce who got the most points and who won the grand prize.

At seven twenty-five, he stood from the bar stool he'd been sitting on, and he was about to go up to her room to check on her when Graham walked in. As soon as his eyes fell on Parker, a sadness washed over him. He walked straight over to Parker, put his hand on his shoulder, and said, "I'm so sorry to hear about you and Kelli."

"You know?"

Graham nodded. "She told me when she came to me last night and asked if she could fly home today instead of on New Year's Day. *Oh.* She didn't tell you."

Alarm shot through Parker, and he'd taken one step on his way to rush up to her room and try to explain everything and convince her not to leave, but Graham put a hand on his shoulder, stopping him.

"She texted a couple of hours ago, saying that she was taking an Uber to the airport early. She's already gone."

Everything closed in on him, crushing him, as everyone else in the room made their way to the couches in the family room to hear the winner announcement. Everything around him didn't quite seem real, and the world seemed very far away.

"You'll have to excuse me," Parker said as he made his way out the door, and hopefully up to his room before he fell apart.

# Chapter Nineteen

KELLI

*B*efore Kelli talked to Parker last night, if someone had told her that she'd be going home today and that because of her late decision to do so, she wouldn't even get to be on the same flight home with all the new friends she had made, she would've been devastated.

But after everything with Parker, she was glad she didn't know anyone on the plane because she didn't want to talk to a soul. Not even the people on either side of her. She went to the back of the line so she could board last, and the moment she sat down, she put on her headphones—the universal "I don't want to talk" signal.

She didn't even listen to the audiobook she had gotten specifically for the plane ride. She just dusted off her *Sad Songs* playlist and wallowed along with Adele and John Mayer. Parker had been so worried about her getting her hopes up too much that things would work out with her dad. Maybe he was right to worry, and maybe he wasn't. But what Parker really should've been worrying about was her getting her hopes up too much that things would work out with Parker.

Because him ending things with her crushed her more completely than her dad not inviting her to Christmas had, which she hadn't even thought was possible.

He had just been so harsh about her dad. Way more than he needed to be. It was good that she got to witness the side of him that saw things as black and white, right or wrong, without considering everything. She could never be with someone where she had to worry if he was going to judge her just as harshly for a mistake she made. She should be happy she discovered this side of him early. She should be thrilled that he broke things off before she got invested even more.

So why wasn't she?

Probably because she had discovered a lot of other sides of him, too. As the plane flew from the east coast toward the west, she couldn't stop thinking about how much she enjoyed spending time with him, how easy it was to talk with him, how quick he was to laugh or tell a joke, and how great it was that she could get him to go do fun things at the spur of the moment.

And how quick he was to help people. When they had spent hours on the cold bench on Christmas Eve, she talked about what she wanted to do to get ZentCube employees to help at the soup kitchen in Denver. Not only had he been encouraging, but he said he'd be the first to sign up.

And he was so cute with the kids at the Christmas Village. And seeing the way he held Graham's baby had made her heart melt into a pile of goo. She wanted to have kids someday, and she wanted their dad to look at them exactly the way Parker had looked at baby Hope.

And he'd been so kind and inclusive at the Tinsel and Tidings Ball. She was so impressed at how he'd looked out for her. He was always looking out for her, more than just at the ball.

She closed her eyes and let the memory of how it had felt to have his strong arms around her when she was scared. His arms made her feel safe and protected like there wasn't a fear in the world that he couldn't quell. Even the thought of it made warmth spread throughout her body, bringing with it the feeling of peace she had when they'd been so close.

That morphed into the memory of how it had felt with his arms cradling her when she was sad. The way he listened and comforted her and made her feel that no matter how bad things got, everything would be okay. She wished those arms were around her now, comforting her and telling her everything would be okay.

Right now, she desperately wanted to see again the way a smile spread across his face whenever she walked into the room, showing that dimple on his cheek.

Then another memory hit her. The very first day, when Merit had introduced Elise, she had wished and hoped and craved to one day have a man look at her the same way Merit looked at Elise. The realization that she had gotten her wish —that the way Parker looked at her was exactly like that— was difficult to bear. She had wanted so badly for things to work out between them.

As she sat in her seat, headphones on and eyes closed, silent tears rolled down her face and fell into her lap. Maybe she would never be able to hold on to a love like that. Maybe the memory of it was all she would ever have.

The plane touched down at Denver International and it hit her that she had been so wrapped up in thoughts of

Parker that she hadn't even thought about where she was long enough to be apprehensive about the takeoff or landing.

She wiped the last few tears from her cheeks, removed her headphones, wrapped them up, and placed them into the side pocket of her bag.

"Are you okay?"

Kelli looked at the person in the aisle seat for the first time—a man in his thirties who looked very uncomfortable asking, yet also very concerned—and she nodded. Although she could still feel his concerned gaze on her, he thankfully didn't ask any more questions.

As she got off the plane, walked down to baggage claim, got her suitcase, got on the shuttle to the car lot, then got in her car and drove home on snow-lined streets, she thought about the guys she had dated before. She had felt a connection with a few of them. She had with James, too, actually, although that connection came very slowly.

She had never felt it as strongly, though, as she had with Parker during their week that felt like two months. Maybe it had been longer than that. Maybe she had felt it from the other side of the second floor of the marketing building at ZentCube ever since he started working there just over two and a half years ago. Maybe that was why their pranks had continued over such a long period when they hardly saw each other through their normal work tasks.

She just hadn't known how strong that connection would grow to be until they both boarded a plane headed to the other side of the country.

When she finally pulled into the parking lot in front of her apartment, right next to a monstrous pile of snow left by the snow plow, she grabbed her suitcases out of her car and headed up to her place. As soon as she opened the door, two warring emotions hit her. Comfort and relief at finally being home again after a long vacation, and a sudden empty loneliness, like a home after everything is packed up in a moving truck.

Normally, she wouldn't do anything before unpacking her suitcase and getting everything perfectly in its spot. But today, she just left them next to the front door, trudged to her bedroom, climbed into bed, and pulled the covers over her head.

# Chapter Twenty

PARKER

*P*arker missed the announcement of the winner at the closing ceremony.

He missed saying goodbye to Graham, Tessa, baby Hope, and the eight other ZentCube Employees who were flying home.

He missed lunch.

He missed Kelli.

It was late afternoon before he finally managed to drag himself out of his room and down to the beach. Not to run—he didn't have the energy to do that. Instead, he just walked along the same section of beach that he and Kelli had walked so long ago. Although it hadn't actually been that long ago. Somehow, it already felt like she had been a part of his life always. He was so grateful that Stephanie had broken off their engagement or he would've never gotten this second chance with Kelli.

He just wished he hadn't blown that chance.

He should've been working on the list that Stephanie had given him from the moment she'd put it in his hands.

Right at the very top of her list had been *Not putting me as the #1 thing in your life*. He hadn't understood at the time why she had that on the list at all because he thought he *had* been putting her first.

But now he got it. Now that he realized he did the same thing to Kelli. If she had been the number one thing in his life, then his issues about her dad wouldn't have taken the driver's seat. He would've done everything possible to keep her radiating that happiness that had seemed too big to contain when she'd first come into his room to tell him about her dad.

In looking back with the benefit—or the curse—of hindsight, he could see so very clearly how much damage he had inflicted when he'd said the things he had.

On the woman he loved.

He couldn't walk any further, so he just sat on a nearby bench, staring out at the ocean as wave after wave came onto the shore. The entire sky was filled with gray clouds that seemed to pull the color from the ocean, and the cool breeze bit into his skin.

He thought back to the carriage ride and how it felt to have her snuggled up into him, her head on his shoulder, her breath on his neck, his arms wrapped around her. He thought about sitting next to her on the bench in the center of The Royal Palm's grounds in the middle of the night, the two of them huddled together for warmth, spending hours sharing their hopes, their fears, their pasts, and their dreams.

He would give anything to have her sitting next to him on this bench right now.

Or to see the way she quirked one eyebrow when she was amused or pulled on the corner of her bottom lip with her teeth when she was concentrating. Or to watch the way she led with her heart on every decision. The way she looked out for others. The way she let herself feel everything deeply, yet never dwelled on the shortcomings of others. The way she immediately saw the best in others, whether it was her first time meeting them or someone she had known her entire life.

No matter how many times she got knocked down, she stood back up. Even at times when most people would've stayed down for a while.

And then his breathing hitched when he thought about the moment he'd looked across the Christmas Village and had seen her holding baby Hope. He had known his whole life that he wanted to be a dad and have kids, but he'd never actually been able to picture anyone he dated as being the future mother of his children until that moment.

She was soft and compassionate, organized and playful, trusting and non-judgmental. She was terrified of spiders and complete darkness, yet she showed incredible inner strength and resilience time and time again. She was someone not to be underestimated. She was an enigma that he wanted to spend his life figuring out.

Darren had said he thought Parker was ready to open his heart again. And the surprising thing was, Darren had been right. There was one missing piece still, though. Parker hadn't already become the man who was worthy of her.

# Chapter Twenty-One

KELLI

$\mathcal{A}$ knock sounded on Kelli's front door, but she was too sick to get out of bed to go answer it.

Then she heard "I'm using my old key and coming in" loudly enough that she was pretty sure any neighbors who were home heard Valeria's voice, too. A moment later, her friend walked into her room.

"How are you feeling?" Val asked while setting down various bags and putting things on her nightstand.

Kelli paused the Hallmark Christmas movie she'd been watching. "About as awful as I look." And then a coughing fit hit, and she grabbed a tissue to cover her mouth, her brain feeling like it was getting beat up inside her head with every cough.

"Well, I guess getting the world's biggest cold is one way to distract yourself from the heartbreak."

Kelli shrugged and dropped the crumpled tissue on her floor with the others. It hurt her soul to have them all just making a mess of her floor, but she had been too exhausted to get out of bed and move her trash container closer. "If I'm going to feel awful, I might as well deal with them both at the same time."

This was the worst cold she had gotten in a whole lot of years. On second thought, she probably wouldn't have chosen to double it up with anything.

Valeria placed the back of her hand on Kelli's forehead. "No fever still. That's good because I brought soup." She pulled from a bag two containers of soup, a stack of napkins, and two spoons. She glanced once at the Hallmark movie-watching blanket that was spread across Kelli, but instead of bringing it up, she asked, "Have you heard back from Liz yet?"

Kelli was grateful Valeria wasn't bringing up Parker. Everything was still too bright and painful and fresh. Liz, she could talk about. Liz, she could even smile about. "I did. She hadn't already gone in to look at the ad campaign yet, but she looked and told me not to stress out, that these things happen. It's all part of the game. You win some and you lose some, and I have a track record for winning more than I lose, so it's all good."

Valeria grinned as she carried the soup to the other side of Kelli's bed and put it on the nightstand furthest away, then climbed onto the bed and sat down next to her. "I told you it would all be fine. Now push play." She grabbed both containers of soup and handed one to Kelli.

They watched and ate soup, commenting only on the movie, for several long minutes before Valeria said, "Remember when Rhett and I broke up and I barely got off the couch for three days?"

"I think I've got your look beat. But yeah—you were a mess."

"Yet, that didn't stop you from loving me, and it didn't make you kick me out of BFF status."

"Of course not!"

"And I still love you, too. Your name is practically tattooed as my BFF."

Kelli grinned at her, unsure why her friend was getting all sentimental on her but liking it all the same.

"Since I was your roommate for two years, I've seen you be imperfect plenty of times."

Kelli looked back at her, wary. Whatever turn Valeria was taking this conversation on, she no longer liked it.

"I mean, it wasn't often. But you think your less-than-perfect moments only happen when Parker's around? What about that time you decided to make scones for the first time and thought the oil needed to come to a boil to show that it was ready? I'm surprised you didn't burn the kitchen down when you dropped that first one in. And I'm pretty sure that we could find something in the apartment that still carries the stench of The Smoke that Permeated Everything."

Heat flamed to Kelli's face just remembering it. Now it seemed so stupid that she ever thought the oil was supposed to boil, yet at the time, it had made perfect sense. It still surprised her how quickly that scone flash-burned to black.

"And the time you couldn't sleep during the night so you got up and rearranged all the furniture in the living room but didn't tell me. So when I woke up and shuffled toward the kitchen, groggy and still half asleep, I stumbled into the corner of the armchair and fell and nearly sprained my wrist."

Maybe she did have a fever because her face was on fire. "Thanks, Val. I'd been doing a pretty good job of repressing those things."

Valeria put her soup container on the nightstand and turned to face her, sitting with her legs crossed. "The point is, I still love you. In fact, those things made me love you more because I got to see the real you. I like when you're imperfect."

Kelli smiled. And might have gotten a little teary. But that might have just been the watery eyes from her cold. "That's why you're the best, Valeria."

"It's not just me." Valeria huffed out a breath, her eyes aimed at the ceiling, thinking, like she was frustrated that she wasn't getting her point across and trying to figure out how. "Okay, do you know what? I'm just going to come right out and say it." She took a deep breath. "Your mom didn't leave because you're imperfect. She did because *she* is imperfect."

Kelli gasped as the blow of talking about her mom hit her.

"Your dad didn't keep from inviting you to join him, his wife, and his new stepdaughters for Christmas because *you're* imperfect. They did because *they* are imperfect. We all are. Every single one of us. That's what makes us human and beautiful and yes, even *lovable*."

Tears were falling in earnest now. Kelli set her soup on her nightstand.

Then Valeria whispered, "And Parker isn't going to stop loving you because you're imperfect or because you make a mistake. And he isn't going to stop loving you just because *he's* imperfect, too."

Kelli grabbed a tissue and started wiping at her eyes. "I want to believe you, Val. I do. And I totally believe in the concept. About other people. I'm just... not sure that I believe it deep down. About me."

"All right. I'm going to list off all the embarrassing things that have happened around Parker, just on this trip alone. Now, you might have to help me if I don't remember all of the ones you told me. But in my defense, the list is *long*."

Kelli laughed through her tears and swatted her friend with the back of her hand. Then she blew her nose.

"The water landing in your lap on the plane, making it look like you didn't make it to the bathroom in time. Drooling all over him when you accidentally fell asleep on him. Taking your poor row neighbor's luggage, flinging a mushroom into his water, tripping with the cookies while caroling, singing the wrong verse while caroling, twisting your ankle at dinner—"

"Okay, stop! You don't need to name them all—I think we've established that lots of embarrassing things happened." Her face was flaming hot all over again.

"But he still kept falling for you, through it all."

Kelli closed her eyes. He had. No matter how many embarrassing things happened, he still kept wanting to be with her. Right up until the end, when he ended things with no real explanation. "Val?" she said, her voice quivering. "He was so upset about my dad."

"Kelli." Valeria paused until Kelli met her eyes. "It's because he's in love with you and doesn't want anyone to hurt you."

She studied her friend's eyes, trying to figure out if what she was saying felt true. "I don't know if he's in love with me. He broke up with me, Val. That's not what 'in love' people do."

"Sometimes 'in love' people get a little scared."

Kelli flinched back in surprise. "Why? That makes no sense."

"When Rhett and I broke up, part of the reason was because he was scared and a little insecure. I didn't find out that part until after we got married and he told me." Valeria shrugged. "Maybe Parker worries that he's not good enough."

Kelli shook her head. "He's perfect. That can't be it."

Valeria chuckled. "How much do you want to bet that he feels the same way about you?"

Kelli's head was pounding and her sinuses ached, so it was a little more difficult to think, leaving her feeling slightly bewildered. "We broke up, Val. *He* broke up. Do you really think there could still be a chance for us?"

Valeria got off the bed and walked back around to Kelli's side. "Sweetie, I think you're two amazing people who are perfect for each other, and soon you'll both figure that out."

Kelli studied her friend for a long moment and then grabbed a tissue just in time to block a gigantic sneeze. "So what do I do?" Her nose was stuffier from the sneeze and the words didn't come out quite right.

"Get better. Right now, getting better is your only job."

Valeria crouched by the sacks she had set on the floor. "Now, I don't know if you've noticed the passage of time as you've been dwelling here in your cave of broken hearts and mammoth colds, but it's officially New Year's Eve, and I," she said, pulling items out of her bags, "brought decorations!"

# Chapter Twenty-Two

PARKER

When Parker finally pulled himself out of bed, he went downstairs to the mansion's kitchen to try to find something for breakfast. He didn't want to leave the place to go find food—there was so much festiveness going on at the resort, and he felt anything but festive.

Addison was sitting at the island counter on a barstool, reading on her phone and eating an apple. She glanced up as he walked in. "Hey, Parker."

"Morning."

She sat her phone down. "Parker. It's been three days, and you're still looking like you belong in a movie about an apocalypse."

He let out a single huff of a humorless laugh. "It's not a movie." He turned his back to her, looking on the rear counter for any more fruit.

"I might have been a little jealous of Kelli when we first got here."

Parker turned around at the mention of Kelli's name.

She shrugged. "But I've gotten to know her, and the truth is, she's a pretty cool person."

"I know."

"And she deserves a good guy."

He was very painfully aware of that. "I know."

"And it was obvious from day one that you're a good guy, Parker."

He studied Addison for a moment. The comment seemed genuine, but she hadn't known him well enough to know all of his shortcomings. Instead of responding, he opened the fridge.

"Read this before you look for food. It was here on the counter when I came down."

She tossed a piece of paper in his direction, and he caught it before it drifted off the edge of the counter. It was a note from Merit, asking Parker to meet him at the Green Olive in the clubhouse at nine for breakfast. He glanced down at his watch—it was already eight-forty. He probably shouldn't have chosen this as the one day to sleep in.

He thanked Addison, hurried upstairs to shower and change, and then jogged over to the clubhouse, trying to ignore all the work going on to get the place set up for the New Year's celebration going on tonight. The dinner, live music, and dance that was going to be outside under the stars, with fireworks and a toast to the new year, along with kissing at midnight. The event that he was supposed to attend with Kelli.

Darren, Adam, and several other friends had texted or called since the morning Kelli flew back home. He hadn't responded to any of them—he just hadn't been ready to talk. Yet Merit was sure to bring everything up.

He glanced at his watch as he stepped into the lobby. It

was a few minutes after nine. The place still had the Christmas tree and most of the Christmas decorations that had been there when he came with Kelli, but some had been switched out for gold, silver, and black New Year's decorations, and somehow, all of it looked right together.

The hostess directed Parker to a table where Merit sat, just as the waiter was setting down several plates of food.

Merit looked at Parker and said, "Oh, good, you made it," before thanking the waiter. "I'm glad you got my note. I ordered food already. I hope that's okay."

"Of course."

An empty plate sat in front of each of them, and all the plates with food were in the middle of the table, filled with eggs, bacon, pancakes, hash browns, fruit, and toast.

"I didn't know what you'd like, so I got a little of everything. Dish up."

As they put food on their plates and started eating, Merit asked him questions about the retreat. It felt mostly like small talk, but he figured the guy probably wanted to know if things needed to be tweaked for their next retreat. So he pushed his feelings of sadness and remorse aside, focused on the conversation, and answered everything honestly and openly. It was better to talk about this stuff, anyway. He could convince himself that they were just two guys chatting about a work thing without a care in the world.

He was caught completely off guard when Merit asked, "So have you decided whether or not to take that other job?"

He had *almost* forgotten that he had told Merit about the job offer. Not that he couldn't remember telling him—it was just that neither Merit nor Graham had brought it up a single time on the retreat, so he just hadn't thought about it.

He nodded. "I turned it down. I'm going to stay at ZentCube."

A smile spread across Merit's face. "We're glad you're staying. You're good at what you do, and we're fortunate to have you." Merit looked down at his plate for a moment, a small smile on his lips, before he looked back at Parker. "Although I'm sure it wasn't just a matter of us convincing you that this was a good company to stay with. I'd bet that Kelli had more to do with your decision than we did."

"You convinced me," he reassured Merit. "This is a great company."

Merit raised an eyebrow in a look that told him that he didn't like it when people just said what they thought he wanted to hear. He liked it when they told it straight. Parker knew enough about Merit to know that already; his response had been less about protecting Merit's feelings and more about protecting his own.

"Okay, she did have a lot to do with the decision. If I can someday be good enough for her, then I want to see her while I'm at work, too. If I can't, then I deserve to be reminded daily of what I lost."

"Ouch." Merit flinched, like that pain hit him, too. "Do you love her?"

Parker's nod came quickly. "More than I ever thought I could love another person. She's funny and thoughtful and has the most incredible inner strength. Just being around her makes me want to be a better man."

"So what happened?"

Parker exhaled slowly, trying to figure out how to tell Merit. He was embarrassed and didn't want to admit how foolish he'd been, but he realized that not responding to any of his friends who had reached out hadn't been working out so great for him, either. He just really needed to talk it out.

"If you would've asked me what Kelli's biggest fear was before we came on this trip, I would've guessed spiders. I've realized that it's a fear of people walking out of her life. But I didn't understand that until I said some stupid things that made her believe that she needs to fear that with me."

"Does she?"

"No!" Parker swallowed hard. "Except I kind of did when I ended things with her. I didn't even want things to end."

Merit picked up his glass of orange juice and swirled it around for a moment before he drank the last of it and set the glass back down. He met Parker's eyes. "Graham and I are both surprised that you haven't come to me asking if you can get your flight changed to an earlier time. He's been texting several times a day, asking if you've come to talk to me yet. It's New Year's Eve already—why are you still here and not back in Denver, trying to convince her that she doesn't need to fear that with you?"

"Because I want her to be with someone good enough for her." Parker swallowed down a lump in his throat. "And I don't think I am."

"Do you want to be?"

"Of course I do."

Merit's phone lit up with a text, and he typed a response before continuing. "I've noticed that Kelli is a bit of a perfectionist."

Parker chuckled. "You could say that. Which is crazy, because she's perfect even when she's not trying to be."

Merit studied him for long enough that it made him flinch. This wasn't his boss studying him—this was the CEO, the co-founder, and the co-owner of the huge company

Parker worked for. This was by far more intense than any time Adam's focus was on him. It made him feel exposed, as if Merit could see anything about him that he wanted to.

"Have you ever noticed that you're a bit of a perfectionist, too?"

Parker rubbed his forehead, frowning. He hadn't ever thought that of himself.

"Parker, if there's anything I've learned by falling in love with Elise, it's that Kelli doesn't need you to be perfect. *Nobody* needs to be perfect. It's only ever about recognizing your shortcomings and working to overcome them. You have your own incredible strength of character. Graham and I wouldn't have brought you on this trip otherwise. Every amazing person I've ever met has gotten there by continually working to become better. Never because they're working to become perfect, only that they're working to be better today than they were yesterday.

"So work to be better. Make it a habit to apologize sincerely when you're wrong. And let her know how you feel about her already."

Parker shook his head. "I don't know." All of that made sense logically. And he could see it working. But what about the long term? "I'm just... not good at being able to tell when things start to go wrong."

"This ex-fiancée of yours—from what you told me, you were blindsided when she gave you this list, right?"

"Very much so."

"Okay. Were you blindsided when things went wrong with Kelli?"

"Yeah."

His answer had come quickly, but Merit was still looking at him like he was waiting for him to think it through, so he did. Things had been going well. But he'd had his own fears he'd been working through, and looking back, he could easily see when those things were impacting things with Kelli, even before their disastrous conversation.

And from what he knew about Kelli's mom leaving and her dad's new family, she had plenty of fears she was working through, too. He knew all of that and knew it could be an issue.

And then he thought about the conversation in his room about her dad. He had looked at her face several times during that conversation and saw what it was doing to her. Yet he still kept talking, still kept saying things about her dad.

Had he even meant everything that he had said? Had he forgotten that she was much more important than any negative opinions he had of her dad? Or had he simply been allowing his fears to take over, and subconsciously sabotaged everything with a single, terrible, hurtful conversation? He wasn't sure, and the weight of what he'd done hit him anew.

He shook his head. "I wasn't blindsided."

Merit nodded, and then he picked up his phone, touching several things while he spoke. "Graham wanted in on this conversation. And since he's Graham, he sent his contribution in the form of a slideshow."

Parker chuckled as Merit turned his phone toward him. Graham must've had the slides set to a timer because each one switched to the next on its own. The first slide was of the twelve of them who had come on the retreat—the same bobble-headed images from the slideshow Graham had presented on the first day—standing in front of the limos, holding their luggage, with sounds of cheering.

Most of them had a bag and a suitcase, but Parker seemed to have the most luggage of them all. He had the bag and suitcase but also wore a huge backpack like the kind hikers take when they want to stay overnight somewhere and they have to pack in all of their bedding, shelter, clothing, food, and cooking supplies. It was big enough that it even rose higher than his head.

Then it switched to the second slide, and a slow, instrumental song played through Merit's phone's speakers as bobble-headed Parker and bobble-headed Kelli danced, which wasn't easy with their bodies that were so much smaller than their heads. The luggage was gone, but Parker was still wearing the giant backpack.

The next slide came with the sound of forks clinking on plates, and bobble-headed Kelli was smiling at bobble-headed Parker as they both served food at the soup kitchen. The backpack was still on Parker's back.

As the next slide came on the screen, the song that Merit and Graham had sung to wake them up Christmas morning —*We Wish You a Merry Christmas*—played, as all seventeen of them sat around a Christmas tree, including baby Hope in Tessa's arms. Parker was holding a Christmas present out to Kelli and, of course, he was still wearing the backpack.

The next slide was split into two. On the left was an outline of the state of Colorado, with a bobble-headed crying Kelli in the middle of it; on the right was South Carolina with a bobble-headed crying Parker, still wearing the backpack. He couldn't say he'd cried, but the image still captured how brokenhearted he felt.

The next slide was of a plane on a runway. An animated Parker threw off the backpack and then ran with his suitcase to the plane. Then it switched to bobble-headed Parker and bobble-headed Kelli kissing, a love song playing in the background.

The visuals, fun and cartoony as they were, hit him hard. But at the same time, they filled him with hope.

Merit smiled, shaking his head, as he closed out of the slideshow. "Graham is nothing if not theatrical in his slideshows. I think the point he got across without using a single word was that it's easy to project the baggage from a past relationship onto the next, Parker. We've all done it. Just remember that Kelli and your ex aren't the same. *You* aren't even the same. So don't let your past ruin something pretty great in your future."

Parker swallowed, letting Merit's words and Graham's pictures sink in. "I can see why ZentCube is so successful. You're pretty wise."

Merit laughed. "I wouldn't go that far. It wasn't that long ago that I made my own monumental mistakes when it came to falling in love with an incredible woman, and I was grateful to have someone step in and help me get past it." He reached into the pocket of his jacket, pulled out a folded piece of paper, and then slid it across the table. "The earliest flight I could get you leaves this afternoon. A car will be by to pick you up at two."

"Thank you, Merit." He couldn't express how grateful he was, but he hoped Merit could see it on his face. He seemed to be good at that.

He picked up the paper without opening it, his mind racing to figure out what he should do once he landed in Denver.

# Chapter Twenty-Three

KELLI

$\mathcal{A}$ knock sounded at Kelli's door. She glanced at her clock—it was after eleven p.m.—then shook her head. She thought she'd fully convinced Valeria that she was just fine and didn't need her babysitting all night and that she should go celebrate New Year's Eve with Rhett.

Before the trip to the Royal Palm Resort, before the plan to extend the trip over New Year's, before everything with Parker happened, and before this cold decided to take up residence in her body, she had planned to go to the same party and had been excited about it. The place was even going to have a light show in the ballroom as they counted down to midnight, and as much as she didn't want to be alone tonight, she didn't want Valeria to miss it even more.

She cleared her throat the best she could in its current state and called out, "Come in! And you better be coming back only because you forgot something!"

She heard the key turn in the lock, but she started coughing because yelling that loud had been too much for her poor, scratchy throat. The coughing made her head pound and angered her sinuses. She was just blowing her stuffy nose when Parker appeared in her bedroom doorway.

"Parker!"

She stared at him with her mouth open, wondering if she was really seeing him standing in her doorway, holding bags, snow in his hair and on his shoulders, the light she'd left on in her living room backlighting him and making him look like an angel. Was she seeing things?

"What are you doing here? Aren't you in Myrtle Beach? You don't even know where I live! And how did you get into my house?" More and more questions filled her mind, but they were coming too fast to get any of them out of her mouth.

He took one tentative step into her room. "I just got back an hour ago. I emailed Valeria to see if she knew where I could find you. She had me meet her at some party and gave me your key. She told me you were sick and that I should come tonight and let myself in so you didn't have to get out of bed." His eyes quickly scanned the room and then fell back on her. "Is it okay that I'm here?"

Kelli gave him a slow nod, and then closed her eyes, thinking about how much she wanted to strangle her best friend. Just because Valeria thought Kelli needed to realize that she didn't have to be perfect didn't mean that she wanted Parker to see her like this. She had managed to shower last night, but hadn't even blow-dried her hair; she had just let it do whatever it wanted to do, and then she'd pulled it into a crazy bun on top of her head.

She hadn't so much as put on moisturizer, let alone the makeup she always put on before ever leaving the house. She was sure her nose was red and dry, especially from blowing it right before Parker appeared in her doorway. And her eyes were probably giant bags from crying earlier. Likely bloodshot, too, based on how itchy they had been and how terribly she'd been sleeping.

And she was wearing flannel pajamas, in bed, and her room looked like a bomb went off in a tissue factory. This was not the way she had wanted to see Parker again, especially after so many embarrassing things had happened in his presence.

But he was there. When he was supposed to be celebrating New Year's Eve on the beach. What did that mean? Her brain was feeling too sick to be able to figure out things like that. She needed Valeria there to translate.

"Can I come in?"

She nodded and motioned to a reading chair she had on the other side of her nightstand. He put his bags down and then sat, but he scooted the chair so that he was facing her. Her overhead light wasn't on, just her two lamps, but it was plenty to see his face in their soft glow.

So many emotions were battling it out inside her, right alongside her massive cold. A thrill had gone through her at seeing him, and it was coursing through her even more madly now that he was so close and his eyes were on hers. There was also an overwhelming sadness that he had ended things. Panic and embarrassment were fighting for dominance, too, and making her wish she'd never said he could come into the room to see her like this. And there was curiosity as to why he had come. That one seemed to be winning.

"I'm sorry you're so sick." He reached a hand forward like he was going to brush his knuckles down her temples. He pulled his hand back, seeming unsure, but her skin was still on high alert and practically tingling with anticipation of his touch. "When did it hit?"

"Not long after I got back. Hopefully, I didn't give it to you before I knew I had it."

The awkwardness was crowding in the room, causing uncomfortable silences and uncertainty. Like they both were bursting with so much to say, but didn't know how to say it. Like they didn't remember how to be around each other since they had officially broken up.

"How's everything with your dad?"

"Good. Some crazy weather delayed his flight, so he doesn't get home until tomorrow afternoon now, but we're going to spend the evening together." Just like her dad had promised. He might not make choices that she agreed with, especially when it came to JoAnn, but he didn't lie. He didn't make promises he couldn't keep. She wished that Parker understood that about him.

Before it had a chance to turn into another awkward silence, she hurried to ask him a question. "When do you start working at your friend's company?" She didn't want to hear the answer. She didn't want to face the idea of him not being at ZentCube daily to become a reality. But she had to know how much time she had left. Hopefully, his answer wouldn't be the day they were supposed to go back to work after the holiday break.

What she wanted to do was ask him to explain why he ended things. She wanted to tell him that she was working on her fears and that she loved him and wanted him to be with her through it. And if he had fears, that she wanted to be with him as he worked through his. She wanted to keep trying to make it through whatever they faced together. That she loved him for who he was.

But she couldn't think straight. Not with this cold and not with him unexpectedly there, sitting so near. She grabbed a tissue and rubbed at her nose. She'd asked Valeria what she needed to do, and all her friend had said was for her to get better. Since she hadn't done that step yet, she hadn't worked out what came next.

Parker moved to the front of his seat, barely sitting on it, leaning forward with his arms resting on his knees. "Kelli, I was wrong. About so many things—most of which I hadn't even realized at the time. I was wrong to say all the things I did about your dad. You were right. I didn't know him well enough to say what I did.

"But I did know you well enough to know that I shouldn't have doubted you. I shouldn't have worried that you would get hurt. I should've just been there for you."

Her breath hitched and a warmth spread through her as his earnest words wrapped around her. He stood and moved to the edge of her bed, sitting by her knees, like he was too far away and needed to get closer, and she could barely breathe.

"Kelli, I am so sorry. I know that what I said hurt you, and I don't ever want to hurt you again. I want to be the one to protect you from anything that could ever harm you. I am every bit as scared that I'm not nearly good enough for you as I was back in my room at The Royal Palm. I wish I was already the kind of man you deserve. All I can do is promise you that I'll never stop trying to be."

Maybe it was the cold, but she was so confused. She reached a hand up and touched his face. "But you're perfect already."

He smiled and leaned into her hand. "I think that's the cold talking."

She laughed. "You were perfect before I got sick."

He just looked at her in dazed awe, like he thought she might be perfect, too, instead of looking like death came by for a visit. "And I think you're amazing every second of every day."

"Even if I cover your work area with cats? Or steal the conference room?"

A smile spread across Parker's face, showing his dimple. "Even then."

He reached for her hands, but she jerked hers back. "Wait!" She was sick, and she didn't want Parker to risk getting what she had. She grabbed the bottle of hand sanitizer from her nightstand and rubbed a generous amount on her hands, then waved them back and forth so they'd dry.

Then she reached toward him and, chuckling, he took her hands in his. "I love you, Kelli. Please tell me that you'll give me another chance."

*I love you.* He'd said, "*I love you.*" The emotion swelled up in her so much that she could barely keep the tickle it had caused in her throat from turning into a cough.

"Well," she said, "I think that's a distinct possibility because it just so happens that I am madly in love with you, too."

The look of happiness on Parker's face made her feel warm down to her toes and made her wish that she had mistletoe hanging right above her bed. And that she wasn't sick, obviously. She also wanted to get up and pretend that they were at The Royal Palm Resort like they had planned, dancing the night away—this time as an actual dating couple. Her first dance with him had been so amazing that she wanted to spend every chance she could get for the rest of her life dancing with him.

Instead, she motioned to the bags. "What did you bring?"

Parker smiled like she imagined he did when he was fifteen and his little brother realized that Santa had come, and he pulled the bags toward him. From one, he pulled out a mini Christmas tree and set it on her nightstand. She scooted closer to look at the ornaments under the glow of her lamp.

"I found a shop on the boardwalk that had a bunch of unique ornaments."

There was an airplane, a person sleeping, a couple dancing, a cooked turkey, a lamppost with Christmas lights wrapped around it, a train, reindeer antlers, a gingerbread house, a little bottle with sand and seashells inside, a horse and carriage, a group Christmas caroling, a cat, and even a mushroom. Seeing all of them made her want to laugh and sigh and cry happy tears and snuggle up in his arms.

"This is amazing, Parker. I've—" She was speechless. Words couldn't express all that she was feeling.

He reached down into the sack and pulled out a present wrapped in beautiful red and gold paper with a tag that read *Kelli* and placed it under the tree. "This one isn't actually from me, but you once accused me of practically gift-wrapping it and putting it under the tree with your name on it, so it felt appropriate to do just that."

She gasped and stared at him for one heartbeat before grabbing the present and opening it. A plain box was inside, and she lifted off the lid to see a single piece of paper that looked like a certificate and read, *THE GRAND PRIZE WINNER OF OUR CHRISTMAS CONTEST IS KELLI ELLIS! AND, AS THE WINNER, IS HEREBY AWARDED THREE EXTRA VACATION DAYS, PARKING SPACE C7 FOR A FULL YEAR, AND LUNCH FOR HER TEAM EVERY WEEK FOR A YEAR.* It was signed by Merit Casselman and Graham McNeil.

Her eyes flew to Parker. "I won?"

He grinned. "Of course. No one could come close to doing all you did."

She leaned back against her headboard. "So I get you *and* parking spot C7, all on the same day."

He leaned forward and gave her the sweetest kiss on the forehead. "And you get my grandma's famous 'Cold Begone.'" She gave him a questioning look, and he bent down and picked up one of the bags he brought. "It's a warm drink with honey, lemon, apple cider vinegar, cayenne, and ginger. Not only will it speed up your recovery time, but it'll make your throat feel better practically instantly."

"No offense, but that sounds pretty gross."

He smiled big again, showing off those dimples. "I know, but it isn't. Trust me. I'll even drink a cup with you." Then he walked out of the room, and she could hear him doing things in the kitchen. He hadn't even brought her the warm drink yet, and already her chest felt warm, just knowing that she and Parker were going to work out.

He came back a few minutes later, holding two mugs, still steaming, and she scooted over in her bed. He handed her one mug and then sat beside her, putting an arm around her shoulder. She snuggled into him, just like she had on the carriage ride, laying her head on his shoulder and cradling the mug in her hands.

She smelled the drink—it didn't *smell* awful. But still, she waited until he took a drink and watched his face for any signs of it being awful. When she saw none, she blew on hers.

But before she took a sip, he said, "Wait. Hang on." He put the mug on her nightstand, then pulled out his phone and opened the browser, then set it between them and picked up his mug again. It was the official New Year countdown, and it only had about thirty seconds before the year would end and a fresh new one, full of possibilities, would rush in. When only ten seconds were left, they counted down together.

Right as the New Year started, they clinked their mugs of Cold Begone together and each took a sip. It wasn't exactly sparkling champagne, but to her surprise, it actually tasted good and made her aching throat rejoice.

Parker kissed her temple, his warm, soft lips pressing into her skin so gently and so sweetly that it made her sigh. "Happy New Year, Kelli," he whispered, and she knew it would be.

# Epilogue

Parker felt like he'd waited his entire life for this day. Guests were filing in and taking their seats on both sides of the aisle, his bride-to-be was in the bride's room with his mom and Valeria, he was surrounded by loved ones, and his tux fit perfectly. The excitement bubbling up in him to see Kelli walking down the aisle was too much to contain, so he went from person to person, chatting, hoping that would use some of the energy.

His dad put his hand on his shoulder to get his attention. "We're going to go say hello to the Garlands." Parker nodded and smiled as his dad and Ethan, who was now as tall as he was, headed over to greet their family friends just as Kelli's dad, Richard, stepped over to him.

"With as many last-minute hiccups as we've had, it looks like this is coming together."

"It is." Parker looked around the venue that was filled with white Christmas trees, the silver and gold lights on them casting a warm glow through the room, and he defi- nitely felt some Christmas magic at work. He had always wanted to get married at Christmastime, and since that was when he and Kelli had fallen in love, it felt exactly right.

He turned to his soon-to-be father-in-law. "Thanks again for agreeing to be my best man. It means a lot to both of us."

Richard nodded. "Thank you for asking me. It means a lot to me as well."

He hugged the man. The two of them had come a long way in the past year. Although Parker still thought Kelli's dad had made a terrible mistake by not celebrating last Christmas with his daughter, he was hardly the only one making mistakes. Parker had been so worried that Kelli had been setting herself up to get hurt again, but he knew now how much he should trust her judgment on matters like that. Giving people the benefit of the doubt the way she did had made his life richer as well.

Besides, if Richard hadn't left Kelli alone last Christmas, the two of them might not have ever gotten past their fears enough to even go out on a second date. So maybe he should've been thanking the man all along.

As Richard went off toward JoAnn, Parker found himself pulled toward the other three men in tuxes: Valeria's husband, Rhett, who had become his best friend over the past year, and Merit and Graham. He shook their hands and thanked them for being part of the wedding party.

Merit was wearing a wedding ring now, which made Parker smile. Baby Hope was now a toddler who was walking around, charming everyone in the room. Both men were beaming, yet looked so relaxed and carefree.

"Were you guys as wired as I am when you got married? You look so calm."

"I was wired," Rhett said.

"Me, too," Merit said.

Graham nodded. "But being a groomsman is easier. We're practically pros at it."

Graham and Merit shared a mischievous smile that made him wonder how many couples the two of them had a hand in getting together. He knew that Joy and Thomas had gotten married in the fall, and Addison and Davis had a date set for next summer. Three couples getting married, all because of the same Christmas retreat. And Merit and Graham had been doing the retreat for years.

"When do you leave for this year's retreat?" he asked them.

Merit answered. "Tomorrow morning, bright and early. We are headed to the Royal Palm again, and I can't wait."

"Me, neither," Graham said. "We've got another good group joining us."

Parker chuckled, wondering if any of the people in that group had any idea what they were in for.

He felt a buzz from his phone, so he pulled it out of his pocket and then excused himself from the group. It was a text from Kelli that read, *I'm nervous.*

He typed back, *Having second thoughts?*

A year ago, he might've been afraid to ask that question. But now he could ask it, knowing that she would take it as a light-hearted joke. Now he was confident enough in their relationship, and confident enough to know that he always put Kelli first and would know if anything was going off track long before it became a problem.

KELLI: Haha. Not that kind of nervous.

Come into the bride's room?

PARKER: You want me to see you in your wedding dress?

Isn't that bad luck or something?

But he was already on his way to the bride's room. He'd wanted this wedding to be perfect for Kelli, but, of course, not everything went according to plan. When the flowers arrived, they were missing a boutonniere, several trips had to be made to run back and grab something that was forgotten, one of the tiers on the wedding cake was dropped and practically exploded when it hit the floor, one of the band members got sick, and an entire tray of food was dropped at the rehearsal dinner.

But they pulled together pieces from the other flowers and made another boutonniere, retrieved everything they needed, made the cake look incredible with one less tier, the band found a substitute, they enjoyed the meal served family-style at the rehearsal dinner, and his bride was happy through it all, which was all that mattered.

KELLI: We already used up all our bad luck.

There's nothing but twinkle lights and Christmas magic from here on out.

So come. Calm a girl's nerves.

He was already at the door, knocking.

Valeria opened the door, wearing her pale gold maid of honor gown, smiling. "I'll leave you two alone." Then she turned her head back toward Kelli and said, "I'll be waiting in my spot with your sisters. Don't forget to put that lipstick on before you come out."

Then Valeria walked out the door and Parker stepped

into the room to where he could see his bride next to his mother. Kelli stood in front of the full-length mirrors, that smile he loved lighting up her beautiful face and nearly blinding him to anything else. Her hair was a cascade of curls spilling down her back, and her white dress hugged her figure down to her hips before flaring out. She stood tall and confident, shoulders back, looking like a dream come true and quite literally taking his breath away.

His mom turned to Kelli, putting her hands on Kelli's shoulders, and smiled. "Only a few more minutes, and I get a daughter! I'm so happy I'm going to cry!"

"Don't do it," Kelli warned, brushing a fingertip under her eye.

His mom ran a finger under her eye, banishing any threatening tears. "I won't. Okay, I'll leave you two alone. Remember, next time you see me, I'm 'Mom' to you."

The two women hugged, and then his mom gave him a smile before ducking out of the room.

"Wow, Kels. You look incredible."

Her smile was brilliant. The only hint that she was experiencing any nervousness was the way she ran the tip of her thumb over the tips of her first two fingers at her side. In three strides, he was next to her, lifting that hand with his, brushing a kiss across her knuckles. Then he turned her hand slightly and kissed the inside of her wrist. "Tell me what's making you nervous."

She stared at him for a moment, like she'd forgotten her train of thought, and he loved that she still reacted to his touch like that.

Then she glanced toward the door. "I don't know. There are a lot of people out there. I'm afraid I'll trip over my dress and fall or something." She lifted it a bit as if to show that the length and the bulk could be problematic.

"You won't fall. Your dad will be at your side and he has your back—he always does. Besides, even if you trip a little, we still get to be married in less than fifteen minutes."

Her grin was as wide as he was sure that his was. This was really happening. Soon.

"True. The only thing that needs to be perfect is my choice of who to marry. And I'm one hundred percent sure I made the perfect decision."

"I know I did." He closed the gap even more and wrapped his arms around her waist as she reached up and wrapped her arms around his neck. She played with the hair at his neck, and the touch sent even more electricity coursing through his body. As if he hadn't already had more than he knew what to do with. "So how can I help with those nerves?"

A corner of her lip twitched up. "There's a reason why I don't have lipstick on yet."

She pulled him closer to her, and he responded by closing the little bit of space between them, pressing his lips against hers. It didn't matter that they had been together for a year—a kiss from Kelli made his breath catch and his knees weak every single time. He couldn't imagine anything being better than spending the rest of his life with Kelli. The love he felt for her had grown more every single day, filling him to bursting, and he couldn't wait to see what tomorrow brought. Or the next year. Or the next ten years, or fifty, or seventy-five years.

And he would get to spend them all with a woman as amazing as Kelli.

As they kissed, he pulled her closer, their bodies pressed

together from their chests nearly down to their feet, and he never wanted to let go.

But then there was a knock at the door just before it opened a bit and Richard poked his head in. "Are you ready, Kelli?"

She pulled back from Parker just enough that he could see her beautiful face and that smile that felt like it was made for him. "As much as I'd like you to stay in here forever, I don't want anything to delay you becoming my husband."

He grinned and gave her one last peck on the lips, then headed toward the door. Right before he walked out, he called back, "Don't forget the lipstick."

"Oh! I nearly did!"

He chuckled.

A few minutes later, he was standing at the altar as his groomsmen walked up the aisle with Valeria as Kelli's maid of honor and her three sisters, whom she had managed to form a pretty tight bond with, as bridesmaids. When they had reached their spots and were facing the guests, the wedding march sounded, and everyone turned as Richard walked Kelli up the aisle.

At one point, Kelli's foot caught on her dress and she faltered just a bit, but her dad held her arm firmly, so it was barely noticeable. She gave Parker a wink, and he knew that no matter how either of them stumbled through their lives, everything would be okay if they had each other.

As she reached the front and he took her hands in his as they looked into each other's eyes, grinning like kids at Christmas, he knew that life was going to be imperfect, but that was okay. They were perfect for each other, and that was all that mattered.

Author's note:

I hope you enjoyed both of these Christmas romances!

If haven't read my other book that is set at The Royal Palm Resort, make sure to get *A Kiss at Midsummer* (Merit's and Elise's story).

If reading these books got you in the mood for Christmas romances, check out *The Christmas Pact.* It is the start of a 3-book Christmas series filled with loads of chemistry and small-town charm and packed full of Christmas romancey goodness.

Happy reading!

—Meg

# Get more Nestled Hollow romances

*Coming Home to the Top of Main Street*
*Second Chance on the Corner of Main Street*
*Christmas at the End of Main Street*
*More than Friends in the Middle of Main Street*
*Love Again at the Heart of Main Street*
*More than Enemies on the Bridge of Main Street*

Listen to the audiobooks on YouTube

## About Meg Easton

Meg Easton is the *USA Today* bestselling author of contemporary romances and romantic comedies with fun, memorable, swoon-worthy characters, and settings you'll want to pack up and move to. She lives at the foot of a mountain with her name on it (or at least one letter of her name) in Utah. She loves gardening, bike riding, baking, swimming before the sun rises, and spending time with her husband and three kids.

She can be found online at www.megeaston.com

Sign up to receive her newsletter and stay up to date with new releases, get exclusive bonus content, and more.

If you liked this book please leave a review. Your review can help other readers find books they might fall in love with.

youtube.com/@megeastonauthor

bookbub.com/authors/meg-easton

instagram.com/megeaston_author

facebook.com/MegEastonBooks

tiktok.com/@megeaston_author